Ingot Publishing Books by Adrian V. Diglio

The Blacksmiths series:
The Ravenous Flock (short story)
The Soul Smith

The Apotheosis Saga:
Beyond Reach (short story)

THE SOUL SMITH

Book One of
The Blacksmiths

Adrian V. Diglio

**Ingot
Publishing**

THE SOUL SMITH

The Soul Smith: Book One of The Blacksmiths
Copyright © 2011 by Adrian V. Diglio

Cover art created by Natalie J. Salvo, copyright © 2012 Adrian V. Diglio

Map of Thornwall copyright © 2012 Adrian V. Diglio

Edited by Derek Bowen

Ingot Publishing
www.ingotpublishing.wordpress.com

ISBN: 978-0-692-42894-8

Library of Congress Control Number: 2015906022

First Edition: April 2015

Printed in the United States of America

ACKNOWLEDGMENTS

First, I would like to thank my editor, Derek Bowen, for his caring, careful and sometimes ruthless editing and advice.

Second, I would like to thank my family and friends that have supported me throughout this incredibly long journey – and especially to Natalie J. Salvo for creating my cover art.

Last but not least, I would like to thank everyone that supported me on Kickstarter, and give special thanks to:

<u>Goma Enchanter Tier</u>:
Deidre Braun
Donnie Karns
Jeffrey Boiles
John Weber
Jose Delio Guzman
Maureen & Daniel Smith
Chad Shaffer
Chad Bowden
Rhett Walker
Luis Then

<u>Blacksmith Tier</u>:
Clinton Hatch
Becky Wiley
Bob Piranio
Donna Diglio

<u>Elkin Warlord Tier</u>:
Marc & Ashely Merrill
Stephanie Diglio

THE SOUL SMITH

MAP OF THORNWALL

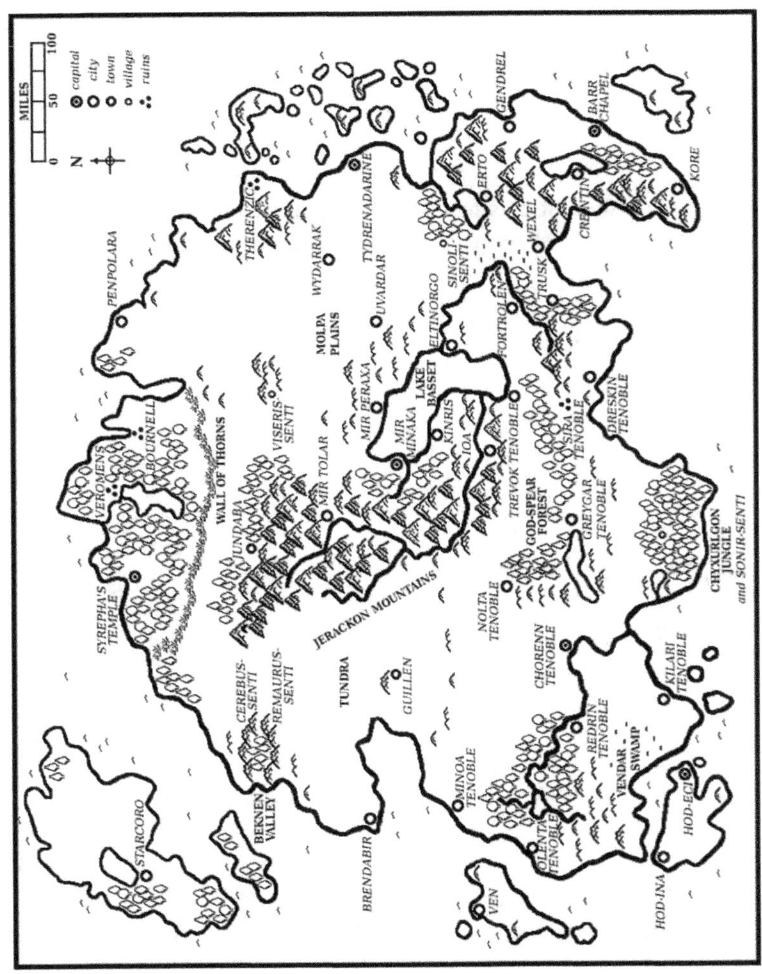

For my wife Stephanie and daughters Haley & Sophia,
who always share their beauty with me – of moon flowers
in full bloom.

CHAPTER 1

It was excruciating; my monstrous skeleton was raised from a rocky, fiery bed and slammed onto a cold hard surface. Everything was black, I couldn't see, couldn't move. I was just bones and cartilage, yet I was awake. My four legs and tail dangled from the metallic slab I lay upon. Every inch of my skeleton felt as though it were still burning from the pool of fire I had been drawn from. My head was seized and locked to the table, clamps grinding into my skull. I felt their final ratcheting squeeze just before the first hammer blow crashed into my jaw. I felt it grow longer with each agonizing impact. Then my chin was gripped by pairs of unseen tongs and my mandible was torn asunder. I wanted to scream, but I had no control over my body, let alone throat or tongue to shape a sound. Then a leg was clamped. Then the hammer moved on, and the tongs, and other tools I could only guess at, and with them the drawing and the wrenching. Every swing of the hammer altered my physical form. Someone was changing me, annealing my skeletal structure, molding it into a new creation the way a blacksmith would forge a sword.

The reknotting of sinew and joint, the welding of a weighted metal ball to the tip of my tail, and riveting of bony plates to my shins, neck, and spine melded into seamless agony. Then I was picked up and thrust into a pool of foul liquid. The icy fluid tempered my bones. Pulled from the pool, dripping oil and water, I was flung back atop the metallic surface. Relieved of the heat, I felt an almost peaceful moment, but the reprieve didn't last. Innards were thrust inside my rib-cage, followed by the binding of slabs of muscle and flesh to the bone. All of a sudden, the aroma that filled the room charged into my nostrils, overflowing them with the odor of smoke, charred flesh, and burnt hair. What was happening to me? Why was I conscious through this?

I could now work my aggrandized maw, but every movement was stiff and sore. I ran my new tongue across multiple rows of flesh-rending teeth; when I dropped my lower jaw open, my split mandibles showcased serrated death. I had just begun to wonder what would happen next, when gelatinous orbs were thrust into my eye sockets, and I felt the optic nerves worm into my brain. I had to blink a few times, as the sensations of light and shadow cleared to become normal vision, but I could now observe my surroundings. I was lying on my side atop a massive iron anvil within a dark room, lit by the flickering firelight of a furnace. The sight of tongs, bellows, chains, vises, and other instruments that lay among the wavering shadows confirmed what my body had already told me: I was within the forge of a blacksmith. It seemed so familiar, as if I had been here once before. Or more than once. I searched through my memories, but, like trying to recollect a distant dream, there was nothing. I rolled my head over and peered into the darkness. I strained my eyes to resolve another form glimpsed across the room. At the edge of the shadows, sprawled across another anvil, lay the lifeless, skinless, and bloodless corpse of an unrecognizable creature. Is that what I am going to be, or what I am being created from?

Two hands grabbed my head, twisting it about to face a shadowed figure. Beyond him, my gaze was drawn to a cubed mass of translucent flesh on a short, thick handle, with veins and a beating heart inside. The Forging Hammer. I still could not make out any details of the man before me, but that hardly mattered: I knew now where I was, who my tormenter had to be. As He cupped his hands over my eyes I could feel His fingertips seep into my skin. His fingernails anchored into my skull as He began to drag my eye-sockets into a more centered location upon my face. I struggled to squirm away, but I was still bound to the table. After a guttural, approving grunt, He removed his fingers and my depth perception improved. He picked up the Forging Hammer and began affixing scales to my exposed flesh, beating them into place with titanic blows. I feared my ribs would break under the impact.

The relentless pounding finally ceased. The craftsman lifted his living mallet of flesh above me and began chanting in a language I didn't understand. A jolt of power arced from the Hammer to me, sparking life within my heart as it began to beat in rhythm with that of the Hammer. Blood and energy pumped through my veins, yet I felt weak—as if I didn't have the strength to lift my enlarged limbs. He stepped back and repeated his words, louder, and the torrid smithy air grew cold. He slammed the Hammer into the dead creature adjacent to me and an emerald wisp of smoke separated itself from the corpse. As it rose out of the body, it swirled around itself, suspended in the air, emanating an eerie green hue that tinged the shadows untouched by the forge's dancing orange. I watched as the man directed it with the Hammer, guiding it from that body toward mine; and with one final blow He drove the essence into me. I could feel it possess me, bind itself to me, adjoining its vitality to mine; we became one. I felt a surge of strength and a sense of consummation; I felt powerful. I felt complete.

I felt Him release the bindings around my legs and I stood up atop the anvil. I turned to face my maker, who I now saw to be but a fraction of my monstrous size, only to have a white-hot poker pressed against my forehead. With a loud sizzling, it branded an unknown symbol into my scales. I squeezed my eyes closed, howling and moaning in pain. I tried to scratch it away with my massive, blade-like talons, but then, in a flash, the pain and smell of burnt hair was gone. I opened my eyes to see a lush green forest, abundant ferns littering the floor about the bases of massive redwood trees. The dirt was moist under my paws; drops fell from the leaves above. It had just finished raining. I was ravenous. And I was free to hunt.

***

Everything stopped.

The echo of a grievous howl ascended from deep within the forest of the Beknen Valley below. The elkin, a savage race of men with antlers sprouting from their skulls, gathered in the center of the village of Cerebus-Senti. Proud hunter-warriors exchanged anxious glances at a wail unlike that of any beast known to man.

One boorish warrior grimaced as he approached; the stalwart legs distinctive of elkin carried him with confidence. All of Clan Wyndlyn turned their attention to the husky brute as he stepped into the center of the gathering. His broad, ferocious antler rack seemed a tangible echo of his raucous voice. "The Soul Smith has sent us a new devil to add to our trophy collection," announced Herlidrek.

A second voice echoed his. "Gear up and follow my lead if you want your blade to see this demon's end!" The woman's boldness drew a few supporters.

"Shall we make this a competition then, Megna?" Before giving her a chance to take him up on the offer, Herlidrek continued: "Come on. This is what we're here for. Let's end this demon before it knows its ass from its head!"

Eager for the taste of battle, the rugged veteran drew his weathered war axe from his belt and strangled its wooden handle in his calloused hand. Muscles flexed as he shifted the weight of a massive wooden shield studded with sharpened antler tines. His dirty brown hair was long and uneven, if combed and straight. Eyes cold as flint well matched a jaw that might have been chiseled from it. His torso was bare, apart from several slender leather straps that encircled his shoulders and chest; teeth and small bones were braided into the straps like little trophies. Damp wool trousers were matted to his brawny legs by air humid with recent rain.

Many more courageous warriors donned shields, slung quivers of javelins, and formed teams to hunt the new demon of the Soul Smith, which continued to howl from the depths of the forest below. As they charged down the stair from the plateau on which their village rested, others took up vantage points along it to ensure nothing escaped the valley… or entered.

Overlooking the mouth of Beknen Valley sat two elkin villages, poised above either side of a narrow pass like sentries guarding a vault. The pass was shaped as if the mountains had been wedged apart the way an axe splits cordwood. It was the only entrance to the inner valley by foot. Unscalable mountain ranges surrounded the valley, jutting near vertically out of the earth in solid curtains of shale and slate, cradling the forest within their walls.

Clan Wyndlyn, along with their neighbors of Clan Hortyr in the village of Remaurus-Senti, regularly turned away fortune-seekers and risk-takers from the valley's mouth, never granting entry to outsiders, to spare them almost certain death, as well as a fate the elkin regarded as worse than it. Though after being refused passage through the valley's door, most adventure-minded humans would depart more resentful than gracious, their curiosity only further piqued. Throughout Thornwall the elkin had become wreathed in mystery, and rumors abounded as to what treasures and relics the elkin might guard within the confines of the forest.

Less regularly, Clan Wyndlyn was obliged to deal with what it actually held.

A dozen hunters sped toward the source of the creature's groans. Even as they ran, these diminished in frequency and volume, trailing off altogether and leaving the forest in foreboding silence long before they could near their prey. They glided along a mudded trail through the undulating terrain of the valley floor with silent precision, slipping past towering ferns and tumbled splinters of the surrounding ridges without so much as a whisper. When the path split, the elkin warriors did as well. Each squadron of six contained equal numbers of men and women, some wielding hand axes and shields, some carrying javelins; a few carried no weapons at all.

Herlidrek raced at the point of his band; only a lifetime of training restrained him from outpacing them altogether. Even this failed when, in the near distance, loud snorts and a heavy rustling became audible over the trickle of a nearby stream.

***

Hunger drove me to gallop through the forest as fast as my four legs would carry me, toward a scent of cooked meat. The metallic ball anchored to my tail furrowed the moist forest floor behind me, ricocheted from trees as I zigzagged through them. I bounded a small stream and came upon a large scorched area. Small embers still glowed hot on the ground amid ashes of fern and moss; some sort of antlered humanoid lay in the center of the blast. Its skin was riddled with blisters. Its torso was separated from its legs; ribs were exposed, entrails and stomach contents strewn about. Roots had already begun to emerge from the burnt land and entangle the corpse, secreting an enzyme onto its flesh. I was hungry, but I had no appetite for a decomposing corpse.

I stared at the bark of the tree in wonder, watching it tinge a darker hue as the roots drank the blood of the corpse. Nearby, there was a strange circular metal object upon the ground; it looked like a metal mouth of pointed teeth, stretched open as wide as possible. I flexed my dual mandible as I roared at it in challenge, grinning at the fact that mine was bigger. I was about to touch the object, but I detected some movement out of the corner of my eye. A third humanoid arm, severed at the shoulder, was being coiled by more snakelike roots. It seems more than one humanoid was killed here. But what caused the fire?

My curiosity ebbed rapidly, however, no match for my hunger. It vanished altogether when, to my surprise, I discovered more antlered humanoids had approached while I was distracted: six of them, running toward me. My mouth salivated as it became apparent that lunch had found me. They began to yell words to each other which were foreign to me, though different from the chant of my maker. My barbed tongue shrilled between my trifurcated jaws as I roared and charged the oncoming morsels. I sideswiped the first and largest out of my way with a foreleg. My sword-like talons rattled against his spiked shield as the strength in my arm sent him flying. If he was their best, this would be simple. I pounced at another, mouth agape, and clenched my jaws around his head. Crunch! His antlers jabbed into my gums before I could close my jaws and sever his head; still, my teeth tore gouges in his flesh as I released him. Furious, I jerked sideways and swung the metal ball on my tail at his unshielded side, imploding the dazed humanoid's ravaged face before he could turn his defense.

A slender female advanced, weaponless. She stretched out her arm, presenting her palm. Surrender? Pleading? I hardly cared. Then a flash of white light burned my eyes. I backpedaled, shaking my head to try to regain my vision, but then I felt two sticks impale my ribcage. I scuttled backward faster, until I collided with a tree. Some instinct told me to ascend. My vision was still blurry, but I had little need of it for climbing: that, I could do by feel. I turned, stood upright, gripped the girth of the bloodbark tree with my forelegs, and heaved myself upward. I could feel the palms of my feet suction to the bark of the tree. My body was one continuous, pleasant surprise. I ascended with ease.

***

The hunters set fresh javelins to their atlatls. Their first volley had sunk two into the beast; its formidable armor had turned the rest. Beige bone plating overlapped a thick layer of cobalt scales across its shoulders, spine, and legs, while a crest-of-bone flared about its gullet. The runic emblem of the Soul Smith was branded into the scales above its eyes. Its lower jaw splayed open as the fiend unleashed a throaty wail at its sudden blindness and pain, sending tremors through the muddy earth. The elkin stood undaunted, maneuvered for better angles from which to cast. Then it turned; talons that looked as if they could cleave a man in half grabbed the trunk of a bloodbark. The warriors froze in astonishment as they watched scales and bone shift color to match the bark of the tree. As swift as if on level ground, the beast climbed the bloodbark and disappeared amongst the shadowed canopy.

Emerging from the lush underbrush, the other squadron of elkin arrived and aided Herlidrek to his feet. Only bruised from the beast's swipe, he pointed at the scorched earth whence the beast had attacked. "Not only can this beast blend in with its surroundings, it can breathe fire too." The elkin all turned their gazes to the blackened and grisly remains.

Among their number was Erador, a novice by comparison to the rest, a talented hunter at the prime of his youth, awaiting ascension into adulthood. He stood aghast at the unfamiliar sight of the carnage that the Soul Smith's demon left in its wake. Erador was equipped as most of the Clan Wyndlyn warriors were: fur boots, trousers, axe sheathed on leather belt, linen tunic beneath warm fur cloak, a javelin in one hand and a wooden shield in the other.

Faint strings of smoke ascended from the withering embers and dissipated into the air as if it were the fire's last breath. Gnarled tentacles of roots had erupted through the soil and entangled the dismembered portions of elkin carcasses. Erador gripped his javelin with nervous hands, his jaw agape at the scene of scorched death. He panned away from the cooked landscape to his clan mate, slain by the whip of the demon's tail, left unrecognizable with shattered skull. Erador shook his head in sorrow, but there was no time to grieve. There was nothing they could do for their felled companion now, though he knew that they would honor their fallen later. There was no better way for an elkin to perish than in combat with a demon; to have their remains recycled into the earth was as good a burial as any.

Erador returned his gaze to the root-entangled remains upon the forest floor. After a hard swallow, his youthful voice broke the silence. "Are they ours?"

"No," answered Herlidrek with a cold, short tone. "See the snare on the ground? They belong to Clan Hortyr."

Herlidrek turned slowly, holding his rectangular, antler-spiked shield in the air as if to ward off the heavens as he tried to locate the beast within the towering canopy. The sky was still overcast from the recent rainfall, leaving the treetops shrouded in gloom.

The rejoined squads followed Herlidrek's orders and gathered in two groups of four, all with backs to one other, each monitoring a quarter of the canopy. The remaining three spread slightly apart from the others, to lure the creature with easier targets.

No more words were spoken.

They all abided with patient determination, the hunter's vigil second nature for them. Feet shifted imperceptibly to avoid becoming mired in the mud; eyes darted about seeking movement. Droplets of water plashed upon waiting blades. The peaceful sound of the unconcerned stream imposed a timeless serenity upon their mortal tension.

The respite was broken by two bloodied javelins clattering upon nearby rocks.

***

Hidden in the shadows of the canopy, I pulled the two sticks from my side. The pain was trivial compared to my forging. I tossed the sticks away from me as a distraction. I watched in mounting anticipation as the hunters took the bait, forming a semi-circle around the fallen sticks, scouring the canopy in the wrong direction. My mouth drooled at the thought of tearing into all those juicy morsels.

I descended head-first down the far side of the bloodbark to remain concealed, but I became too impatient to continue in stealth. I rounded the bole and leaped down behind them, landing upon the soft earth with an authoritative thump. They spun in surprise and threw more of their sticks at me, which merely glanced off my bone plating as I bounded toward them. I slavered in satisfaction as I stomped one face-first into the earth while I wrapped my jaws around his meaty leg. The mud and his cries swallowed one another as my jaws sawed into flesh and sinew. The taste of blood drove me into frenzy. I tore his leg loose and began to gnaw meat from bone. I planted myself atop my catch and whipped my tail low across the ground, tripping two would-be rescuers.

They were more cautious of me now. Their communication became less boisterous, more urgent. They repositioned to surround me with slow, deliberate steps, watching as I finished consuming the meat on the leg. Some had even begun to back away to keep their distance. About time they started showing the sense to fear me. Unless... my gaze was drawn to one particular female. Her arms were hanging at her side, palms open outward toward me; her hands were glimmering with white light. That one. Not fear, then: trickery. I didn't care to be blinded again, even if it meant delaying my next tidbit. I crouched, readying a leap.

She clenched her hands into fists; for one moment, her delicate bones and veins were appetizingly backlit. Then she knelt and punched the ground with both fists. Sparks pulsed from the contact, racing along the ground to conjure two large, glowing circles beneath the feet of the two warriors adjacent to her. Brimming with energy, the circles surged upward—lifting the warriors off their feet and propelling them toward me through the air.

I spat the leg from my mouth in preparation to snatch them out of the sky. The flying warriors swung back their axes with a fearless war cry as beaming trails of light arched them through the air. I sat back onto my hind legs and opened my forearms to welcome them both when another searing flash of light sent my vision into a burning blur.

***

The creature was blinded once again as both warriors landed their axes in its neck behind the hulking beast's shield-like bone plating. The two warriors clung onto the creature's back and hacked in a merciless frenzy at any exposed areas of the creature's flesh they could reach. It roared its pain and its frustration at having been blinded again. "Watch out for its fire breath!" shouted

15

Herlidrek as he charged, prepared to deflect any flames with his shield.

A coordinated volley of javelins sunk into the demon's exposed chest just above Herlidrek's head as he gored his sharpened antlers into the gut of the monstrosity that towered above him. The creature fell forward onto all fours and whipped around, bucking both warriors from its back. It lashed its lethal tail randomly in desperation, but to no effect.

Herlidrek, antlers dislodged by the demon's writhing, rolled from under it and to his feet, planting himself face to face with the beast. It twisted its head from side to side, as if trying to decide which of him to deal with first. The veteran warrior wasted no time. He whirled his axe over his head in a broad circular motion, culminating in a backhand that cleaved into the temple of the creature, embedding the entire axe-head into its skull.

The beast fell dead, and the elkin stood there, victorious.

"What is it?" one asked as they all stared at the lifeless carcass.

"You know what it is. A devil, born from the fire of the Soul Smith's furnace. One we haven't seen before. Collect the equipment of our fallen. Be sure to get their antlers so the Soul Smith can't collect their souls. We will remember them in song, that they fought valiantly in today's triumph over this… this demon," intoned Herlidrek, hesitating as to what to call the beast.

"You killed it, you name it," reminded Erador. He produced a set of shears from his belt pouch and went about the task of severing the antler racks from each of the fallen elkin. Another hunter used a similar tool to prize forth a dozen of the demon's teeth for trophies, one per hunter, including the slain. Theirs would feature in the memorials later.

Herlidrek thought on that for a moment, while one of his clan mates attended his bruised ribs. "Then it shall be known as Thorbryx," he decided.

As the elkin were concluding their cleanup, a single leaf, detached from the canopy above, drifted to the ground among them. It was not one loosened by the encounter.

"The first sign of autumn," murmured one.

"It comes early this year."

"And winter will too soon follow. We must alert Warlord Brynn."

The Thorbryx's blood pooled wide around its lifeless corpse; as if the trees were starving, the roots emerged from the soil to entangle the slain demon. The elkin watched in pleasure, knowing that there would be no bodily remains left for the Soul Smith to collect.

Erador carried the antlers of the fallen and followed the nine other remaining elkin as they marched back to their village perched above the mouth of the valley, where they were greeted with praise. Herlidrek raised his hands to quiet the crowd as he told the story of their victory over the fire-breathing Thorbryx to a captivated audience. As the story came to a close, he added, "Let us all remember our fallen clansmen this day in defeating another of the Soul Smith's demons. One day soon, the Soul Smith will learn his place when dealing with Clan Wyndlyn!" Cheers erupted throughout the crowd.

Amidst the cheer, Erador looked at Herlidrek with envy. *He got the kill so he gets the glory,* he thought. Erador did not join in with the applause. Instead, he wandered further into the village, dragging his feet as he walked. He gave a longing stare at the antlers within his hands. *I wish I could have done more to have spared your lives.* Then he lifted his head and saw movement in the distance, upon the tundra that spread about the valley's enclosing walls. A dust cloud, trailing an approaching band. An unusually large one.

"Look!" he shouted over his shoulder to his gathered clan mates, pointing. *So much for vigilance,* he thought. *Victorious, we take our eyes from our charge to celebrate. That group should not have come half so near without being spotted. And* I'm *supposed to be the one too young to know what he's doing?* The fact that he only spotted them because he was sulking had no impact on affronted youthful self-esteem.

The celebration ceased as, one by one, Clan Wyndlyn saw the oncoming threat nearing the mouth of the valley. The troop seemed to number near as many as the clan, mostly warriors with spears pointing to the heavens, though no few were far smaller. Children?

"Are we under attack?"

"Is it the Brenzwik Tribe again?"

"No. I see antlers!"

"Another clan of elkin? From where?"

It wasn't long before both Clan Wyndlyn warlords joined Erador to look upon the visiting clan. Each Warlord had donned a distinctive suit of armor that had been forged by the Blacksmiths themselves and bore the markings of their divine inscriptions upon its surface. Warlord Frodden wore a suit of plate-and-scale produced in the forge of the Sky Smith, while Warlord Brynn wore the heavy full plate armor of the Onyx Smith. The holy runes of the Blacksmiths were believed to contain god-like power locked deep within their cryptic runes—a forgotten language lost by the passage of time. Each set was a most rare and prized possession.

They were a sight to behold. Standing adjacent to his father, Erador looked ill-equipped by comparison. Erador eyed with awe the heavy sword sheathed at his father's side, then studied the golden runes etched into the armor's rugged jet surface. His eyes were drawn from one to the next, roving across helm, breastplate, bracers and greaves, as if each symbol beckoned for his attention.

Warlord Frodden's armor appeared to be crafted of cloudy glass, yet it was a match for any steel. Rows of fine scales cascaded from each shoulder and around his waist, over sleeves and leggings of even finer chain, connecting the plates covering chest, forearms and shins. Runes of royal blue, small and delicate compared to those of the Onyx armor, seemed to dance upon its faces. Unlike Warlord Brynn, Warlord Frodden lacked weapon and helm to match.

Clan Wyndlyn was not alone in having noticed the newcomers. From the far side of the valley, a party from Clan Hortyr was descending. *At least they weren't ahead of us*, thought Erador. He'd spared his clan *that* embarrassment.

Below, the approaching group had neared enough that details could be picked out. Yes, there were youths and children scattered amongst the adults. Though the most surprising detail was the elkin who strode at their head. For he, too, was dressed in armor of the Sky Smith.

"Shall I sound the call for battle, father?" asked Erador, even as he wondered: *What clan would bring its children to a battle?*

"No, wait here," commanded Warlord Brynn to the crowd. "We're going to hold a Meeting of the Warlords."

CHAPTER 2

Erador had never heard of a Meeting of the Warlords before. *Was this another secret that was kept from me?* he wondered. He was determined to find out more.

Erador watched his father and Warlord Frodden depart. They met two representatives from Clan Hortyr who had separated themselves from the rest of their party. One would be Hortyr's Warlord, Korin. He wasn't sure about the other. As he peered down onto the valley, a slender, younger clan mate came up beside him. "How many of them do you think there are?" asked Zimmerik.

"It looks like sixty adults, plus youngsters and children. Maybe fifteen of those? Twenty? Too far away to tell how many are our age. Not many."

"Do you think they traveled far to get here?" asked Zimmerik.

"Have you heard of any other elkin tribes living nearby?" Erador thought too late to soften his sarcasm, decided to cover it by moving on. "Anyway, there's only two reasons why anyone *would* travel here."

Zimmerik scrunched his brow. "Really?"

Erador's eyes continued scanning the approaching elkin. "Same as anyone else we get. They're either here to attack, or because they want something from us."

"Well, if they were here for battle, wouldn't they have attacked already?"

"You think I have the answer for everything, don't you?" Erador jested.

"Well, uh, zeesh. It's just that your dad is our Warlord, so you usually know this type of stuff."

Erador did not want to admit that he was becoming increasingly aware he knew far less than his friend imagined he did.

"But if they aren't here to fight, then what do you think they want?" asked Zimmerik, rubbing the back of his head.

The combined delegation stopped in a flat, clear area, readily visible from both villages. The approaching Warlord halted his clan and came forward to meet them alone.

"I'm not going to wait to find out. I'm going down for a closer look." Erador bolted down the stair from Cerebus-Senti toward his father. Zimmerik shouted one last phrase, but the words were lost to Erador's ears.

As Erador reached the clearing, he slowed to a walk. He could feel the stares of all Clan Wyndlyn on his back as they watched him from their perch atop the bluff. He studied the visiting clan of elkin as he approached. They wore wild garb and their faces and arms were streaked with dirt, though the patterns seemed deliberate, like war paint. They wore long cloaks, knotted from something that looked like hair. Their own? Leaves and ferns were worked into the knot-work: it looked as if they carried a forest floor on their backs. They looked hungry and tired, resigned, their body language hinting at desperation. Erador's eye caught up briefly on one female in particular, about his own age, who appeared more alert to the proceedings than the rest of her clan mates.

The new warlord was not as the others. His skin, where it showed, was free from dirt and grime, and his shoulders free from any camouflaged cloak. He bore a sinister frown across his face. His straight black hair was sleek and trimmed below the shoulders. The Sky Smith Armor he wore was almost identical to Warlord Frodden's. Not until he was almost up to the meeting did Erador's keen eye notice that there were subtle differences in the inscriptions.

As Erador neared, he shifted his focus toward their conversation. Erador was careful to tread softly so as not to interrupt. With each step, their words became clearer.

"…jungle turned to stone and we are in need of a home. Plus, I hear there is a Channeler that can provide training," said the visiting warlord.

"He must be talking about you, Clan Wyndlyn," stated the elkin from Clan Hortyr who accompanied Warlord Korin. "We haven't any Goma spell casters…"

"…since anyone born with the ability leaves us for *them*," added Warlord Korin begrudgingly, addressing the stranger. "But you could still come with us if you have no problem letting go of your Goma enchanters."

"That is not an option," stated the visiting warlord as he shook his head. "I will not separate my daughter from my clan."

Warlord Brynn smiled. "So you have proclaimed fathership of your daughter? She must be talented. Our Channeler will be pleased; she is always looking for new pupils."

"Who's this!?" barked the visiting warlord, glaring contemptuously at Erador's arrival.

Warlord Brynn turned in surprise and Erador froze in place, searching for something to say that might excuse his presence. His father gave him a look which let him know he was going to pay later for interrupting their meeting.

"Warlord Dryden, this is my son, Erador," Warlord Brynn said, gesturing to him. "Erador, this is Warlord Dryden of Clan Grondyr from Sonir-Senti within the southern jungles of Chyxurlgon."

"Does this stripling think he belongs at the Meeting of the Warlords?" growled Warlord Dryden. "This is insulting."

"I come with pressing news," stated Erador with feigned confidence. "During our hunt, we saw the first sign of autumn."

"Already?" asked a surprised Warlord Frodden, as the elkin of Clan Hortyr looked at one other in concern.

Warlord Dryden raised his brows in confusion. "What's so important about autumn?"

"Because winter will soon follow," answered Erador.

Warlord Dryden glowered at Erador's facile reply. Erador offered a swift, silent prayer to the Onyx Smith that he hadn't just started a war.

"He's right," stated Warlord Brynn as he straightened his posture. "We must begin preparations immediately. As I stated earlier, Warlord Dryden, we could use the extra hands. I think our village has enough room. Plenty of empty huts, though we if we need to build more next spring, we shall. If you will have us, we will have you. But if you do join us, there can only be one clan, and there can only be one leader."

Warlord Dryden scoffed. "Then clearly, this Meeting is not yet finished."

"Clearly," Warlord Brynn agreed. His face was chiseled into an unreadable expression as his stern gaze returned Warlord Dryden's. "Erador, leave us."

Not daring to question, Erador turned to leave. After five steps, he glanced over his shoulder and watched Warlord Dryden slide the Sky Smith helm around his antlers. Erador froze in bewilderment. *Are they going to duel?*

"Put your helm on!" ordered Warlord Dryden in fury.

"Are you challenging me?" asked Warlord Brynn, apparently not expecting this response to his hospitality.

"I don't see any other choice. Words won't solve anything," said Dryden, confirming Erador's suspicions.

Without a second's thought, Warlord Brynn slid on the dark helm of the Onyx Smith and braced for combat. "You will regret this," he promised.

The warlords circled each other, knees bent, leaning forward to point their antlers at their foe. A motionless overcast, dark as storm or stone, hung above them. The onlookers, from their varied vantages, observed in tense silence. Their collective fates were hanging in the balance.

With a war cry that rang throughout the sky, Warlord Dryden dug his feet deep and lunged in a powerful burst. Warlord Brynn rooted himself to receive the charge. Antlers and helms collided in a crash that rolled across the tundra, echoed back from the valley. For some moments, neither could find an advantage against the other; they grunted and strained, bucked and twisted, vying for leverage in a duel of raw muscle.

Warlord Brynn appeared to stumble, as if one knee had suddenly betrayed him. It had not. He sensed an opening low in the other's guard, got beneath it, and took step after heavy steps forward. Warlord Dryden was driven across the ground, feet scrabbling to find traction. His opponent unbalanced, Warlord Brynn surged upward and sent the challenger flying backwards to land upon his backside.

Warlord Brynn removed his helm and shook free his hair, standing tall and ominous in his Onyx armor as he surveyed the faces of the visiting clan. Satisfied with whatever he saw there, he looked down at the defeated warlord and offered him his hand. After a moment's pause, a clouded white gauntlet reached up and clasped his onyx one. Warlord Brynn pulled his opponent to his feet. Warlord Dryden spat at the ground, humiliated by his loss. Warlord Brynn looked him in the eye and said, "That is no longer your clan and they are no longer known as Clan Grondyr. They are my clan now, and you will all be known as Clan Wyndlyn. You will still be a warlord, but it is I and my lineage that will rule here and lead this clan."

Erador felt a smile tug at the corners of his mouth in pride. Warlord Brynn turned to face all of the elkin and continued. "You should put off those cloaks, for they will not serve you in this terrain. You should bathe in the waters of our river and dress yourselves in the linens and furs of our clan. Then you can satisfy your hunger by joining us at feast, and afterward in song and revelry. You shall dine this evening as guests of honor, then go to your beds tonight as kindred."

Erador watched their reactions. Many looked to one another, searching for reassurance. After a long, silent moment, the first elkin removed his cloak of knotted hair and leaves and folded it over his arm. With just the slightest glance toward his former leader, he stepped forward and shook Warlord Brynn's hand.

"Welcome to your new home," said Warlord Brynn. "Welcome to Cerebus-Senti."

One after another of elkin did the same, then all followed Warlord Brynn as he led them up the slope to Cerebus-Senti. The representatives of Clan Hortyr returned to their own, to tell of what had passed. As the old and new members of Wyndlyn mingled for the first time, Warlord Brynn raised his hands and spoke loudly so all could hear. "These elkin needed a home, as theirs was taken from them. They have agreed to join us under the banner of Clan Wyndlyn and learn our ways. So tonight, we host a ceremony! We will celebrate the slaying of the Thorbryx and the merging of our two clans!"

Smiles and greetings were exchanged all around. The newcomers did as they had been bidden, bathing and washing their clothes, disposing of their cloaks. The streaks of mud that once mottled their skin were scoured away and their hair was scrubbed clean. They emerged from the river refreshed and with new-found hope. They were handed new linens—after a hasty search to find enough to fit them all—and were shown about the village, shown which dwellings were empty and which might house another elkin or two. Despite the hospitality, there was an uncomfortable awkwardness as the new elkin settled in small, silent groups to await the feast.

The clouds finally gave way to reveal the sun setting beyond the mountainous ridges that rose about the valley. The sun's orange glow bled down the sharply-defined horizon as the first sounds of the night were swallowed by the rhythm of leather-skinned drums filling the muggy air. Old and new clan mates danced into the sunset.

The ceremony teemed with life. Aloof from the celebration, Erador perched upon a stone at the periphery of the activity, motionless as a pondering statue. Deep in mournful contemplation, he stared into the fire as if he were alone.

Out of the darkness, a weathered hand gripped Erador's shoulder. He jerked with surprise, twisting from the grasp to confront the other. Before him stood a towering man wearing the light tan linen tunic, dun trousers, and fur boots common to the clan. Twin antler branches, tines sheathed with metallic tips, loomed in the dancing firelight.

"Father?" asked Erador, stunned at being approached unaware.

"I did not mean to startle you," stated the warm familiar voice.

"What are you doing here?"

"I wanted to congratulate you on your hunt today, but you do not seem yourself. What's troubling you?" asked Warlord Brynn.

"The Soul Smith's demons are getting larger, and more dangerous!" Erador stated his concern in boisterous tones, oblivious to his surroundings. "I need to master my vanquisher training! I need you to teach me—"

Warlord Brynn glanced around at the disdaining glares the exchange had attracted from the newcomers within earshot. Their eyes were full of jealousy, mingled in a few cases with distress from those who grasped the deeper import of Erador's words. Warlord Brynn whispered, "Lest you desire animosity to grow between you and your peers, I suggest you not complain about your already preferential treatment."

Erador glanced up just as three adolescents looked away. Warlord Brynn continued in his wise, heart-felt tone, "It is rare enough for a youth to hunt alongside the adults. Rarer still for a blood-father to claim his child as I did you. Something you might wish to remember when remonstrating with that father in front of those who cannot."

Erador took a deep sigh and spoke at a careful volume. "Two of us died this day. If only I were stronger… I could have reacted faster, or thrown my javelin more accurately, could have prevented our clansmen's deaths. And now, we celebrate our victory over the Thorbryx instead of mourn their loss."

Erador looked into Warlord Brynn's dignified eyes and noble expression, seeing a look that only a proud father could give to his son. All Erador could manage was a half-smile in return. Erador had begun to wallow back into the loneliness of his mind, staring once more into the flickering fire. The rhythmic music, far from commanding attention, transported him into a distance. Warlord Brynn could see by the furrow of his son's brow that the deaths of their fellow clansmen weighed heavily upon Erador's mind.

Warlord Brynn spoke with a gritty undertone. "It is their fate, Erador. They fought with courage until the end. Any elkin would have been proud to have done the same."

"But fates can be altered…"

Warlord Brynn appeared impressed by Erador's train of thought. "You speak of matters that only the Channeler can answer, but you must remember our oath: 'May we bleed so others will not. Honor the fallen and covet their bravery. Revere the gods, and embrace your fate. Defend our lands to your last breath.' That is our oath. You know this. Every elkin lives and dies by those words."

Erador smiled as the familiar words soothed his worries. "The gods can be cruel."

"While we must respect the gods, we don't have to trust them. Thus we collect the antlers of our slain, trusting ourselves rather than the gods to preserve their souls from the Soul Smith. None of us wish our soul to be in his hands again," uttered Warlord Brynn. "In fact, Warlord Dryden has already visited Clan Hortyr's village across the way to deliver the antlers of their deceased, so that they may do the same. That was the way of our ancestors and so it is the way of our people. There is much wisdom to be discovered from the methods of our ancients."

"The one set of antlers we found," reminded Erador. "We found nothing of the second elkin other than the arm. The Soul Smith may have lost his latest demon, but he won something as well." Erador's gloom returned full force at that memory. "There is also much of our ancestors' wisdom that lies concealed from me until my ascendance to adulthood," Erador prompted, hoping his father might have some other reassurance to offer.

Warlord Brynn's face grew sour. "You are less than a year away from that now," he said. "For now, we must prepare for our retreat to the Willow Cave before the arrival of winter." Warlord Brynn shifted his weight. "Erador, you know I must punish you for your intrusion into our meeting?" Erador opened his mouth to respond, but Warlord Brynn didn't wait for an answer. "So it is your task to collect firewood and turn it into charcoal. Enough to last our entire clan for the winter. You start at sunrise."

Erador nodded in agreement. "Father."

"Hmm?"

"Well fought today."

With a smile, Warlord Brynn departed and rejoined the celebration. Erador put an effort into doing the same—his father's none too subtle reminder about politics still fresh in his mind—but his heart remained elsewhere.

As the ceremony and song came to a close, Erador wandered to the edge of his village, perched high above the mouth of the valley, and looked out over the tundra that stretched in an endless expanse before him. The light of dual full moons, one a dull gray, the other an icy blue, could do little to illuminate subtle differences in its monotony. The moons hung in the starry sky like the ripe honey-filled melons that dangle from leudinar trees.

As he contemplated the countryside below, and the realms beyond it he'd never seen, a sense of ownership, of responsibility and—at last—of accomplishment flowed through him. The valley at his back was small; a vast open world lay before him. The land seemed so peaceful, so serene and quiet that it looked fragile to him. A land worth protecting… that needed protecting. Whatever their loss this day, Clan Wyndlyn had prevented the Thorbryx from rampaging unhindered across it.

Before Erador retired, his eyes glanced across the mouth of the valley toward Clan Hortyr's village. From afar, they were just shadows and silhouettes amongst the firelight. He studied them until the last of them put out their camp fire, wondering at what emotions they might be feeling right now. As with every winter, Clan Hortyr would be entrusted with the protection of this land during his clan's voyage to the Willow Cave. Clan Wyndlyn did so to fulfill the traditions of the ancients… traditions which were kept secret from children, secrets that Erador was impatient to attain.

Just before he went to turn in, he glimpsed a streak of light against the night sky. It seared just above the horizon, like a flaming arrow—then vanished as suddenly as it had appeared.

"Did anybody see that?" he asked in an amazed voice as he pointed at the sky. Only the sounds of the night answered him. He realized he was talking to himself: everyone else had retired.

"What *was* that?" he thought aloud. Erador searched the horizon a moment longer in hope that it would reappear.

"It must have been a shooting star," he decided, then returned to his hut for the night.

CHAPTER 3

Erador jolted awake with his arm drawn back, ready to punch the intruder from his horrid dream. His forehead was drenched with sweat, and his chest heaved in heavy, sporadic breaths. His eyes darted about in wild confusion, assessing his surroundings, teasing apart everyday detail from dreamscape, as the false reality that had imprisoned him within his mind fought a tenacious rearguard battle.

Soft rays of daylight filtered through the reed roof and around the hides draped across the doorway of his hut. Erador fell back into his fur bedding and sighed in relief. The familiar moss-covered stone walls comforted him as he admired the expert stonework of his ancestors. The round stone enclosure accommodated a bed and sitting stone within its walls, with just enough room left over to permit his personal effects to be strewn about the floor in jumbled disarray. A comb whittled from bone lay next to a pair of wool trousers. A long tunic, bundled with a cloak and brooch, lay scrunched beside his mud-covered boots. A leather tool pouch on a matching belt rested next to the sitting stone. Only his armaments showed any indications of attention. His war-axe was kept propped against the raised stone slab of his bed. Its wooden handle was weathered and worn, wrapped and rewrapped with a leather grip; its crudely sharpened iron head showed use and care in equal proportion. His shield leaned against the wall next to the door, holding his quiver of javelins upright behind it.

Erador's unrest bagged under his eyes. He threw off his fur blankets and sat at the edge of his bed to don his trousers and boots. He brushed aside the thin deer hides of the doorway and walked out of his hut pulling his trousers up around his waist. Erador shielded his eyes against the sun, still low on the horizon; its bright light glistened off his tan muscular physique. The clouds of yesterday had vacated the sky.

While his eyes adjusted to the illumination, he surveyed his village. It was quiet. It looked almost empty to him, as no one had yet awoken from their night of revelry. The village's numerous scattered huts gave no semblance of any order. While his was among the smallest, most of the other dwellings were as modest as his; the few that were not were just large enough to bed a child alongside a mother. Only one structure differed from the others: the Armory. Its sheer size stood out amongst the elkin huts: three full families could live within its confines. Four solid megalithic granite slabs formed its rectangular walls, roofed by a fifth. It stood near the center of Cerebus-Senti like a monument, yet it bore no markings upon its surface, nor was there a single entrance. The immense stone walls encased its mysterious contents like a tomb. Clan Wyndlyn's banner flapped gracefully from a spar above the Armory, displaying metallic antlers behind a depiction of the Onyx Smith's legendary Forging Hammer, upon a forest green background.

Erador returned to his hut. He ran the comb through his long dark hair. Its fine teeth parted tangles left by his thrashing from the dream and combed out a single head louse. He considered the tunic, but decided he'd have it off five minutes after he began chopping, so he might as well leave it. He tied his belt around his trousers, settled the pouch in the small of his back. On the way out the door again, he paused: he wasn't going hunting, and he wasn't going far, but… he slung the javelins across his shoulder anyway.

Erador picked up a wood-cutting axe from the village's store of common tools. Seating himself on the bluff at the edge of the village, he drew an oblong whetstone from his belt pouch and addressed the axe's dulled edge. His eyes burned a vibrant bronze in the daylight. Through the thinner trees near the valley's mouth, he noticed other elkin returning from the depths of the forest carrying a metal trap dangling from a short chain. Its steel teeth had closed around the body of a blood-soaked white rabbit. Erador's eyes never left the elkin as they ascended the long stairway carved into the opposite mountainside.

Clan Hortyr, Erador thought with disgust. *How do they call themselves hunters when that contraption does all the work? Their crystal would have been better spent buying weapons from the human traders, rather than their toys.* The elkin from Clan Hortyr seemed to sense his gaze, looking across as they ascended, but made no sign. Erador continued sharpening his axe. *Their traps were of no aid against the fire-breathing Thorbryx, and their warriors suffered because of it. Are they helpless in battle without Goma enchanters?*

From a nearby hut emerged a tall, thick, broad-shouldered adolescent, one of the newcomers from Clan Grondyr Erador had met last night. His dark brown hair was cut short and complemented the rounded face beneath his compact antlers. Though he carried more weight than most elkin, he looked like he would be a brute in battle and a valuable asset to their amalgamated clan.

Erador grinned at the sight of him. "Perfect for dragging back piles of wood," Erador thought aloud. He fished for a name, unaccustomed to having so many new ones presented in so short a time. For anyone less memorable he might have failed… Baltor. That was it.

"Baltor! Grab an axe! Let's chop up some firewood."

Without hesitation, Baltor reached back inside his hut and retrieved a double-bladed iron axe. Its massive head was bound atop a lengthy 'S'-curved handle that cradled comfortably within Baltor's oversized hands. The handle consisted of three vines that intertwined as if they were one.

Erador gripped the rope of a nearby sled and dragged it behind him as he approached Baltor. "I know of a fallen tree not too far from here. Follow me. We'll need to go out of our way a bit first, since it's too steep here to haul the dray up and down."

Erador led westward along the inner wall of the valley. A narrow trail sloped down from the plateau upon which Cerebus-Senti perched. Anyone looking up from below would see only scrub-covered slope rising from the valley floor. The elkin rarely used this path, most often for tasks such as this, where the rock-carved stairs were less practical. Upon reaching the lower end, Erador and Baltor turned back toward the valley mouth, working along the edge of the bluff where the forest began, taking in every detail, remaining alert for any dangers that might be lurking within.

More leaves had fallen since yesterday, speckling the soft earth with the green-gold of birch and alder, the occasional orange spark of an early-falling oak. The red-edged parchment of bloodbark would come later, after most of the others had gone to brown. Birds sang their songs to each other from shaded branches. Rabbits and squirrels dashed through the underbrush. Game trails wandered amongst the trees and shrubbery, challenged by grass and weeds. Near the base of the bluff lay a magnificent bloodbark tree; its fall had opened a gap through which the village could be glimpsed.

"Its wood hasn't rotted yet," said Erador as they approached the tree. "See? You can tell by the color of its bark. There's still a shade of red to it."

They stared at the tree, as though uncertain where to begin. "Well, let's get to it," stated Erador. "We need to haul in more wood than usual, and winter is impatient this year."

They began swinging away with youthful vigor. As chips of wood popped into the air with every chop, slow tears of blood trickled from the gouges of their axes. It didn't take long before the bark lost the remainder of its color, exposing tawny wood within. They first severed the branches from the trunk, trimming the heavier ones to be placed onto the dray. The humid heat intensified as the sun had made its course to the highest point in the sky. Their shirtless bodies glistened with perspiration.

Between the dull thuds from the strikes of their axes, a sound not of the forest danced at the edge of Erador's attention. He took a moment's rest, one foot on the fallen tree, hands atop the axe handle. Peering up through the window in the canopy, he saw a group of young girls—both familiar and new—watching them from the village in adoration. Or at least he hoped that was what it was. Erador smiled back and flexed a pose. Even with the distance, he could tell they were embarrassed to have been noticed. He relished the attention, regardless of their age. He brought his show to a close when the girls twisted around as if startled, then disappeared from sight.

A new face emerged from atop the cliff. A beautiful maiden, near his own age, peered over the ledge to see what the girls had been ogling below. Her light blonde hair was tied into a series of intricate knots around the crown of her head. It was the girl who'd caught his attention when the tribe had arrived yesterday. Carra. Hers was one name he'd taken care to learn. At the first sight of Erador, she shook her head in disbelief with a smirk of amusement. Erador waved, and she rolled her eyes in response and walked away. Erador snickered and turned to Baltor.

The thick-set elkin was still chopping away silently, almost aggressively; his lips hadn't released a grunt all morning, let alone a single word. Erador watched his impressive exotic weapon sever branches clean from the trunk with each swing. "Hey Baltor, what was it like beyond the tundra?"

Whack! "What d'ya mean?" he asked as he continued swinging his large axe. *Whack!*

"I meant, what was the world like when your clan migrated here?"

Baltor paused, displayed a puzzled, cautious look on his face. "Wait. So ya never left Cerebus-Senti?"

Erador shook his head and resumed chopping. "Except for our journey across the tundra to the Willow Cave each year, this place is all I know. The village, the valley and the tundra."

"Why d'ya go to the cave ev'ry year?"

"It's always been that way. We pack up what we need for the winter and go. When we get there, the adults leave all the youths behind to practice the ways of the ancients while they disappear for seven days."

"Where do they go?" *Whack!*

"The adults? I wish I knew." Erador wiped the sweat from his brow. "If I was just one year older, I could travel with my father this year and see it myself."

Erador instantly regretted his words as he realized that Baltor probably wasn't as fortunate to know the identity of his blood-father. Erador eyed the hefty elkin, searching for the slightest sign of jealousy or irritation. If Baltor had taken offense, it didn't show anywhere upon his plum face. After a silent moment, Erador thought it best to change the subject. He glanced at the treblevine haft within Baltor's hands. "Is that axe-handle from Chyxurlgon Jungle?"

Baltor gave a single nod. "A piece o' home."

Erador was about to lift his axe to return to work, but his curiosity didn't fade. "Is it true? That your *whole* jungle turned to stone? How could that happen?"

Baltor stopped swinging. The massive adolescent elkin turned and stared deep into Erador's eyes, his heavy glare seeming to lean into him physically. Erador stood there in uncomfortable ignorance. Baltor stepped close to Erador, towering over him. Erador's eyes darted back and forth in vulnerable confusion.

"Ya tryin' to irk me?" prodded Baltor.

Wide-eyed, Erador shook his head from side to side in a slow rhythm.

Baltor squinted a bit. "Ya really don't know?"

Erador repeated the same genuine response. Baltor seemed satisfied, returning to his work.

Whack! "I wasn't a part o' the vanguard squad, but they discovered a God-Dragon livin' in our jungle."

"God-Dragon?" Erador asked with shock. Such a name should belong only to some creature of great legend. But his tribe's legends did not speak of them at all. *Not the legends I've been allowed to hear*, he amended bitterly.

"One o' the original creations o' the gods, before the time of the Blacksmiths. More powerful than anythin'. Bigger than our village. It can breathe fire even."

Erador's tone switched from horror to confidence. "Sounds like the Thorbryx we killed yesterday. Not so tough."

"No," Baltor stated, concerned to convince Erador of his error. "The Soul Smith hasn't made anythin' as dangerous as a God-Dragon. Our Mother of Clan Grondyr told us that they make even the Blacksmiths afraid. She said that the Soul Smith can't create life the way the old gods did… that's why He needs bones an' bodies an' stuff to build from. Just imagine what He could do if He ever got His hands on somethin' like that."

Erador couldn't believe his ears. Of the many things that his father had told him about the world, he had never heard such tales about the Blacksmiths before. "But the Soul Smith has made life of His own creation before. Creatures that have no resemblance to any other. That's His power, it's what He does!" protested Erador.

"True," stated Baltor, "but as impressive as they may be, He still can't *create*, like the old gods did. Only put parts together an' change 'em. Mother said that even the first elkin were made from humans."

Erador felt dumbfounded. More than ever, he felt keenly aware of how sheltered his life had been. "It must have been an honor to have listened to the wisdom of your Mother."

Baltor closed his eyes and nodded his head once in agreement.

Erador muttered, "Vorkus, the Father of Clan Wyndlyn, was supposed to be one of the first elkin, that's why he had metal antlers… But he passed centuries ago. We were never fortunate enough to study under someone as old as Mother. What happened to her?"

Baltor took a deep breath. "Mother told us all to get out o' there, that turnin' the land to stone was the only way to defeat the God-Dragon and prevent the Soul Smith from collectin' its remains. Warlord Dryden never got a chance to fight it. I remember hearin' the argument, that our weapons couldn't pierce its scales an' it was better to lose one life than all of us… So she stayed behind an' did what needed doin'."

Erador couldn't conceive of a power that could turn an entire jungle to stone. Why would someone capable of that be afraid even of the Smiths? "But how did she do it?"

"I dunno. No one really knows for sure… Warlord Dryden refuses to speak of it."

Erador stood in silence; it was a lot to take in. "So… when you evacuated, where did you go? What was the world like on your way here?"

The look on Baltor's chubby face lightened. "Ya should see the human capital! Bronze walls, an' a huge onyx castle loomin' over it. I never seen anythin' built bigger! Ya could get lost in it, I figure. Never mind the whole city. None o' their other villages can compare." Baltor's eyes gazed at invisible horizons. "Though we didn't go in there, just saw it as we passed."

Erador laughed. "That sounds too unbelievable, even for me." *Whack!*

As it neared time for their evening meal, Erador called a halt and surveyed the day's work. They'd cut far more than one load's worth, though much of that was discards, branches too small to be made into charcoal. Things would slow down when they started on the trunk. He'd have to see if he could find someone to collect the leavings for firewood—so that he and Baltor wouldn't get stuck with that, too. After the dray was as loaded as seemed practical, they began the roundabout drag back up to the village. Baltor did most of the pulling; Erador followed, retrieving any logs that slid off. The Cerebus-Senti they returned to was as bustling with life as it had been quiet when they'd left.

Clan mates bustled about in all directions, usually in pairs, one new and one native, so nearly even had the two groups been in number. The children from the southern jungle may have had much to learn, but friendship they seemed to have little trouble with. Lingering exhaustion from their journey was a bigger barrier than newness. Erador marveled yet again at Baltor's strength. Others nearer Erador's age were more hesitant, where he saw them: Carra was not in evidence. Probably cooped up with the Channeler, he supposed. Most of the adults from the south looked ill at ease. Still, they were weary, and it was only the first day. Erador tried to imagine himself being ripped away from all that was familiar to him. And failed. *How could I imagine it*, he wondered, *when I never have been away from this place?*

Not all the activity dealt solely with preparing for winter. There was a great deal of measuring and sewing of linen and wool, since the clan's store of garments had effectively been halved, and of spinning and weaving fresh thread to replace the cloth in turn. Clan Grondyr's timing had been favorable in that respect, as the late shearing had just taken place, and it was still the right time of year to gather flax. The flax seeds were separated to be ground into linseed oil to condition leather and hides against the weather. Many a strong back hauled fresh clay up to the village: few pieces of earthenware had survived the trek. Bundles of reeds were brought up to be woven into wicker… especially baskets, to haul more of everything else. Fetching water and firewood became tasks for any pairs of young hands caught momentarily idle.

As the season wore on, emphasis would shift to slaughtering animals, some of which would come from the clan's goat flock but most of which would require hunting. The meat would be salted or smoked. The hides and pelts would be cleaned, cured, and tanned, in most cases with the fur left in place. Old hides would be sorted through and the least satisfactory destroyed… though Erador anticipated a dip in the clan's standards this coming winter. And while oak bark was available in any quantity they desired, he could see no way for the clan to avoid sending a party around the outer wall of the valley to where it met the Western Sea. They would need to make more salt, something they usually did only once a year, in mid-summer.

Baltor dragged the dray to a place Erador pointed out, unfortunately on the east side of the village, the side farthest from the path, but where the prevailing winds would blow smoke away from the village. The ground there was clear; a careful look showed traces of several large circles. The two of them unloaded the wood and stacked it beside the first of these. Erador shook his head. His father had said he was responsible for making the charcoal, not just gathering the wood. "Once we have a half dozen or so loads, we'll need to chop them to size. Then we get to dig a pit, stack the wood again, and shovel the earth back over it."

Baltor shrugged. "Then what?"

Erador grimaced. "Then some elder will light it and sit by it to make sure it burns properly, while we get to start collecting another load. First one should be done burning and cooling off around the time the third's ready to be lit." He paused for dramatic effect. "Then we get a day off so we can remove the earth from the pile, sift out the good pieces of charcoal, stuff them into baskets, and shovel the waste away so we can load it all up again."

"Same thing tomorrow, then?"

Erador didn't think Baltor looked sufficiently put upon. He nodded. "Rest well tonight. We're going to need a lot more timber to last a clan of this size for the whole winter."

Which was how it went. There were days Erador forgot that his task had been given to him as punishment—though he usually remembered it again the next morning as he got out of bed. Luckily for him, the best cure was the cause: a quarter hour of axe work and everything had loosened up again. He wondered if he was going to look like Herlidrek by autumn's end.

One of those days, Baltor interjected out of the blue: "Warlord Dryden said somethin' to me about ya last night."

That wasn't the most promising opening Erador had ever heard.

"He said when he first heard you was bein' punished by havin' to chop wood, he thought that was pretty lame. But now, he's impressed at yer dedication and doin' without a fuss. Plus, he said seein' as how the other Warlords keep sayin' 'More wood!' he figures it was smart o' ya to bring me along." Baltor finished with a huge grin.

Erador smiled back, but was troubled all the same. "So, you don't… uh, mind that I dragged you into this?"

Baltor snorted hard enough to scatter chips of bark. "Ya kiddin' me? I look around, see everyone's got a job o' some kind. Me? I hate milkin' goats, I ain't much at weavin', and my needlepoint reeks."

A few of the jungle elkin had garments ornamented with fine thread when they arrived, but no one was wasting the short autumn making more. Some of Clan Hortyr had taken up the hobby, though, always fascinated with what the humans had for trade. Erador couldn't understand that at all. Why would someone pay for pretty thread made from worm dung?

Baltor went on between swings. "With you, I get to chop things. I like choppin' things. Best job on offer." His grin was infectious. Fortunately, so was his energy. Otherwise, Erador would never have been able to keep up, and the last thing he wanted was for his new friend to think he was shirking. That much he could figure out even without advice from his father.

The days seemed to blend together; their routine was repeated day-in and day-out, matching the rise and fall of the sun. But with each new day, more leaves had fallen from the day before it. As they changed colors from a lush green to a mix of yellows and reds, Erador knew that time was running out. The impatient winter was fast approaching.

CHAPTER 4

The valley floor was carpeted in gold and red leaves, the canopy still dense with orange, crimson and parchment, when the weather turned. Gentle, temperate currents coming up from the south, steered by the spine of the Jerackon Mountains, gave way to stronger, sharper winds coming from the northwest. Gathering force and moisture across uncharted miles of the Western Sea, these too would be caught by the Jerackon—after they had their way with the tundra.

The change was impossible to miss. Though the early gusts still only hinted at the chill to come, the walls of Beknen Valley seemed greedy to snag more than their fair share, yet were unable to hold it once they did. Wind piled on wind, forming a howling blast which tore the remaining leaves from the trees and hurled them toward the valley mouth, where they gathered in unseasonable drifts. A cold, spitting rain followed. Within days, this was replaced by the first snow.

For the elkin, everything now came down to a question of timing. The sleds carrying the bulk of their supplies could not make the two-day journey until there was sufficient snow on the ground for the runners to glide. Too much snow, and the elkin would be unable to tow them. Warlord Brynn chose to err on the side of safety. Faced with leading a clan half of whose members had never seen snow, he decided it was better to leave sooner, even if it meant the going for the sleds would be more difficult.

In the quiet calm before dawn, chill winds whispered upon crisp air. The village came alive with torchlight as the clan awoke and readied themselves to depart. The last loads were piled on sleds and secured beneath furs with braided leather rope. Food was stuffed into travel packs, cloaks fastened, baskets and bundles shouldered. Stars could be seen through gaps in high, thin clouds, holding out the promise of at least one day of decent traveling weather.

Erador grasped a cylindrical wicker basket filled with charcoal and put his arms through its looped handles, settling it on his back. On his way down the steps from the village, he saw Warlord Dryden below, shaking hands with someone from Clan Hortyr. The other man locked eyes with Erador for a brief moment, then looked back at Warlord Dryden, smiled, turned and left. Erador was surprised to see Warlord Dryden wearing his armor. He, in turn, seemed surprised to discover that Warlords Brynn and Frodden were not, as he returned from his leave-taking.

Erador got to the bottom and greeted his father. "I'm ready to go."

A grin of gratification grew on Warlord Brynn's face. "Good. Erador, I know this is your last year staying within the cave, but it is the first year for all those born of Clan Grondyr. You must make sure that they learn the ways of our ancients. Can you do that?"

"Absolutely."

"Good. And it looks like I'll get to teach Warlord Dryden what the cold can do to our swords and plate armor," Warlord Brynn said with a wink. Warlord Frodden, standing nearby, got a good chuckle. Warlord Dryden projected irritation, wondering what information was being kept from him now.

"What did you say?" he grumbled, removing his helm as if to unmuffle his hearing.

"Let's have it be a surprise," answered Warlord Brynn with a smile.

Anger overcame Warlord Dryden as he thrust a finger at Warlord Brynn's face. "I will not tolerate this mockery. I only joined you so that Carra could be the understudy of your Channeler. Don't forget that you needed us just as much as we needed you." He looked like he had more to say, but he took one look at Erador and chose to bite his tongue. He turned and stalked to the head of the group.

Erador looked at his father with concern. "What did he mean by that?"

Warlord Brynn's smile vanished. "We were too few in number to keep up with the influx of the Soul Smith's beasts. We needed to bolster our ranks. Clan Grondyr's arrival was well-timed in that respect. But Warlord Dryden is something else. Even after three months, he's still having trouble adapting to our ways."

Erador thought Warlord Dryden was not alone in that regard. Few of the adults from the south seemed willing to take wholeheartedly to Wyndlyn's ways. Erador wanted to inquire further, but the entire clan was gathering and sorting themselves into marching order. Of all the clan, only the aged Channeler rode. Mothers bore infants and toddlers swathed in furs, sharing body warmth. All the others walked, taking shifts towing the burdens across the fresh snow: the clan had no draft animals. All but the children bore baskets or bundles upon their backs as well.

Erador picked Carra out of the cluster. Her flowing blonde hair was as stunning as the craftsmanship of the Blacksmiths. She was wrapped in a white fur coat that accentuated her fair skin and ice-blue eyes. As the clan organized into a double file, Erador shuffled through the crowd to take the place next to her. A handful of warriors formed a loose perimeter. In addition to their usual tasks of guarding against predators and seeking the easiest routes for the sleds, this year they also had to keep track of the more adventurous among those children experiencing their first taste of snow. The caravan started its march.

Erador adjusted the basket that he shouldered and cleared his throat. "Are you eager to see the Willow Cave?"

Carra gave a polite nod.

"It's beautiful inside. Wait until you see the willow trees our ancestors planted."

Carra cracked a smile. "Are we just going there to escape the winter?"

"No. We're going to teach the youths the ways of the ancients while the elders are gone," he stated.

"Really? Where are they going?" Carra responded with interest.

Erador found it odd that the Channeler hadn't explained such basic things to Carra. "It's a tradition that we've followed since the days of our Father, Vorkus. But I don't know where they go, just that they are gone for a week. They won't tell us until we are of age to experience it ourselves."

"I take it that you've asked them, then?"

Erador laughed. "Many times."

Carra brushed some of her hair behind her ear. "And how long until you go with them?"

"This is my last year, but we shall see," said Erador with a smile. "I hope my father will make an exception. I am almost upon my twentieth soul keep; being a few weeks off can't hurt anything."

"You'd rather break tradition than wait? Why is this so important to you?"

"I want to know all that they know. Their secrets surround us! I mean, aren't you the least bit curious to know what's inside the Armory, for instance?"

Carra shook her head. "I never really thought about it."

Erador scratched at his nose. "Well, I want to know about our past. Where we came from. Those sorts of things."

"But, if not of our heritage, what are *we* supposed to be teaching the children?"

"Oh, we tell them stories and traditions, too—the ones we know," he punctuated with a wry grin, "but most importantly, we teach them to how fight and survive in the cold."

Just at that moment, they both noticed Warlord Dryden arguing with Warlord Brynn at the front of the drove.

"I think your father just found out that the winter frost will reduce his armor's mobility and make his blade stick in its sheath," said Erador. He thought his knowledge would impress, but Carra seemed suddenly downcast.

"It wouldn't matter. Not about the sword, that is. No one has ever seen him draw his blade," she said with a sigh.

"Ever? Truly? Then I wonder what the commotion's about."

Her voice, though gentle and barely above a whisper, freighted each word with an inner burden. "My father hasn't been himself since the loss of our Mother. He's grown distant. At first, before we came north, he used to venture into the jungle to pray to the Blacksmiths every day. Now, he doesn't pray at all any more, I don't think..." She trailed off.

"I'm sorry to hear that."

Carra didn't give so much as half a smile and Erador realized he needed to steer the conversation in a new direction. "How did Warlord Dryden obtain the armor and sword of the Sky Smith?"

"I'm not sure. He's had it for as long as I can remember," she answered with little enthusiasm. "I've never heard anyone else mention a time before he had it, either."

Erador nodded, letting an awkward silence settle in. Carra glanced over to see the flustered look about Erador's face. "How did Warlord Frodden acquire just the armor, and not the weapon or helm?" Carra asked in an attempt to keep the conversation alive.

Erador answered with excitement. "It was won in battle a few years back. I was too young to fight at the time, but a legion of erethizons known as the Brenzwik Tribe came up from somewhere in the south, and laid siege against us at the mouth of the valley. Their leader was dressed in the armor of the Sky Smith and wielded a great runic bow to match."

"Erethizons?" she asked in earnest. "I've heard of them, but never seen any."

"You never encountered any in the Chyxurlgon Jungle? They're a race of men covered with sharp quills on their arms, legs, and head—so you can't get too close. My father says they must have been sent by the Sky Smith himself, because the wielder could unlock the magic within his runic bow." Erador acted out the story as he spoke. "They say that when he drew the bowstring back, without an arrow nocked, he would aim and release. Then a bolt of lightning would strike down from the sky at the target."

Carra was flabbergasted. "Wait, the wielder knew how to read the runes? Impossible! The language has been lost to time; its magic lies dormant within those runes. How could he have possibly learned to read their inscriptions?" exclaimed Carra in disbelief.

"I do not know. If the Sky Smith had given the armor to him in person, perhaps He taught him to read the language."

"And you would have me believe that the gods walk among us again?" Erador's only response was a blank expression. "Never mind that," she continued. "How did you defeat them?"

"Our hunters, and especially Warlord Frodden, were instrumental at winning that battle. They scattered across the plateau our village sits upon, arcing their javelins as far as they could, raining down upon the erethizons as they struggled to climb up. With a masterful throw, Frodden struck their leader a mortal wound, his javelin plunging into the gap between chestplate and helmet. When the erethizons retreated, they were able to grab the Sky Smith bow and helm, but they couldn't take the body before our counterattack drove them off. My father awarded him the armor and named him a Warlord for his accomplishment."

"Why did they attack you?" asked Carra, perplexed.

Erador shrugged his shoulders, not knowing how to respond. "Perhaps they wanted my father's armor. Or perhaps they were just another group of fools convinced our valley was filled with hidden treasure."

They were as good as any guesses he'd ever come up with, and were apparently enough to satisfy Carra. Erador noticed that the argument between their warlord fathers was still going on. One sentence, in Dryden's voice, carried back to them on the wind: "We have to entrust our runic armor to a bunch of youths?!" Erador barely noticed, however; he was lost in his own thoughts.

He thought of the God-Dragon, a jungle turned to stone, a magnificent human city, and that fireball in the sky he'd seen that final day of summer. Hours passed, and despite the sun shining from the heights of the clear sky, the chill winds encouraged them all to a brisk pace. Tall grasses, unbowed as yet by winter's early efforts, rippled in the biting breeze. The thin snow was turning muddy beneath their sleds' runners. Warlord Brynn gave permission for the files to loosen into staggered rather than straight lines.

As evening came on the Jerackon Mountain range came into sight, their rocky summits already shrouded with snow. Menacing storm clouds piled against their barrier for much of its length. More could be seen scudding in from the northwest, and behind those, in the far distance, a wall of unrelieved gray. The second day would not be as pleasant a stroll as the first. Apart from the rare crow passing overhead, the elkin seemed to be alone in this desolate land. Erador blessed the current empty skies. No doubt the first glacial bats were already stirring from their hibernation somewhere among those peaks.

Mostly, Erador kept his gaze low, searching out signs of animal burrows beneath the early snowfall—doubly important now that the line of march was twice its normal width. The footing for those towing sleds was difficult enough without such complications. The basket grew heavy on his back through the long hours. Fatigue had begun to set in, most clearly amongst those unaccustomed to the conditions, but there was no time to rest, no time for breaks.

Warlord Brynn was determined to see them cover as much ground as possible while the fortuitous weather held. As the sun dropped, so did the temperature. Erador took little note of the familiar cold, but he could tell Carra's teeth were chattering.

A halt was finally called once there was no longer light enough for them to see by. The moons provided little help. Brightly though they reflected from the snow, they were of little use when they were ducking in and out of clouds. The exhausted elkin drew the sleds into a circle to form a low but invaluable windbreak. Several gathered snow for the Goma to melt so the clan could fill their empty water skins. The elkin settled in groups within the shelter of the sleds, and clustered together beneath multiple furs to share body heat. Warlord Brynn posted a minimum of watchers, all of them veterans of winter; a few of the new members seemed inclined to take this as an insult, but he would permit none of them to do aught but rest. In other years, this would have been the extent of the night's arrangements. This time, the warlords and the Channeler held a conference, then the crone summoned the other Goma enchanters and gave them instructions. Soon, a soft glow emanated from the gathered Goma and filtered out across the camp. The huddled elkin felt the furs grow warm around them. The comforting warmth relaxed their weary bodies; for most, its soft glow was the last thing they noticed until they were roused the next morning.

The dawn revealed a ceiling of gray, broken only in rare patches. The mountains, though nearer, were lost to sight behind lower clouds. The wind was no colder nor stronger than the previous day's, but the air was heavier. Snow was nearing, and would be no trifling matter when it arrived. This it did before midday, falling in heavy, wet flakes. Warlord Brynn ordered the clan to double up on the tow-ropes to make as much time as possible during the short window where the deepening snow improved conditions, before it began to work against them.

It was a good choice. By late afternoon, the wind was picking up, and seemed more and more inclined to come at them head-on. The clan had by then reached the minimal foothills along the Jerackon's southern flanks, however, and before the dwindling light failed them, they caught sight of the cavern mouth.

Half of the clan was within before the clouds finally shrugged off all restraint.

CHAPTER 5

Thick snow came down in heavy blankets, sticking to Erador in a white coat as he was among the last to enter. The familiar warmth within the cavern was an immediate comfort and thawed Erador's fingers. A small cluster of shallow hot spring pools was situated at a back corner of the cavern. The walls dripped sweat from the steam that emanated off their surface, now enhanced by the snow rapidly melting off the elkin. Eight mature willow trees thrived inside this cave. Their foliage dangled to the floor with gentle grace, while their bark oozed with thick plumes of amber sap. Carved into each trunk was a single unique runic symbol, one tree for each of the eight Blacksmiths.

The cavern was a large open room, rising well above the crowns of the willows, capacious enough to house the entire enhanced clan. Stalactites studded the ceiling, their smooth surfaces glistening with condensation, dripping water onto the willows and keeping the ground moist. The glow of the gomabeetles scattered across the ceiling mimicked the stars across the heavens. The tenebrous illumination revealed a time-worn cloth draped upon the cavern wall, displaying the faded but still-discernable outline of a forging hammer and antlers—the distinct markings of Clan Wyndlyn's banner. *Looks untouched since our previous stay,* Erador thought.

The adults began to unpack and spread out fur blankets across the floor. Many elder elkin bedded down between the furs as soon as they were laid out. Erador went to help start fires in small stone rings scattered about the cavern. A few strikes of flint against steel sent sparks dancing amongst small piles of kindling; a few gentle puffs brought forth hungry trickles of flame. Erador fed it a taste of charcoal. The fire grew, and its light proliferated throughout the cavern. Erador watched as the soil around the fire wiggled to life as worms and other scavenger insects fled its heat.

Erador looked about the crowd of elkin, watching as they aided one another in shedding the snow from sodden cloaks and clothes. Many of the women withdrew the bone-combs that held their hair in buns, letting it fall like waves to shake out the clinging snowflakes. Within the bustle, Erador noticed Carra amid a cluster of youths, all originally from Clan Grondyr, standing in astonishment at the marvel of the cave, ogling the sumptuous willow trees. He walked over beside her and knelt to the height of the smaller children as he introduced the youths to the symbols of the Blacksmiths, pointing at each tree as he spoke. "This one here is the Radiant Smith, lord of light and the sun; the Flood Smith, ruler of ice and water; the Gaia Smith, lady of trees and nature; the Scorch Smith, overlord of heat and fire; the Sky Smith, master of weather and air; the Chromium Smith, forger of alloys; the Soul Smith, creator and recycler of life; and the Onyx Smith, with dominion over stone and shadow."

The children stood frozen in awe until a splintered voice broke their concentration. "Come here, children, and bring your bowls with you," exclaimed a veteran warrior standing amidst the willows.

Carra smiled at Erador. "I guess I should go too."

Erador's eyes followed her as she departed, but his gaze stopped on the Soul Smith tree when he recognized its rune to be the same mark he saw branded into the Thorbryx's forehead, conjuring forgotten grief of the Thorbryx's wrath. The loss they suffered that day plagued him with regrets. *It wasn't your fault,* he reminded himself as he tried to shake the memories away.

The trees were now surrounded by weary children scraping sap into their polished clay bowls, their longing to sleep after such a tremendous journey forestalled. However, among the garden of willows, Erador also spotted Warlord Dryden standing near the Sky Smith tree. Its symbol was wispy and soft, embodying the essence of air in the rune's design. Warlord Dryden looked upon it in admiration, the same look Erador has seen him give to Carra from time to time—though not often enough, in Erador's opinion.

The remaining adolescents were unbundling the wooden handles of their weaponry and shields for the elder's journey through the winter and distributing these among the children. The children's dreary faces expressed their discontent as they lacquered the sap of the willow tree onto any exposed wood. A veteran warrior supervised the youths, walking with a javelin to support the limp in his step, its shaft stained black by the blood of his victims. His strong voice instructed them as they worked, "The sap from these willow trees has been used since the time of our ancestors to strengthen our wooden hafts and shields. Once the sap hardens, it becomes safeguarded from shattering in the cold. You wouldn't want to strike your enemy only to have your weapon shatter in your hands, now would you?"

"No," said the children in unison.

"So coat it on nice and thick, because that's what the numbing cold is capable of. Now, hold up your weapons to show me your work. If you've done well, you can go to sleep. If not, then you'll keep doing this until you get it right."

The vulnerable arms the southern elkin brought with them received priority, lengthening what seemed an already interminable task to the children. The veteran walked behind the row of children, inspecting their work. As the sap began to crystallize, the weapons turned a brilliant golden hue. Once the bulk of the weaponry was complete, all the children were permitted to retire for the night.

The most urgent tasks of establishing their winter domicile completed, an exhausted Erador did the same.

***

Erador awoke relaxed and rubbed the sleep from his eyes. He lay still, remaining in the warmth of his bear hide blanket, staring at the several narrow, vertical crevices which penetrated the outer wall of the cavern. Already these were sealed over with barriers of ice, as the warm moisture from the cavern's springs met cold stone and winter air. Wan light filtered through them, illuminating the cavern in a bluish haze; on days the skies were clear, they would take on a vibrant inner glow, graced by occasional refraction rainbows. He could hear the steady commotion of his brethren already awake, sorting and storing supplies, making final preparations for the adults' pilgrimage. He sat up and felt rejuvenated, thankful for his extended rest.

Everyone was gathered in small clusters, trying to talk over the howl of the heavy blizzard that was underway outside. Erador surveyed the activity. A few children were coating the last of the wooden weaponry with thick layers of sap. To his right, some elders were sitting around a fire, enjoying a meal of spotted salmon that had just finished cooking over the spit. As their elongated canine teeth tore into the cooked meat, they relished in the benefits of pre-dawn spear fishing in a nearby brook.

Erador got to his feet and wandered through the grove of willows toward his father, his courage building with each step. Erador kept a keen eye as he approached the far side of the cavern, pausing once he realized his father was no longer alone.

Beneath the frayed banner of Clan Wyndlyn stood three wooden crosses hoisted upright on square bases, each as tall as a man—two showing signs of age, the third clearly just assembled from fresh wood. Standing beside them were the three Warlords. Frodden and Brynn were already at work setting the pieces of their runic armor on the stands. Warlord Dryden remained hesitant to part with his.

Settling the chest plate of his Sky Smith armor on the display, Warlord Frodden looked at Warlord Dryden, who just stood there, frozen with apprehension. "If you stood that still out in the blizzard, you would freeze to death," commented Warlord Frodden. "Even without your armor drawing the chill to you."

With a guttural grunt of disapproval, Warlord Dryden set his helm aside, shed his chest armor and slung it over the arms of the cross with bitterness, then placed the helm above it. The austere, heavy wool tunic he wore beneath his armor did not hide the gouges and scars that painted his arms, the marks of a true veteran. "Must I leave my sword as well?" he groused.

"It won't prove of any use to you frozen in its sheath," smiled Warlord Brynn.

Reluctantly, Warlord Dryden acquiesced and hung his sheathed Sky Smith blade from one arm of the cross. Warlord Brynn moved to do the same, then hesitated, choosing to draw his blade from its mundane sheath to take one last look at it. The broadsword appeared hefty and cumbersome, yet seemed light and agile within his hand. Its entire length was edged in mystically flawless diamond, capable of cutting through solid rock. The golden runic symbols etched into the face of the black blade glittered in daylight, were invisible in shadow or night.

"Our weapons will be missed," he said as he sheathed and hung the Onyx broadsword.

Two hunters emerged from the curtain of snowfall, hauling in their catch: each held one end of a javelin that had skewered the neck of a mountain goat. "Children! We have your first meal," one of them boasted as they shook the snow from their white furs.

"Well done, and just in time, before the blizzard froze the meat on its bones," exclaimed Warlord Brynn.

A big smile and a hearty laugh came from the pair of hunters.

This is it, he thought. *I have to ask him now.* Erador cleared his throat. "Father, I have something important to ask of you."

"Can it wait?"

"No, I've waited long enough. I want to go with you on this excursion. Please allow me to accompany the elders this year."

Erador stood tall, but felt vulnerable. He stared into his father's eyes, searching for a hint of compassion. There was a long pause. His father seemed to be planning his next words carefully, never breaking Erador's gaze.

"No. I cannot allow it," said Warlord Brynn. His words were as blunt as a rock.

Erador's heart sank. "Why can't I learn of your destination? Of what you do there? Of what's inside the Armory? It feels like I am being sheltered from the world."

"Erador, your vanquisher training is incomplete; neither have you undergone the rite of adulthood. There is still much left for you to do. You are not ready. The secrets we keep cannot be entrusted to the ill prepared. There are those out there that would go to great lengths to learn of our knowledge; to guard the knowledge of the ancients is more a burden than a blessing."

"But I *am* ready. You've seen me fight. I've proven myself more than a capable hunter and warrior and I am not far from my twentieth soul-keep. I feel like there is a whole side to our clan, to who we are, that I am not privy to, and I want to know."

"You implore me to let you learn the deepest secrets in our traditions, yet cannot bring yourself to observe this one? Is this your evidence of readiness?" Warlord Brynn scowled. He held his son's gaze until Erador lowered his eyes. Then he exhaled slowly. "I cannot deny your talent in combat. You were born a warrior. Your

axe is as much a part of you as your antlers are. And you have
proven a capable marksman with the javelin too. You've hunted big
game successfully even when measured against those chosen by the
Fates to be hunters. So, I will give you the same treatment that my
father, Warlord Synder, gave me."

Warlord Brynn paused and searched the crowd of elkin,
while Erador grew more curious by the second.

"You two. Come here," called Warlord Brynn as he
motioned for the newly-returned hunters to approach him. The
hunters divested themselves of the skewered goat and huddled close.
Brynn placed his heavy arm on the shoulder of Erador and
whispered, "I want you and a wing-guard of your choice to be in
charge while we're gone. You'll have to hunt for food and protect
the youths. In doing so, we can give these two a break, so that they
need not remain behind this year. Can you do that for me?" Both
hunters' eyes widened with excitement as they awaited Erador's
response.

"Consider it done," stated Erador.

"Thank the Onyx Smith!" exclaimed one. "Here, take my
javelin and get it a nice fresh coat of sap." He offered it to Erador,
who gladly accepted the auspicious weapon.

Warlord Brynn continued, "Better still, choose two wing-
guards. One should be experienced in winter, the other from our new
clan mates. They need to learn our ways as swiftly as we can teach
them. I know you will choose wisely. This will be a trying time for
you. One day, you may inherit this armor and the responsibilities
that come with it. Don't disappoint me."

"Yes, father," he replied confidently.

Leaving the armor stands, Warlord Brynn donned the thick
hide of a two-headed Torren Dog—a trophy he alone of Clan
Wyndlyn owned. Putting the hide on like a vest over his everyday
garments, he slid one arm through each of the gaping jaws and then
fastened its fur closed over his chest. Each head of the beast rested
on one of his massive shoulders, brandishing flesh-rending yellow
teeth; their thick craniums made excellent substitutes for shoulder
plates. They were a fitting complement to Warlord Brynn's
immense antlers, in which the stories of battles of years past could
be read where metal capped cracked or broken tines.

Erador saw his blood-father anew. The father he had known belonged in the suit of armor on display. Standing before him was something *more.* What he saw was a descendant of a long line of hardened hunter-warriors, the embodiment of a champion, the culmination of everything an elkin's enemies feared. Erador looked upon him with utter respect, looking up to him as his leader, the way he imagined all other elkin in Clan Wyndlyn must see him. In that moment, Erador's assignment of responsibility filled him with pride, as it had not come from his father, but from his Warlord.

Erador had seen nineteen cycles of the seasons and knew the routine well. The children were to stay in the safety of the cave for the entirety of the winter. While their elders were away, the teens would be responsible for keeping them all fed, warm, and protected. Normally, one or two junior adults would remain as well, as a safety measure, taking no action they did not need to: it was a time for the teens to learn how to lead and to cope with matters on their own. Leaving the leadership to Erador was a tremendous affirmation of his father's faith in him. The more so since, with this year's new additions, there were twice the mouths to feed. That brought a troubling thought to his mind: *What is Warlord Dryden's reaction going to be when he hears* I'm *to be left in charge?* He tried to put it out of his mind, concentrating on sifting through the faces of the crowd to choose who he would use as his wing-guards.

While he was doing so, chatter amongst the clan was brought to a halt. One by one, they all got down on one knee. Erador chose a spot on the outside of the gathered circle, near one of the banked fires, from which he could see most of his clan mates' faces—and all the faces of a certain group he was particularly interested in. Only the Channeler, the eldest practitioner of Goma incantations, remained standing. She was a feeble old woman, though her mastery over the manipulation of light earned her tremendous respect amongst Clan Wyndlyn. She was hunched over, leaning upon the staff that she held in one hand, while she managed to cradle a newborn boy in the other. Apart from the runic Blacksmith armor, the Channeler's Staff was regarded as the greatest relic among their clan. The body of the Staff was formed from the interwoven, melded antlers of all of Clan Wyndlyn's Goma spellbinders of centuries past... with the exception of one. Those antlers crowned it: a scythe-like metal rack in its original, unaltered glory was fused to the top of the Staff. It had belonged to Vorkus, the Father of Clan Wyndlyn.

As the Channeler spoke, all of Clan Wyndlyn listened. Her squinted eyes paid special attention to the newer faces as her raspy voice echoed throughout the cavern. "Wrought in the deepest of traditions, every newborn is destined to fulfill a role within the clan. Once of age, *every* elkin, man or woman, takes the oath and fulfills that role as a lethal combatant on the battlefield. Let us Call the Fates to see where this child's destiny lies."

She placed the little boy on his back atop a light blanket on the cavern floor. With no teeth or antlers, the baby looked human. The Channeler then placed four artifacts evenly around the boy. An axe represented the role of warrior; an atlatl that of hunter; an incandescent gomabeetle in a clay cup covered by a piece of clear quartz to represent the role of Goma incantatory wizardry; and most salient of them all, a smith's forging hammer to represent the one that could read the inscriptions upon the runic armor.

Erador always played a game during this event: his eyes scanned the faces of the crowd to try to determine who the blood father is. Every parent was always hopeful that their son or daughter would be the one to choose the forging hammer. Some believed it meant more than just the ability to wield runic items: they believed it would mean that their child was the reincarnation of Vorkus. Though the crowd was twice as large, it was actually easier for Erador to play his game this time, since the adults still mostly grouped themselves to their old allegiances… and of course he knew who the child's mother was. Which is why he'd taken up the position he had.

Eyes closed, the Channeler raised her staff into the air and began muttering the language of the ancients to summon the Fates. With a downward jerk, she thrust her staff into the cavern floor with an authoritative thud. As the butt of the staff connected to the earth, all light throughout the cavern peeled away from its source as it was pulled into the tips of the metallic antlers atop the staff. For a moment, there was blackness. Erador could still feel the heat of the flame despite the absence of light. A ghostly figure materialized above the boy, looking down at him. Its aura shed light, but masked all colors, imposing only shades of gray throughout the room. It appeared as a delicate floating sheet of smoke, suspended effortlessly in the air. From within its grey mist, an arm reached down toward the boy, as if someone was on the other side of the wispy sheet trying to reach through. A single finger stretched out and touched the center of the boy's forehead. Without hesitation, the little boy rolled over and used his muscular legs to crawl toward one of the objects. It was the atlatl. It was at this moment that Erador's attention was caught by the face of a warrior across the room. He saw the battle-hardened warrior's mouth make the faintest grimace. It was only the slightest of reactions, but Erador knew it was a sign of disgust. Erador smiled with satisfaction as he knew he had discovered the baby's blood-father. To witness the grimace of disappointment reminded him of how honored he was to have been claimed by his.

The Call of Fates was over. As the grey aura diminished into the air, light and color were restored to the cavern. There was no clapping or cheering, just emotionless warriors going back about their business. All of the adults began to don fur coats and grab their sap-coated weaponry to prepare for their seven-day journey. Erador paid them close attention, trying to discern the purpose or destination of their journey based on their supplies. They gathered furs, food, weaponry, and charcoal, but beyond the obvious gear for survival in the snow, he could find no indication.

I have to follow them... at least far enough to see what direction they take, he thought.

Erador stood near the cavern's exit and watched. The earlier blizzard winds had largely subsided. As the long line of adults ventured out into the thickly-blanketed landscape, into the silence of the falling snow, nervousness crept up within him. He balanced the weight of his axe in the palm of his hand to try to distract his mind from his worries. He watched with anxious anticipation as the three Warlords were the last to depart. Erador's father gave one last look back, no words, just a simple nod of approval before they all vanished from sight amidst the heavy snow fall.

Erador wasted no time in snatching an extra fur pelt and wrapping it around his shoulders. He sheathed his axe and exited the cave to follow the elders into the biting cold. He took but two steps into the snowbank before the awareness of his new responsibilities fully caught up with him. *If something happens to me, who will hunt for the children in my stead? Would they be safe if attacked?*

His conscience rooted his feet in place. Erador watched as the tracks of his elders' feet were swallowed by fresh snowfall and exhaled in disappointment as his opportunity passed him by. He turned back toward the cave and looked up in shock to see Carra standing at the cavern entrance.

"I'm glad you chose to stay," she said.

Erador was puzzled. "You weren't going to try to stop me?"

Her voice was as sweet as spring. "No. I was just observing to see what you would do."

Erador felt guilty, ashamed by his intent to abandon. "Keep this between us, won't you?"

Carra nodded her head and Erador returned to the warmth of the cave. He began inventorying the supplies, focusing on the work as a distraction, oblivious to the boredom of the children. He counted and then recounted each pile to avoid any error… and to avoid thinking. It felt like hours passed as he made his rounds, but once he came to the three sets of Blacksmith armor, he stopped. Staring in admiration of their craftsmanship, his eyes were drawn to the unique runic symbols engraved upon each set of armor. He traced his finger over the cryptic writing as if trying to connect to the forgotten language of the Blacksmiths. They were an impressive collection to say the least: any of the creations of the Blacksmiths were considered rare and prized possessions throughout Thornwall.

Erador focused his gaze on the Onyx armor until it was all he could see. Originally given as a gift to Vorkus by the Onyx Smith Himself, the armor had been passed down through the generations. As Erador stared into its dark, craggy surface, it reminded him of his father, of how Warlord Brynn had once told him that even the secrets of his clan couldn't compare to the value of these suits of armor that stood before him. Erador brushed the back of his hand along the hilt of the Onyx blade. His admiration turned to fascination as he began talking to himself. "Not since Vorkus has there been an elkin of Clan Wyndlyn that could properly wield the power locked within its cryptic runic symbols."

His concentration was broken by Carra's soft voice, and he turned, drawn to her natural allure. She had gathered all the younglings around in a circle underneath the long vine-like arms of the Gaia Smith's willow tree. He noticed the children did not share his admiration: all of them cast jealous stares upon Carra. He recognized that look well. It was not because of Carra's egregious talents for Goma-incantations nor her rare opportunity of apprenticeship with the Channeler. That glare was familiar, for it was the one given to any of the select few claimed by their blood-fathers. A fact of which they had recently been reminded by the morning's ceremony.

She appeared, or pretended, not to notice. "Do you all want to hear the story of creation?" she asked with a smile.

The children scooted closer impatiently, nodding in unison. Erador had heard this story a hundred times and didn't care to hear it again. He stood leaning near the cavern entrance, directing a blank stare toward the drifting snow outside, but there was nothing to listen to other than Carra's soothing voice and the occasional cackling of the fire.

"First the gods created the stars, the sun, and the two moons. Then the gods created the flat ground for us to walk upon, the world we know as Thornwall. Soon after, the gods created man, and then man created tools, buildings, roads, walls, weapons, and armor. The gods grew curious to see what man could build if given their power. They summoned the eight best blacksmiths in the land and gave them each a unique Forging Hammer imbued with their divine power. Wielding the Hammers gave them unnatural long life. In fact, these ageless willow trees were planted to pay homage to all the Blacksmiths. Clan Wyndlyn favors the Onyx Smith for His generous gift of blade and armor to Vorkus, our clan's Father.

"Unfortunately, the Blacksmiths abused their power. Destruction ensued, and wars erupted. The gods did not foresee the destructive will of man and abandoned Thornwall after realizing their mistake. All that you see today is the product of the Blacksmiths."

The children were wide-eyed and full of curiosity, seeking Carra's attention to answer some particular question. Carra was still trying to decide who to pick when a flash of light outside flared across the immense tundra, overwhelming the dimness within the cavern; a beam of purest white through the entrance warred with lightning blue from the ice-windows. Then it was gone, leaving only afterimages burnt into dazed eyes. The room turned silent. Erador stood tall, mouth open, staring into the distance. A low rumble shook the earth beneath their feet and an echo as of thunder resonated upon the air.

All eyes were on Erador. The rumbling continued to escalate. "Get down!" he yelled. Too late to retreat deeper, he placed one foot behind him and braced for impact as an explosion of wind and snow blasted into the cave, extinguishing the fire and tearing the fur hide from his shoulders. Above the basso roar, a thousand tortured screams sang overtones. A cacophony of horrified cries throughout the cave echoed them. The children covered their ears and tucked their heads between their knees. Cracks raced through stone, stalactites broke loose and fell, part of the ceiling collapsed along the back wall. A cloud of dust billowed through the air, inducing heavy coughs.

The rumbling stopped. Erador had withstood the blast, his stalwart legs holding him firmly in place. Now waist-deep in snow and debris, he looked up—only to see another wave of force racing across the snow. Erador frantically strove to pull himself out, but it was upon him too quickly for him to do more than twist to protect his exposed face. Goosebumps surged across his body as the snow all around—and on—him crisped into a sheet of ice, locking him in place.

Carra rushed to his aid. As she clenched her hand into a fist, a bright red glow radiated within it. She closed her eyes and focused. When she stretched her fingers flat, hazy red light poured forth from her palm. She waved it in a sweeping motion over the ice. The light circled Erador, emanating heat akin to the warmth of the summer sun. The ice cracked and melted. Erador pulled himself out of the resulting hole, dripping wet. He stared into Carra's worried eyes. "The blast..." he muttered. "Was that..."

"The Blacksmiths?" finished Carra with a hushed tone, as if she couldn't believe it herself.

"The elders! They were exposed!" exclaimed Erador.

Carra's eyes turned red as she tried to hold back the tears. "Our fathers," her voice cracked.

"I'm going after them." Erador grabbed a tall rectangular shield crafted from bloodbark in one hand and his hand axe in the other. He was on his way out when Carra snatched his arm to hold him back.

Erador looked her dead in the eye. "You can't stop me. That could have been me out there!"

Carra dropped her eyes and replaced the fur over Erador's shoulders. Then she looked up at him, her gaze intense. "It could *still* be you. Make sure you come back."

Erador was taken aback, surprised at her empathy, and was uncertain how to respond. "Thanks," he murmured.

Sheathing his axe, he clenched a handful of the fur across the center of his chest and ran out into the blistering cold. Erador raced across ice thick enough to bear his weight with ease. Remaining upright became a challenge all its own: he glided as much as he ran. He was alone on the open tundra with no wing-guard to watch his flank, something he was taught to never do. His eyes were alert, scanning the ground as he ran, looking for signs of his clansmen frozen in the ice.

Nothing.

How long were they gone? I don't even know what time of day it is.

He ran for as long as his heavy legs would carry him, but elkin were not built for running long distances. Breathing heavily, he slowed to a walk. His mouth was dry, his lips were cracked, and every exhalation turned to mist. He sought evidence of the source of the blast, but the relentless snowfall limited his vision while erasing traces. The cold had already seeped beneath his garments and into his skin. He felt lost. He felt defeated. But he pressed on.

"Father! Anybody!" he shouted in desperation.

He yelled into the vastness of the tundra against his better judgment and instantly regretted it. The absence of a response brought reality back to him. His adrenaline ebbed, and suddenly he became acutely aware of his solitude. He was alone, vulnerable, and couldn't see ten feet before him. The beasts of the Jerackon Mountains were much bigger than in the rest of Thornwall. Images of all the various creatures that must be sizing him up for dinner filled Erador's mind. He thought of how easy it would be for glacial bats to pinpoint his position through echolocation and sweep in without warning. Nervousness got the better of him. He slung his shield onto his back and he began to retrace his steps back to the safety of the cave as rapidly as possible, with only the looming range, indistinct through the snow, to guide him. Darkness threatened to overtake him before he finally made it back.

As the cavern entrance came within sight, Erador was consumed with fresh worries. *Everyone is going to be looking to me for an answer. Could the elders have even survived the blast?* His mind began to jump to conclusions. *The children would be devastated by the loss of the elders, Carra worst of all. What do I tell them?*

Anger rose inside of him at how helpless he felt, for the children that he would let down, but most of all for what the gods had done this day. Carra greeted him at the entrance with a look of worry. "What did you see?"

Beyond her, everyone was staring, waiting for his answer. He took a deep breath to regain his composure, and with an expressionless face, he shook his head.

"What do we do now?" asked Carra.

"We wait," Erador replied. He glanced at the children's troubled faces. He felt his cheeks flush from fury as the inconceivable potential loss of the elders crushed down on his mind. Erador threw his shield to the floor, whipped off his snow-battered fur, stalked to the chopping block at back of the cavern, and began to take his frustration out on the mountain goat brought in that morning.

"Zimmerik," he called to his friend. "You're my wing-guard."

CHAPTER 6

Erador plopped himself onto a rock in front of the chopping block with the lifeless goat upon it. He pulled the carving blade from the block and raised it in the air. He swung and buried the blade in the goat-meat, severing its hind leg from the body with a few deft strokes. He turned the carcass to do the second leg, and swung again.

Zimmerik, a seventeen-year-old hunter with a slim athletic build and dexterous reflexes, approached him with a confused look on his face. "What do you mean I'm your wing-guard?"

Erador didn't look up from his work. As he continued severing the other legs of the goat, he uttered, "Warlord Brynn said that I and wing-guards of my choosing should do the hunting this year."

"What? You mean we have to catch our own food?" exclaimed Zimmerik nervously.

"Look around. You see anyone else who's going to do it?" *The gods can be cruel. If I hadn't pressed father so hard, there would still be two elders with us now.* Erador wasn't sure whether he ought to laugh or cry, so he chose neither. "Relax. It's only for a week, and then everyone will come back," he continued calmly.

Zimmerik, flustered with the weight of the responsibility laid upon his shoulders, began pacing back and forth. "And what if we aren't successful? What if we don't bring in enough food for us all?"

"Then we eat the worms and beetles from the floor."

Zimmerik made a face of disgust. "That's your plan? And what will those from Grondyr think?"

"Don't worry. We'll find food," Erador quipped.

Zimmerik leaned in and lowered his voice while maintaining a fierce tone. "What if you and I don't survive a hunt? How will the other ten adolescents manage to feed the thirty-two younglings without us? They aren't hunters. They're all warriors or Goma… except for Valen or Neriya, but they can't solo hunt: they don't know the winter." Erador stopped cutting the meat and glowered at his friend, yet Zimmerik continued, "Or worse, what if the elders don't return? What then? We all saw the size of that blast. What did you see out there?"

Listening to such detestable thoughts made Erador furious inside. Zimmerik's lack of confidence in his skill to hunt made Erador second-guess his decision. *But he is right to be concerned. Zimmerik didn't ask for this,* Erador thought to himself, *and that explosion, what if there is another one?* He wiped the thought from his mind. What might be didn't matter. They had no choice but to deal with what was.

"Nothing. I saw nothing," said Erador. Never breaking his gaze, he stuck the cutting-blade into the meat of the goat and stood up. "Tonight we eat and keep the fires burning; tomorrow we hunt." Erador began to walk away as if to conclude the conversation.

"Why?" Zimmerik asked to Erador's back. "Why did you pick me to be your wing-guard? Why not Gressyn or Dorgeeryn, or even the twins?"

Erador turned around to face him. "Because I know who your blood-father is."

Zimmerik's jaw dropped. He couldn't muster a word, nothing but a blank stare of disbelief. His mind began racing; "An answer like that could only mean—well, could it be? Warlord Frodden?" Zimmerik cleared his throat. "Is it—"

Erador nodded his head in affirmation. "And now I need your advice." At that, Zimmerik's astonishment reached new heights. "Warlord Brynn said I should take *two* wing-guards, one of them from our new additions, so that they can learn our ways as rapidly as possible. I had thought that I could manage with just you, but your words rang true. It *is* dangerous out there—we'll need both of our flanks covered, so we can hunt farther from the cave, and go after bigger game. So we need to decide who to take with us tomorrow."

"Well, uh, Baltor's the one you know best…"

"No, not him. Not the first time, at least. I want his strength here. Though it might be worth—Baltor!" he called his massive friend over.

"Yeah?" Baltor came over. His face was set in the same lost expression they all wore at the moment.

"I need your advice." *And I thought* Zimmerik *looked amazed...* "I need to decide who's going to act as my wing-guards tomorrow. Zimmerik's one, but I need to take someone from Grondyr as well, so that they can start learning how to hunt in winter. I want you to stay here with Carra, to look after the younglings. Who do you think should I should take?"

Baltor humphed. Without hesitation, he said, "Ya gave me an easy one. Neriya's the best hunter we got here."

"Isn't she a bit young?" Fifteen soul-keeps, if Erador remembered correctly.

"Ain't you a bit young to be leadin'?" It didn't quite come out as a joke. "Ask Carra if ya don't believe me."

"No, I believe you. I just need to be sure. I—*we*—can't afford any mistakes. Zimmerik?"

"Huh? I mean, yeah, I agree. I partnered with her a few times—" Zimmerik stumbled and blushed, abruptly aware of the double meaning, "—uh, hunting, that is, back in the village. She's small, but she's quiet and sneaky. A lot like me. Good throw with a javelin. Unless you wanted to take a Goma..."

He realized the problem the same time Erador said it out loud: "Carra's the only Goma we have. We can't risk her. She stays." The other two nodded. "Neriya it is, then." He looked at the half-disassembled goat carcass. "Baltor, you want to finish up here? Zimmerik and I need to go talk with Neriya."

Baltor grunted, pulled the chopping knife, and set to work as the other two walked off.

***

Carra walked back into the cavern. Snowflakes glistened upon her lengthy blonde hair, upon her petite antlers which grew inward in a faint defensive stance. She made her way to the hot springs at the back of the cavern. Several of the clan's youths were there, setting out uneven clay mugs and bowls that they had made themselves before the migration to the cave. All of these were filled with the ice and snow she had been liberating from the impenetrable frozen layer outside. She was exhausted. Never had she used her powers for that long at a stretch. Elsewhere, children scattered mugs with careful precision throughout the cavern to patiently collect the water dripping from the stalactites. "The water of the spring is not the best for drinking," Carra instructed the children, "but we can make use of its heat to melt fresh water from the snow. We could set our vessels near the fires, but it is better not to put them near something that hot when they're filled with something cold: they could crack and break. Warming the snow slowly is better." She was amazed at the words emerging from her mouth. Just one season ago, *she* would have placed the pottery next to the fire as the obvious thing to do. She held back a tear, hoping she hadn't had her last ever lesson from the Channeler. She finished supervising the laying out of the pottery, wiped her hands against her fur vest and looked about the cavern.

Her eyes stopped, curious as to the dumbfounded look upon Zimmerik's face.

"What happened? Are you all right?" she asked, interrupting his thoughts.

"Uh—" wanting to keep his information private, he realized he had to say something quickly. "Can you and the others cook the goat tonight? I need to prepare." He bolted over to the furs, began flipping through the pile, wanting to hand-select the best equipment to prepare for tomorrow's hunt.

He knew he needed to stay warm, so only the thickest of furs would suffice. *If the piercing chill could shatter tree branches, exposed skin would turn black in about ten minutes,* he thought to himself. He turned through the piles of hides, their soft furs warm to the touch from the camp fire nearby. The thickness of the fur wasn't his main concern; he wanted it to be white to blend in with his surroundings.

None could be found. "None of these will do. If only those hunters didn't leave with their albino-furs," he murmured to himself.

"Why not use the fur of the black bear?" suggested Carra.

He started, not realizing she'd come with him. He forgot he had planned not to talk about it. "Because I'm *Erador's* wing-guard. He's counting on me. The whole clan is. I can't mess this up. It has to be perfect."

Carra laid a hand on his shoulders to calm him down. "You need your fur to be white? All you needed to do was ask." She picked up the top black bear skin and laid it across a low flat stone that served as a table. She extended her arms over the hide, hands open, palms down, and began waving her arms in concentric circles. The fur became blurry and strained Zimmerik's vision; he turned away and rubbed his closed eyes. Upon opening them, a snow-white bear hide lay before him on the table. Astonished, Zimmerik picked it up to inspect it closer.

"Is it permanent?" he asked.

"No, I can't alter the refraction of light on an object forever. At some point nature will override it and return it to normal. So be sure to see me just before you leave tomorrow—"

"To maximize the duration of the effect," Zimmerik remarked, completing her sentence.

Carra smiled out of the corner of her mouth. "Yes. If I had the Channeler's Staff, I could enhance the effects. I could increase the longevity of the refraction, or block all light entirely."

Zimmerik was amazed. "You mean I could walk in a permanent shadow? Like the legends of the Onyx armor?"

"It's possible, yes. The staff channels the power from all the past Goma practitioners whose antlers have been woven into its creation."

Erador snuck up behind them. "What about the stone jungles of Chyxurlgon? Will nature override that?"

Carra wasn't amused by Erador's wit, nor his eavesdropping. "No, because it's not a manipulation, it's not artificial. All trees, animals, houses, God-Dragon and our Mother are now solid stone, through and through."

Zimmerik's head dropped in sorrow. "Carra, I know it must have been hard on you to lose your home, and Mother." He paused, contemplating the possibility that Clan Wyndlyn's entire heritage could have been lost in that explosion. "While Erador and I are out during our hunting expeditions, we'll keep our eyes open. Our elders are out there somewhere."

"I'm sure they'll return safely within seven nights from now," Erador stated as if it were a matter of fact. "When I was out there, I didn't get very far, and we don't even know where they go every year. I could have been looking in a completely wrong direction. So, let's sharpen our weapons for the morrow's hunt and then grab a bite once the goat meat finishes grilling."

Carra received the assistance of two youths, Ressy and Serlin, in gathering up the now-ready cuts of goat and skewering the meat to grill over the fire pit. The less appetizing parts were tossed into a pot to boil for soup. The beetles wasted no time cleaning up the remnants from where the carcass was butchered.

All the youths gathered around the spit to get their share of the goat meat. Before any meat was served into their empty clay plates, they all turned and faced the exhibit of Onyx armor. Carra intoned, "Onyx Smith, thank You for this bounty we are about to receive, and thank You so much for Your protection over Clan Wyndlyn. We pray that You will watch over us and our elders, and for their safe return." Once she finished paying respect to the Onyx Smith, they all served themselves small portions, mindful of the number who had to eat. Their elongated canine teeth tore into the well-done meat to their stomach's content. Erador made sure to savor every bite and relished the moment, as it might be their last delectable meal. He kept his concerns to himself. *Was there even any game left to hunt after that blast?*

***

It was the dead of night; Erador and Zimmerik opened their eyes and awoke like clock-work. Zimmerik went to rouse Neriya. They moved amongst the sleeping children in total silence, like weightless spirits drifting through the dark. They headed toward the back of the cave and took a dip in the hot springs to cleanse their scent. Then they dressed, took up their weapons and draped themselves in their furs. They tied these off with leather straps at wrists, ankles, and waist, so that the furs would move with them.

Zimmerik shook Carra to awaken her so that she could disguise his fur. Erador shook his head and laughed to himself about Zimmerik's nit-pickings. Erador knew his friend was always peculiar about the details. "You shouldn't rely on such superstitions, Zimmerik. Carrying a back-up is all you need." Erador slung a quiver with three spare javelins over his back. He held a fourth in his hand, leaving his axe sheathed at his side.

Carra ignored him. "You didn't tell me Neriya was going out with you. Should I do hers, too?"

Zimmerik was about to reply, but Erador headed him off: "Yes." Just that, flat and definite. Three pairs of eyes widened behind him as he walked away.

The fire had been reduced to glowing embers during the night; Erador grabbed some more charcoal and fed it. As Carra finished up her incantations, Erador looked at all the sleeping children that depended on him. *Such peaceful faces*, he thought. *Sleep on; forget yesterday's frights for a while longer.* It dawned on him that all their fortunes rested in his hands. He didn't want them to go hungry on his watch; he wanted to bring them a feast like never before.

Carra approached Baltor, tired and cold, standing guard by the cavern opening. "Thanks for taking the first shift. You can catch your sleep within my fur-wraps." Baltor went to relieve himself before he slipped into her fur blankets, still warm from her body.

Zimmerik, Neriya and Erador stepped out into the open tundra. The air was crisp and clear. The snowfall had broken, the grey and azure moons illuminated the ground before them, and the snow crunched as it compacted underneath their heavy steps. Carra watched as they traveled off toward the lowering moons, away from the sunlight that would soon begin to paint the peaks of the Jerackon Mountains. It seemed as if the Blacksmiths smiled upon them this day.

They traveled north and west along the line where the tundra met the sheer mountainside. Keeping the cliff near to hand as a ready defense, Erador focused on the land ahead, seeking the slightest signs of movement; Neriya, two steps behind him, was responsible for their wide left flank; Zimmerik, two steps farther back, swept his eyes across their right, as well as above and behind… and from time to time to Neriya, to ensure she wasn't having trouble with this new environment. As far as he could tell, she wasn't.

Who would have imagined that chill blast did us a favor? There's only a few inches for Neriya to become accustomed to walking through, instead of a couple feet. Zimmerik was more surprised she had no trouble with the ice beneath—until he thought about walking on mud. *Guess there's plenty of that in a jungle.*

Their training took over. Movements were made in sync so their footsteps sounded as one. Each trod in the footprints of the one ahead, masking their numbers. The camouflaged furs on Zimmerik's and Neriya's shoulders blended so well into the backdrop of the snow that, from a distance, they would even look like a party of one.

There were no signs of any animal droppings or any recent activity in the area. There weren't any tracks to follow, and most of the tall grass had drowned beneath the thick covering of snow. Zimmerik's thoughts filled his mind as only the sound of wind filled the air. *This is looking bleak*, Zimmerik thought to himself. *Hardly any reasons for animals to be here. Perhaps Erador is leading us to the watering hole. No trace of the elders either.*

For a great distance, they continued their methodical trek through the near-barren tundra. Then, out of his peripheral vision, he saw that Erador squatted down; he and Neriya did the same in unison. He and Erador began to eat small amounts of snow, to prevent their breath from being visible; Neriya mimicked them, whether she knew the reason or not. Out of the corner of Zimmerik's eye, he saw Erador slowly fit the back end of the javelin into his thrower. Zimmerik refrained from glancing over to determine why Erador was loading the atlatl; his training dictated that he keep his vision on their flank, so that their unified awareness would not be compromised. Even the slightest of head movements could give away their position, if predator or prey spotted their undisguised antlers. On occasion his eyes would move to glance upward to monitor for aerial predators. *What does Erador see?*

Utilizing minimal movement, Erador placed the atlatl's flimsy metal strip with a nipple on one end into the groove at the base of the javelin. He bent his arm back until his fist was adjacent to his ear. The center of the javelin shaft, pinched between thumb and forefinger, rested across his other knuckles so that the javelin, the handle, and his eye-sight were all parallel. Zimmerik and Neriya likewise prepared javelins—Neriya was actually the first ready, for all that her motions seemed no faster than those of the other hunters. *Guess she was the right choice*, he thought. Then, they waited some more.

It began to snow again. They squatted without movement, as if petrified, for what seemed like eternity. Gray daylight slowly began to displace twilight. Concern overwhelmed Zimmerik at their imminent loss of concealment. *Erador's dark hide will give us away and we'll have no option but to fight*, he thought. *Erador must have noticed it too. Though* as luck would have it, Erador's brown fur coat was accumulating a healthy covering of snow, as it began to pile up to their belts around their crouched poses. Even his sap-coated javelin collected snow along its length. With no nearby cover to retreat to, whatever it was that Erador spotted, they would have to kill it here. And with the chill of the harsh winter seeping in to their bones, they would have to do it soon. Zimmerik's fingers became so numb that they were burning in pain. Determined to not let Erador down, he forced the sting of the cold from his mind as he concentrated to stay as inanimate as Erador, to maintain their element of surprise. He couldn't even imagine how Neriya was feeling.

The creature grunted, and Zimmerik knew the beast's identity. *A badger-ox,* Zimmerik thought to himself, *but what was it doing way out here, away from the Molpa Plains?* Then it moved to within his vision, not close enough to charge with an axe, but within range of a javelin. It was a bulky beast, large enough to carry a man atop its back. Its thick grey hide was blanketed in snow, with savage claws capable of rending a man in half: a dangerous animal indeed. Its face had the distinct white and black stripes, with small beady eyes beneath two short, thick horns pointing toward the heavens. Zimmerik watched the beast, remembering to check the skies every now and then. The badger-ox began to burrow, its rear end facing the sky, shoveling the snow behind it. *It must have been burrowed under the snow for it to have survived the blast.* Then there was another grunt, not too far away, followed by a high-pitched squeak brought to an abrupt silence. *They must dig down to eat the little critters that burrow just beneath the top-soil. As long as we maintain the element of surprise, we stand a chance.* Then Zimmerik's worst fear became a reality; his fur lost its artificial color and darkened to a deep black. Even with the snow on and around him, he realized he'd become noticeable: one of the beasts turned its head to stare straight at him, and gave an alerting snort to the other. Zimmerik checked his grip, knowing that the blitz was imminent.

Erador's powerful legs catapulted him toward the target, sending his snow-coverings flying off his shoulders and back. In mid-air he gave a fearsome roar, casting his javelin like a ballista over the body of the beast nearest him. The metal strip of the atlatl whipped massive force into the flat trajectory. Then he dropped his head and pointed his antlers, aligning his spine to put all his body weight into his thrust. Blood spewed out of both beasts as his antlers impaled one in multiple spots across its neck and face, while the javelin penetrated through the other's shoulder and buried itself in its heart. Erador kept pushing his antlers deeper into the beast's neck to ensure he had inflicted a mortal wound. After it had stopped moving, he withdrew his axe and swung it into the beast's neck to use as leverage to wrest his antlers from the corpse. With one pull, Erador dislodged his antlers from its tough hide. They were dripping with blood steaming away into the frigid morn. Erador grinned, breathing heavy. "We have food for our clan!"

Zimmerik went to check the other: half of Erador's javelin was ensconced inside the beast. "You know, you used more strength than required, Erador. The atlatl only requires finesse." He tapped a second javelin, protruding between ribs a hand span away. His had never left its thrower.

"Well, I like to make sure I kill them with my first toss," answered Erador, followed by a hearty laugh. "It seems your superstitions worked against you this time Zimmerik. Carra's spell almost gave us away."

Zimmerik continued to joke with Erador, hoping that detail would be forgotten. "You're the one with pieces of badger-ox in your hair. We need to get home quick to wash up, before the scent attracts scavengers." He cast about, suddenly worried once more. "But… wait: where's…?"

Then he spotted a pair of antlers and a javelin not a dozen feet behind Erador. "Oh, right: *her* cloak's still white." Which only made Erador laugh harder.

They began to tie ropes around the chest of each beast. Once tied in the center, they each grabbed both ends of the rope over their shoulders and dragged the dead weight behind them. Neriya offered to help Zimmerik, but Erador told her to keep an eye out around them instead.

"We're leaving a trail of blood behind us," she mentioned.

"The intense cold should suppress their bleeding soon enough. What little trace they left behind will be covered by the falling snow," stated Erador confidently.

Much like our elders, if their fate was as grim as it seems, thought Zimmerik before he wiped the thought from his mind. "This could… feed us… for days," he panted.

"I can't wait to see their faces. Especially my father's when he hears the tale upon his return. I knew I wouldn't let him down."

Zimmerik looked over to see the joy covering Erador's face, but he wasn't as optimistic. It saddened him to think that he might not get to speak to Warlord Frodden as father to son. Perhaps he would have more confidence in their return if he had known his father the way Erador had.

Zimmerik closed his eyes and made a private prayer: *Onyx Smith, please continue to bless Clan Wyndlyn with your guardianship and bring the elders back to us unharmed.* He stopped for a moment to look into the heavy skies above, as if searching for a sign that the Onyx Smith had heard him. For now, he tried to feel fortunate enough to have secured such a bounty for the children during this harsh winter.

CHAPTER 7

Carra stood watch at the cavern entrance, waiting until everyone else awakened, staring into the shrouded distance where her friends were out hunting. Little by little, the children awoke with grumbling stomachs. They each grabbed small portions of yesterday's leftovers and gathered around the fire like moths to a flame. They dangled the goat meat above the low simmering fire just long enough to reheat it. The children chatted and laughed amongst themselves, able to enjoy the moment. Carra envied them for it. They were able to forget the looming possibility of their elders' misfortune.

Baltor began snoring. One of the children who'd finished eating snapped off a leaflet from a willow tree and tickled his nose. Baltor slapped himself in the face with his enormous hand and woke up mid-snore. All the children laughed and dispersed in all directions, expecting him to give chase. Even Carra laughed, though Baltor just grumbled and pulled the fur blanket over his head and rolled over back to sleep.

Then something strange caught Carra's eye. The dangling foliage of one of the trees was gently swaying, as if in a breeze—but it was one of the trees farthest from the entrance, not nearest it. With slow, curious steps, she approached the tree, watching the movement intently to make sure her eyes weren't deceiving her. She walked past the mounted runic armor, past piles of stores, and stood near the small hot spring pools. She could feel it; one strand of hair, then another, was stirred by whispers of air coming from somewhere behind the fallen rock from the cave-in. She moved her hands across the piled stones, seeking its source.

The seven other teens had gathered the children into three small groups, educating them about their budding antlers. The twins, Vynocent and Wiltyn, raised and trained together with the axe and shield since their youth, had impressed even the elders with their unique teamwork fighting style. Wiltyn commanded the group's attention. "Your antlers will become your most valuable weapon. In battle, you may run out of javelins or lose your axe, but you'll always have these," he said as he grasped each of his own antlers. "Right now, most of you only have the soft velvet coating covering your rounded antlers, but they'll sharpen, and harden, and grow in time to become your most lethal weapon."

Vynocent cut in, "Yes, and the smooth velvet helps them grow. We never shed our antlers the way deer do, an improvement the Soul Smith implemented when creating our race."

One of the youths blurted out a question, "Why does the Soul Smith create such dangerous demons?"

"Are you a dangerous demon?" asked Vynocent. After the group had a giggle, he went on. "I'll answer with another question. Why do you think there is a cobra to eat the mice?" he challenged their fertile minds.

"We are the mice?" the student asked, confused.

Vynocent chuckled. "No, we are the mongoose that stops the cobras from eating all the mice. Clan Wyndlyn shields Thornwall from the demons He conjures from within Beknen Valley, the way Clan Grondyr did at Chyxurlgon Jungle. The Soul Smith has grown reckless, vengeful even. That is why we train and dedicate our entire lives to become the greatest warriors in all of Thornwall. We take great pride in defending the world from dangers they will never know." The children listened to the lessons in earnest, despite being taught by teens only a handful of years their seniors.

Gressyn and Tysyra noticed Carra's peculiar fascination with the stone pile, and brought their instruction to a halt. "Okay, children, that's enough for now, you can go play," Tysyra told their group. They didn't need to be told twice.

Gressyn fiddled a comb through unruly hair as he approached Carra. His slim athletic build was hidden beneath oversized garb, as if he were meant to grow into it. He had the rune of the Onyx Smith tattooed to his forearm, a decoration he'd acquired to match one Tysyra bore, an impulsive decision he now regretted. Tysyra followed at his heels, her braided locks swaying to her knees. The end of the braid was knotted around the hilt of a dagger. In close combat, with a simple twist, she could whip its flat, spade-like blade around and slit her enemy's throat.

"What's wrong?" Gressyn asked Carra.

"I think there is more cavern beyond these crumbled stones. Feel the breeze coming through the cracks."

Gressyn and Tysyra held out their hands. Moving air tickled their fingertips. They looked at the cracks running up the walls on either side, the ceiling where the shock wave of yesterday's blast had loosened the stones.

"Let's see what's on the other side," Gressyn enthused, beginning to pull a stone away from the base of the pile.

Carra laid a hand on his arm. "Wait! We don't want to cause a further collapse. Let's take the stones from the top first."

Tysyra jerked her head back as if that was the most absurd idea she'd heard in a while. "First, how are we going to reach that high? And second, if we pull from the top of the pile, there could still be more unsecured stones above waiting to fall."

"There could still be stones waiting to fall no matter *which* ones we move first," Carra observed.

They all stood there, dumbfounded at how this simple pile of rocks had turned into a nightmare of a puzzle. The wall here had not merely collapsed, but shattered: a few chunks were massive, but most would be easy enough for them to drag and push. Even those were substantial enough to crack a skull with a short fall, or break a limb caught beneath them. Several minutes of silent contemplation on how to remove the boulders in a safe manner failed to spark fresh ideas.

Gressyn said aloud what was on all of their minds. "What if it's a secret left behind by the ancients?" They felt growing conviction that he was right—and that they had to see what mystery their ancestors might have hidden on the other side.

They analyzed the pile of stones meticulously, trying to determine which ones could be removed without destabilizing others. Gressyn looked around for a way to gain access to the top of the rock pile. Nothing in the cavern stood out to him. The children were all climbing and playing in the willow trees. He picked up a javelin, placed the flat end against one of the stones near the top, and began pushing with all his might, hoping that anything he loosened would fall away from him instead of toward him. Carra and Tysyra took a few steps back, just in case.

With one final grunt, he convinced his rock to move. Others on the top of the pile shifted… most, but not all, in the direction he'd hoped. Then, as Carra had feared, more stones began to separate from the cavern ceiling, grinding into the top of the stone pile and tumbling to the floor. Gressyn leapt backward to avoid having his feet smashed. Dust rose into the air and into Gressyn's eyes. He rubbed them in annoyance, then allowed tears build up to flush the dust out. By the time he regained his sight, Carra had already climbed gingerly to the top of the pile and was peering into the darkness of the newly discovered space beyond. The gap at the top was big enough to crawl into.

The trickle of air that had attracted Carra was now a steady breeze against Carra's face as she peered through the unobstructed clearing. Carra picked up a small stone that fit inside her hand. She rubbed her thumb on its surface in a small circular motion until the rock began emitting light as bright as a lantern. She tossed the rock into the darkness ahead of her. The small stone skittered to a halt, revealing a tunnel which continued beyond its illumination.

"What do you see?" asked Tysyra.

"It's just a tunnel, but it's smooth, not rough. It might be manmade," replied Carra.

Tysyra and Gressyn could see the light trickle through occasional crevices in the pile of stones, suggesting how thin the collapsed wall had been. Carra slid carefully down to the floor. She turned and faced her companions. "We should organize a scouting party to see what's in there. I'll see if Baltor's awake; you two can go grab some weapons. We want to take this carefully."

The light coming over and through the pile of stone began to come and go.

"Uh, Carra—"

She ignored Gressyn's interruption and continued describing the plan. "We'll have the other teens stay to guard the children, two at the entrance, the rest here."

Gressyn interrupted, "Carra, does your light spell blink off and on?"

"No, but I can turn it off. Just like this," and with the snap of her fingers the light died out.

Gressyn and Tysyra's mouths dropped open and their faces turned a pale white. "Carra, step away slowly," whispered Gressyn. Tysyra motioned with her hands for Carra to step towards her.

Carra watched as Gressyn's fingers tightened one by one on the javelin in his hands. Fear didn't strike Carra until she saw Tysyra draw a serrated dagger from her boot. Carra turned to look at the pile of rocks behind her. Her gaze rose toward the opening at the top. Amidst the blackness, there were three glowing yellow eyes, seeming to hover above the heap of boulders, fixed on her.

All activity in the cave had ceased when the stone pile shifted. The children stopped playing, frozen in place, quiet and motionless, some still hanging in the tree. A couple made tentative moves toward the back of the cavern, but the other teens signaled them to stay put. Now Vynocent, Wiltyn and Hammynt took up axes and shields, Dorgeeryn and Valen shield and javelins. They were but fifteen or sixteen years of age, old enough to be an adult in other societies, but only just beginning the vanquisher training that distinguished elkin from other warriors. Hammynt shook Baltor, still snoring near the camp fire, to rouse him. The cave became completely silent, apart from the occasional plash of a water droplet.

Gressyn, and Tysyra spread out to flank the cave-in, their knees bent, waiting to spring into action. Carra continued to back away, her hands crossed behind her back, pulsing with light. Tysyra wielded her dagger in the pikal grip, her thumb covering the pommel. Gressyn held his javelin in both hands, as if bracing to resist a cavalry charge. The concealed creature made a rapid clicking sound, which echoed throughout the cave. Everyone held their breath. Silence fell once more as the echoes died. Carra could feel her heart fluttering inside her chest.

The glaring yellow eyes withdrew into the shadows. The disappearance was celebrated by nervous exhalations, as everyone relaxed their guard, relieved by the withdrawal of the creature. Baltor rolled out of bed and retrieved his double-bladed axe from where he'd propped it against a wall near his furs.

Carra suppressed the pulsing energy she'd held ready—and immediately became aware that she'd done something wrong. Pain shot through her hands. She began to massage her fingertips. "That thing must have been ten feet tall," said Carra. She turned to look at the children still motionless in the willow tree and around the cavern. "Everyone get down and get back into that corner, as far away from this pile as possible. Now!" The children dropped from the tree onto the soft soil, scurried to huddle in the corner. Carra looked at Vynocent and said, "Grab javelins and lay them on the ground at the children's feet." She turned to Dorgeeryn and Wiltyn. "You two, grab some pelts from that pile and drape them over the children."

The children huddled together, backs to the cavern wall. Their antlers, small and short, quivered with their fear, but they were well-trained and made no sound. Carra stopped massaging her fingers to look at them. With her hands trembling, she turned her fingernails to face her; they all appeared bruised underneath, as if something heavy had crushed them. She clutched her hands together and pulled them close to her stomach, gritting her teeth. *I shouldn't have contained the energy for so long without expelling it,* she thought.

Vynocent distributed javelins at the feet of each child. Dorgeeryn and Wiltyn began tossing the furs over the shaking children. Carra shouted to them, "You all are going to have to stay perfectly still. I'm going to make the furs look like the cavern wall." The last fur was thrown over a little girl with tears welling up in her eyes, cradling the newborn that had undergone the Call of Fates the day before.

Carra shook her hands rapidly, trying to shed the lingering pain so she could invoke her illusion. The rapid clicking sounded once more from the cave-in. Carra froze in terror: she wasn't ready.

"Carra! Protect the children, we'll hold it off!" yelled Baltor, exuding confidence. The other teens formed an arc around the stone pile, crouching low so that only their eyes peered over their large rectangular shields.

The newborn began to whimper in distress underneath the furs. *Oh no,* Carra thought, opening and closing her hands into fists over and over to help the pain subside.

"Hold it together, children," she murmured, fear undisguised in her voice. She inhaled deeply, wove her arms in intricate gestures…

A thunderous crash exploded from the stone pile.

Several of the children gave brief shrieks of terror in spite of their training and fervent desire to remain unnoticed. Fragments of rock went flying across the room. Dust billowed outward, forcing the teens to turn their heads or duck beneath their shields. The continued grinding and shifting of individual stones warned them they had little time to recover.

What pushed its way out of the rubble stood to the height of the new-found tunnel. It was covered in a thick grey carapace. It had four arms. One of these palmed a loose stone and hurled it toward Hammynt, still huddled behind his sap-coated shield. The force of the impact shattered his defense, snapped the arm that held it, and sent him sprawling. Lying on his back, he dropped his axe and clutched his shield-arm in pain.

As the towering creature began to step free of the remaining boulders, two of its hands gripped the edge of the cavern walls, while the other two picked up fresh stones. Its three eyes moved independently of each other, darting back and forth between the elkin. A pair of antennae twitched above its head. Two long metal tusks protruded from its chin. Its bulbous carapace was rounded like a beetle's, providing additional shields across its back. Its fearsome mouth was drooling onto the stones that it held in its hands. The saliva bubbled and fizzled, eating away at the surface of the stones. A lengthy tongue drooped out of its mouth to lap at one of the stones in its hands. The saliva had dissolved the center of the stone, turning it into a bowl containing a soup of liquefied rock.

"Carra!" Baltor yelled, annoyed by her delay.

"Okay. Okay," Carra replied. Her fingernails still bothered her. The combined surface area of the animal pelts was daunting, her largest concealment attempt yet. *If only I had the Channeler's Staff,* she thought to herself. She held out her palms toward the hiding children, thumbs touching, intoning the words of her spell out loud, almost chanting them, to aid her focus. The image of the pelts began to haze. She gritted her teeth as her hands drifted outward, spreading the blurring effect across all the pelts. No matter how hard she focused, her hands wouldn't stop shaking. Her spell began to fragment and she couldn't maintain it any longer. She clutched her hands in agony, ending the spell prematurely.

"Damn it!" she cursed. "Keep holding him off, I can conceal the furs one by one."

"There's no time for that. Carra, get over here!" shouted Baltor.

The creature finished slurping up the liquefied rock and made its chittering noise again. It took two steps toward the prone Hammynt, who was still clutching his forearm. The other elkin enclosed the creature in a semi-circle, each taking a step forward to close in and protect Hammynt. The sight of the elkin moving in unison caused it to hesitate, and that was all the elkin needed to strike. Gressyn and Dorgeeryn, on the creature's flanks, launched their javelins at the creature, only to witness them glance off its hardened carapace. Valen sent a third into its torso; the chitin cracked slightly, but held, and the javelin fell to the ground.

The beast retaliated. Retrieving one of the javelins, it lunged toward Dorgeeryn and brought down the javelin in a stabbing motion, piercing through Dorgeeryn's muscular thigh and driving the point into the ground. He cried out in pain. The creature's back was turned to Gressyn, revealing the brand of the Soul Smith rune.

"It's another demon of the Soul Smith!" warned Gressyn.

"Think we're ahead of you on that one!" Tysyra shot back.

The demon loomed over Dorgeeryn. It drooled with anticipation as it slowly applied pressure against his ribs with a metallic tusk. The tip of the steel tusk was cold against Dorgeeryn's skin; his ribs strained not to break. The demon's eyes darted back and forth as it studied its victim, all the while making the same rapid clicking. Its tusk held Dorgeeryn at arm's length, preventing him from jabbing it with his antlers.

Carra watched helplessly as Tysyra ran forward with ruthless determination and sliced between layers of chitin at the tendon above the creature's heel. It let go of the javelin in Dorgeeryn's leg and limped around to face its attacker in frustration. It threw a bowl-shaped boulder at Tysyra, missing her face by inches. She paid it no mind as she maneuvered nimbly about it, looking for a new vulnerability in its defenses. It remained hobbling on one leg for only a moment longer, then the creature's back shell split open, revealing wings beneath that lifted it into the air, raising the recently-fallen dust in a fresh hurricane. The pressure of the droning wings bored into the elkins' heads and rattled their bones. The bulbous creature hovered there, assessing, beyond the reach of their axes.

"We should spread out—we can surround it now!" cried Valen.

"No!" Vynocent called back. "Get over here with us—we need to cover our wounded!"

Dust and dirt began to stick to the bleeding wound on Dorgeeryn's leg. He struggled to free the javelin from the ground, but he couldn't get the proper leverage and the pain was too great. While the monster hovered in the air, the elkin repositioned to guard their wounded, three around the immobilized Dorgeeryn and two around Hammynt; shieldless Tysyra continued to dance in the open, trying to distract it. Gressyn had retrieved his javelin. Shielding her eyes from the dust, Carra ran to Hammynt's aid, grabbing him beneath his armpits and dragging him toward the wall opposite the huddled children.

The creature spewed a powerful stream of saliva toward Tysyra, who tumbled to avoid the spray. It turned its attention to Dorgeeryn's continued groans of agony. Vynocent and Wiltyn aligned their wooden shields to create a barrier between the demon and their wounded companion. It sent another stream of saliva splashing across both shields, which sizzled and began eating away at the sap coating. They both threw their shields to the floor before the acidic saliva got onto their skin, and stood there, exposed, with only their axes. Valen flung his javelin alongside the line of the stream, hoping to catch the demon's open mouth, but the gusts from the wings caused it to go wide. Gressyn launched a skillful javelin throw toward its gut as a last-ditch effort. The demon snatched it midair, grabbed it with another of its hands and snapped it like a twig.

"Now what?" asked Gressyn.

"Retreat into the new tunnel. We can force it to walk on its gimp leg and bring it within reach of our axes!" shouted Vynocent.

"But what about the children and the wounded?" yelled Carra.

They could barely understand one another above the pulsating drone of the demon's wings. Hammynt staggered to his feet, cradling his broken forearm, and bellowed, "I'll stay to safeguard Dorgeeryn and the children. They need you in there, Carra, so they have light to see by. Go!"

As the uninjured elkin scrambled over the dispersed pile of rock and into the darkness, the demon's eyes tracked their movements, confused by their actions. Its attention darted back and forth as it clicked in counterpoint to its buzzing wings, first to the seven elkin running into the tunnel, then to Hammynt pulling the javelin from the ground, freeing Dorgeeryn, and then it turned its full attention to three figures that entered the cavern from another direction, dragging a pair of carcasses, all of them covered in snow.

CHAPTER 8

The cavern entrance was now within sight. The hunters visualized the coming celebration for their success, bragging about their accomplishment the entire trip home, reliving the moment.

"It seemed like we were motionless forever. The snow was so cold, it almost gave me the black-foot," Zimmerik joked.

Erador smiled. "We stayed still for as long as we needed. We must bathe in the hot springs to get the blood flowing again."

"Carra said something about black-foot." Neriya strove to keep her concern from her face. "She told me the Channeler made her practice melting ice in different ways, so she could do it inside the body. You don't, uh, think that we…" She looked down at her boots.

"Do your toes hurt?" asked Erador.

"Yeah. A lot."

"Then you're fine," he reassured her. Then, since he realized he hadn't said it yet and ought to have: "You did well out there. I could not have asked for a better wing-guard." Zimmerik seconded the sentiment. Neriya's concern fled her face at the unexpected praise.

Zimmerik was excited in expectation of a fervent welcome. "I can't wait to see their faces when they realize the feast we will have tonight!"

"Yes, and to commemorate this moment, I will make us each a necklace of the claws of these badger-oxen," stated Erador.

They entered the cave with wide smiles across their faces only to be greeted by no one, as if the cave had been abandoned. Their expressions altered from bliss to confusion. Then to concern: the willow trees were whipping about as from a gale blasting them from the far side of the cavern. Instead of the calm they'd expected upon leaving the moaning winds behind them, they heard an obnoxious, throbbing drone. They peered upward only to discover a gigantic flying four-armed monster hovering near the back of the cave, just visible above the crowns of the trees.

The hunters threw down the ropes they had been dragging and took up their javelins. In the corner of his eye, Erador noted the display of the Blacksmith runic armor. Without a second thought, Erador ran toward his father's Onyx armor with its matching broadsword sheathed at its side. As he reached it, the exposed opening in the back of the cavern wall came into view. Boulders were strewn about on the cavern floor in front of it; the flying creature hovered nearby, producing a ratcheting vocalization. Without hesitation, Erador grasped the hilt of the Onyx blade and withdrew the masterfully crafted blade from its sheath. The sword sang with a metallic *zing*, as if announcing its presence. The diamond-tipped single-edged blade glistened in the bluish light of the cavern.

The creature answered the sword's challenge with a hideous screech. Muffled cries came from beneath a peculiar pile of bear furs along a nearby wall of the cavern… some of which quivered and twitched. Erador instantly realized the peril. "The children!" he cried. The demon's three eyes all turned, attracted by motion where there should have been none. Erador shouted back to his companions. "Go protect the—"

Wumph! The Soul Smith demon dropped from the air and landed on the ground in front of the hidden children. The droning cut off as wings folded in tandem beneath its grey exoskeleton of its back. The beast was between Erador and the children, hobbling on one of its legs. "No!" shouted Erador as the monster reached for the pelts. It clutched one of the fur blankets and ripped it off, revealing a frightened child swaddling a crying newborn. She shrieked. Erador ran forward, closing on the hulking demon. Suddenly, a wave of furs erupted as the older children threw off their cover and seized javelins from the floor. Filled with desperate courage, the children screamed high-pitched battle-cries, filled with a blinding instinct to protect the newborn.

Startled, the demon hobbled back a step as the youths threw their javelins with amateur accuracy at the demon. A dozen javelins produced thudding sounds in rapid succession as they ricocheted harmlessly off the demon's exoskeleton armor. As the children took up fresh weapons, the creature grabbed one of them around his waist, lifting him high into the air in preparation for a smashing swing. The child struggled in futility to escape its death grip. Then the beast jolted stiffly upright. The child stopped struggling as he saw Erador standing at its back with his hands upon the handle of the Onyx blade. The blade was inserted so deep into the creature's back that the hilt was flush with the demon's shell. Erador pulled the blade free, smothered in its blood, and took two steps back.

The demon turned to face his attacker; Erador responded with a swipe that severed the arm holding the child. The child fell to the soft soil, still within the grip of the severed arm. Three of his friends grabbed him and pulled him to safety behind their skirmish line. As the demon roared in fury, its back shell and wings fanned out in a fearsome threatening display. The creature had four translucent, round-tipped wings, laced with wire-thin grey lines. Its right wings were punctured from Erador's strike, and were dripping with the creature's blood. The demon lumbered toward Erador, limping as it came on. Erador danced back, easily able to keep distance between them, while he calculated his next move. The demon suddenly began whipping its wings downward on alternate steps, launching itself in half-leaps to overcome its handicap. With each lunge, it whipped its head forward, trying to gore Erador with the two metallic tusks protruding from its chin.

Backpedaling, Erador parried each swipe with the Onyx blade; sparks flew and the clang of metal on metal echoed throughout the cavern. Neriya regrouped the children into a tight hedgehog around their younger peers. Zimmerik, always the patient hunter, waited with readied javelin, watching as the demon drove Erador back toward the runic armor display, waiting for a vulnerability to reveal itself. As the creature crossed in front of him, he seized the opportunity of an exposed back… with carapace opened around extended wings. Zimmerik leaned back, putting all his weight on his back leg, holding the atlatl above his antlers, to the full extent of his arm. His throw began from the earth, force driving up from foot to leg to waist to shoulder to arm to wrist. The metal launcher grazed the surface of the ground with his follow-through. The javelin whipped through the dusty air with lightning speed, straight and true. The hardened, sap-coated missile struck squarely between the join of wings to body, sinking deep into the back of the creature.

It dropped to the floor.

Erador stopped, breathing heavily, and watched as the demon writhed in pain, until its antennae stopped twitching. He glanced over to the youths, several of whom were now helping free the child from of the grasp of the severed arm. Erador then stared at Zimmerik, nodding his head. "It's about time you joined the fight," Erador said. His look of impressed approval belied the understatement of his words.

The youths gasped and drew back as one of the beast's legs twitched to life. And another. The demon scrambled into a crawling position, struggling to support its weight on its remaining limbs. It snatched at the legs of the nearest child, only to find it curtained behind a thicket of javelins. Erador snapped. He leapt on top of the creature and went into a hacking frenzy, yelling with every strike. The Onyx blade sent shreds of carapace and chitin-covered flesh in all directions. Erador didn't stop until his arms strained from swinging.

Zimmerik went to check on the children, but the sight of Hammynt and Dorgeeryn, both wounded, stopped him in his tracks. "Hammynt, what happened? Where are the others?!"

"That demon came from the other side of the cave-in. The others ran in to try to draw the creature away from the children, but then you arrived—thank the Onyx Smith," said Hammynt, gritting his teeth in pain.

"Erador!" Zimmerik yelled. "Go into the tunnel and find the others. We have two wounded here!"

Erador, gasping for breath, wiped the demon's blood from his face with the back of his hand. Erador could feel himself sweating beneath the hides he wore to keep the chill of the hunt at bay. He had never wielded the Onyx blade before; its keen edge and effortless balance left Erador in awe at the masterfully crafted blade. *This sword isn't mine, I should put it back. I must clean it first... perhaps I should put it down and clean it later. But it feels so comfortable in my hands... I'll just hold onto it for now. No knowing what else might be down that tunnel,* he rationalized.

He wiped excess blood from the blade onto his already blood-covered fur, verified that the children were fine, then headed toward the tunnel to find the others. As he neared its entrance a glow appeared from within it. Then Carra was racing toward him, an illuminating rock in her hand, with the others close behind her. Erador, standing at the edge of the cavern's bluish light, was smitten with joy to see her. He couldn't wait to tell her of the successful hunt and the demon slaying.

Carra stopped running and rested her free hand on Erador's gore-covered shoulder as she tried to catch her breath. "Erador, is everyone alright?!" she asked in a panic.

"Everyone is fine, the demon is slain. Though it looks like Hammynt and Dorgeeryn will require time to heal."

She breathed a heavy sigh of relief. Erador noticed that the nails of the fingers on his shoulder were as black as night. He snatched her hand to inspect it. "What happened to you?" he asked.

She yanked her hand away and crossed her arms to hide her hands. "It's none of your concern. I'm fine," she said in a tone of finality.

Erador scrunched his brow in concern, but decided to let her be. "Why were you all so deep in the cave?" he asked.

Baltor spoke up first, "We turned a corner an' Carra couldn't make a light at first. Then we heard the creature's roar echo ev'rywhere. We thought it was right behind us, an' we couldn't see, so we kept goin' deeper into the tunnel to buy Carra time. As we got deeper, all we could hear was the sound of rushin' water, it was so loud."

Erador held up his hand to stop the story. "Wait, there's running water in there?"

"We didn't find it, but we had to be close," Baltor responded.

Erador's head dipped groundward as he delved within his mind, trying to find a way to use this information.

Carra, arms still crossed, interrupted his planning. "Erador, don't think too hard. You might hurt yourself," she said, eliciting a few chuckles amongst the group.

Erador couldn't help but feel a bit embarrassed. He smiled out one side of his mouth and spoke in an arrogant tone, "Well then, perhaps we should all just stick to what we do best. I'll stick to hunting, while you can stick to cooking!"

His quip evoked belly laughter from the rest of the group, while Carra squinted at him with a menacing glare. "Oh yah? What am I going to cook, the filthy carcass of the Soul Smith demon?"

"We only eat bugs when we have to." Erador winked at Zimmerik. "How about roasting the meat of the badger-oxen that we brought back?"

His statement was followed by blank stares of disbelief, as if his claim was too good to be true. He nodded his head in reassurance and Baltor began to drool.

"But first, Carra, we need your talents to help with the wounded." His implied confidence in her was apology enough for his previous insult. She smiled and replied, "Absolutely," as she headed over toward Hammynt and Dorgeeryn.

Tysyra took over allotting responsibilities. "Vynocent and Wiltyn, go skin the badger-oxen and prepare the meal. Gressyn and I can clean up the demon's remains."

Gressyn concealed his disappointed look from Tysyra's eyes, perturbed to be paired with her yet again.

Tysyra continued uninterrupted. "Baltor and Valen, you tend to the children and calm them down. Check to see if any got hurt. Erador, you're covered in blood. You and the Onyx blade need a bath."

Erador laughed in agreement.

"And all three of you need to get out of your hunting garb and warm yourselves properly in the springs." She received no arguments there, either. "And while you're there, keep an eye on the tunnel. And don't forget to check yourselves for black-foot."

Zimmerik nodded. "That sounds great. It'll be good to get a little rest while staying on watch." Neriya nodded, too; after her first hunt in the cold and snow, she seemed too exhausted to produce words.

Erador concurred and they all went about their assigned tasks. Baltor approached the youths, with a proud smile on his face at the uses they'd made of their javelins. Their calm composure, after the fight they'd just been in, would have surprised anyone other than another elkin. He bent down to their height—a long way, for him—and asked in an uplifting voice, "How'd you like to study the demon's weaknesses? That way if we ever meet another, it won't be so scary." They all seemed receptive to the idea, bobbing their heads up and down. He led them to the weapons stash so they could collect a few axes. The children that were big enough took turns chopping at the demon's exoskeleton until they found the soft spots in its joints. The others watched intently, giggling from relief of their pent-up terror whenever one of the axe-wielders struck flesh. Valen, a young, quiet hunter who had come north with Baltor, contributed occasional comments about the anatomy their efforts revealed.

While the demon's carcass was undergoing vulnerability testing, Gressyn and Tysyra were wrapping themselves in furs, preparing to venture out into the snowy tundra.

"Tysyra, I got an idea," said Gressyn.

"What is it?"

"Let's use the rope tied around the badger-oxen to drag this demon outside."

"Too easy," she replied, as she began untying the ropes from the heavy badger-ox bodies. As each of the carcasses was liberated, Vynocent and Wiltyn hefted it between them—barely— and shuffled it to the butchering area. "Besides," Tysyra continued, "looks to me like by the time Baltor's done with his lesson, there won't be anything big enough to use a rope on."

Carra arranged a bed of pelts for Dorgeeryn to lie upon. Carra elevated his wounded leg while inspecting the sap-hardened javelin that had been driven through his thigh. "I'm sorry, but there's no way we can break the javelin. I'm going to have to pull it the rest of the way through."

He shook his head in a dramatic fashion. "No, no, no, no. I thought you can heal me with a spell."

"Not with the javelin still in it, I can't!" Carra looked at his dirt-caked bleeding wound. She looked back at him disheartened, wishing she had better news. "I—"

"Hold the javelin as still as possible," interrupted Erador, on his way to re-sheathe his father's now-clean weapon. "The Onyx blade should be able to cut through the sap coating."

Dorgeeryn turned to lie on his side so that the longer section of the javelin rested against the ground. Erador instructed Carra to brace it with her weight, then hovered the large Onyx blade above the horizontal javelin, aligning his chop as close to the leg as possible. Dorgeeryn closed his eyes tight, preparing for a searing pain. Erador readjusted his footing and raised the blade high above his head. He swung with speed and precision, easily severing the shaft of the javelin and burying the sword-tip inches into the ground.

"Woah, keep that far away from my antlers," Carra said. With careful focus, she pulled the javelin through Dorgerryn's leg. Blood flowed out the gaping wounds on both sides of his thigh like water from a bucket. The hole was so large that they could see through it; the javelin had just missed the bone. For a moment, Carra feared it had *not* missed an artery, so great was the initial flow, but the bleeding slowed as soon as what had built up in the wound ebbed out. Hammynt, with his one good arm, arrived with a bowl of water to clean the wound, then aided Carra in wrapping a shredded tunic tight around Dorgeeryn's muscular thigh. Erador, satisfied that he was no longer needed, went about his delayed clean-up.

Once the wound was tied off, Carra folded a couple furs into a raised pillow. "This is to keep your leg elevated," she said.

She draped additional furs over her pale patient, who had begun shivering from shock. "These will keep you warm. You're going to have to rest now. We've done all that we can do. If only I had the Channeler's Staff I could mend your wound with a spell," she stated in sincerity.

Breathing heavily from his nose, he nodded his head and closed his eyes. It was obvious he was in pain but didn't want to let it show.

Half an hour passed. Vynocent and Wiltyn finished skinning the large bodies of the badger-oxen. Wiltyn delivered the animal's claws to Erador per his request, while Vynocent put two entire badger-oxen legs on the spit. In an hour's time, Clan Wyndlyn had their feast, and Erador had his necklace. The aroma of the cooked meat filled the cavern, making everyone's mouth water. Those that did not eat the steak with their hands used their daggers, stabbing juicy slabs of meat and biting into the filets atop their blades. Their elongated canines tore through the tough meat with every bite. Juices from the fat dripped onto their faces.

Whilst chewing, Baltor attempted to tease Erador. "This makes for a late lunch, what'll ya catch us for dinner?"

"This is an early dinner," he replied with a smile "You slept through lunch."

Everyone was rejoicing over the victories today; everyone except for Zimmerik, who stood guard at the tunnel's entrance. Erador finished his meal and headed toward Zimmerik. He sat perched on a stone like a statue, leathery hands gripping a javelin, cold blue eyes gazing into the tunnel. The cool breeze coming from within the tunnel raised goose bumps on Erador's skin.

"Zimmerik, I made us each a necklace to remember this day. I already gave Neriya hers."

Zimmerik remained motionless, never removing his sight from the tunnel just like a good wing-guard should.

"You haven't moved from that spot since you finished cleaning up. You should at least get yourself a serving," exclaimed Erador, troubled by his friend's stillness.

Zimmerik remained silent a moment more, then said, "We need to go in there."

"What for?"

"Shh! Did you hear that?"

They both sat in silence, staring into the blackness of the tunnel, trying to ignore the happy cacophony of conversation behind them. Zimmerik shifted his javelin to his other hand, holding it like a spear in a defensive stance. Erador heard it now: a sound like rats squeaking back and forth, but in a slightly lower pitch. Erador realized he didn't have a weapon and improvised, making a fist around the necklace he held, three badger-ox claws protruding between his fingers.

A dozen pairs of glowing silver eyes winked into being within the tunnel, staring back at them, no more than three feet off the ground. Then a dozen more appeared further within the blackness. The eyes were huddled close together, and then one pair began to approach; they appeared to be hovering in the darkness.

"Clan Wyndlyn! Arm yourselves!" shouted Erador with a commanding tone that he did not know he had.

"If it's not one thing, it's another," whispered Zimmerik beneath his breath.

The festivities stopped. The children brandished the daggers they were using for eating while the adolescents ran for weapons and shields. All attention was on Erador and Zimmerik, who stared into the emptiness of the tunnel. Distressed at the prospect of yet more troubles, they all stood still and tense.

The creature behind the eyes was not alarmed by Erador's booming voice, and continued approaching without hesitation. As it moved near enough for the faint ambient light to reach it, its outline became clear. A humanoid, small, no taller than a mature elkin's waist, with a bald head and long pointy ears. Its arms and legs were slender when compared to its large hands and feet, and its body was the shape of a pear. The creature stopped within the shadows at the edge of the light, and began to sniff the air.

Just above a whisper, Erador stated, "They must have smelled our cooking."

The creature inched a chalky white-skinned hand out of the shadows and into the cavern's bluish light. Short, tough, rock-honed nails tipped the fingers. The hand remained visible for only a brief moment before the creature jerked it back and withdrew into the shadows. A burst of bickering squeaks ran between the creatures, then they retreated out of sight.

The elkin relaxed… a little. Zimmerik said, "This cave is getting less safe by the hour."

"Well, we can't leave, we must wait for the adults to return. We still have five days remaining."

"Have you heard of Warlord Brynn or the Channeler speak of those creatures before?"

Erador frowned with disappointment. "There are a lot of things I wish my father had told me."

"Well, if it's our cooking they want, then let's give them some."

"Some? Did you see how many of them there were? Besides, we need that food for our own survival."

"Let's rebuild this barricade and prevent them from returning."

"It's late in the day, and we're all already tired. No way we have enough energy between the lot of us to move all these heavy stones into place. Some of these I don't think we *can* move."

Zimmerik took a deep breath. "Okay. So we fight. Why do you suppose they wouldn't come into the light?"

"I don't know. Either they can't see in the light, or they are sensitive to it. Either way, Carra will be our advantage and we should prepare for them to return."

"We'll be outnumbered, Erador. Do you expect the children to fight as well?"

Erador took a brief moment to consider the idea. Zimmerik noticed the glimmer in his eye and began shaking his head in a dramatic fashion. "No, no, no. That's a bad idea Erador."

"They'll fight if we need them to fight. We should at least prepare them for it. Those creatures are smaller than most of the youths."

"No. Let's head after them right now, and we won't need to involve the children."

"And fight them in their own territory?" Erador extended his hand, offering the necklace of badger-ox claws to Zimmerik. "What do you say we hold them right here?"

Zimmerik took the necklace and donned it. "I'm with you Erador, but we can't entirely rely upon Carra. If we are to hold them here at the tunnel, let's make what wall we can out of these stones to slow them down. Maybe narrow the opening, force them into a bottleneck. They'll be fodder to our javelins."

Erador nodded in agreement and swept his gaze across the vast cavern that was supposed to be their shelter. His eyes stopped upon the three sets of Blacksmith runic armor. "Zimmerik," he said with a sense of ingenuity, "let's prepare for battle."

CHAPTER 9

Carra, Erador, and Zimmerik stepped up to the stands holding their fathers' runic armor, intimidated by the power contained within. The daunting suits seemed to look down at them, judging them. Standing before Warlord Brynn's Onyx Smith armor, Erador's mind flooded with memories of his father. They were of sun-filled days, full of joy, hope, and promise. He remembered the day that Warlord Brynn stepped forward into the Channeler's circle in the presence of the entire clan to claim Erador as his son. No other elkin of Clan Wyndlyn dared question his claim as they had no reason to suspect a lie. He remembered learning the javelin from him, how well his aim improved just after one lesson. He remembered their first hunt together. He remembered testing his strength against his father's when they crashed their antlers together. He remembered the day his mother died in a battle with a demon of the Soul Smith, and the song his father wrote for her. He remembered how his father entrusted the survival of the youths to him just before leaving the Willow Cave. He remembered the blast. Erador felt weak, hesitant to put the armor on. The empty eyes of the dark Onyx helm seemed to be staring at him in disapproval.

Carra stood before the cloudy, shining surface of Warlord Dryden's Sky Smith armor. Her attention was drawn to the sword as she adored the intricate runic inscriptions upon the metallic sheath that hid the famed blade. She caressed her fingers across the pommel and down the hilt. "No one from my clan has ever seen Warlord Dryden unsheathe this sword."

"Let's have a look then," said Zimmerik, feeling a bit jealous as he stood before Warlord Frodden's weaponless and helmless Sky Smith armor, hoping it could be adjusted to his lanky frame.

Carra shook her head. "I don't think that would be right, but I don't see how I could make use of it this battle."

Zimmerik pounced upon the opportunity that Carra lay before him. "May I use it then? Just this once?" he asked.

Carra, ignoring Zimmerik's request, grabbed her father's helm from atop the display. It had two slits that run from the top of the head to the back of the helm, allowing it to be slid around the antlers of an elkin. Erador noticed the similarity to his father's Onyx helm. "Did Warlord Dryden have his helm modified, or was it built for him?"

Carra slid the massive helm onto her head. Her voice was muffled within it. "Like I've said before, he's had the armor as long as I can remember."

"And no one has seen him unsheathe the blade in all that time?" asked Zimmerik.

Carra turned her head toward Zimmerik, the oversized helm bobbling loosely on her head. She shifted the helm about in an effort to steady it, then removed it. "Take this helm. It obscures my vision and keeps slipping. Let's hope it will be snug upon your head," she said, handing him the helm.

Zimmerik took it and put it on with excitement, blanketing his smile with the helm's ghastly visage. "Thanks!"

"Glad it fits you better than me," smiled Carra.

This called their attention to an additional complication. The heavy, layered cloth that the Warlords wore beneath their armor was somewhere out on the tundra, on their bodies. The teens had to make do with scrounging extra tunics and trousers from their peers. The padding provided was barely adequate; the effects on the way the armors fit ranged from insufficient to inconvenient.

The light that filtered through the blue ice was dwindling. Erador spotted the first gomabeetles lighting up upon the cavern ceiling and knew that time was short. He looked over at Baltor, Gressyn, Tysyra, and the twins, watching them building the small rock blockade at the tunnel entrance. They were exerting frantic energy, yet the stack was still only waist-high. Erador could see their strength drain with each boulder. "Take a rest," he shouted. "Save it for the battle. Have the children build a couple of fires near the wall; perhaps the light will help keep the creatures at bay."

"We don't need the fires for their light, we need them for their heat," shouted Tysyra with her tiny voice. "How about we lay a blanket of burning charcoal on the ground on our side of the stone hurdle?"

"Even better," approved Erador.

Erador returned his attention to the massive black stone armor of the Onyx Smith standing before him. He took a deep breath and summoned the courage to begin donning the armor. *Only the greatest warriors of Clan Wyndlyn have worn this armor*, he thought. His father Warlord Brynn, and his father before him Warlord Synder; all the way back to Vorkus. And now he was about to join them in this honor.

His concentration focused on the importance of this symbolic moment. He used all his energy just to breathe in and out while his heart raced, beating so loud that he fell deaf to all outer noises. His vision was locked onto the armor, all else blurring away. He stretched out his arms to pick up the helm when he felt a small tug at his trousers. His concentration broke, and the busy noise of the clan came rushing to his ears. He looked down to see a small girl, Lora, originally from Clan Grondyr. She clutched a doll and, judging by her small, velvety antlers, could not be more than six years of age.

"Excuse me," she said with an innocent high-pitched voice. "Can we go home? I don't like it here anymore."

Erador felt conflicted. *I don't have time for this*, he thought as he glanced upward to check for more gomabeetles. He looked back down to her; her hair was braided with meticulous detail, parted in the center with long bangs curving along the shape of her face; the hair style of an elkin princess. This would have been a grave offense, were there a princess to speak of. The only time a family would monogamously unite their bloodlines in the presence of the Channeler's circle is when a product of their lovemaking chose the forging hammer during the Call of the Fates, thus declaring the parents royalty and their child a true heir of Vorkus.

His concerned gaze met hers, and he could see the fear behind her big brown eyes. He got down on one knee and placed his hands on her shoulders as he spoke in a sincere, soft voice. "This cavern is as much our home as Cerebus-Senti. It was built by the ancients and is worth protecting. I know these monsters are scary, but soon there will be no more creatures left to harm us here."

"You promise?" she asked with the naïveté only children can muster.

"With the armor that's behind me, I will be able to protect us all; I promise."

She smiled and ran off. Gressyn approached him right after Lora's departure. "Erador, we will have to use at least a week's worth of charcoal to cover a big enough area. I hope we have enough to last the winter."

Erador sighed as he recollected all the extra work he had done to prepare enough charcoal. "Use what we need to."

Carra jumped in. "We're going to have to ration it, then, have smaller fires until we feel that we're caught up."

Erador nodded once in approval. Gressyn ran back toward the stone wall where Tysyra continued dumping and spreading charcoal from woven baskets. Wooden thudding and whacking sounds echoed from Vynocent and Wiltyn's last-minute combat class. They were instructing the eldest of the youths on how to keep their guard up with a shield.

Time for me to put on this armor, Erador thought, but his attention was distracted by Carra helping Zimmerik adjust the fit of his armors' greaves. "What do you plan on naming the Soul Smith demon you slew?" Carra asked Zimmerik with a flirtatious smirk.

"It hadn't even entered my thoughts. I've never named one of the Soul Smith's new creations before," he replied, contemplating the matter. "How does Gorrotin sound?" he asked.

Why is she giving him the credit? That was my *kill.* "It has a good ring to it," interjected Erador. "You have a talent for naming creatures as quickly as Herlidrek."

While strapping on his greaves, Zimmerik asked, "Speaking of creatures, didn't those little critters remind you of the gremlins in the Channeler's stories?"

"Impossible. The Channeler said gremlins were driven to extinction ages ago by Goma the Radiant Smith, during the Cleansing."

"Perhaps they were driven into caves instead, to hide from his light?" Zimmerik insisted.

"If they did as you say, they would have had to stay there for many, many years to adapt to the darkness the way these creatures have," stated Erador, as he donned his chest plate and began tightening its straps.

"And if that's true, then there would be many, many more of them than we saw," exclaimed Zimmerik.

Erador stood bewildered, dumbfounded, and shocked all at once. Zimmerik's words evoked horror that shook him to his very core. Erador's courage has been tested against monstrous demons, faced with the potential loss of the elders from the blast, but Erador has not tested his prowess against an entire horde. "No, you're right," Erador said in a panic. "That was their scouting party we saw. Gremlins or not, they're going to be back in numbers far greater than we have javelins to throw." He looked toward the ceiling as he watched gomabeetles light up before his eyes. *Time is running out,* he thought. *Darkness is upon us.* He felt paralyzed by his realization, scanning the room, taking in what may be his last memories of his clan, his family. His gaze stopped upon Lora, so young, so innocent, yet she was trading her doll for a dagger. He remembered his pledge to her, *With the armor that's behind me, I will be able to protect us all; I promise.*

A fire burned inside him; a rage had been awakened. This wasn't going to just be a battle, this… was going to be a war. A war with the odds stacked against them: possibly his clan's final stand. Erador hurried to strap on the Onyx Smith plate. Carra and Zimmerik had already finished gearing up—his armor not as snug as he would have liked, hers almost absurdly loose, even after stuffing spare fur mittens beneath its shoulders and behind its knees and elbows. Erador at least had the advantage of being near his father in size. As he slid the black Onyx helm around his antlers, his face was masked with the visage of the Onyx Smith Himself. Every inch of him was covered with black stone. In full armor, Erador felt a surge of confidence; the transformation was complete.

Erador marched toward the wall where the fires had yet to be lit. "Get every javelin we have and stick them in the ground here in a long line for faster reloading. Anyone that can hurl a javelin, stand here now," Erador pointed at the soft soil beneath his feet, fifteen feet away from the wall. His voice found new levels of masculinity; the armor's very presence evoked trepidation and commanded unquestionable authority. All eyes were upon him.

"As soon as I give the word, you let loose and don't stop. Throw volley after volley until there are no more javelins left to throw. Then we'll lock shields and push forward, shoulder to shoulder, and stand at the edge of the fire. We will hack them to pieces with our axes while we watch them burn. No matter what, we will not let them step one foot into this cavern. We will fight throughout the night, without sleep, whatever it takes. Now *get that fire lit!*"

***

They waited. Dozens of javelins stuck out of the soil before them in a long line like a poorly crafted fence. The breeze from within the tunnel cooled their brows as the heat from the charcoal made them sweat. Only the eldest of the youths joined the teens at the front line; the rest took up daggers and axes, guarding the hastily snow-packed badger-ox carcasses near the butchering block. Nervous tension filled the air as the first vermin-like squeaks echoed from within the tunnel.

They were close.

At the last minute, Carra came up behind Zimmerik as he stood beside Erador, facing the darkness. Her arms went around his waist, and he looked down in surprise—then was even more surprised to see her tying a belt above his hips, a silver sheath dangling from one side. "Here. I can't imagine having any use for a sword. You might as well see what can be done with it." Then she stepped back again.

He was too amazed to think of a reply. Then he didn't have time to.

At first sight of their foes' reflective eyes, Erador drew the dreaded Onyx blade so that its diamond edge shrilled against its metal sheath, sending the sword's war cry ringing down the tunnel. Zimmerik did the same, drawing the Sky blade from its silver sheath.

"Is this some kind of a joke?" demanded Zimmerik in a fury.

He held the hilt firmly before him, but there was no blade attached to the guard. He looked inside his empty sheath and couldn't believe his luck. "This stupid thing!"

Zimmerik flung the handle at the tunnel in frustration just as the first intruder rose up over the stone partition. Its chalky face and silvery eyes were illuminated by the simmering glow of the charcoal. The handle spun past to one side of the creature; its pale head and shoulders fell forward into the charcoal, severed clean from the rest of its body, which slid into the darkness beyond the wall.

"Did… did the sword do that?" asked Zimmerik in disbelief. He turned to Erador. "Get me back that blade."

Erador's eyes filled with intensity. "Volley!" he roared, raising the Onyx blade toward the tunnel. The elkin hurled javelins into the blackness beyond the wall, raining death upon the unseen creatures. Shrieks of pain stung their ears. Erador charged; despite his armor, his muscular legs launched him over the fire and the wall. He swung blindly into the darkness as he landed. The blade was so sharp the gremlins' bodies seemed to offer no resistance to it. But their speed and numbers surprised him, swarming him and immobilizing his arms. No matter how sharp, his sword did little damage when merely twitched by his wrist. Claws pried at his armor, seeking ways past it.

"Volley!" he yelled from within the shadows of the tunnel, knowing full well that he might get hit, choosing to trust his armor.

Another slew of javelins sleeted into the blackness. More shrieks tortured the air, while two of the javelins thudded against Erador's back. The force of their blows toppled him over face first upon squirming bodies. He heard a voice behind him—Zimmerik's, he thought—yell, "No! Don't!"

Stubby claws were tearing into his neck, elbows, knees, underarms, everywhere the plate's protection gapped of necessity. Other hands were holding down his arms and legs, and he could feel them tugging at the blade and plying at his fingers, attempting to disarm him. Erador flailed about with all his strength, trying to free himself from the scrum. He bucked his head with lethal force, goring the occasional gremlin incautious enough not to avoid his antlers, but his efforts proved useless against their numbers. They were swarming him like bees to honey, and still more ran past him—he could not even begin to guess how many, only that it was worse than Zimmerik's gloomiest pessimism had conjured. The never-ending train of shrieks eclipsed all other noise.

"Carra!" he yelled through his pain. "I need your light!" His voice couldn't have traveled far, as it sounded muffled even to his ears. The overwhelming squeaks of these creatures filled the tunnel like a massive swarm of bats. *Why hasn't there been another volley of javelins?* he thought. *Have we been overrun already?* The gremlins finally got hold of and pinned his antlers; one or more others found purchases on his helm, working it off around the antlers by trial and error. He was immobilized. The only positive he could find was that he no longer felt anything prying at the death-grip he maintained on his sword's hilt. *They're so thick now they're crowding one another out.* He recognized the irony of his mental sneer. *Not that I have any tactics which could take advantage of that. Where by all the Smiths is that light? Did Carra's incantations fail her again?*

Even as he thought it, a wave of golden light washed overhead and past him. The creatures shrieked and scattered in a wild panic. Lifting his head, Erador saw a vibrant, glowing javelin sticking out of the body of its victim like dawn's own flag pole. *Onyx Smith*, he swore silently at his first good look at the opposition, *there must be hundreds of these cave dwellers.* His helm lay on the ground in front of him, coated with blood—not all of it theirs. Erador lurched to his feet. When he went to draw back his sword-arm and give them another taste of the Onyx blade, he discovered why he still had it: around his death-grip were the literal death-grips of two gremlins, both with javelins in their backs. Their corpses had blocked further efforts by their comrades. He had no idea where those carefully-placed javelins might have come from, nor did he care. He pried the hindrances loose and smote about him with wild retribution as frantic creatures ran in all directions. With each swing of his enormous blade, the tunnel got a little quieter.

Erador pulled the illuminating javelin from the corpse and held it sideways in front of him at waist level, using its light to keep the gremlins that were still within the tunnel at bay. Hundreds of eyes stared back at him, packed close together. They were edging backwards, deeper into the tunnel, away from the light. Erador heard the sounds of battle behind him, and he could only pray that his clan was able to contain the creatures and let them burn in the fire as they hopped over the wall.

***

Beyond the tunnel entrance, gremlins swarmed the elkin inside the Willow Cave. The creatures had poured over the wall in a flood, faster than any had anticipated. They cascaded over the wall and attacked with unrelenting fanaticism. The flood ebbed after Carra hurled the illuminated javelin deep within the tunnel, but that had no effect on those gremlins already through. The fire had swallowed up many of the first wave, but its band was narrow, and the press simply stormed over the charred carcasses and smashed against the heavy wooden shields of the clan's front line. The gremlins were vicious, clawing and biting like rats fighting over scraps of meat. Baltor loomed like a giant in the center of the wall, more than double the height of the attackers, though many of the gremlins were as tall as the youths who alternated along the shield wall with the teens, doing what they could to extend it.

Carra's hands felt refreshed after illuminating the javelin, the pain gone from her fingertips. She stretched her arms wide, palms cupped, and announced, "Feel the wrath of the Radiant Smith's light!"

Blinding bursts of focused light flashed from her hands, pulsing on and off in rapid succession. Gremlins struggled and clamored to escape it. Their panic seemed to take place in slow motion, the creature's movements seemingly broken down into a series of frozen moments in time. The gremlins caught directly by the pulses of light covered their eyes and buried their faces in the dirt. Shrieks of terror mingled with squeaking battle-cries as the attackers scrambled in unthinking flight all about her. Carra turned constantly, gesturing as if conducting a symphony of hysteria throughout the cavern. The light from her spells diffracted along near-invisible veins in the feather-like scales on her shoulders and hips, shimmered down the fine chain that draped the insides of her joints; she seemed to be cloaked in rainbow. None of the gremlins dared to approach her.

Carra targeted her repeated flashes of light at the backs of the elkin warriors, still standing and hacking in a wild frenzy in front of the smoldering pile of bodies. The gremlins piling against them released claws and jaws and scrambled blindly away, tripping over stones and colliding into each other. But the wall had been unable to stop the entire surge, and gaps had begun to appear in it. Masked by the shadows, small detachments of gremlins collected the badger-oxen meat, several of them together beneath the larger portions, like so many ants. Others grabbed whatever was at hand. They scuttled back toward the tunnel, shrieking and bickering, not dropping their plunder even when swept by Carra's flashing light.

Behind the shield wall, Tysyra spun in circles like a whirlwind of death, twin daggers inflicting mortal gashes on any creature that got too close. Her blade-tipped braid lashed all around her, carving wounds into the gremlin's pale flesh. "None of your grubby claws will touch me!" she shouted as she twirled like a serrated tornado.

Sprays of blood from Tysyra's dagger slashes caught Carra in the face. As she wiped it away, she realized they'd been flanked. A hole had appeared in one side the wall. Valen and at least two of the youths were down, and now Vynocent and Wiltyn were struggling to keep it from being turned altogether while the remaining youths shifted to the far end under Gressyn's direction. Carra swept her gaze around the room. Where the youths once stood, where the children had huddled for safety, she saw only dog-piles of gremlins. She directed both hands toward the piles of creatures, blasting frantically away with rapid pulses. The gremlins scrambled up and rolled backward into shadows as if pummeled by palpable force, then darted about seeking safe routes of retreat. Those pinning the elkin warriors began to flee as well. *Releasing an elkin of Clan Wyndlyn is a terrible mistake,* she thought. As her blasts blinded the gremlins one after another, freed elkin warriors swung axes and daggers in fierce retribution. Many a disoriented gremlin learned the full wrath of an elkin's arms.

***

Erador continued facing the darkness of the tunnel, his back to the Willow Cave, holding the creatures at bay with the illuminating javelin. He could feel blood running down his back beneath his armor. Though he could hear the battle behind him, he was still taken by surprise when fleeing creatures struck him down from behind, half-smothering the light he bore—though they did not stay to take advantage of his position. As he struggled to regain his

101

feet, he saw groups of gremlins hoisting the partially-butchered badger-oxen carcasses over the barrier and hastening into the darkness as if he did not exist. Erador gasped. *How did we fail?* He put his back against the wet tunnel wall and slumped on the floor, too staggered by the defeat to challenge the gremlins running past him.

If they succeeded at getting our food... he dared not even finish the thought, dreading the massacre he might find within the Willow Cave.

More and more gremlins ran past him, many with some or another of the clan's carefully hoarded supplies. Their squeaking and shrieking seemed to bear tones of victory. "They're mocking me," Erador muttered. Then he howled: "We weren't ready for this! My father never prepared me for this!" His words echoed throughout the tunnel. Wallowing in defeat, his attention turned to the Onyx helm still lying on the floor. As he picked it up, the tragedy became immediate and personal: two paces beyond the helm lay the body of Neriya... weaponless. He looked at the carnage around him, at the two gremlins that had been so neatly skewered while they pried at his sword. And he knew. *I could not have asked for a better wing-guard,* he'd told her just... hours ago? It couldn't have been. Erador turned the Onyx helm so that it was face to face with him, its mask dripping with his own blood mingled with that of his enemies. He addressed it in forlorn tones: "Tell me how to use your power. Tell me how to read the runes. If I am to protect my father's clan, I *must* be able to wield the power of the Onyx Smith."

"Erador?" The soft voice carried to him from within the cavern.

Erador lurched to his feet. "Carra?" he yelled in confusion. "You're still alive?"

"I was going to ask the same thing of you," she said.

Erador walked back toward the cavern with dragging steps. He spotted the Sky Smith sword-handle near one wall of the tunnel... next to a gremlin foot, presumably severed during their headlong retreat. He picked the handle up—gingerly—and continued. Zimmerik stood beside Carra atop the barricade, the clouds of their fathers' Sky Smith armors shedding raindrops of blood. "How many of us are left?" asked Erador as he handed the Sky blade back to Zimmerik.

Zimmerik sheathed the weapon and contemplated the ground, afraid to look into Erador's eyes. "We have many wounded—"

"How. Many!" interrupted Erador, irritated by his indirect answer.

"Not many," said Zimmerik in subdued tones. "We lost a lot of the children."

"Was Lora among them?" Erador asked in a stern voice.

Zimmerik nodded his head.

Erador's infuriated eyes met Carra's distraught gaze. "Summon the Fates. I need to talk to them."

CHAPTER 10

It was the dead of night. The cavern stank of blood and charred flesh, of opened innards and other odors of death's entourage; of smoke and singed fur, as some of the embers from the charcoal moat had scattered into the elkins' supplies—what remained from the gremlins' predations. Erador's mouth tasted of dirt. A long period of time went by where not a word was spoken; no more than a few coughs and groans of pain could be heard. Erador had never felt the sting of true defeat before. The loss of clan mates, one or two at a time, yes… but always accompanied by victory for the tribe as a whole. *This…* he had nothing to compare to. No precedent to draw upon. He welcomed, all but celebrated, the uncomfortable silence. He knew that this memory would haunt him forever.

Even the willow trees seemed to share in the depression, their branches drooping lower than before. The few remaining members of Clan Wyndlyn were tired, battered, and broken. Erador knew there needed to be a mass funeral, yet no one could muster the energy to gather the deceased and clip their antlers. The elkin moved about mechanically, tending what few tasks remained within the scope of their energy, mourning in their own separate ways, or else simply passing out from fatigue. Erador sat on the ground, back to the tunnel wall, knees curled to his chest, still covered by the protective plates of the Onyx armor. Here, he could pretend he still guarded his clan. Here, he did not have to see… He sat for hours in silence, glaring into the Onyx helm that he perched on a rock before him. Peering into its empty eyes for hours, searching for his father's wisdom from somewhere within. He missed the transition point where his head fell heavy against his forearm, his eyes no longer met the helm's gaze and he fell fast asleep.

The morning was icy and gloomy. Erador's body ached from armor worn throughout the night… finding it odd that his wounds were a lesser discomfort. The tunnel showed no change from his last bleary glimpse. He collected the uncommunicative helm and returned to the cavern. He noticed that Baltor had awoken early as usual, and had almost completed the grim task of collecting the fallen youths' velvety antlers. Erador approached him, stepping over gremlin carcasses. As Baltor reached for Lora's antlers, Erador grasped his arm.

"No, I should do it." Baltor shrugged.

As Erador knelt over her, he stared at her in remorseful adoration. Tears welled in his eyes. "I have failed you," he said to her in a soft voice. "I failed all of us… I'm sorry." The battle had ruffled her hair. He took his hand and gracefully brushed her bangs to either side of her innocent face. He took her lengthy braid and began twirling it around her head to restore it to the way it was before. Erador began to mutter the words to the song his father composed for his mother's death as he continued arranging her hair atop her head:

"Broken beneath—my soul to keep,
Guardian my heart still beats,
Voiceless the sorrow sinks too deep,
In life eternal, we shall meet."

He finished winding her hair, set the comb in to hold it, then used the shears his father had obtained from human traders to clip her antlers away. Lora looked human without them, which only reminded Erador of how removed they were from Cerebus-Senti, how much further from the nearest trading village. Clutching her small, soft antlers, he closed his eyes, contemplating the choices and events that led to her demise. At that moment, he held her unfortunate fate to no faults but his own, and a burning determination smoldered to life within him.

"I vow that her death will not be in vain; that I will find a way to protect the clan, and do whatever it takes so that her memory will live on," he asserted to himself. With the last of the antlers collected, Erador turned to Baltor. "Let's give them the burial only a Warlord of Clan Wyndlyn should receive."

Confusion crossed Baltor's face. "How d'we do that?" asked the brute.

Erador gave a solemn look at the soft rounded antlers within his hands. With a calm and serene voice, he said, "We give them over to the willow trees. Their bodies are consumed by the roots, and their antlers absorbed into the trunks by the sap."

The icy chill from the exterior began to awaken the rest of the wounded elkin from their slumber; they had allowed their fires to burn down in the night. The handful of elkin who remained all assisted Erador in giving their fallen the honor of a Warlord's burial. The willow trees seemed to work in tandem with them, as if they knew the routine. Roots rose from the ground, entangling the bodies and secreting their enzymes, while the bark of the trees released thick plumes of sap, encapsulating the tiny antlers pressed against them. The coating soon hardened to bark, studding the willows with new branches.

The gremlin corpses they would throw on the offal pile, later, and wish the carrion beetles joy of them.

Dried blood stained Erador's face as he looked at the small number of children that remained: Asordin, Evey, Vyranys, and Abby. They ranged from eight to eleven years of age, and had survived as much due to fortune as to any other reason; both Evey and Vyranys had come away wounded, though neither badly. Clan Wyndlyn had buried twenty-eight youths, including the newborn, who had no antlers to clip—Erador did not care to imagine what might become of his soul—plus Valen, and Neriya, his wing-guard of one day. *What will my father think of me after this?* Erador thought. *Will he disown me? Is he even still alive? I don't see how anyone could have survived such an explosion in the open... Why did I survive this battle? I should be buried along with them... I disgrace this armor, and I shame the Warlords that wore it before me. Even with this armor, the others won't listen to me now.* His confidence dwindled that the elders would ever return to relieve his torment.

Gressyn and Carra left to check on Dorgeeryn's wound. He had managed to remain hidden throughout the battle beneath his bear skin coverings, along with Asordin and Abby—which seemed miraculous, given how thorough the gremlins' rampage had been. Dorgeeryn's face was pale and his forehead dripped with sweat, yet he was shivering even beneath the furs. Carra knelt down and laid the back of her hand across his forehead. "He has a fever. A bad one. His wound must have gotten infected," she said to Gressyn.

"Isn't there anything you can do?" Gressyn replied helplessly.

Still facing the ailing Dorgeeryn, she said, "Go get something fresh we can use to change the dressing, and water from the springs so we can clean the wound. I'll go melt some snow for him to drink."

As Carra and Gressyn rose, Erador intercepted her. "I need to speak to the Fates," he said. "Can you summon them?"

"Not now, Erador. We have more important things to do. Besides, that would require the Channeler's Staff. The only way to Call the Fates without it is to offer a sacrifice, altering someone's fate by ending their life before their time. But there's no way we should even consider it."

"I know the sacrifice ritual, but there must be another way."

"No," Carra said heatedly.

"I'll do it," said a weak voice.

They all turned to stare at Dorgeeryn in disbelief. "No, you can't," cried Carra.

"It's okay," Dorgeeryn tried to calm her. "I want to. I can't take a few more days like this, and we don't have the Staff. I'm a hunter; my death should be on the battlefield. I don't want to die slow. If there's any way I can help, I want to do it."

Erador half-smiled, in spite of his stomach twisting at the offer, thankful and surprised for such a willing sacrifice; perhaps the Blacksmiths had heard his prayers. Carra rounded on Erador in fury. "Did you put him up to this!? You better not be doing this for your own selfish reasons!"

"Hey!" shouted an enraged Erador. His voice boomed throughout the cavern, silencing all else, a fact which did not escape Erador's notice. He breathed deeply, then spoke in a soft but irritated tone, "I made a promise to Lora that I would protect us with this armor, a promise that I didn't keep. How will we survive another attack like that? The Fates *must* tell me how to use this armor."

"And sacrifice a life to do so? Isn't that counterproductive?" Carra replied in acrimony, challenging the intelligence behind Erador's logic. "Do you intend to sacrifice a clan mate every time *you* fail to keep *your promise*?"

Erador reeled at the vitriol behind her accusation. "You heard the man! Dorgeeryn wants to end his suffering and help us in the process."

"And what if the Fates don't have the answer, Erador?" taunted Carra, her words biting like ice.

Erador snarled at the thought of such an opportunity wasted. The others, all attracted by the argument, joined in.

"What if the elders return?" asked Gressyn. "Dorgeeryn is my friend; if he can hold out until the Channeler gets back, then she can mend his wounds."

"Yah, and what if Dorgeeryn's condition improves on his own?" challenged Hammynt, still gripping his broken arm.

"The elders aren't returning!" Erador boomed in fury. "You all need to open your eyes. Do you imagine they would *not* have returned *at once*, after that blast, to see if *we* needed to be rescued? That they would *assume*—that the cavern still stood, that its entrance was still open, that we weren't pinned beneath rubble? That they'd simply go on about doing… whatever it is they *do* do?" That he had not reached those conclusions prior to uttering them in no way diminished his offense that his peers might think such things of their elders—of his father. His rage spiked… then flowed away, as his own words sank in. "They aren't coming back. One of the Blacksmiths took them from us with that explosion. Can't you see? We're all that's left!" Erador stared at faces aghast at his sudden pessimism.

There was a brief moment of silence before Erador sighed in defeat. "I'm sorry," he said. He looked at the floor, averting his eyes from their disapproving stares.

Tysyra walked over to comfort him. "It's okay, Erador." Her voice was soothing and therapeutic. "We're all shaken up. None of us know what to do. But whatever it is, we're going to have to do it together, or we've got *no* chance. None at all."

Her words held little real comfort, but they brought Erador's focus back from the depths. He scanned the cavern, gaze stopping at the unnumbered pasty white bodies tossed rudely to one side, and an idea struck him.

"Everyone, let's let these gremlins know that they messed with the wrong clan. Collect all their heads and put them on staves throughout the tunnel. Send them a message that they shall not soon forget."

Tysyra smiled. "Now that's the Erador I remember."

"Teeth wouldn't be good for trophies anyway," Wiltyn added, looking forward to a bit of vicarious payback.

The business of severing heads and stacking the corpses more neatly out of the way kept the clan busy for a time. Even the four youths joined in to help out, carrying javelins and sweeping the detritus of the battlefield away from the living area.

It was just what the clan needed to keep their mind off of their defeat, Erador thought. *Feed their thoughts with dreams of redemption and retribution so they may escape the sorrow and depression that drains one's soul.*

Erador trailed behind the last load of gremlin heads disappearing into the tunnel, looking around to make sure none had been missed. He was about to follow them when an unexpected sound caught his attention.

"Psst!"

Erador saw slight movement out of the corner of his eye and turned to see Dorgeeryn weakly beckoning him over. He hastened to his ailing friend, fearing some turn for the worse.

He was right to fear.

"Please, Erador. I can't take any more of this. End my suffering. Summon the Fates. Save the clan." Dorgeeryn expended all his energy getting out those words; then he began coughing spasmodically. He stretched out his arm to offer Erador his dagger.

Though it was what he believed necessary, he still shrank from the doing. "You realize that this ritual will cause you to forfeit your soul to the Soul Smith; you'll be reincarnated into one of his creations. Your soul might even be used in one of his demons."

Dorgeeryn nodded his awareness before he began another round of uncontrollable coughing.

Erador looked about tentatively to see if anyone was standing witness, but they were all gone, deep into the tunnel. He searched the cavern for the shears and placed them at the base of Dorgeeryn's antlers. With a *crunch* and a wail of pain, they were removed.

"Thank you, my friend. I will pray that you will remember your past life in your new one."

A single tear rolled down Dorgeeryn's cheek. "Do it."

Erador then took the dagger and plunged it deep into Dorgeeryn's chest.

***

"Carra?" asked a faint, sheepish voice, muffled by the reverberating sound of running water from somewhere further along the tunnel.

Carra looked down to see the young and timid Abby standing behind her. She had a turned button nose and high cheek bones. Her hair fell straight down to hide her ears. Abby's hands shook with nervous tension, and once she had Carra's attention she clutched them together against her body to keep them still. Vyranys stood behind her, a boy who habitually avoided bathing and presently had smears of soil and grime on his face and hands. He gave Abby an encouraging shove. "Go on, ask her."

Abby took an unwanted step forward from Vyranys' push. "Um, can you please show me…" Her voice trailed off as her nerves got the better of her.

Carra smiled sweetly. "Go on Abby, you can ask me anything. It's okay."

"Can you show me some Goma incantations?" she asked, feeling vulnerable and exposed. "I want to help fight if they come back."

"Did the Fates choose you as a Goma? Why haven't I seen you at any of the Channeler's exercises?"

"Yes, I was chosen, but I didn't go because…"

"Because she was too scared," blurted Vyranys.

"No!" she said, "It's because I'm not good at it."

Carra's words were as soft as silk. "Everything takes practice if you want to excel, and your courage here proved to me that you want to get better. So let's find a private place, and I can teach you a few things right now. Okay?"

"Okay," she said with a hint of excitement.

"Wiltyn!" Carra called. "I'm taking Abby back to the cavern, so please keep everyone busy for a little while. Can you search for a way to access the rushing water we keep hearing? If we find it, we might find food."

Wiltyn finished slamming a decapitated head atop an illuminated stave propped between large loose rocks. Light poured out the creature's mouth and produced a bright red glow beneath its cheeks. "No problem," he replied, as he attempted to wipe the grime from his hands.

Carra began escorting Abby toward the privacy of the Willow Cave. The long tunnel was illuminated in ever-shifting light as black blood trickled down the glowing staves, each of which skewered two or three heads. The tunnel floor was lined with the corpses of the creatures that had fallen there, along with more severed heads awaiting mounting. Some carrion beetles had already found their way to the bodies.

Carra began the lesson during the eerie trek back. "Goma is the practice of manipulating light, named after Goma the Radiant Smith. The Channeler told us of the event that led up to how the elkin got their powers, known as the Cleansing. The Radiant Smith had tried to use the sun to burn out all life from the earth's surface, but the Soul Smith stopped Him with a powerful blow from His Forging Hammer. It is believed that some of Goma's blood was mixed in when the Soul Smith later created the first group of elkin, Vorkus among them. That is why only some of us can use Goma incantations."

"How could you know that to be true?" Abby asked.

"You should direct that question to the Channeler when she gets back," Carra replied. "I have my suspicions as to how such knowledge could be gained, though I imagine we will discover the truth once we ascend to adulthood."

"Are there other types of magic?"

Carra looked intrigued. "How do you mean?"

"Are there other elkin throughout Thornwall, or perhaps humans, or erethizons, or any other manner of creature that can manipulate things other than light? Like..." Abby pondered for a moment, then her face lit up with excitement. "Like the wind! So they can fly alongside the avians."

A smile broke across Carra's face as she shook her head. "Other than the rare runic weapons and armor crafted by the eight Blacksmiths..." she stopped walking and they both paused; her beautiful smile faded. Abby watched as Carra dove into deep recollection.

"I think I remember Mother of Clan Grondyr saying something about runic rings. That they contain the power of a spell." Carra let the memory slip from her mind. "But the wearer would still have to read the rune aloud, and the language has been lost for centuries."

"Why don't you have to speak when you cast Goma enchantments?" Abby asked.

"You do need to speak the words initially to learn them, but you will soon discover that after practice, you can conjure up the same incantations with just your will—by your thought alone. We are unique from those wearing runic armor because we can learn more powers and even create new spells," said Carra. "Though Goma incantations have their drawbacks."

Abby nodded, acknowledging the seriousness of the matter.

"You must first learn the simplest of Goma incantations, and learn them well. Many more difficult enchantments are combinations of the easier spells. It requires practice to convert these spells to memory so that you can build off of them later. This is why magic is a discipline, and you must learn to conjure your incantations *correctly*," Carra warned.

Abby looked timid, almost frightened. Carra took a deep breath. "I know this seems like a lot to take in at once, but it's important. Casting improperly or mixing spells to your own design could poison the mind or cause your powers to slip into darkness."

"Darkness?" peeped Abby.

"Yes. The Channeler warned us of a few whose powers altered over time to control only the absence of light. Others have experienced terrible things; some go blind, others go mad, while one elkin even lost his soul," Carra said, covertly massaging her blackened fingernails. *They don't hurt now. Maybe they really are just bruised,* she tried to convince herself.

"What happens when you lose your soul?"

"Without the essence of life, you cannot wield magic. You don't sleep, you don't eat, and you become dead inside, cold and emotionless." Carra leaned in close and spoke in a whisper, grinning in adoration. "But that elkin did it on purpose, to challenge the Soul Smith to a duel! The Soul Smith's powers proved futile against the elkin. After a masterful battle, the Soul Smith surrendered, asking that His enemy spare His life in exchange for one wish," Carra remarked with pride over the elkin's ingenuity.

"What did he wish for?" asked Abby, mesmerized.

"I'll have to save the story of the War of the Wish for our second lesson," she said with a wink. "Here is an easy first spell for today. Grab your horns and repeat after me: Shor tu urluk ma."

Carra's antlers grew into an enormous size, thickening and doubling in stature from the pedicle to the crown tine. New tines with thick, sharp spikes forked off the beam as they grew. Shimmering and pulsing with radiant light, they almost reached the height of the tunnel. The size and shape of her antlers were reminiscent of the metallic surroyal antler rack of Vorkus atop the Channeler's Staff. Every movement of the glimmering antlers caused shadows to dance along the cold stone walls.

Abby stood amazed. "What are those words you spoke?"

"They are phrases passed down from the ancients, the words of the Blacksmiths."

"But I thought you said it was a forgotten language."

"While we can *speak* these incantations, we cannot *read* the runes they scribed on their creations. No one knows what word goes with what symbol any longer. Now you give it a try."

Abby took a careful grip on her soft, rounded antlers; she took one last glance up at Carra's massive and intimidating rack of antlers before she closed her eyes and shouted, "Shor tu urluk ma!"

Carra watched and cheered with great enthusiasm at Abby's success. Her antlers grew and mimicked the shape of Carra's.

"Now charge!"

Carra and Abby bowed their heads and ran through the tunnel toward the Willow Cave, laughing with every step. As soon as they flew over the stone wall and into the cavern, they were enveloped by a thick grey light and stopped dead in their tracks. Both sets of radiant antlers returned to normal, their effulgence swallowed by the monochrome gloom. Carra stared in disbelief at the sight of Erador standing before the smoky apparition of the Fates. Abby dared not move, unsure as to why Carra suddenly looked so devastated: she had been told only the Channeler could summon the Fates—did that mean she'd returned? With the others?

Her eyes darted back and forth between Erador and Carra, anxious to discover the meaning of Carra's reaction.

As the Fates dissipated into the air, the bluish glacial haze of the cavern returned. Erador turned to Carra with a brilliant smile on his face. "Carra, I know what we must do."

Carra's eyes glanced in horror at Dorgeeryn's lifeless body, confirming her worst fears. Tears poured from her eyes. "How could you!?" she roared as she thrust a pulsating fist into the ground. Beams of light erupted beneath Erador's feet, launching him high into the air. Erador crashed into a small pile of bowls, shattering the hardened clay into tiny pieces.

"How could you!" she shouted through sniffles, wiping tears away in fury. "He could have lived!"

Erador got to his feet, his face and hands covered in dirt. "I think I deserved that."

Carra dropped to the ground, cupping her face with her hands as she wept.

Abby decided this was an excellent time to practice being very, very small.

Erador approached and sat beside Carra. "Dorgeeryn was my friend as well, but he was too sick for any help we could give him and none of us wanted to admit it."

Carra leaned against Erador's shoulder. "I know... but how many more of us must we lose?"

Erador placed his armored arm around her shoulder to comfort her. "No more will be lost if we find the Channeler's Staff."

She lifted her head from her hands, eyes red and forlorn. "What... what did the Fates tell you?"

Before he could answer, Wiltyn came bounding over the wall and into the cavern, bursting with joy. "We're rich!"

CHAPTER 11

Wiltyn sprinted ahead into the tunnel, the light of his Goma-illuminated hand axe glinting from damp walls long past the last of the staves. "Wait up!" Carra yelled, keeping pace with Erador, whose bulky armor weighed him down. Her own Sky Smith armor seemed hardly to hinder her, in spite of its poor, improvised fit. The ground beneath their feet became rugged, the walls and ceiling uneven; whatever shaped the tunnel they'd begun in evidently had no hand forming the one they were in now. The sound of rushing water reverberated throughout the passage, sounding as if it came from every direction.

Wiltyn stopped in front of a slender crevice in the wall ahead of them, and shouted something at Erador and Carra.

"What!?" shouted Erador. "We can't hear you! The water is too loud!"

Wiltyn didn't respond, just slid into the side passage; the light from his axe illuminated the hidden crevice, which cut the cavern wall like a deep scar. Carra and Erador arrived, panting. They could see the other elkin huddled within. Erador entered first, obliged to turn sideways by armor and antlers, followed by the much-smaller Carra. The elongated crack opened out into a room lined with violet crystals from floor-to-ceiling. They had just stepped into the heart of a giant geode.

"My mother told me about these in one of her fairy tales," smiled Erador. "I can't believe it!"

Laughs of uncontrollable ecstasy erupted from Erador and Carra; they couldn't conceive the volume of wealth that surrounded them. Zimmerik put a hand around Erador's shoulder; while his masked helm hid his smile, Zimmerik's eyes were eloquent. "Can you believe it, Erador? There's nothing the humans have that we can't afford now!" he yelled over the roar of rushing water. "Even their most advanced weaponry."

"Have you ever seen anything like this before?" asked Hammynt. "We could purchase animals from the human trainers! We could get mules to haul all these crystals. Or beasts of war, like an osprey to warn us of danger. Or even a saber-tooth to help us in the fight!" He grew more excited with every word.

"Since you love animals so much, it'll be your job to feed them all," joked Vynocent.

Erador took the axe from Wiltyn and began directing its glow along the crystalline walls. The outer walls leaned inward, meeting an arm's length or so above the tops of Erador's antlers. He strode deeper into the crystalline cavern, wide enough for two persons to walk shoulder to shoulder. The sound of rushing water was even louder here. As he walked, his light revealed a narrow split running across the cavern floor. Erador knelt down to direct the axe's light into the broken ground; droplets of mist gathered on his gauntlet. The river was directly beneath the ground upon which he stood.

The crystalline cavern continued deeper than his light would show him, so Erador returned to the others. "I can see the river beneath us!" he yelled over the roar of the rushing water. As they huddled together so they could hear one another, the light of their weapons upon bandage and bruise reminded them of their vulnerability. "We should stay here for the night," Erador said. "We have water to drink, and there's no way the gremlins will hear us chiseling the crystals away with the water being this loud."

Baltor chimed in. "Plus, the entrance can be easily blocked. Onyx Smith knows I barely fit through there!"

Guffaws burst from the crowd. "Let's collect our belongings and bring them in here. We should still have some dry jerky left; only four more days now before the… elders return," Zimmerik trailed off.

Erador mustered a small grin, but his face was still riddled with doubt. They meandered back toward the Willow Cave, their lightened mood fading as they reached the rows of staked gremlin heads. "Those bastard things," grumbled Baltor. "I can't wait to get me a second chance at them. My double-bladed axe is still thirsty for their blood!"

Conversation turned to the topic of revenge and retribution. They spoke of deadly machines and weaponized wagons that they could purchase from the humans to rid this mountain of the gremlin infestation. As they rounded the last bend in the passage, they spotted little Abby standing at the entrance to the cavern, waiting. Carra stopped dead in her tracks as the painful memory of Dorgeeryn's sacrifice returned.

"Carra, what's wrong?" asked Tysyra.

Everyone was now staring at Carra. She was clearly distressed, and equally clearly did not want to say why.

"No, you should hear it from me," said Erador as he stepped through to face them all at once. Claw marks and dried gouges too small to bandage littered his face and neck; he'd left his helm where he and Carra had been sitting. Picking it up, he toyed with it in both hands a moment, searching its unfathomable gaze. His Onyx armor almost seemed to be absorbing the light. Raising his head, he told them bluntly, "I spoke to the Fates." Expressions of disbelief and dismay spread through his audience. "I believe you all know what that means."

Gressyn began shaking his head in anger and in denial.

Erador continued, "He was beyond healing; it was his dying wish to help us, and help us he has."

"No!" shouted Gressyn in outrage. His voice cut through the distant noise of the river crisp and clear. "I don't believe it. What you have done is unforgivable!"

Erador stood tall and confident within his intimidating Onyx armor. "You were not there when he handed me the knife. You were not there to see the way he coughed; he had trouble just breathing."

"You killed one of our own needlessly!"

"It was Dorgeeryn's choice!"

"No! You put the thought into his mind, with your selfish dreams of power, of wielding the magic of the runes!"

"It's selfish to let Dorgeeryn suffer a painful, slow death, just because you want him to have a small chance to live, even against his own wishes!"

"Erador, you chase after the impossible. Trying to read the runes after the Fates chose otherwise for you is a foolish ambition."

"An ambition turned to reality!" His claim stunned even Gressyn into momentary silence.

Before either could start up again, Carra interrupted, "Why don't you tell us exactly what happened?"

There was a pause as everyone waited for Erador to speak. All ears were hanging in anticipation of his next words. Erador gulped and took a deep breath to soothe his inner tumult, then recounted what had transpired.

***

Erador severed the antlers from Dorgeeryn's head. "Now your soul has no place to rest." He plunged the dagger deep into Dorgeeryn's raggedly beating heart. Blood spilled out around the blade. Erador stared into the dying teen's eyes, awaiting the moment that the soul departed the body. As soon as the life fled them, Erador smeared his hands with the blood, then withdrew the dagger from the wound, lifting it high into the air with blood-covered hand, the severed antlers with the other.

As Erador began shouting to the cavern ceiling, the light seemed to retract from the cave. "Fates! With this weapon, I have ended his life before *your* choosing. With these antlers that I have severed before his death, even his soul was sacrificed. His fate is now at the mercy of the Soul Smith instead of your own.

"Holding these instruments with his blood upon my hands, I have changed his fate and completed the sacrifice. Fates! I call upon you!"

Small streams of Dorgeeryn's blood spiraled upward above his body, forming a rotating column suspended in the air. The tips of the antler rack seemed to inhale the light of the room, and as darkness coated the cavern, the Fates' grey mist emerged. Its dim glow shadowed the room, suppressing all other colors.

The apparition floated in the air like a banner in the wind, not the vague human semblance they had before. This ragged shroud rippled like water in time to their words. "Why have you summoned us?" queried three distinct voices in unison, two male and one female. Though they were little more than whispers, they conveyed deep-rooted anger at the preemption of their prerogatives.

"We have no sanctuary from the perils of this cave," cried Erador. "With what few of us remain, we will not be able to survive. I must know how the elders fared against the blast."

Their united condescension battered him: "Not. Well."

His tongue caught in his throat and he dropped to his knees. He had suspected as much, but the confirmation made his heart sink. Kneeling in disbelief, Erador stared at the blood on his hands while he struggled to reason past churning emotions. He needed more. For this sacrifice, this pain, this loss… "You. It was you that stopped me! Why did you keep me from following the elders? I should have been at my father's side in the blast!"

"Do you wish yourself dead? You might have had that any number of times. You need not have summoned us. You need not have changed the fate of another to have altered your own." Their accusation was palpable—he felt the dagger as Dorgeeryn must have, the numbness that followed, the emptiness… "That is not what your father would have wanted. Or can you not recall his last words to you? 'Don't disappoint me,' he said." When the Fates intoned his father's words, it was in a single voice… his father's.

Erador grasped after threads of composure while he gathered his thoughts. "Then you must tell me how to harness the power contained within the Blacksmith's armor if we are to survive. Teach me to read the runes of their forgotten language."

The sheen of mist floated in silence for a moment, as if considering the matter. "The forgotten language. A strange request to make of us," said the voices.

"Do you know it?"

"We are older than humanity; we know all its languages. Though how did you expect us to read the inscriptions upon your armor when we are blind?"

Hope drained from him. *My luck can't get any worse than this*, he thought. He rose to his feet, dangling a hand's-breadth from despair. "There must be another way."

"There is always another way," said the rippling mist, its tones defying a human's range.

He waited.

"Very well. We shall deliberate."

The greyness seemed to… turn around and face itself, without ever changing outline. Erador knew he was being judged, but it was over things he hadn't yet done. It bothered him to be judged for things over which he had no control, rather than being judged over his actions in the past. *Though considering my most recent ones, I might fare better that way.*

"We have arrived at a decision," announced the Fates.

Erador perked up and stood tall to receive their decree. "What is my fate?"

"Mortals are to never learn their fate. There is one that can help you, but you must carry his weight. To find him, let the Staff lead the way."

***

Erador concluded the story, though the clan's eyes lost their focus on him long before the end. They stared into private abysses as the information sank in. Hammynt cradled his broken arm and began to weep. "We're all alone," the youthful hunter murmured as tears rolled down his cheeks.

Zimmerik looked at Erador in despair. "Our elders and fathers… gone?"

Erador nodded.

"A riddle?" Gressyn asked. "You performed the sacrifice ritual and killed Dorgeeryn, and all you got was a *riddle*?" Gressyn stormed past, a vengeful look upon his face.

"Where are you headed?"

"I'm going to go pay my respects to Dorgeeryn," he muttered.

The rest of Clan Wyndlyn followed one by one, into the bluish light of the cavern, now grown so unfamiliar. The willow trees extended solace. The elkin gathered around Dorgeeryn's body and stared at his fatal wound in disbelief.

Gressyn repeated Erador's words. "There is one that can help you, but you must carry his weight," he said with spiteful sarcasm, followed with a condescending snicker.

Erador yelled after him, "Gressyn! You know me never to tell a lie!"

Gressyn spun in anger; his voice boomed throughout the cavern. "*Know* you? I don't know you! I don't know one single elkin who would do *this!*" Gressyn pointed at Dorgeeryn. "It's not lies, it's your mistakes! And every one of them is getting us killed! First, your tactics at the last battle cost thirty of us their lives! You relied on your armor and charged into the tunnel by yourself when we should have relied on Carra's incantations!"

"But Carra wasn't—"

"*I'm not finished!*" he spat as he yelled; his eyes were wide with fury. "Second, not only have you ended Dorgeeryn's life, but you surrendered his soul to Xorbyk with the summoning sacrifice!"

Gasps erupted from his audience. Tysyra approached him and placed a hand onto his shoulder, trying to calm him down. "You shouldn't say the Soul Smith's name; He hates being reminded of his human life."

Gressyn noticed the tattoo of the Onyx Smith rune upon her arm and was reminded of his regrettable decision to get a matching one. He batted her hand away. "Don't touch me," he growled through his teeth. He stabbed accusations at Erador with his finger. "You tried to be a hero, jumping into the swarm of gremlins, breaking formation. If it wasn't for Carra, you would be dead. Neriya *did* die, because she thought her place as a wing-guard was at your side! You are reckless and we're paying the price for it! Any of us could be the next casualty to your folly!"

Erador's eyes snapped toward a large figure standing at the entrance to the cave. It stood upright, about seven feet tall, covered in snow. "Is that a snow mauler?" he asked in wary disbelief.

The group spun around, retrieving weapons from their belts, ready to strike.

The creature lifted its hands to the side of its head, then pulled back a large fur hood to reveal a rack of antlers. Sheets of snow slid off the furs as it began to remove an overcoat. Clan Wyndlyn relaxed from their battle stances and jogged across the battle-worn soil eyeing the intruder in curiosity.

"Who is that?" whispered Carra as she hurried toward the entrance.

"I don't know," replied Zimmerik, trying to hustle whilst in the unfamiliar Sky Smith armor.

"Are the elders back?" asked Tysyra.

"Father!?" Carra yelled in astonishment.

As they neared, they saw that it was indeed a smiling Warlord Dryden. He had an axe and dagger sheathed at his sides, tucked behind his thick black leather belt. His brown woolen travel pack was slung across his back, its straps crisscrossing his shoulders. Without his armor or coat, his lengthy battle scars were visible across his forearms. The scars were a raw, bright red and looked as if they were straining to hold his skin together.

Carra sprinted and leapt into his open arms with a hug that spoke volumes of their kinship. "I'm so glad that you're safe," she said. The others glanced at one another as they shared the awkwardness of their hug, not privy to such open affection with their blood fathers. "Then the Fates were wrong," Carra said with glee. "Where is everyone else?" Expectant smiles spread amongst the gathered.

"The Fates?" he asked, confused.

Carra's joy vanished as swiftly as it had arrived. "The… others?"

Warlord Dryden shook his head. "I'm sorry to tell you, but the others didn't make it."

The celebratory mood shattered into disappointment and despair. Warlord Dryden looked around at fallen stalactites and fissured walls, peered in wonder past the willow trees at the new tunnel-opening at the back of the cave. He noticed the bandages, the spatters of blood dried upon torn garments, flecks of unrecognizable gore from recent charnel tasks. "What happened here? Where are the rest of you?" No one seemed willing to meet his inquiring gaze. He exhaled in solemn disappointment. "I see. Then my worst fears are realized," he said whilst glancing at Erador in contempt. "We both suffered similar catastrophic losses."

His eyes fell on Zimmerik, clad in the cloudy glass armor of the Sky Smith flecked with congealed goblin blood, with his Sky blade sheathed at his side and helm tucked under his arm. "Zimmerik," he said, his voice full of disgust. "I forbid you from touching my equipment ever again. You disgrace it with your touch. The blood you have spilt upon it doesn't merit the tongue of a vomit-spewing bottom-feeding bloagus. Take it off at once! I'll deal with you later."

His quick shift in personalities caught Zimmerik off guard. "My apologies," he said as he set down the helm upon a sitting stone and began doffing the armor.

Erador stepped forward. "You're the only survivor?" he asked with a last beacon of hope.

A long exhalation escaped his lips. "Regrettably, yes. The others were frozen beneath that thunderous blast."

Erador grew suspicious. "I see you are empty-handed save your travel pack; you didn't collect their antlers to save their souls from the Soul Smith?"

"They were covered in snow, and then encased in ice. I had to save myself, I couldn't take the time to dig them up," Warlord Dryden replied with barely-contained irritation.

"How did you survive while the other's didn't?"

"Sheer luck," he answered boisterously. "I was flung partly into the lee of a boulder, and so was only partly covered by the ice. I guess the Fates decided it wasn't my time," he said with a sneer. "But what of you, Erador? I couldn't help but overhear Gressyn just now. Did you perform the sacrifice ritual to summon the Fates?" His voice held no sympathy.

"Yes." Erador looked him cold in the eyes, and as when he would play the game with himself during the Call of the Fates ceremony, he noticed the faintest indication of a smile upon Warlord Dryden's face. It was the most subtle of reactions, but Erador realized that he was hiding great pleasure.

"Clan Wyndlyn," he said so all could hear. "Were Gressyn's accusations true?"

Erador looked about at his clan mates and grew worried as no one rose to his defense. "Carra!" he turned to her in desperation. "You tended to Dorgeeryn's wounds. You know that he was beyond saving. Say it, they'll believe you."

Carra looked at her father and then ducked her head in silence, avoiding Erador's eyes. Erador shook his head in disbelief. "Zimmerik, you're my wing-guard; you know that I only jumped into the gremlin horde to retrieve the Sky blade for you."

Before Zimmerik could open his mouth, Gressyn interrupted, "Sounds like you cared more about saving the Sky Smith sword than saving us."

Erador stood speechless, mouth agape at the one-sided dissent against him.

Warlord Dryden proclaimed, "Erador, your peers have reached a unanimous decision. Your actions and decisions to place artifacts before the lives of your fellow clan are responsible for the deaths that occurred here."

"What occurred here is *not* my fault. We were attacked."

"Then tell me why everyone else thinks otherwise."

Erador was at a loss for words.

Warlord Dryden took a look about the disheveled cavern. "Too many lost their lives under your watch. Many of whom were just children! Your failures cannot be forgiven. You are expelled from the clan!"

Erador remained where he stood. He dared not move or else admit his own guilt. "No," he said as he clenched his fists.

Warlord Dryden's head cocked sideways at his defiance. "Oh, you think you can best with me with a feat of strength?"

Erador drew in a long breath; the air was cool in his lungs, but ignited his adrenaline. As he slid the dark Onyx helm over his face, Warlord Dryden could see the flame in his eyes, as if the helm incited in him a new, intrepid persona. The dark helm's grimace asserted mutiny, challenge accepted. Erador bent his knees and lowered his head, angling his antlers into lunging position. He sidestepped to circle his challenger, his eyes burning with contempt.

"Give me my helm!" Warlord Dryden shouted with arm outstretched, waiting it to be placed in his hand. He never broke Erador's gaze, his face as chiseled and frozen as the Onyx helm. Zimmerik placed the Sky Smith helm into his hand, and then backed away to watch the duel.

The clouded glass appearance of the helm seemed to awaken as Warlord Dryden slid it over his face. The clouds within the mask twisted and compacted, growing darker like a brewing storm. A squint of his eyes heralded the lunge. Both combatants leapt high in unison; the storm clouds within the Sky helm seemed to shimmer with lightning as their helms thudded together. Their arms gripped each other's shoulders, pushing and vying for the upper hand.

Warlord Dryden pushed with all his might, but Erador was heavy in his Onyx plate. Grunts, roars, and spit emerged from both contenders; they were at a standstill, unable to budge one other. They twisted in circles, their antlers interlocked, trying to throw the other off balance until, with a fit of rage, Warlord Dryden roared something unintelligible. Erador caught a glimpse of clouds spinning within his mask like a hurricane, sparks of lightning flashing, and then Erador flew backward, muscles no longer responsive to his orders.

Erador lay upon his back ten feet from his opponent. He looked up to see the Warlord laughing in a wild rage of victory between his heavy breaths. The twisting clouds within the Sky Smith helm seemed to slow in concert with his breathing, and a tiny blue flash arced between the tips of his antlers. Erador blinked a few times, trying to comprehend what just happened. He looked about the crowd and all eyes were upon him. "Did anyone see that?" he asked.

"You mean see me throw you across the room?" mocked Warlord Dryden. He laughed some more, but none of the teens joined in his amusement. Erador, flustered, got to his feet and turned his back to Clan Wyndlyn, and proceeded to the cavern's exit.

Steps into the snow, Erador heard a faint voice. "We can't let him take the Onyx armor from the clan."

"Eh, let him wallow in his own disgrace. The frost will stiffen his mobility. Let it be a punishment to him; a constant reminder as to why he was expelled," said Warlord Dryden.

Erador didn't look back once, and continued walking until he disappeared into the snowfall.

CHAPTER 12

Erador ventured onto the blanketed tundra, snow crunching as it compacted beneath his footsteps. Even with the added weight of his armor, he did not break through the ice layer left by the blast. Heedless, he walked in the open, no wing-guard to watch his flank and no camouflage to conceal him. His breath clouded in the air; the doubled clothing he'd put on in a hurried, makeshift attempt to pad his armor was all that kept him somewhat warm. He brushed snow from his shoulders often, to keep it from melting and running down inside. It was a losing effort.

I can't let the frost stiffen the joints. If I stop moving, I'm dead.

His thoughts whirled in his head much as the snowflakes did around him. *Where should I go? Where* can *I go? Remaurus-Senti? What would they think—a lone Wyndlyn clansman coming in from the tundra? They wouldn't believe a thing I say.* Erador played with his badger-ox claw necklace as he walked. *Will I ever get to see my friends again?*

Warlord Dryden seemed pleased at the thought of expelling me from the clan... How did he shock me? He must have known how to use his Sky helm, but that's impossible! Or is it? The Fates told me that there is always another way. Then, the realization coming far too late to do him any good: *That... that Smith-dross bloagus whelp... he cheated! I should—*

He reined that thought in. *No, I shouldn't... not now. Not yet. I must find the Channeler's Staff and collect the elders' antlers before it's too late.*

With a new sense of determination, he considered his location. *But what direction to head in? I don't even know where the elders were going.* He realized he had lost track of time in his introspection. He looked to the sky to try to locate the sun, but the clouds were too thick for even an educated guess. He cursed himself. *Idiot! You should have followed Warlord Dryden's tracks!* One look behind him and his rush of hope had vanished. Even if the snow had not erased them, it was not likely he would be able to find them with what remained of the day. Another realization too late to be of use.

It's getting late, he thought as his stomach grumbled. *I'm going to need to find shelter before nightfall. With any luck, I might find some food along the way.* Frost highlighted half-cleaned gremlin-blood spatters on his plate armor. His toes were beginning to grow numb from the cold; his gauntleted fingers, lacking the benefit of exercise, were well on their way. He feared for his ears, which had become tingling agony beneath his helm. A mixed blessing: the snow was becoming lighter as the air grew colder.

He looked at the Jerackon Mountain range, an indistinct shadow looming behind drifting snow flurries. *I know the mountain range runs north and west; I can use that to keep my bearings.* He continued trekking across the large flat expanse of land, keeping the range in sight on his right. The wind picked up; the powdery snow was now falling sideways, driving in from his left. Erador could feel his lips drying as the wind whipped through his visor. He realized that the armor was beginning to lose mobility: he couldn't bend his left arm.

I must keep moving, to keep my blood flowing and prevent the joints from freezing, he thought. He tried bending his arm in, but the armor was locked stiff. He strained with all his might to break the elbow joint free from the grasp of the frost, then put his right hand against the joint and his left wrist against his thigh; with a *snap* he could move the elbow again. *I don't know how I'm going to escape the cold,* he thought. *If I go to sleep, I'll freeze to death. And even if I survive, my armor will be useless by morning.*

Though with this armor weighing me down, I'll tire soon anyway if I try to keep moving. He slowed his walk to conserve energy. *But if I do that, I won't get anywhere in time to do me any good.* He looked at the mountains upon his right. He knew there were pine trees on the lower slopes. "Fire," he said aloud, "I need to make a fire." He was out of other choices, if he wished to see another day.

He turned to the mountains, picking up his pace once more. Fortunately, he had never strayed far from them, and he was soon scrambling up a steep slope. Or trying to: the ice from the blast underlay fresh snow here as well… and spelled his defeat. Though he clutched at every protruding bit of shrubbery, sometimes even used his hands to crawl, he soon realized the trees he sought were unattainable. He cast about, wondering if he could make enough of a fire from the thin, green branches of the bushes within his reach. He had to try. Clinging with one hand to the nearest bush, he grasped the hilt of the Onyx blade.

It wouldn't budge.

"Damn it!" he shouted at the blizzard. "I can't believe I'm doing this right now. I was correct about the elders, but they didn't listen. So what did I do? I did what needed to be done because no one else would. Oh, and I risked my life to protect the artifacts that are as much a part of Clan Wyndlyn's heritage as the willow trees. They are worth protecting! Otherwise we should have just run away from the cave gremlins… and they expelled me for it! Now I have to deal with this! And I can't cut the branches because my blade is stuck in its sheath!" He grasped the branch with both hands and bore down. It snapped off neatly, right at the ice layer.

Without the branch to hold him in place, Erador went sliding back down the slope, powder fountaining around him. His curses were borne away on the indifferent whistling wind. Clinging to his prize with his right hand, he finally arrested his descent as his outstretched left snagged a new purchase. That snapped off as well, but not before it had brought him to a halt.

Erador removed his snow-filled helmet and shook it out. He wiped flakes of ice from his eyes and looked upward to see how far a distance he'd fallen. Most of the way. What was more depressing was how short his skid-path actually was: his climb hadn't taken him nearly as far as it felt. And all he had to show for it would barely serve as kindling… if he could get it to light at all, if he could find somewhere to set a fire to begin with. *Perhaps there's a crevice somewhere, an overhang, anything. I'll take a badger-ox den. And the badger-ox, too.*

He'd chosen this slope to harvest because of its greenery, not its geology. He looked at the nearby flanks; to his left the scrubby vegetation that protruded from the snow continued. To his right the slope soon jogged slightly northward, out of sight, but where it turned back there was a section where jagged slabs had detached from a near-cliff and slid into a jumble below it. There had to be *something* there he could wedge himself into.

He began to work his way thence, gradually yielding as he went what little elevation he'd retained. He estimated his destination at perhaps half an hour's hike away—then halted in surprise when he realized he *could* see that far, that there was no longer snow in the air. He hadn't noticed when it ended. *Can't afford to pass up a good look around,* he grumbled inwardly. *Might be the last one I get.*

The sky to the north and west hinted at clearing—or at least the clouds seemed thinner there. The contrast also revealed how far west the sun was. He had maybe two hours of daylight left to him, maximum. The mountains still looked like mountains; the pine stands still looked unreachable; the tundra still looked empty; the rocks he was hoping to find shelter in...

He saw a patch of brown amid the grey and white.

It was near a jutting boulder, in a slight dip perhaps a quarter mile from where he stood. It appeared to be lying nearly flat upon the snow... but only dusted, not covered over, by it.

Erador approached cautiously, aware that if he had to fight his options for weaponry consisted of his antlers plus two pieces of brush and a sheathed sword. He also kept a crude hunter's knife along with his shears in his tool pouch. He tried drawing the sword again; it still did not budge. He removed the sheath from his belt: using that as a club was still better than not at all.

He was within ten paces of it before he could identify the object: the pelt of a bear.

He was within five paces before it moved. He froze.

Bears didn't move like that. Something was beneath—

A scurry of rats shot from beneath the pelt, fleeing his step. *Dead.* He heaved a sigh of relief. *But how...?*

He stirred the pelt with his sword. No more rats. The pelt lifted away, revealing a partly-gnawed carcass... gnawed down to the ice layer.

Caught by the blast. He felt a hunter's sympathy for the trapped beast. *How long did you struggle to free yourself? It must have been long; you shrugged off most of the snow that came after.* Replacing his sheath and setting the branches carefully aside, he removed a gauntlet. The corpse was cold. For some reason he did not understand, Erador found that a relief.

Most of the bear's hindquarters was encased in the ice, as was one forepaw. The head and one forepaw had remained above it, along with most of the torso. The pelt, where it was above the ice, had been largely liberated from the body by the hungry rodents. Most of the organs were gone, but there was still some flesh upon shoulder and haunch. Erador dug out his knife and flayed away the rest of the exposed pelt; there was enough to make a half-cloak, at least. Were the weather any fairer, it would have been vile to wear, but the cold would preserve it for now. He would have to hold it by one hand, as he had no way to secure it, but it was a vast improvement over nothing at all. Then he dug out as much of the bear's unfrozen flesh as he could, coming up with enough for two light meals.

Even if he had to eat them raw, which looked increasingly likely. *No reason to wait.* He tore into a cold piece with his sharp teeth, chewed long at the predator's stringy flesh, swallowed. *I've had worse. I'll eat the rest on the move.* He sliced a few pieces down to bite size, so that he could pop them in his mouth with a free hand.

Erador stood, draped the pelt fur-inward over his shoulders, held it with his right hand while he picked his meager branches up with his left. He looked around, still saw no shelter better than that he was already headed toward. He resumed his trek, occasionally shifting the grasp on his cloak to his left hand so that he could fish out another bite of bear, trying not to thrust twigs and needles through his visor whenever he did.

As he neared his destination, it began to look as though he'd guessed right. It was hard to be certain since the wind was now lifting fallen snow into his face. Still, between gusts he could see that large vertical sections of cliff had slid down against one another in some distant past; several had crumbled into rubble, while others remained wholly or partially intact, leaning against one another. Dark spots at the bases of several of these suggested gaps between them. *If only this blasted snow would stay out of my eyes, I could—*

Turning his head to shake clear his latest face-full, he caught a ghost of a shadow flicker across the lighter western sky.

Erador dove and sprawled in the snow, holding the broken branches over his head.

It took a moment before his conscious mind caught up with his reflexes.

Glacial bat!

His mind was telling him to get down. His face was telling him he already had.

How long can I wait here before I freeze to death?

After a time, a soft pattering caught his attention—regular, nearby, and getting closer. Footsteps? Something four-footed; the sounds were too close together for a biped. *Does that mean the bat's gone?* He tried to turn his head without raising it...

He caught a glimpse of the creature just before it clamored atop his back. *Argh! Not a bloagus. Not now!*

Bloagi were carrion eaters, well-known to his tribe. One of the Soul Smith's lesser, if more successful, demons, they had survived and spread over centuries. Rumor had it they could now be found in most parts of Thornwall. They were no threat to an armed human or elkin; usually, they would not even approach a living one. Usually. Unless the elkin happened to be wearing a still-fresh bear pelt and was himself pretending to be dead to avoid being noticed.

Erador would have been happy to let the bloagus eat the pelt from his back, except that its digestive bile would melt living flesh just as well. He had to get it off him.

He tried to roll away from it. His improvised cloak left a trail of slime as partly-melted sections sloughed off. The bloagus was surprised by the movement, but didn't back away. It did at least stop to slurp up what he'd wiped onto the snow. Its slimy black blubbery skin hung loose upon its bones. It had very short stubby legs, with no room for knees, and bulging bullfrog eyes. A long tail dragged behind it, and its disc-shaped mouth worked along the ground to retrieve every last morsel. Then it snuffled about, clearly not satiated and scenting more carrion nearby. Its nose was better than its eyes: it could scent death and decay miles away, even in the snow. It rolled one eye his direction.

In the blink of an eye, the bloagus vanished.

Erador felt a powerful downward gust and resumed his rock impression as he watched a miniature cyclone of snow whirl up the side of the mountain, athwart the direction of the wind and far faster than it was blowing. He thought he caught one last glimpse of the bloagus, a black dot rising away from the slope in the clutches of

131

a great white glacial bat. *Should I make a break for the rocks now, while the bat's feeding?* He had no idea how long that might take, or how much a glacial bat considered a meal. He *did* know they would hunt things larger than he was.

He did not know if they hunted alone.

Slowly, he worked his arms and legs beneath him, gathering himself into a crouch while changing his profile as little as possible. Then he rotated his head inch by inch, hoping his antlers looked like shrubs shifting in the wind. He still had the two branches in his left hand, if he could think of a use for them. He'd turned a little when he rolled, so now his head was pointed toward the slope, his feet away from it. To his left, he saw only mountainside. On his right was the cliff, tantalizingly close now, though he'd have to cross a good bit of open ground to reach it. In summer, there was probably a stream weaving along between hillocks of grass as it left the shallow valley it carved into the range. There were a few shrub junipers and leafless hawthorn bushes still peeking through the snow near the jumbled rocks.

Then Erador noticed some dark spots in the distance. Some were moving around. They were more bloagi. A half dozen more, at least. More like eight or nine. Though they were spread out over a good bit of the ground he wanted to cross. They didn't look like they were closing in on a common point, either.

I think I can work my way around to one side... if they're distracted enough. They look like they are. But what lured them all here? A herd of mountain goats, a pack of wolves, some other group of animals caught by that bla—

Oh.

No.

No!

Boots, hands, and antlers protruded from the misty blanket of snow. Erador was about to leap to his feet screaming and charge the bloagi, heedless of all else, but at the last instant something stayed him. The sensation reminded him of the hand he thought the Fates had laid upon his shoulder when he'd tried to follow his father onto the tundra. It also struck him as what it would feel like to be in the eye of a miniature cyclone of snow plummeting down a mountainside at one's back. *Onyx Smith protec—*

He doubted he would ever know if the Fates, or the Blacksmith, or both, had anything to do with it. All he could be certain of was neither cared one whit about bloagi. One bat passed directly over him, low enough his antlers would have gutted it had he been standing, ripped through the center of the group and was gone skyward before Erador could finish his prayer. A second dropped through the ravine, silken wings near vertical, and hit the bloagi farthest in that direction just as they all began to look up from their meals. It rose more slowly, allowing Erador a glimpse of its fine white fur sleeking in the wind. The remaining bloagi turned away from the ravine to run—where a third was met headlong by a bat coming low across the open tundra, rising up the ravine.

Five bloagi scampered as fast as their short legs could bear them, in five different directions, none of them toward Erador.

Erador remained motionless until all were out of sight. He pulled himself to his feet. He decided it didn't make the slightest difference at that point: if there were any more glacial bats around, he would die no matter what he did.

For a moment, he wasn't sure he cared. He knew what his feet now carried him toward.

He was right.

"I found them!" Erador cried. Then, as the putrid smell of foul digestive acids struck him: "I have to collect their antlers!"

Erador tried to bury his nose into the bend of his arm, but helmet and armor would not allow it. He surveyed the field of scattered corpses and realized that they had not all died in lines, as they ought to have if slain as one by the blast. Several were spread about, singly or in small clumps. As he brushed away the snow from a grouping of fallen elkin, he revealed four elders lying face down in the snow; their skin had turned pale blue, but it was not cold that had killed them. Each had suffered a stab wound to their back.

A sneak attack.

"But Warlord Dryden said they all died in the blast. That coward!" Erador grew furious. "He thought first of his own safety and abandoned Clan Wyndlyn!" He fished the shears from his tool pouch and began to work with haste in the dwindling light, collecting the antlers from every cadaver he uncovered. Every face that he found he recognized as an original member of Clan Wyndlyn. Some of the bodies had already been dissolved, leaving nothing to recover or to identify whose it was, nothing but stinking puddles melted into the snow and ice. He turned over one more frozen corpse to see Herlidrek, his face twisted in pain with a javelin through his ribs. *Are there no bodies for those originally of Clan Grondyr? There seems to be many missing, though they are probably too deep in the snow to uncover.*

Erador recovered Herlidrek's massive customized shield, studded with antler tips. He continued his survey of destruction, searching in desperation for his father. In the distance—at what he belatedly realized would have been the head of the column—he saw the snout of a torren dog, barely visible above the fresh blanket of snow. "Father's hide armor!" he said with disbelief as a single tear broke away from his eye.

He dug and dug, flinging snow out behind him until he saw the slit across his father's throat. He studied the cut in great detail; he could tell that the wielder of the blade stood behind Warlord Brynn to slice open his gullet. "You never saw it coming. It must have been someone you trusted," he said. Erador knew he would need extra layers for warmth, and the thick hide of the torren dog was the optimal choice. He removed the heavy wrap of fur and the travel bag from Warlord Brynn. He had already allowed the remaining scraps of disgusting bear skin to fall from his shoulders; now he slung the travel bag over his armor, then draped his father's cloak so that each head of the torren dog sat atop one shoulder, closing the fur across his chest.

He shook his head, then checked the contents of the bag. "Jerky!" It had never been such a pleasure to see before. He ought to collect all he could from those lying about him… but he had little light and less energy left, and more pressing tasks to complete. "Father, for the honor of your memory, the honor of Clan Wyndlyn, and to all those before me that wore the Onyx armor, I will avenge you," he intoned as he cut away Warlord Brynn's antlers. Then he continued through the insufferable graveyard.

Things were not adding up for him. *How did Warlord Dryden survive the blast? How could he, unless he knew… unless this was somehow his doing? And if this was his doing, what took him so long to get back to the Willow Cave?* he wondered. *We're only a couple of hours travel away, unless… Did he travel back to Cerebus-Senti?*

Confusion mounted Erador's distraught face. He addressed the gathering gloom: "But if Warlord Dryden mounted the attack, how did he cause such an explosion? Surely power of that magnitude could only come from a Blacksmith." His eyes darted back and forth as he began piecing it together the only way he could figure. *But he knew the runes on his helm… which he could have learned only from meeting with the Sky Smith Himself! Could this have been a coordinated attack? But why Clan Wyndlyn? Why would the Sky Smith care about us?* He had more questions than he had answers.

Then an even more terrible thought gripped his mind.

"Were the others part of this, too? I have to get back to the Cave and save the *real* Wyndlyn— No. Stop. Think! They didn't do anything before Warlord Dryden returned… and they could have, could've stabbed us all in the backs while we fought the gremlins. They supported him against me, but so did my own kinsmen. No, that's still unfair. *Only* my own kinsmen spoke against me. Those from Grondyr stood silent. Dorgeeryn gave up his soul to save Wyndlyn. *Damn it!*" he roared to the sky. "Why must everything be so complicated? I can't—" Erador sobbed out between gasps, "—I can't, just can't be everywhere at once, everywhere I need to be. How did you lead, father? How do you choose? How?"

He looked at the rimed carnage all about him.

"Start where you are. Do one thing at a time. Then move on." It was his voice that spoke the words, but the sound that reached his ears was his father's. Or maybe he heard the words first, and repeated them.

It wasn't what he wanted to hear… but it sounded right.

It was the only advice he could follow anyway.

Already he had far too many antlers to carry. He made a trip to the nearest of the crevices below the cliff, not caring how deep it went. He could move them after he was finished. After the second such trip, he began to worry. He still hadn't found… the snow turned blood-red; Erador whirled, dreading what new peril assailed him now. Of all things that passed through his mind in that instant, this was the least expected: the sun breaking through low, scudding clouds, already no more than half its disc above the horizon. Erador almost forgot where he was for a moment, almost stayed to watch it set. Almost: then he spun again, eyes flicking about, looking for shadows, for a glint upon metal—there! Near another of the crevices, well away from the center of the slaughter, he found it. He thrust his gauntlet into the snow beneath a pair of upthrust steel tines, and yanked free the massive fused-antler Staff of the Channeler. Vorkus' metallic surroyal antler rack arched like dual scythes atop it, rising higher than his own antlers did. It was heavier than the Onyx breastplate he wore. "Fates! I've found it!" he yelled into the chilling wind.

He dug deeper, seeking the Channeler's body—her antlers were almost as important to him as his father's. The Staff contained the history of Clan Wyndlyn's Goma enchanters in their intertwined antlers; hers must be joined to it, though he had no idea how to accomplish that. He hoped Carra might be able to—

He found the Channeler, uncovered her head. Her antlers were gone.

There were no sharp bases to show they had been cut away. Instead, there were small, velvet-covered buds… as if she were a child, her antlers just beginning to come in.

He looked at the Staff again, looked back at the aged face of the Channeler. It seemed younger, somehow, in repose. Looked at the velvety buds. *How…?*

It was a mystery he had no time to contemplate. In the last vestiges of twilight, Erador rushed to scout the taller caves between rock-slabs. For once luck was with him, and the first he tried went back a good fifteen feet. He still could not rest: he needed fire. One thing he did not lack was spare weapons—indeed, so burdened had he become that he'd already discarded first one than another when he found smaller ones. He cut as much from the minimal exposed brush as he could haul in one load. It would not make much of a fire, but it would have to do; his adrenaline had long since been exhausted, and instincts born of long training were all that forced him to lay and kindle it. He tossed a couple extra furs near the back of his refuge. Herlidrek's shield just spanned the crevice, so he set it as a windbreak in front of the fire. As he removed his sheath and set it beside him, he had one final flitting wish that he'd gathered a couple mouthfuls of snow before lying down. But the wish fled along with his consciousness.

CHAPTER 13

Carra stood at the entrance to the Willow Cave, watching Erador disappear into the snowfall. She waited for him to look back so he could see the guilt upon her face. He never did.

"Carra!" Warlord Dryden snapped. "I've been calling you for the last two minutes. Are you going deaf?"

Only half-heeding, Carra gave her default response to her father's infuriated tone. "My apologies, Warlord; I will try better next time," she said, still staring into the distance.

Gressyn, grinning at Erador's banishment, spat on the ground once he was no longer within sight and shook his head in disgust.

Carra's unintentional impudence was not the respect Warlord Dryden believed he deserved. Still surging with adrenaline after tossing Erador clear across the room, he demanded veneration, and turned to Zimmerik to get it. Zimmerik had managed to unbuckle only one shoulder plate before he stopped to watch the altercation unfold.

"My Sky helm will not wait any longer for its counterparts," Warlord Dryden rasped. Beneath his wool tunic his chest still heaved with every breath. The rippling of corded muscles was apparent even where they were not exposed.

Zimmerik, without hesitation, removed the sheathed Sky blade from his waist and offered it to the Warlord.

Warlord Dryden accepted his Sky blade, grasping the cold polished steel sheath, up which intricate inscriptions spiraled. He grunted and said, "Now finish doffing the armor and have it cleaned."

"Yes, Warlord," Zimmerik groaned.

Warlord Dryden attached his weapon to his waist. "So what happened here in my absence?" he asked.

Gressyn reported. "The blast created an opening at the back of the cavern, exposing us to creatures within." That statement caught his full attention. "Our losses… we lost too many," finished Gressyn as he struggled to find the right words.

The Warlord sighed in disappointment. "Were they given a proper burial?"

"All except Dorgeeryn," answered Gressyn.

"The clan has suffered *greatly* under Erador's leadership," he said. "But now that I've returned, there won't be any further *amateur* mistakes. I don't suppose there is any good news, is there?"

Wiltyn jumped at the opportunity and approached Warlord Dryden. "Warlord, I have discovered an entire treasury's worth of crystal."

"You must be exaggerating." The Warlord's voice made it clear he'd reached the end of his tolerance for childishness.

"No sir, I'll escort you myself. We just came back here to gather what remain of our possessions to move camp."

Warlord Dryden's irritation relented slightly at the youth's confidence, but he didn't comprehend the need to relocate the entire camp. "Why can't we sleep here?"

After a moment's silence while everyone balked at the thought of admitting fear, Carra stepped in. "This cave isn't safe. A horde of gremlins lives within this mountain, and possibly other cave dwellers." She pointed at the offal pile, into which the carrion beetles had only begun to make inroads. "We need to sleep in a secure area, and we can easily barricade ourselves within the crystalline cavern."

"Yeah, there was even a new Soul Smith demon we killed," added the injured Hammynt.

Zimmerik scowled at Hammynt's "we" as he undid the straps of the final leg-piece. *Erador and I killed it. Without this Smiths-damned armor. All* you *did was bleed.* He fingered his badger-ox trophy necklace and regretted his silence.

Warlord Dryden looked ready to bite Hammynt's head off. "What fable is this? There could not be a new demon here—the Soul Smith can only send his demons into the world in certain places, and elkin guard them all!"

"Maybe that's why the ancestors created this cave," Zimmerik said dryly as he presented the doffed armor. He forbore mentioning who had done the slaying.

The Warlord looked as if he were about to strike Zimmerik, then noted the other teens all indicating that the account was true: there really had been a demon. He shrugged the puzzle off as something to deal with later. Taking a deep breath, he turned his attention back to Wiltyn. "You must take me at once—" he said, spirits rising at the thought of uncountable wealth, though a brush of embarrassment crossed his face, as he realized he did not know who he addressed. He looked at the adolescent standing before him, and glanced over at his twin. "Which one are you?"

"Wiltyn, sir."

"Wiltyn, I don't want to confuse you with Vynocent. So you shall escort me there as my new wing-guard. And since there is no reason to allow it to go to waste—Carra! Remove the Sky Smith armor at once." He tilted his head toward Wiltyn's ear and lowered his voice to a whisper. "You've just been promoted."

The words were music to Wiltyn's ear. He grinned in excitement, eager for his chance to deck himself in legend. He ogled the royal blue runes dancing upon the milky white clouded glass as Carra presented piece after piece, as if he were present to behold the Sky Smith's forging it. Vynocent aided him in buckling on each piece as it was handed over, pride for his twin mingling with envy… and concern: how should they fight as one now?

Meanwhile, Warlord Dryden looked about him, scowled as his gaze swept over the image of Zimmerik washing the last of the armor. *Those* hands would never touch his armor again. He pointed to the injured teen. "You. Hammynt. Assist me. Give me a hand and help me with my armor." He did not even notice the implied insult. Hammynt did, but was ashamed rather than angered; he hid his feelings behind obedience.

Baltor's deep voice called attention to a new problem. "These baskets o' charcoal burnt up." Baltor picked up a handle from one of the woven baskets, showing the ragged remains of a rim which had escaped consumption. The piles of ash he stood next to testified to disaster.

"All of them?" asked Vynocent. "We don't have *any* charcoal left?"

Baltor sifted through the pile, causing clouds of ash to rise. He coughed as he tried to swat the dust away. "Ow!" he exclaimed at one point, yanking his hand back and shaking it. "Guess it ain't all done burnin' yet." The four children, who'd huddled together a bit apart from the teens—and away from the terrifying Warlord— giggled at Baltor's whimsical ways, then continued talking amongst themselves; Abby had them all captivated with a story. Baltor grabbed a javelin to stir the pile more cautiously, seeking any pieces that remained unignited.

"During the melee, some of the burning charcoal must have been kicked around into the baskets, and we didn't even notice," said Tysyra.

"We've been so preoccupied," tried Hammynt. "How will we stay warm, or cook food?"

"Furs will be plenty to keep us warm. There's no winter inside the tunnels," answered Gressyn.

"I don't think we should be cooking anything anyway," added Vynocent. "Not if it was the smell which drew the gremlins. We should stick to eating jerky."

"Yeah, well, that could be a problem, too," Tysyra added, gesturing about the plundered cavern. "Those crummy knee-biters swiped whatever they could carry… and I guess packed jerky was easier to haul off than bear skins or charcoal baskets."

"You mean we don't even have *that* left?" Vynocent paled. "Not much."

Warlord Dryden brought an end to the quibbling. "Enough! What you need is a real leader. From now on you will do as I say; are we clear?" he demanded. Everyone nodded their agreement. Carra knew that he was insulting Erador's leadership and she seethed with contempt. She wanted to tell him what lengths Erador went to in order to protect the clan. That he summoned the Fates in an attempt to learn to read the runes, and that he was doubtless searching for the Channeler's Staff right now, as they had bidden him. But she bit her lip, knowing to choose her battles wisely. Especially where her Warlord was concerned. She should have stood up for Erador when she was given the chance. She reserved a portion of her contempt for her own reticence.

Warlord Dryden grew impatient with these delays and indecisions. "We're going to that crystal cavern *today*, blast it, so grab your things! We will amass as much crystal as we can garner, and figure out the rest later. You've got a couple of minutes; I will leave you behind if you're not ready."

"But sir," whispered Wiltyn so others couldn't hear, "we must honor the deceased." He gestured across the cavern.

Warlord Dryden's eyes spotted Dorgeeryn's defiled body. "Wiltyn, see that he be treated with propriety, then bring up our rear. We need to get moving."

"Yes sir!" said Wiltyn.

***

Wiltyn collected Tysyra and Vynocent, wielding his newly-minted power to carry out his assignment with a haste he hoped would please his Warlord. He and his twin bore the body to the circle of willows; Tysyra brought Dorgeeryn's severed antlers. Wiltyn looked from willow to willow, wondering which might be most appropriate. Well, he now wore the Sky Smith's armor…

As he moved toward the Sky Smith willow, Tysyra snapped, "No." Wiltyn was about to invoke his authority, then saw a look of rebellion on his twin's face. "She's right. Honor the Sky Smith yourself if you want, but we're supposed to be honoring Dorgeeryn here."

"You can't be suggesting we give his body to the Onyx Smith… not after he was killed by someone wearing the Onyx armor," Wiltyn growled. "Or maybe you'd like to give him to the Soul Smith? It was His demon laid Dorgeeryn out, and He's already got Dorgeeryn's soul—"

Tysyra hissed at him, "You are going to make one *lousy* leader. Five minutes in that armor and you're already thinking of yourself more than Erador ever did." When Wiltyn opened his mouth to respond, she cut him off. "Don't. Just don't." Her eyes sparked behind tears—for her dead friend, for the future of her clan. "The Gaia Smith's tree. Let Her raise new life to oppose the Soul Smith's death." Vynocent nodded. The willow's roots performed their task, but when Tysyra placed the antlers against the trunk… nothing happened. She moved them about, pressed harder. Nothing.

Vynocent asked, "Is it because… because his soul isn't in them?"

141

"It doesn't matter," interjected an impatient Wiltyn. "We can't stand here all day."

Tysyra looked at the antlers in her hand, head bowed. Then she carefully slid them into one side of her belt and walked off wordlessly to join the others gathering their depleted supplies.

Wiltyn watched her go, followed by his twin. *I can't believe I'm wearing the Sky Smith armor,* he thought. *I've dreamt of wielding such power. I understand Erador's affinity toward it now, but I won't make the same mistakes he made.* He walked back to the Warlord to see what other orders he might have. "Sir?"

"What? Oh, you're done. Good. I want to see this crystal covered room sometime today. Go get the others moving faster," he said. Wiltyn scurried off, eager as a favored dog.

Hammynt was having difficulty adjusting the straps and buckles of the Sky armor to fit Warlord Dryden. His hand was slippery with sweat, and trembled from nervousness at the unfamiliar task.

"You must be doing it wrong, my armor doesn't feel right at all," complained Warlord Dryden, tugging at one piece and another to adjust the way it sat on his body.

"My apologies, sir."

With a sigh, and a sudden sense of compassion for the wounded teen, he suppressed his anger. "Perhaps it just feels this way since Zimmerik had adjusted it to himself," murmured the Warlord.

While it was still twilight outside, the ice-light within the cavern had dwindled to nothingness as their crevices passed into shadow. The gomabeetles seemed reticent to make up the difference, shedding less light than usual. Carra hovered her hand over the head of a hatchet and rocked her fingers in a wave; a small glimmer of light seemed to emerge from within the object, increasing in intensity, as if her fingers were coaxing the light from hiding, until it radiated a constant brightness. The remaining members of Clan Wyndlyn, burdened to their capacity, lined up behind Carra. "Let's go."

***

Carra held the hatchet in front of her, keeping her other hand cupped around the back of it, guiding the effulgence into a focused beam. She led the file through the tunnel, cautious and weary, hesitant to make any sudden movements. Even at the slightest hint of motion, she would flatten her cupped hand, and the focused ray of light from the hatchet would expand to fill the tunnel from wall to wall, though at the cost of reducing its range. The carrion beetles were feasting away at the rotting carcasses of gremlins; the stakes displaying their mounted heads glowed only feebly now, some not at all, as the spells on them faded. The sound of running water grew louder as they drew near their destination. Carra paused to reveal the slender fissure in the cavern wall, and Warlord Dryden brushed by the others to enter ahead of them.

With hungry eyes, he grabbed the hatchet from Carra and slithered inside. The adolescents tried to listen for his reaction above the roar of the river, but they couldn't hear a thing. Carra cleared her thoughts and cupped her hands together in front of her mouth. She whispered words that none could hear, drowned in the sound of running water, and blew into her hands the way a man would breathe life into a flickering ember. Something inside her hands began to radiate with light; her hands glowed a dark pink as the light tried to escape through her skin. Only she noticed the shadows where it did not glow through her fingertips. She opened her hands to reveal a delicate floating orb of yellow radiance. She blew it away from her and it floated weightlessly into the crystal cavern, illuminating the way. The others followed it, admiring Carra's new incantation.

Warlord Dryden was frozen in awe, crippled in disbelief, dazed by the vast abundance of crystal. Wiltyn strutted up in his Sky armor beside him. "I told you, an entire treasury's worth."

Warlord Dryden's face was eclipsed by the Sky helm, though Wiltyn knew he was smiling. The children chased after the radiant orb, and once they surrounded it, they blocked most of its light. Carra urged them away, so she could adjust the height at which it floated, but the dirty Vyranys would not budge.

"Go on, Vyranys, move."

"Only if you tell us what he wished for," he said. His voice cracked from puberty. Carra was confused by his demand.

"Carra, what did that elkin wish for?" asked Abby. "I told everyone the story, and now we all want to know."

"Yah. What happens next?" asked Asordin, the youngest survivor, a strapping boy of about eight. His vibrant green eyes stood out beneath his sandy blonde hair. Abby, Evey, and Vyranys were nodding their heads in agreement.

"Alright, you four. But Abby, you better show up to your next lesson, you promise?"

"I promise," she said.

"So the elkin had the Soul Smith begging for mercy, and the Smith offered him one wish in exchange for his life. But the elkin was not his normal self without his soul, and could only think selfish thoughts. He asked the Soul Smith to give him one reason why he should not kill Him and wield the divine Forging Hammer himself. The Soul Smith, with all His cunning, reminded him that he did not have a soul, and thus couldn't harness the powers of the Forging Hammer. Without the ability to wield its powers, he would be an easy victim for anyone else desiring the Hammer.

"The elkin dreamt of wielding great power, and wanted to stop himself from dying. He knew that with the loss of his soul he could not wield magic, so he wished for the Soul Smith to return his soul and grant him the ability to stop death, so he may live forever. Some might have seen this as more than one wish, but the Soul Smith raised no objection. He granted him his wish, and forged the Armor of Souls, a set of armor unlike any the world had ever seen. It was forged from the bones of a black phoenix, and was accompanied by a helm forged from the skull of a cyclops, and a staff more powerful than the Channeler's. But the Soul Smith tricked him; the armor was a curse.

"He made the elkin cut off his own antlers so he could wear the Skull helm, which He had fashioned without slots to slide it over them. Then the Soul Smith gave him back his soul, but not truly. He placed the elkin's soul into the helm so he was forced to wear it. If he ever lost his helm, he would no longer be able to use the power of the armor and staff. And that power was a hungry one: to achieve immortality, he had to kill over and over again, so the armor could feed off the souls of his victims. Then with his staff, he could stop death by animating the dead.

"With his soul returned to him, he could cast Goma incantations again, though his powers fell to shadow, able to manipulate only darkness. With his expertise in combat, and his new arsenal of spells, he went on a murderous rampage, raising an entire army of undead—"

"Carra! Children!" yelled Warlord Dryden, "Stop telling stories and get to work. We can get a few hours of chiseling in before we rest for the night."

She smiled at Abby. "I guess I'll finish the tale of the War of the Wish on your next lesson," she said with a wink. She glanced over at the other youths. "And once we finish here, the rest of you should talk to Wiltyn or Vynocent and ask them about starting your vanquisher training. I know you are young, but circumstances have changed."

Evey, Asordin, and Vyranys were wide-eyed with excitement.

Carra continued, "Perhaps they'll even teach you some of their signature moves from their teamwork fighting style."

"Okay, we will!" they said with enthusiasm.

Carra picked up her tools and set to work with the others. Baltor had already broken away some crystals over the entrance, then driven in some javelin heads and draped thick furs over it so Carra's light wouldn't give them away to anything passing by in the tunnel. Hammynt, who could do little else, sat guard by it to give warning in case something chanced upon them anyway. Tysyra went to sit by Gressyn to begin chiseling off the crystals, but as she sat down, Gressyn stood up and moved further away. Tysyra felt alone. She wondered where Erador was just then, sure he must be feeling the same way. With a sudden emptiness, she realized that she missed him and wished he was still here.

The work was tedious, especially with few real tools, let alone the right ones. Most of the elkin had to place the blade of the axe near the base of a crystal, then hammer the butt of the axe with the rock until the crystal dislodged from the wall. Sometimes one would get lucky, and find a section where the crystals grew in more or less even rows, so that freeing the crystals of one row would expose the bases of the next. Most had to be worked free individually. They all chiseled for hours, the vociferous river preventing talk and concealing the *chinks* of their hammering.

Warlord Dryden allowed a halt only when Carra's spell on the axe faded. It was obvious she was too fatigued to cast fresh spells, and was better to get themselves settled before her orb dissipated into nothingness. Few remained awake longer than it took them to pull their furs atop aching shoulders.

***

One by one, they awoke to complete darkness, locked deep within the mountain, though their time-sense told them it ought to be morning. The first couple had the decency to allow their comrades extra minutes. Finally, someone with less patience shouted, "I can't see."

"Is it morning yet?" groaned another.

"Ahh, I feel sore all over."

"Someone wake up Carra."

"Where is she?"

"I can make light by growing my antlers!" volunteered a far-too-cheerful Abby. "Shor tu urluk ma!" she shouted, and her antlers grew into a graceful royal antler rack, shimmering with light. The light seemed to play among the violet crystals along the walls, skipping about the cavern as she turned her head back and forth.

After one piece of jerky each, Warlord Dryden had everyone back to work.

"Can you please illuminate this axe for me?" asked Wiltyn, who looked uncomfortable after sleeping in the armor. "I like having my own light next to where I work," he pleaded.

"No problem," she said absently. She enchanted the axe head, then picked up her own axe, badly dulled and notched, and the rock she was using as a hammer. Wiltyn turned to where he had worked the previous day, only to be confronted by a massive bipedal shape seemingly composed of the same crystal as the walls around him.

"What magic is this?" Wiltyn asked in horror.

As the crystalline figure raised its club-like arm, Wiltyn's reflexes responded with a hasty chop of his axe. With a loud *chink*, small shards flew into the air as the axe wedged between larger crystals above where a heart would have been. The light in that part of the room dimmed to a deep violet as the axe illuminated the creature from within. The construct displayed no signs of pain, but snapped the golden sap-coated handle off, leaving the head still lodged within its body. With no room to maneuver, Wiltyn couldn't evade as it punched him square in his chest plate, sending him flying backward against a wall.

The crash alerted everyone; they leapt up, axes at the ready, strung out along the narrow cavern. Warlord Dryden pushed through to the front of the group. The crystalline construct directed an arm at him, then chunks of the arm broke away and flew toward him like arrows. The shards of crystal scattered off the protective cuirass of the Sky armor; a couple of elkin were struck by ricochets. The construct placed its stump against a wall and fresh crystals merged with it to reform the arm.

Warlord Dryden grinned and barreled toward the creature on his powerful legs. Just before his shoulder made contact for a tackle, the construct dispersed into a loose pile. The Warlord skidded on them and slammed headfirst into a wall. The shards of crystal shifted behind him, rising first into a column, then reforming limbs, the glowing axe head now at its feet. The nearest adolescents pounced forward, chopping and hacking away at its shoulders and neck. The construct twisted in a sweeping kick that savaged the legs of two opponents in front of him and dropped them on their backs. It turned toward those on its other side.

Abby, her antler rack still enhanced by her spell, saw the construct had its back to her and reacted. Before she thought what she was doing, she placed one foot in front of the other and bounded forward, stepping between her downed clan mates and driving like a spear toward the creature. Her radiating antlers, grown to half her own height, pierced its solid body, lodging deep within its torso.

And stuck there. From the corner of one eye, Abby saw it bend an arm thick as a club in an impossible direction, preparing to deliver a crushing blow. She closed her eyes tight and screamed in terror, "SHOR TU URLUK MA!"

Clan Wyndlyn watched in astonishment as her antler rack thickened and extended; new tines radiated throughout the construct, searching out gaps between crystals. Their light turned a burning red, and they began to shed heat. Then the whole thing splintered at once and it fell into pieces at her feet, the magical bonds that held it together shattered. She stood above the broken construct, her antlers glowing as if about to catch fire. Then the spell faded away until the only light remaining was from the axe-head at her feet.

Carra was agape at the magnificent sight. "Abby, that was amazing!" she shouted.

Abby noticed Warlord Dryden staring at her the way he first set eyes upon the crystal cavern. Then she turned about to see the looks of bewilderment on all the other faces. "What did I do?" she asked.

Carra stepped forward and placed a comforting hand upon her shoulder. "You defeated the creature with your incantation, an impressive one at that! How did you do it?"

Abby looked embarrassed. "I don't know. I—"

"I've never seen anyone cast a spell like that before."

"Nor have I," stated Warlord Dryden with an intrigued grin. "You have some talent, Abby."

Wiltyn inspected his armor for scratches from the blow that it absorbed. There were none. "What was that thing?" he asked.

Warlord Dryden got to his feet. "It is a remnant of Old Magic, lingering here from the time of the Gods. There are still forces left behind, here and there, untouched by the Blacksmiths."

"What? The Channeler didn't mention any of this to me," stated Carra, standing beside a confused Abby.

"What did you think the Fates are?" he asked the dumbfounded youths. Staring at his audience, he realized such a question had never crossed their mind before. "They too were left stranded here when the Old Gods abandoned Thornwall. The Channeler didn't tell you because she knows very little compared to our Mother. It's a shame that you did not get the opportunity to study with her more."

"She was always busy," exclaimed Carra. "Goma enchanters never progressed in Clan Grondyr the way they do here with Clan Wyndlyn."

Warlord Dryden sneered. "How can you even call us Clan Wyndlyn anymore? Warlord Brynn has perished, I'm in charge, and we haven't even the Onyx armor."

"We still have the banner," cried a defiant Hammynt.

"Perhaps you ought to fetch it. We have more wounds to bandage," the Warlord said. Gasps and confusion swept the adolescents, only to be repeated when he added, "We won't be bringing it with us when we leave this place."

"Where will we be going then, in the dead of winter?" Carra challenged.

"We are Clan Grondyr now, so we will head south, heading toward home, to our Mother. I had thought it best that we leave at once, but this wealth could not be passed up. Now with this crystal, we will be making some extra stops along the way."

"But Mother is turned to stone, along with Sonir-Senti and most of the Chyxurlgon Jungle. What sane person would go back there?"

"Perhaps it's time I tell you more about our Mother. She was one of the first, along with Vorkus. In fact, they were once a couple with similar noble ambitions of protecting the weak from the demons of the Soul Smith. But Vorkus wanted to move on, so they separated just before the War of the Wish. They formed their separate clans and much later, Vorkus died gloriously in battle, while Mother discovered a way to prolong her life."

"Is that what the Blacksmith runes inscribed upon her antlers were for?" interrupted Carra.

He nodded.

"Could she read them?"

Warlord Dryden smiled. "Our Mother was always busy because she had found a translation stone. It had the runic markings of four of the Blacksmiths. She spent all her time studying it. She kept it hidden. In fact, she kept many secrets to herself, more than you would have ever learned in a lifetime with Clan Wyndlyn."

Baltor looked down at the treblevine handle of his axe. "Why are we going back home?" he asked.

"Mother was born among the ancients, and she has lived for centuries; she still has some secrets to tell me," stated Warlord Dryden.

"But she's turned to stone. How could you possibly get her to speak?" asked Hammynt.

"You will see," he said as he turned into the shadows. "You will see."

CHAPTER 14

Erador was startled out of a deep sleep, from which he could remember no dreams. He sat upright, grabbing the hilt of the Onyx sword and easing it a few inches from the scabbard. Then, carefully, he crouched past the ashes of his feeble fire and pushed Herlidrek's shield aside. He stepped out of the crevice onto fiercely brilliant tundra, and realized that was what had awakened him: the sun glaring off the snow. The sun was itself as brilliantly white as the snow from which it was reflecting. *Guess the Radiant Smith got tired of it being yellow*, he thought.

Then he looked at his partially drawn blade. Then he woke up the rest of the way.

His laughter and the blade's song rang as one across the morning.

Erador felt as if the Fates had spared him. He checked his scavenged supplies. Food, travel packs to carry it. Water skins. Javelins and an atlatl. Extra furs. Rope.

What he needed was a way to transport all of it, along with over two dozen sets of adult elkin antlers. Plus the Channeler's Staff, his runic armor, his sword, his shield, his camp supplies and tools. He looked at the daunting pile once he had finished gathering it near the crevices.

I need something to drag it with... perhaps a dray? No; I don't have the right materials, and it would take too long to make. A travois might work. Lash a couple javelins together—better make that two per side; one won't be long enough. Something to tie them together. Belts would work. Tie another javelin crosswise near the bottom to keep it stable. Spread a couple furs across it and tie them down, load the supplies and tie a couple more furs across the top to keep everything in place... It was far from an ideal solution, but he could not bring himself to leave any of it behind.

He got busy.

Once he had his travois built, he loaded the antlers on it; these by themselves threatened to overspill it. He started packing the other items. The one thing he kept all of was the food, which fitted easily enough into a couple of packs after he filled the one he meant to keep on his back. One water skin on his person, two on the travois. A hatchet, a couple extra belts and some rope on the travois, in case he needed to make repairs; a half dozen javelins as well, plus a quiver on his shoulders. He could use the furs lashed across the top if he needed them for bedding.

Which only left the Staff, Herlidrek's shield, and the Onyx sword to be carried in the hand not dragging the load.

He was highly reluctant to resheathe the Onyx blade, as he had no idea if he'd be able to draw it again. If he didn't, though, he wouldn't be able to bring along everything else he was unwilling to leave behind. With a sigh, and a last look at the golden runes blazing in the mid-morning sun, he slid it back into its scabbard. He considered tying the shield to the travois, but feared it would take too long to free if he needed it. So it stayed on his arm.

That left the Channeler's Staff. He slid the Staff through the top of the travois, antlers to the back, then laid the Staff over one armored shoulder. *Not the most dignified use to put it to, but it works, and it'll be easy enough to slide out if I want to use it... or drop and draw something else if I don't.*

"Time to head home," he announced to the day, then began to march in a southwesterly course. He wasn't exactly sure where he was, but he knew it wasn't far west from the Willow Cave; he'd be in sight of the walls around Beknen Valley long before he could go too far off course.

The day remained fair. The wind that cleared away the clouds the night before had shifted around to the north and displayed no hints of bringing more in the foreseeable future; it was cold, but not bitter, and being at his back was a distinct advantage. As he marched through the morning and into the afternoon, he thought of his father and wondered again where it was the elders went each winter, where they'd been going when they were slain... a place he might never see now. He wondered how his friends were, and how they would respond to the news of Clan Wyndlyn's demise, especially if he were the one bringing it to them. He knew he would need evidence to convince them of his suspicions. Most of all he thought about what he would say if he were to see Warlord Dryden again. He dreamt of retribution and vengeance, for his clan and for himself.

The towering peaks of the Jerackon fell below the horizon late in the afternoon. For a time, there was nothing but the position of the sun for Erador to navigate by. He glanced back from time to time at the twin lines his travois left in the snow; they always appeared straight, but were hard to see for any distance. He stopped just once, to switch to a full water skin and move some jerky into his pouch so he could fumble strips out with one hand while he held the pole over the other shoulder with his shield-arm.

Erador knew it was possible for an elkin to walk the distance from Cerebus-Senti to the nearest foothills of the Jerackon range in the course of a single day, but that was without snow on the ground, without dragging a burden, and during the long days of summer. Nor was the place he'd left this morning the point the mountains ran nearest his valley home, though at least it ought to be no farther than the Willow Cave, if his reckoning were correct. A certainty grew within him that he would not reach the valley before nightfall. At that point he would be faced with equally grim choices: to camp on the open tundra with no meaningful shelter, or to press on through darkness and exhaustion. He decided that as long as the skies remained clear and he could navigate by the stars, he'd press on. He hoped he'd still feel that way when the time arrived.

He jerked awake, chills coursing through his limbs, certain a glacial bat was sweeping down upon him from behind. He stopped walking. It was still dark, still clear; there was no shadow-shape of a bat occulting stars. He looked behind him: his barely-visible trail showed no evidence of wavering that he could see. *Onyx Smith*, he swore silently. *How long have I been walking? Was I asleep just now? How long? This is not good.* He tried to estimate from the march of the stars how long it had been since nightfall. *At least... three?—no, at least four hours. More like five. And I don't remember anything clearly beyond the first one. Just footstep after footstep on featureless snow... If I kept moving at the same speed, I should be able to see the valley walls in front of me by now.* His eyes strained to locate the familiar outline picked out in shadow upon the horizon before him.

All they found was level emptiness.

Oh, Smiths, I must have turned while my mind was adrift! Or have I just been standing here for hours, asleep on my feet? Now I'm going to have to wait for daylight before I can figure out where—

Something loomed on the horizon over his right shoulder.

Erador was so stunned he dropped the Staff. He'd almost walked right past it, perhaps two or three miles from the valley's mouth. He grabbed the Staff, started driving himself forward as fast as his burdens and the snow permitted. *Half an hour. Just let me stay awake for half an hour.*

Half an hour later, he was looking up at the steps to his home, wishing he'd asked for a bit more time than that. He decided he'd best settle for what the gods had given him, and that the remainder was his problem to cope with. Digging deep to find every drop of energy he could muster, he trudged up the stone staircase, regretting every step, the Channeler's Staff jouncing and jarring his shoulder. Even with the Onyx armor he wore, he expected it would be thoroughly bruised come morning.

He fell flat on his face when he tried to take one more stair than was actually there. He pulled the Staff from the travois and used it to lever himself up and brace himself, grabbed the travois in his shield hand, bounced it over the final riser, and let it drop.

He made it to the nearest hut. He'd try to remember whose it had been tomorrow.

***

Erador tossed and turned in his sleep, sweating and groaning from the torment of another nightmare. The grasps of the false reality clung to his mind, trying to keep him from breaking free. Bright white light melted the snow atop the hut's roof, dripping icy cold globules upon the floor and his armor. Even though the light pierced the thatched roof and danced upon Erador's face, he remained locked within the dream state, asleep within his Onyx plate. Neither sun nor the discomfort of his armor, nor the terrors of his dreams could penetrate his fatigue. The day dragged on and the sun moved to the west.

There was a rumbling through the earth. Erador's eyes snapped open. He was freed from the anguish he'd been imprisoned

153

in, so abruptly he could not recover any memories of it. A familiar foul stench reached into the hut, and he could hear the snorts and heavy breathing from a large animal just outside. He stood, body aching from his labors and slumbering in the armor. He inched the hide back from the doorway, wondering at the sun's position high in the sky. Its light seemed brighter than usual.

"Was I asleep for that long? Most of the daylight has already past."

Then he felt the rumble through the floor once more, and realized the creature's footfalls were responsible as it jogged further away. It ran on two legs, Erador knew for certain, but he couldn't remember where he had smelled the thick, musky stench before. He looked around the hut and grew alarmed. There was nothing there except Herlidrek's shield, lying just inside the doorway where he'd slipped it from his shoulder before lying down. "Where are the antlers and Channeler's Staff?"

Then it hit him as he stood stiff with realization. "I left them out in front of the town." He peered past the leather hide draping over the entrance peeling it further and further back, trying to see if the Staff and antlers were still where he thought he'd dropped them. He saw the back end of the travois, and almost allowed himself to feel relief. But something was wrong; it wasn't loaded the way he'd carefully stacked things the morning before. *Did some of it fall off while I was walking unaware out on the tundra? Did one of the furs over the top come undone? Or one of the bottom ones, letting everything fall out?* One of those appeared to be the case—probably the second: where he expected to see a fur-covered mound, instead he saw pelts lying all but flat. He peered out farther.

The Staff was missing.

That, he *knew* he still held when he reached the top of the stairs last night. He'd used it to stand, to take some steps…

Erador's eyes darted around frantically, trying to spot it. "Where did the Staff go?" he muttered. It pained him to sit still. He wanted to run out of his hut, but the loathsome stench of whatever beast wandered his town was still heavy in the air, and he knew better than to risk giving his position away without knowing his enemy.

It took him a moment to notice that something else was missing, too. And a longer one before he realized what it was.

He was could see across the valley mouth to Remaurus-Senti. Where Clan Hortyr should have been watching during Clan Wyndlyn's absence. Where their banner should have been flying. Where someone ought to have noticed that there was someone, or something, on the northern plateau. But he saw no motion there; it too looked abandoned.

Shock and horror hit Erador. "Has Beknen Valley been left unguarded?"

Then, his keen eyes did spy movement—not in front of the hut, not across the valley, but out on the tundra. A pair of humanoid figures, apparently heavily laden, moving southward. Erador was struck with an epiphany: *They must have taken the Staff! And the antlers!*

Erador's emotions got the better of him again. He couldn't lose the Channeler's Staff, not now. His fears melted away before anger; anger fed confidence; confidence, determination. He was becoming a Warlord, fighting to save the relics of his clan, things that were worth defending, just as he had in the Willow Cave.

He swept his blade from its scabbard and leapt toward the stair down from the village. The sun's dazzling light fell dull against Erador's ebony armor, as if he was a moving shadow.

Then a shadow moved on its own, swallowing his. A large, pale blue leg thrust itself into his vision, bare foot spattering slush as it landed. The ground trembled beneath his feet. Erador turned, gaze rising to take in the massive figure towering above him—and the object it held. "Oh, I guess you have the Staff," said Erador to the colossus.

The creature's soiled blue skin reeked even through the clean winter air. *A vyceptor,* he groaned inwardly. *How could I have forgotten their smell?* It stood hunched over, casting its immense shadow as it loomed in front of the gaze of Goma's sun. Its jaw hung open with a green tongue dangling out the side of its mouth. Its teeth seemed attached to the mandible with no gum line, much like the crocodiles from the murky river within the Chyxurlgon Jungle that Baltor had told him about. It had the tusks, furry face, and snout of a boar, and a long white dreadlocked mane that ran from the back of its head down the length of its spine. Their hands had two rending talons and an opposed hooked thumb. Their long strides granted them speed, though their stench scared away any prey. They were clever creatures, able to clothe themselves, even wield weapons with some cunning. They could stay reserved in combat, waiting for an opportunity to present itself. Though given their natural advantages, their skills with weapons were scarce needed.

There were even tales of a Vyceptor Lord, conqueror of a small region of human lands far to the east. Legends said that he was near unstoppable, that he bore runic armor and a double sided axe, too large for any man to wield, given to him by the Scorch Smith. His skill with the axe was paramount, and he had laid waste to many towns and keeps. There were many tales of vyceptors passed down from the elders, and Erador knew them best; above all, he knew about the one that had slain his mother. Though this demon seemed much bigger than the one he remembered.

Erador took a glance at the Channeler's Staff clutched within its grasp. *And I left the shield inside, too,* he scolded himself. *If he swings the Staff at me, I won't be able to parry his blows without risking damaging it.* Erador took a couple steps to one side, moving so that the sun would no longer be at the creature's back. Recalling his vanquisher training, he crouched low, waiting to launch an overhand thrust that would puncture clear through the vyceptor's right knee, immobilizing it. Erador visualized the attack, ready to duck and spin away from the vyceptor's first swing; then he heard another snort from behind him.

"There are two of them?" he asked himself. "I've left one hell and entered another. Where is my wing-guard when I need one?" Erador couldn't leave his flank exposed, so he acted first, abandoning his training. Realizing that risks would have to be taken to gain an advantage in this fight, and that he'd have to depend on his armor to a dangerous degree, he leapt into the air with his powerful legs, both hands gripping the hilt of the Onyx sword as he prepared to stab through the top of the vyceptor's giant foot. The prodigious creature took a single step back and raised the Staff high into the air for a swing. Erador had anticipated as much, and as he landed where the vyceptor's foot once stood, he feinted a strike and tumbled toward the other foot with a spinning chop. The vyceptor roared in pain as the Onyx blade severed several of its toes. As expected, Erador felt the full force of Vorkus' steel antlers crushing into his back as the vyceptor's swing came down.

Erador blacked out for a moment from the impact as the wounded vyceptor hobbled backwards in pain, off balance. He shook his head as his senses returned to him one by one. Just as his hearing came back, a furious roar boomed from behind him. Erador rose to face his other challenger. As it ran toward him from across the town, snorting with every step, its bounding run cleared stone huts with every stride. Erador thought to wait for its wild charge so that its defenses would be lax, but wearing the Onyx armor instilled reckless confidence in him. All his fears were purged, and, with a crazy look in his eye, he bolted toward the other vyceptor. Sprinting full out, in one fluid motion Erador placed one foot on a sitting stone and then leapt onto the edge of a stone hut. He flew through the air like a spear, antlers-first toward the vyceptor's jugular.

It was moving too fast to avoid him; it tried smashing him out of the air, but Erador slashed in return and split its hand open just before he felt the impact of his antlers tear into its throat. The beast hunched over, its throat gurgling with blood as it braced itself with its good hand against a stone hut. Erador remained dangling between hut and demon, antlers lodged deep within its throat. Blood poured down Erador's head and seeped between the interlocking plates of his armor. Erador couldn't keep the blood out of his eyes; every time he wiped it away, more would follow. The odor of the huge creature's blood was enough to suffocate him. He tried wiggling himself free, but his antlers were stuck. The vyceptor fell to its knees, holding onto every moment of life as it struggled to breathe. Erador's feet still couldn't touch the ground, and he now heard the thunderous steps of the limping vyceptor approaching.

Erador didn't know what to do; he was exposed, and about to receive the full wrath of the oncoming vyceptor's revenge. He starting hacking at the vyceptor, but had no leverage to lend strength to his blows. Through his blurred vision he saw the Channeler's Staff coming toward him. In a chaotic fumble, Erador reacted.

It was instinct.

It was a mistake.

Erador peered out of one imperfectly cleared eye and past his hastily-raised blade. He noticed that the Channeler's Staff in the vyceptor's claw was missing something. He looked toward the ground and saw Vorkus' metallic antler rack lying in the snow, sundered from the Staff. *Fates... what have I done?*

The vyceptor cast the broken Staff down and grasped the dangling Erador's arms. It began pulling his arms in opposite directions, stretching him like a rack. Erador resisted with all his might, but the strength of this massive creature far outmatched his. Just when he thought that his arms would be torn from his shoulders, the bleeding vyceptor fell lifeless to the ground; it rolled atop him as it fell, forcing the other demon to release his arms. Erador was now lying in a puddle of warm, fetid blood, crushed beneath the massive corpse's weight. He struggled to turn his head so that its blood would stop pouring into his face; he was having enough trouble breathing without it.

Erador heard the other vyceptor bark twice, followed by a response from somewhere far out in the distance; then he felt the earth rumble as it lumbered away. "This place is flooding with demons," he coughed between spitting aside mouthfuls of blood. "It's as if the Soul Smith knows that we aren't here."

If the Onyx Smith armor had not prevented his ribcage from being crushed, Erador would not have lived long enough to free himself, he was certain. It took several minutes of squirming and pushing with his one free arm, biting back the pain from the other vyceptor's attempt to yank it out, before he could inch himself far enough to one side that he could turn the creature's neck and get his face out from beneath it. By then, it had all but stopped bleeding anyway. *That figures*, he thought. His antlers were still lodged against its spinal column... firmer than before, thanks to the twisting. *And why did it have to land on the arm with the sword in it?* After clearing his face as best he could, he began the struggle to free his other arm before it went numb and he lost his grip on the blade. His legs *were* numb by the time he pulled it free, and he was beginning to become concerned that if he moved his neck any further, it might break. Or his antlers might. With Onyx blade in hand and no room to swing, he began sawing.

After several awkward, agonizing strokes, the vyceptor's spine parted and Erador's strained neck abruptly snapped back, antlers tearing through the monster's blue skin and decapitating it. Erador's head whipped back in the released tension, striking the ground with a crack. He lay dazed for a moment, then began coughing in dry heaves, almost on the verge of vomiting. He worked his helmet off, then scrabbled for handfuls of clean snow to finish removing the demon's nauseating blood from his face. Then he spent the next few minutes enjoying every shallow, constricted breath of the cool winter air.

Then he set to work cutting free the rest of his body. It wasn't pretty, but it was successful. Eventually.

When he could finally sit up again—and feeling began to return to his legs, its own special agony—Erador looked over the dismantled demon. Something embedded near one shoulder caught his eye. He reached up and felt along his antlers… one tine was two inches shorter than it had been. *Guess that crack wasn't just the helmet hitting stone. Now I'll need to get it capped.* He rolled to his knees with determination, intending to crawl toward the severed pieces of the Channeler's Staff. Then promptly sat back down again. He couldn't believe the world hadn't exhausted its ability to shock him after the experiences of the past two days. But he'd managed to underestimate the world yet again.

This time it granted him a long-held wish.

The Armory was open.

Not merely open: demolished. As soon as he could rise, he hobbled to the collapsed structure. *What in the world could even have the strength to move these slabs?* he wondered. Too beaten to climb atop one of the fallen megaliths, he worked his way around until he found a space between two of them. Through that space he saw no floor, only what looked like the walls of a pit. Stepping cautiously forward, he reached the inner edge of the enormous smooth slabs. "This is what the slabs were covering?" He peered over the edge. The pit bored deep into the stone of the mountain. It was empty.

If anything was ever kept in there, it's been taken… and with the death of the elders, I will never know what it was. Erador shook his head in disappointment and bewilderment. All four of the massive walls had toppled outward, a couple of them crushing huts beneath them. The roof had come down to one side and now rested half on, half off one of the walls—though given its immensity, he doubted both vyceptors jumping up and down on it would cause it to fall into the pit.

It was too much for him to wrap his mind around. Besides, it was nothing he could do anything about. Other duties required his attention. He walked back to the scene of his battle, legs feeling almost normal now, and considered the ruins of the Channeler's Staff once more.

He grasped the cold steel of Vorkus' antlers, realizing for the first time how significant their heft truly was. He studied the small imperfections in Vorkus' antlers, minor nicks and scratches from battles past. He was relieved to see that they had remained intact, that the Onyx blade had cut them away cleanly just below where they had been entwined by the antlers of his tribe's Goma enchanters. He scrambled to his feet, picked up his helm and then recovered the rest of the Staff; though he'd expected it, he was still surprised how much lighter it was now than before. Erador tried fitting Vorkus' antler rack back atop the Staff, in the futile hope that the antlers would grow back together. Then he grew further depressed as he remembered that he'd also lost his clan's antlers that day. "As long as they're not in the hands of the Soul Smith," he said aloud, attempting to cheer himself up.

The Onyx helm was covered in blood inside and out, and Erador dared not don it now. In fact, the entire suit needed a thorough cleansing as it reeked of the vyceptor's stench. *The warm waters of the springs could get the stench off,* he thought with regret. *I know I wouldn't be welcomed back. But I must warn the others of what Warlord Dryden has done to Clan Wyndlyn! They're in danger, and Hammynt's arm is still broken. And maybe Carra will be able to fuse Vorkus' antlers back on and fix the Staff.* Erador turned and faced northeast, looking across the snowy tundra, then westward at the descending sun. He sat for a moment and looked at the empty blood-coated Onyx helm within his hand. He stared into its eyes and said, "I marched through the night last night; I can do it again. And I won't be dragging a load this time." Though this would be a later start, he was already worn by the previous trek, and was badly strained and battered from combat. The sensible part of him told him that setting out without resting again was a terrible notion.

As he stared at the helm, Erador grew curious. He slid Vorkus' metal antler rack through the slits in the Onyx helm. With both hands, he gripped their thick trunks; the helm was left suspended in the center, fitting perfectly around their bases. As

Erador stared into the helm, then lifted his gaze toward the massive surroyal antler rack protruding from it, the words of the Fates came to the forefront of his mind:

> *"There is one that can help you, but you must carry his weight. To find him, let the Channeler's Staff lead the way."*

Erador got an idea.

CHAPTER 15

Confined deep with the recesses of the Jerackon Mountains, the reinstated Clan Grondyr was hard at work chiseling the short, stubby, violet crystals away from the cavern walls. All of the elkin labored at liberating the crystals—all except one: Warlord Dryden declared that Abby had met her quota. Collecting the loose shards and chunks of crystal from the defeated crystalline construct was the easiest harvest of their day. Abby's reward was a crystal of purest violet, bigger around than her thumb and as long as her longest finger. She tied it within a leather thong and hung it about her neck. The Warlord himself had selected it from the ruin of the construct: her first trophy, he'd told her. She would sometimes pause and brush her hand against her newly acquired necklace, then hold it up to admire its beauty.

Carra was through with illuminating axes. She wanted to conjure the orb once more, but bigger this time—the way Abby had done with her antlers. She whispered into her cupped hands and could see its pulsating light emanating between the cracks in her fingers. She whispered some more and felt the surge of light rush down her arms and… get stuck at her fingertips. *No,* she thought. *I know I used the proper command.* The pain under her nails started to sting and she started shaking her hands—still cupped together—while wincing in pain. This caught the attention of some others. The power she conjured to add to the orb was not expelling from her fingertips. She felt she was about to cry, the pain was so great, then she finally felt it release. She clutched her hands against her chest as she watched the misshapen orb of golden light warp and churn as it hovered in the air. Despite its mutations, the orb emanated sufficient light for all in the vicinity. Carra checked her nails, but the pain subsided immediately. She felt a wave of relief, picked up her axe and rejoined her clan mates at work.

Even with hands callused and leathery from years of combat training, the elkin found mining to be a taxing chore. Every strike of the rock stung the joints of their fingers, and the pain grew with every hit. As they continued hammering rocks against the butts of their axes, their blades grew dull, and the time it took to chisel one crystal from the wall increased with every strike. They often had to pause from chiseling to run their axes against a whetstone under Carra's illuminating orb. It was monotonous, tedious work, performed without rest. No one was permitted to leave their barricaded vault. The crystalline cavern grew warm and humid from the elkins' breath and sweat. The continuous obnoxious sound of rushing water dwindled from their awareness over time. Without any daylight as a frame of reference, it was impossible to judge the passing of time; as with their harvest, it merely piled up… slowly.

Slow or not, their piles of raw wealth continued to stack up, and it became evident that even a single dray could no longer handle the spoils of their drudgery. Vynocent wiped the sweat off his brow as he took a moment to rest. "How will we manage to carry all of this out of the cave?" he asked.

"Yeah, we can't carry every crystal from this cave. There's too many," called one of the bored youths. When can we stop chiseling?"

Warlord Dryden stood and searched the shadows to try to find where the voice came from, though to no avail. After a brief moment, he answered, "We will need to purchase mules to haul the riches, so we'll be stopping in a human farm town along the way." Hammynt smiled in glee at the chance of acquiring animals as Warlord Dryden continued, "Until then, we'll need to devise a way to haul them through the snow."

Looking for busy work, Hammynt offered, "I can turn the blankets into rucksacks."

"I can help," added Abby.

Warlord Dryden nodded, and they both set work on converting the furs, using a narrow dagger to put holes around the edges, and then lacing them with hastily-braided strips cut from other hides.

Carra stopped and threw down her hatchet in frustration at her father's lack of attention to detail. "Wait a minute. The nearest human farming town has got to be at least… three days' journey from here? Or more, with snow on the ground, right?" She looked to Vynocent to verify her memory with someone who'd grown up in the region. He nodded. She went on, "Without charcoal, how will we make a fire to stay warm? My incantations can't warm us all night long."

All the sounds of stone-against-metal had ceased as attention was turned toward the argument. If nothing else, it gave them a moment to relax the strain from their hands and shoulders without subjecting themselves to the Warlord's disapproving glare.

Without the blink of an eye, nor the tone of remorse, he answered, "Then we must cut down a willow tree for use as firewood."

Never had the adolescents heard more iniquitous words spoken. This was not something they could possibly fathom as an option, ever. To deface a monument to a god is sacrilege; and to use the resources of that monument for your own selfishness is to mark yourself for death.

They wanted to protest but no words could escape their lips. They turned to Carra in their shock, as if expecting an answer from the one that brought attention to the problem. Carra's cheeks flamed from her father's response, embarrassment warring with outrage. She knew she needed to choose her next words with care, to steer everyone away from such grievous thoughts without insulting her father's intelligence. With only a hint of abrasiveness, she reminded him politely, "Warlord Dryden, firewood will give off smoke which can be seen from great distances away. Our position will be revealed to any predator or thief, which is why we've always used charcoal."

"Consequences are consequences," he dismissed the objection, then went back to chiseling at the crystal as if there was no more to be said about the matter.

"But there must be some other way!" Carra protested. "We can't defile a monument to the Smiths! We could use an abundance of blankets to stay warm, something, anything!"

"That's *enough* out of you!" he roared. "I gave you an order! I thought we had an understanding as to how things are to be run around here? Or would you rather deliberate amongst yourselves for hours of time that we don't have?"

"Looks like we've got nothing but time to me," Zimmerik said… but too quietly for the Warlord to catch it.

Carra was stunned with disbelief. *Why does he not care if he offends the Blacksmiths?* she thought. *And why does he not care for our safety? This is not the father that claimed me as his own.* She looked to Zimmerik for support, but he had already returned to his work. He seemed anxious to leave, and had chiseled away more crystal than everyone, even Warlord Dryden. *Perhaps that is his way at an attempt to impress my father,* she thought. Everyone else still stood aghast, uncertain as to how to handle their Warlord's command. Carra searched their eyes: all gave the clear message that they did not want to defy his order; neither did anyone want to be the one to chop a willow tree into firewood. Her heart grew melancholy as she realized that this task was to befall her.

She placed her aching hand on her chest as she gathered the courage to shout, "I'll do as you command." The words almost got stuck in her throat, but they brought comfort to the ears of her fellow clansmen. As if no more needed to be said, they returned to their work. She had hoped that by volunteering for such a doomful task she would have at least roused a reaction out of her father, to make him think twice about his order if it meant condemning his own flesh and blood. He seemed untroubled by her choice.

Even though it would be me who was to be cursed, she thought, *it would be the clan that suffers. If I were to die, only Abby could provide light and she only knows the one cantrip. Not to mention the unwanted attention that the smoke from the firewood would bring.*

Lost in her confusion and despair, she returned to her mindless work. She placed the hatchet blade against the base of a crystal, and swung a rock down toward its butt. The blow landed not with the usual ringing but a suppressed thud: she'd missed her mark. She gritted her teeth against a cry as pain barged past her shock and streaked up her arm. Her left thumb throbbed, and Carra brought it closer to the light of her floating orb. With each throb, Carra could see a black vein take on greater definition beneath the skin. She wiped the sweat away from her brow, and refocused her vision to see if her eyes might have been playing a trick on her, but still the black vein remained.

"No," she said, as if her words could make it untrue. "No, no, no, no. I thought I had avoided the Poisoning." She squeezed her thumb as it turned bright red, as if trying to cut off its circulation. She thought about the other Goma incantatory wizards before her that went blind or mad from malpractice of the art. *How could this be happening?* Her eyes glanced over at the splendid product of an incantation of her own creation: the golden orb, no larger than Baltor's fist, spinning in place as it hovered. Its outer shell glimmered with the pride of a miniature tumultuous sun. In that one look, she knew.

She had improperly modified her incantation, and couldn't expel her conjured power in the process. She had overstepped her boundaries, a limit that was never taught to her. She began thinking back on all the spells that she had learned, each and every one involved illuminating, manipulating, and blasting light, but never had she tried to magnify their effects.. *Was it truly this new incantation that caused the Poisoning? Or was it from before at the battle with the Gorrotin?*

She allowed the torment to fade from her mind and accepted her fate. She had already signed herself up to destroy a willow tree. *Perhaps this is my curse for the crime I have yet to commit. I wonder which one I should cut down?* she thought, feeling a little bit nefarious, as though she had nothing to lose.

As the pain of her thumb subsided, she looked around to see if anyone had taken notice, then went back to work. Tysyra had inched toward her, and now spoke so no one else could hear, "Carra, we need to find another way. You don't have to cut down a tree. Try talking to Wiltyn, he's your father's wing-guard; maybe Warlord Dryden will listen to him. It's not too late."

"No, it *is* too late, for me," replied Carra. Tysyra's face was cross with confusion; she didn't quite know what to make of Carra's statement. "It's okay," Carra added. "Don't worry about me. Worry about the safety of everyone else when the smoke is ascending from the firewood." With that, they both returned silently to work.

Fatigue began to weigh down upon them as unreckoned hours passed. Carra caught another glance of Zimmerik's impressive stack of crystal and decided that she too should demonstrate her worth to the clan. With a grin of satisfaction and a snap of her fingers, all the lights she had produced vanished. The room was pitch black within the blink of an eye. Grumbles and complaints filled the air, her father's the loudest. *I'll probably pay for that. He'll know I canceled the spells all at once.* She waited a moment, to allow for an appearance of effort, then called back, "I can't. I'm exhausted." It wasn't a lie—which she also knew he'd know. She could do nothing but lie down and fall asleep, a smile tugging at the edges of her mouth. Carra heard his voice rumble something about "…so we can get settled," then the crystal vein lit up once more; but she heard no renewed clinks of metal against rock, so drifted off satisfied her father had no intention of stretching Abby's nascent abilities.

Carra awoke with a grumbling stomach. She pointed a finger in front of her, emitting a faint dim light from its tip so as not to awaken anyone. She was the only one awake. As she moved its beam, trying to locate their small store of jerky, she discovered Warlord Dryden asleep on his side, his arm wrapped around his travel pack, guarding it. Her curiosity was overruled by another round of complaints from her stomach. Her footsteps were drowned out by the constant roar of the underground river. She found the rations. The first salty, juicy bite was nirvana to her palate. After consuming the first strip, she helped herself to another. And another. If she was to defile one of the sacred willows, she might as well indulge.

Carra knew what she was doing, that it would mean less food for everyone else. But her hunger would not end. Maybe the shortage of food would force them to leave; it was the same goal that Zimmerik had hoped for, but this was more direct and might yield a quicker result. For all they knew, Warlord Dryden's greed would keep them here for an eternity. She wanted to leave the crystalline cavern, and with a sudden shortage of food, Clan Grondyr would be forced to depart on their journey. She carefully counted off one piece of jerky for each of her clan mates to leave in the pack—feeling clever to remember to include herself—and went back to sleep to await someone else's discovery of the low supply of food.

Carra awoke to the sound of the river filling her ears, how much later she had no idea; it felt like she'd slept a full night's worth after her brief awakening. Her blurred vision was consumed by the delightful sight of everyone packing to leave. Abby had once more cast her antler cantrip to light the way, and the barricaded entrance had been cleared. Carra stood in excitement and discovered that they had left her pile of crystal alone for her to package. She did so with pleasure. She knew that she was only moments away from chopping into a sacred tree, from committing a sin worse than she'd ever imagined, but she was eager to. She felt drawn to it, the way pollen attracts a bee. The Poisoning had begun, and there was no telling what curse would haunt her for the rest of her days. She looked to Wiltyn. "Why didn't you waken me?" she asked.

He forced a playful grin, but his eyes were full of sorrow. "You're about to be marked for death if the Blacksmiths still have heads on their shoulders. We wanted to buy you as much time as possible."

The least useful sleeping furs, now repurposed as rude sacks, were wrapped around the piles of crystal and cinched at the top like a belt pouch. There were now four times as many rucksacks as elkin. Carra couldn't believe they'd chipped away that much, no matter how long those hours had seemed.

"This is not going to be a subtle caravan," she told Wiltyn. He just nodded.

"This is going to drastically reduce our travel speed," agreed Vynocent. "We should leave some of this behind and come back for it with the mules."

"We won't have time to come back," announced Warlord Dryden. "Once we get there, the mules will do the rest, so stop complaining. You don't see Hammynt complaining do you? And he has a broken arm!"

Carra took umbrage to her father's response, *Erador would not have been so dismissive and disrespectful, nor as vain.* She found herself wishing Erador were here. The thought of him made her forget about her predicaments, at least for a moment.

They squeezed the rucksacks one by one through the slender fissure in the cavern wall, then began hauling the hefty sacks in relays up the passageway toward the Willow Cave. Little Abby led the way with her radiant antlers, bearing one end of a javelin, Vyranys the other, with a sack hanging between them. Asordin and Evey followed, occasionally arguing about who had to carry the pointy end. Hammynt grunted and struggled with the weight of his sack, unable to shift it from shoulder to shoulder due to his broken arm. Gressyn's right leg was still heavily bandaged from the crystal construct's leg-whip. Baltor took two at a time. Warlord Dryden remained at the fissure to guard the balance of the treasure, alone… after requiring Carra to illuminate one of their now-superfluous hammering rocks for him. He was clearly in no mood for excuses, and she obeyed him in silence. As he held it casually in his massive left hand, its muted glow raised shadows upon a sinister expression.

As they increased their distance from the crystalline cavern, the constant reverberation of rushing water diminished while the delightful clamor of jingling crystals from within the rucksacks took its place. They hauled their burdens into the familiar bluish ambient light of the Willow Cave. They could tell from the amount of light that it was near either dusk or dawn, but were not sure which, as no direct sunlight struck the cavern's entrance. No one thought to go and check, only of completing the task at hand as rapidly as they could. Everyone deposited their sacks near the willows, then headed back for another trip. When after three trips the pile at the nether end had dwindled to a handful of bags—few enough that several of the tribe would have hands free to gather up the remaining supplies on the next trip—Warlord Dryden stopped Carra. "You need not return for the final load. You have another task," he reminded.

She met his eyes without flinching, nodded, and joined the file. When they unloaded once more at the far end, Carra halted Baltor, asking him, "Can I borrow your axe?"

"Huh? Sure, but why d'ya… oh. Yeah, sure." He pulled it from his belt and thrust it into her hands, then turned back down the tunnel to cover his discomfort. The others were already on their way.

Carra stared at the gentle yet magnificent willow trees as their dangling foliage swayed in the breeze. She admired their magnificence, their antiquity; she studied each runic symbol carved upon their bark. She looked at the lowest branches, ones she knew they'd not had a week before. Already those were sprouting twigs and their first tiny leaflets. *Not only do I get to commit heresy, I get to violate the graves of my friends.*

She considered her dilemma. *I could cut down the tree of the Gaia Smith; how could She miss one tree when She rules over so many? Or perhaps the Radiant Smith tree, since it's His blood that has Poisoned mine. Though the safest choice may be the Chromium*

Smith tree, since He prefers a seat on a throne to rule over men instead of perform His godly duties, she thought as she walked from willow to willow with judicious determination. She abruptly realized she'd spent too much time in her contemplation: the others were already emerging from their final trip. *No, I think the Sky Smith's the best choice. Let my father object to that sacrilege.* She shouldered the axe and stalked toward her choice, daring her father to reveal himself a hypocrite… hoping he would, that it would save her when all else had failed.

She caught a glimpse of a moving shadow from the corner of her eye. She jerked her head toward the snowy entrance; her sudden movement attracted everyone else's attention. Her green eyes grew wide in incredulity, and her face twisted in perplexity as she saw what looked like Warlord Brynn return, gripping the Channeler's Staff near its top in one hand and bearing Herlidrek's shield in the other. The bulky Onyx plate was covered with the pelt of the two-headed torren dog. The golden runic inscriptions, wherever they were visible, seemed to shimmer in the bright light from outside.

The figure's voice said, "I really don't think you want to do that." Carra dropped the axe as if it had burned her.

CHAPTER 16

Carra recognized the voice, and was astounded how much it relieved her tension and trepidation.

"How dare you return to this place!" shouted Warlord Dryden, in his most contemptuous tone.

"How dare you murder my father!" retorted Erador, as he tossed the pieces of the Channeler's Staff to the ground and withdrew the Onyx blade.

"Lies! He died from the blast, like all the rest."

The jet black helm upon Erador's head turned from side to side in defiance, contradicting Warlord Dryden's claims. In an arrogant tone, calm and bold, Erador added, "He died like all the rest, yes—but not from the blast. I saw the slit you drew across Warlord Brynn's neck while standing at his back. A coward's attack. Tsk tsk."

The others saw the truth in his eyes burning beneath his helm, and began stepping away from Warlord Dryden. He still stood tall, expressions hidden behind his helm, unwavering in his glistening Sky Smith plate imprinted with intricate miniature lightning-blue runes. Wiltyn, in identical armor, still guarded the Warlord's flank. Warlord Dryden moved his hand to rest upon the hilt of his blade at his side in its magnificent and elegant silver sheath. "Can't you all see what he is trying to have you believe?" he demanded of them. "He is an exile, trying to fabricate lies to earn his way back into your trust at my expense! What proof, exile, can you lend toward your claims?"

"I was there. I saw it with my own eyes. I have returned here decked in his hide armor, carrying the Channeler's Staff and wielding Herlidrek's shield as proof."

Warlord Dryden guffawed. "That proves only that you found and looted their corpses. Poorly, too, it would seem, if that staff lying broken at your feet is any evidence. But how, Erador of no Clan, can you prove they were murdered?"

Erador's confidence began to waver. He looked down at the torren dog hide that blanketed his chest; he needed to think of something quickly. He noticed that his peers were reaching cautiously for their weapons. He knew full well that his actions, if he could not justify them, would be reason enough for his execution. His eyes drifted to Warlord Dryden's massive winter cloak, the fur pelt so large it covered his antlers, lying in a heap on the cavern floor near the empty armor stands. Finally, an idea! Erador gestured to it with his shield, and asserted, "Check his winter coat. If our elders died as he says, then no blood should have been spilt upon it. But if it's as I say, then you should find blood on his overcoat."

Tysyra and Zimmerik began searching the fur coat's expanse. It was a huge risk. Erador raised his gaze to meet Warlord Dryden's, staring at him while awaiting the results of their search.

"I found blood!" shouted Zimmerik. "On the cuff of the right arm."

"It's unmistakable," added Tysyra, at which point even Wiltyn began to step away from Warlord Dryden.

Warlord Dryden watched Erador raise his blade at the ready and poised his shield so he could see just over its ridge. "Why did you do it?" Erador shouted.

Warlord Dryden's face hardened to a scowl. "I gave him the option to join me, but he chose death instead."

"Buy why!?"

"So I can prove Mother wrong!" he shouted with fury. "For reasons you're too young to comprehend! For the power that was buried at your feet, yet none of you even knew of."

Erador scrunched his brow in confusion. *Buried at my feet?* "Do you mean what was entombed beneath the Armory?"

"Well, well, it seems you have done a fair amount of traveling in this short time you've been gone. All the way to Cerebus-Senti and back."

"What did you take from the pit beneath the Armory?"

"*I* took nothing" Warlord Dryden was deriving entertainment from his opponent's confusion.

Erador's mouth twisted in frustration. "I will not play any of your games! What was in there, and who took it!?"

Warlord Dryden maintained his cockiness. "I believe it was your neighboring clan that disappeared, yes? Perhaps it is to Clan Hortyr that you should be directing that question."

It was Erador's turn to sneer. "Well, at least we have *that* much of a confession. *I* said nothing about Clan Hortyr disappearing." A piece of the Warlord's arrogance slipped away. The younger elkin continued. "You've been working with them, planning some sort of coup. Did you arrange for them to wait in ambush, to help you murder my clan?"

***

Carra couldn't believe the things Erador was claiming her father was somehow involved in. She began to wonder if he had ever been trustworthy since they'd come north—then to dread whether his treachery might not go back farther still. She was perplexed at how he could have accomplished the feats he stood accused of, and before she knew she was doing it she heard herself ask, "How did you cause the blast?"

Warlord Dryden hesitated long before answering. "By making a deal, a favor for a favor. It was the Soul Smith that caused the blast and eradicated your clan. Now it's time for me to make good on my end of the bargain."

Carra could tell that the fatigue of the past days was making it difficult for Erador to maintain his guard, and he was losing his patience. "Impossible! Nothing but more lies! Whatever plan you're up to, it's stopping right here."

Hammynt told the youths, "Get behind the trees and stay there." Axe in hand, he took up position between Warlord Dryden and the willows. The other teens spread along his flanks, weapons now turned against him. He took an apprehensive step backward as they began closing in.

***

There are too many of them, Dryden thought. He knew the Onyx blade was capable of cutting through his armor, that Carra could blind him with light, and that any well-placed blow from a

173

mundane weapon could knock him to his knees or render him unconscious. Unless he could even the odds a bit, he would be overwhelmed. He turned his head to look at Wiltyn, his wing-guard, still standing uncertainly off to the side. "Wiltyn! Join me now, and you will be rewarded with more power than you could ever wish for."

"Don't do it, Wiltyn!" Erador shouted with every ounce of charisma he could muster. "He will stab you in the back to get what he wants, just like he did to Warlord Brynn."

Wiltyn nodded in agreement and brought a javelin to the ready; with that defection, Dryden had no choice but to flee. He looked over his shoulder, contemplating an escape into the dark recesses of the Jerackon Mountains, but that was no option: he had no knowledge of its twistings, and no way to make light. His only exit from the mountain was blocked by Erador, standing in front of him, stubborn and unyielding in the runic Onyx plate.

"You realize I must get past you," he said in an eerily calm voice as he withdrew the Sky Smith blade. Though it seemed he did not draw it *out* of its sheath so much as *through* its sheath. Where there should have been a length of sharpened steel stood only a silhouette of one, composed of dense, grey, swiftly-turning wisps, as if a miniature tornado stirred atop its hilt. Dryden admired its craftsmanship. "It's been a long time since I've wielded you, Tempest," he said to the sword.

As he waved it back and forth, the grey twisting wind would drag through the air, as if giving off trails of cloud. "You know that there is no armor that can protect you from a strike of the Tempest. It can pass through solid steel and still tear through the flesh beneath. Some would even say that this is the only blade that can pierce a God-Dragon's scales."

"It's a good thing I'm not wearing steel, then," Erador replied, undaunted.

Dryden took another step back. He knew Tempest didn't have the reach of the Onyx blade, but he doubted his inexperienced opponents could tell where it ended. Or at least they were unlikely to risk being wrong. But his retreat was feigned; he had a goal, and he achieved it—the nearest bags of mined treasure. He reached down and grasped the cinched openings of a pair of the gem-filled rucksacks. "Step aside and let me through, unless you care to see

Tempest in action," he said as he hefted the sacks over his shoulder. He now began to advance on the anxious teens.

With every step Dryden took forward, Erador took one nervous step backward, until he was standing once more directly in front of the cavern entrance. Then the Warlord stopped pressing the advance, surprised, as Wiltyn stepped to Erador's side. "I don't think the Sky Smith would make a weapon that could cut through his own armor," said Wiltyn with blind courage. He clamped his hand in a fist and beat upon the chest plate of his Sky Smith armor.

The logic stunned Dryden. "You're either very brave or very stupid, boy." He watched Carra out of the corner of one eye, not wishing to allow her where he could not observe her actions. "No, just stupid," the Warlord amended. "He certainly made a weapon that can cut through a helmet that isn't there."

Wiltyn blanched, but said, "I like brave better." He rolled his throwing shoulder back, and raised his other arm to head height as a shield. "Erador is right about you. It doesn't bother you a bit you're willing to kill all of us here and now. Even your *wing-guard*," he spat the title out as if it were a bite of spoiled flesh. "Even your *daughter*."

Dryden grimaced at the thought. *But the fool doesn't realize that it's not a question of what I'm willing to do; it's what I* must *do.*

Vynocent's voice, cold and tight, came from behind his left shoulder. "And if you're as good as you're trying to make us believe, you would've already done it, too." Dryden realized the twins now stood directly across from one another; they could see each other to coordinate, but he could only keep eyes on one at a time.

Next to Erador, Tysyra swayed as if in the beginning steps of a dance. It was no more than a shifting of her weight from leg to leg, but it was enough that her blade-tipped braid was already gaining momentum. Her long, serrated dagger was held in a reverse grip; her other hand was flipping a shorter, double-bladed knife. "So let's find out how good he really is, eh?" She seemed immune to fear.

Then Baltor, over Dryden's other shoulder, asked in an emotion-thickened growl: "Erador?" His throat was choked almost as much as the axe-handle he grasped. "So does that mean *Warlord* Dryden killed ev'ryone from Grondyr, too?"

Erador didn't respond. Neither did the Warlord.

"Father," Carra pleaded. "You are not as I remember you. What has happened to you? Why are you on this quest of destruction?"

"It is not a quest of destruction, but one of rebirth. Elkin were meant to rule all of Thornwall, not to be the defenders of the weak. Our fighting prowess is unparalleled, yet we live the life of guardians when we should be the ones dominating this world!"

He could tell that his words shook her to her core as tears broke out in her eyes. In a trembling voice, she said, "What you are saying is against everything the elkin stand for and pride themselves in. I cannot allow you to harm another soul."

Each tensed, awaiting the other to make the slightest move. In simultaneous acts, Dryden whipped his sword in circles high above his head and Carra stretched her arm toward her father. Gale-force gusts lifted debris from the cavern floor, while the ancient words tantalizing Carra with their untested potential drew numerous black veins to the surface of her arm. She felt the power surge within her, then she released it in a flash brighter and hotter than the white sun. As she did, Dryden's cyclonic conjuration discharged in an explosion of wind radiating outward from him in all directions.

Most of the elkin were flung back from the force of its gust, thrown to the floor or slammed against a cavern wall... though several managed to react in the brief instant in which standoff became battle. Baltor lunged as the cyclone was released, but could not reach his target through the buffeting; his axe only sheared through one of the rucksacks, spilling violet crystal all over the floor. Tysyra's off-hand knife flew toward the Warlord as she tumbled backward, but it veered away. Zimmerik's atlatl-driven javelin did better, striking home as he dove to the ground, recreating his attack on the Gorrotin, but it glanced harmlessly from the scale skirt of the Sky Smith armor. Erador and Wiltyn were lifted off their feet and well out of the cavern, landing in the snow far outside. Dryden cursed in a rage from his burning eyes. His tormented cry echoed throughout the Willow Cave.

***

Carra was dazed, though she could hear the sound of heavy footsteps accompanied by the jingle of a bag of crystals. She was unable to focus through the aftereffects of her spell, but it sounded as though Warlord Dryden, though blinded, staggered straight forward to the exit he knew he had been facing, then through it and out. Recovering from his conjuration and hers, none of the other elkin were able to stop him.

Moments later, Erador and Wiltyn reentered the cave, powdered snow stuck to their hair. "Where did he go?" Erador shouted.

"You just missed him," Carra called back as she struggled to her feet. "No need to chase after him, though."

"What! Why not?"

"Out in the unforgiving winter alone with no food or warmth? I think that may be the last we ever see of him."

Carra met his cold stare and read his eyes: *Don't you realize that I survived the unforgiving winter alone, without warmth?* She couldn't look at him any longer, ashamed that she didn't defend Erador, and could only imagine what he must have went through.

The tension in the room ebbed as everyone looked toward Erador in amazement for his bravery and everything he must have been through. He was the spitting image of his father, all dressed in the torren dog hide and Onyx plate. She could see that he welcomed their stares of admiration, though she realized that they didn't know the half of it.

Erador's clan mates each began to approach him to welcome him back, to apologize, and to offer him thanks. He cut them off with a dismissive wave of his hand, still steaming with rage from Warlord Dryden's escape. "We don't have time for that right now. We have to go after him and confirm his death! I must see the life drain from his eyes for what he's done!"

Baltor interjected, "But Tempest is too dangerous a weapon. How can ya fight against that?"

Baltor's words reminded Erador of the epiphany that came to him at Cerebus-Senti. "Carra, I need to talk to you about the Channeler's Staff. Now."

CHAPTER 17

"It's broken," Carra stated, staring at the Channeler's Staff lying on the cavern floor. She lifted the antler-fused column that formed the spine of the Staff. The antlers of all past Goma incantatory spell casters were warped and entangled together, spiraling and arching in a masterful weave. Tines thrust outward from various points on the Staff like the thorns on a rose stem. Carra inspected the area where Vorkus' antler rack once attached, noticing that it was a clean break.

"I can fuse it back on," she stated with certainty, "but I don't know if the Staff will work again."

"But it could still be working now," stated Erador. "In all the tales about the Father of Clan Wyndlyn, Vorkus never cast Goma incantations, so it should work without his antlers. Just give it a try."

Carra looked at Erador, intrigued by the possibility. "Hammynt and Abby, won't you come here a moment?" called Carra. They both approached. Little Abby stood half Hammynt's height, draped in a lengthy tunic that drooped below her knees. Hammynt's broken arm still rested in a makeshift sling.

Carra dropped down to one knee to face Abby. "This is your second lesson in incantations, but I'll keep it brief, okay?"

Abby nodded in approval, and Carra continued, "It is believed that when an incantation is cast through the congregation of soul-inhabited antlers along this Staff, that its effects can be magnified, even transformed." Carra got to her feet. "Hammynt, hold out your arm."

Hammynt gingerly removed the sling and held his arm out. Carra removed the bandages and splint from it. The forearm was swollen and discolored.

"I'm going to say these words aloud so that you can remember them. Without the Staff, this spell can turn light into heat. But with the Staff... I sure hope this works."

Carra ordered everyone to stand at a safe distance, then closed her eyes. So did Hammynt, but Abby couldn't look away. "Urma luktu sayir zo."

As soon as the words rolled off of Carra's tongue, black veins surged to the surface of her right arm—extending now from her fingertips almost to her elbow. Abby's eyes grew wide with alarm and she drew in a short gasp from the wicked sight of Carra's veins.

Carra could feel a vibration growing along the length of the staff, and she knew it was working and opened her eyes in excitement. The protruding tines seemed to draw in the light surrounding the staff and feed it upward toward its tip, where a glimmering, ribbon-like tongue of light snaked out from where Vorkus' antlers once stood. The ribbon coiled around Hammynt's swollen arm, encircling it, probing it. With a sudden tug and a snap, the beaming ribbon yanked itself tight and constricted Hammynt's forearm, jerking the broken bones back into place. He clenched his hand spasmodically as he cried in pain. Then the ribbon of light sank into his arm, seemingly absorbed by his skin. Carra's black veins subsided along with it. No one but Abby had been close enough to notice their appearance.

"Woah, that's warm," Hammynt said as he opened his eyes, relieved of the pain. The swelling in his arm began to condense and the discoloration started to fade. He flexed his arm back and forth, opened and closed his hand. "My arm feels great!" he said. Cheers and applause erupted around the room.

Carra spun toward Erador. "How did you know this would work?" she asked in fascination.

"The same way I know that this is going to work," Erador answered as he held up the metallic antlers that once crowned the Staff. "I still need you to fuse this to something."

"To what?"

Erador took a deep breath, then he removed his helm. Carra could see the severity in his cold, fatigued eyes. "To me," he stated.

All sound in the room came to a halt.

Erador slid the helm around the metallic antlers as he had done in Cerebus-Senti, and presented it out to Carra, demonstrating the perfect fit of one to the other. The empty eyes of the helm stared at her, as if pleading with her to do it. "I must carry his weight," Erador added, quoting the words of the Fates.

Gasps and whispers began all around the room. Carra was shocked; no words could escape her throat. She had no idea how to respond to such an insane request.

Erador continued, "I must remove my antlers myself, to prove to the Fates that this was a willful act." Everyone stood frozen in astonishment. They wanted to stop him, but they weren't sure what he might do if they tried. Erador had been through a lot, and perhaps had gone mad.

"Absolutely not!" Carra blurted. "For what purpose, Erador? Your soul would be forfeit to the Soul Smith!" Her voice was heavy with concern and stress.

Erador had anticipated objection. "For what purpose? Because I know your father is going to survive the harsh winter, the same way I have! Because to defeat him, we must find a way to fight against Tempest! Because I need to wield the full power of the Onyx armor to slay him! Because I swore to use its power to protect Clan Wyndlyn! Because being an elkin means that we have also sworn to protect the weak, from perils that they will never know. Because I believe that this is what the Fates were telling me. Because I don't want Dorgeeryn to have died in vain, and I don't want the world to suffer from our failure."

"Erador," Carra said, subdued. "This has never been done before."

"I'm quite aware of the risks that I face," he answered.

"Do you know what you ask of me? You've gone mad."

Erador gave a quick glance at the others. No one made a move to help him. "There is no choice. I must do this, for our elders, for Dorgeeryn, and for the clan," he said as he placed the massive surroyal antler rack of Vorkus upon the ground.

Erador raised one heavy gauntlet above his head and grasped one of his antlers, just above the pedicle. His eyes were burning in intensity as he stared deep into Carra's gaze. His second hand mirrored the first. He tested his grip around the base of his antlers. There was no way he could operate the heavy antler shears with one hand. He might have attempted a blind cut with both hands; in his impatience and frustration, he chose not to even try. Carra stepped back, while the rest of Clan Wyndlyn stood petrified from consternation, unable to move, or even blink, at the inconceivable act that was about to unfold before their eyes.

Erador took two deep breaths and deepened his stance; then with a thunderous roar be bore down on the antlers. His biceps and shoulders strained as he pulled downward. The veins rose to the surface of his temples and neck; his face turned a deep red; his eyeballs began to bulge. He let loose a primal scream; the cavern bellowed back echoes. Strands of saliva flew from teeth and lips. His entire body shook as the mounting tension in his muscles sought release.

His screams ended abruptly when, with an authoritative snap, the dead bone of both antlers broke off at the pedicle. Erador collapsed to his knees.

Only his heaving breath broke the silence that followed.

Erador stared in bewilderment at his own antlers in his hands. Still struggling to catch his breath, he raised his head until he could see Carra standing before him, a horrified look upon her face. He felt numb, almost drunk. "Do it," Erador slurred. "Do it now. Fuse his antlers…"

Before Erador could finish his sentence, Tysyra rushed forward to stop him from collapsing. "Someone help! Don't just stand there. Hold Vorkus' antlers steady against his head. Carra! Do it!" she yelled.

Erador's eyelids became heavy, his muscles began to relax of their own accord, and his antlers clattered from his hands to the ground. Erador could feel his body shutting down from pain and fatigue.

He felt arms struggling to hold him up. He saw Carra's face, he heard voices shouting, he felt someone pressing their hands against his cheeks. The sounds that reached his ears were distorted and fuzzy. His eyes fell shut, but someone slapped his face a couple times and he reopened them. He could see a hedge of feet around him, but the numbness was overtaking him, swallowing him down. The last thing he saw was a wave of light enfolding him before he fell limp to the floor.

***

Erador awoke standing in an endless, featureless blackness, all alone. There were no sights or smells, only silence. He looked down at his rugged hands, callused and dry. He realized that he wasn't wearing the Onyx armor anymore; he was clad in clothes as if it were a summer day. "Is this another one of my nightmares?" he asked aloud. His voice echoed as if he were within a tunnel. He tried to remember how he got here.

He remembered trying to remove his antlers…

He hesitated as he brought his hands up to his head, stricken with fear that he might find nothing. He raised his hands higher and he felt the familiar texture of cold steel. Erador began to smile. "It worked!"

"But where am I?" Erador spun around to look for anything, but there was only emptiness. Then he spun again, surprised to see a massive elkin standing before him. He was shirtless, with rippling muscles, wide shoulders, and many battle scars. He stood about a head taller than Erador.

Erador looked up at him; his face was rugged, with a staunch neck and defined jaw. His features seemed sculpted, while his eyes shone with a bright white light. Upon his head were the same metallic antlers—the ones Erador had seen all his life atop the Channeler's Staff. The ones his hands told him were now upon his own head. All of a sudden, Erador felt very conscious of his young age.

"Are you—?"

"Vorkus Wyndlyn," said the towering elkin. His voice seemed god-like in the echo of this strange room.

"Then where are we?" asked Erador. "Am I dead?"

"Our two souls now occupy your body as a vessel," answered Vorkus' booming voice.

Erador showed a hint of a smile. *I was right,* he thought. *This is it. I'm going to learn to wield the powers locked within the Onyx armor.* Out of respect, Erador took to one knee, as he gathered the courage to address this legend. "Warlord Vorkus, I am Erador, son of the late Warlord Brynn, entrusted protector of the clan that bears your name. I have gone great lengths to ensure the survival of our clan, though a traitor in our midst has murdered my father and our other elders. I stand before you, humbled, to seek your help, and ask your service, for your wisdom and skill shall allow us to bring vengeance upon the traitorous Warlord Dryden."

The intimidating mass of muscle before him seemed pleasantly amused by Erador's respectful request. "Tell me more about this Warlord Dryden."

The words had a soothing tone to Erador's ear, to know that all his efforts weren't for naught. He rose, stood tall, empowered, full of tenacity, and spoke with conviction as he told the story. He told of the petrified jungle, the merger with Clan Grondyr, the blast, the Soul Smith's demons, communing with the Fates, all of it, from the beginning. His words poured out of him like a river breaking a dam, and Vorkus was all ears.

"I see truth in you, young Erador. Therefore, I shall honor your request for the loyalty you have shown to your clan and the troubles that you have overcome. I vow to ensure that Tempest and Warlord Dryden are defeated," stated Vorkus, his voice dark and fearful. "In addition, I shall seek an answer from Clan Hortyr, for their unwarranted abandonment of their duty."

For Erador, all of this was almost too good to be true, to know that revenge was so close. "So you're going to teach me how to read the runes?" asked Erador, full of hope.

"No," answered the god-like voice of Vorkus. "Within a vessel, there is only room for one."

Then the towering elkin took a step forward and punched Erador across the jaw with a force as strong as the swing of a club. Erador reeled, stunned and all but senseless. He felt drained of energy, tired from his sleepless trek across the tundra to the Willow Cave.

This must be one of my nightmares, he thought. Vorkus pressed the advance, and swung again. Erador managed to catch the swing, but Vorkus kneed him in the gut, and Erador bent over, clutching his stomach, the breath knocked out of him. Then Vorkus' heavy fist slugged him straight in the temple, and the darkness enfolded him completely.

***

Carra, Tysyra, Baltor, Hammynt, Gressyn, Vynocent, Wiltyn, Zimmerik, and the four children stood in a circle around Erador's body, staring at him as he lay on the floor. Carra had succeeded: the antlers were now fused to his skull. They all watched in captivated silence. They could not even guess at what ought to happen next.

Beads of sweat formed on Erador's brow, his mouth made the slightest of movements, as if speaking the faintest whisper. This continued for some time, then without warning he spasmed and rolled over. Everyone took a step back. Then Erador curled inward, clutching his stomach. Just as Tysyra moved to tend him, Erador woke up. His eyes snapped open, emanating a white glow; they did not appear to be his own. He began to get up to his feet.

"Erador?" asked Tysyra. The massive antlers made him look like a different person, more mature, older. Far older.

"No. I am Vorkus Wyndlyn, the first of my kind, the Chosen Champion of Brikken the Onyx Smith, Wearer of the Onyx plate, Wielder of Wraith, Warlord of the West, and defender of its inhabitants." The voice that came out of Erador was deep and wise… and not Erador's.

Carra stepped forward anxiously. She was starting to believe this really was Vorkus. "Warlord Vorkus, allow me to introduce us—"

"I know who you all are," he interjected. "Erador has told me about you… and what you have done," he said with finality. Worried glances passed among the youths, wondering what Erador had told him.

Warlord Vorkus turned to look around at his surroundings. "Ahh, the Cave of the Blacksmiths." His voice bespoke familiarity and comfort.

The other elkin huddled around Carra and began whispering in panic, while he was preoccupied. "What does he mean he's Vorkus?"

"Is this some kind of a trick?"

"What happened to Erador?"

"Why did he call this place 'Cave of the Blacksmiths?'"

"Shh, I don't know," answered Carra. "Just be quiet, let me think."

Warlord Vorkus turned and looked at the small gathering of young elkin. His gaze stopped on Wiltyn, and his expression turned to disgust and disdain. "You. Why do you wear the Armor of Akai, adversary to my Lord Brikken? Explain yourself," he said with contempt.

Wiltyn looked down at the clouded glass armor of the Sky Smith, and then looked back up in alarm. "Warlord Vorkus, I mean no offense. I was instructed to put this on when I was the wing-guard of Warlord Dryden. He has a full set just like this one, but now he's the man we're after—"

"Yes, Erador told me about him as well," Warlord Vorkus cut him off. "Erador pleaded for my help and I have vowed to assist him. So, where is Dryden now?"

"He mentioned that he was heading home," said one of the teens.

"South. To the stone jungle of Chyxurlgon," said another.

"But he said he would make stops along the way, to spend our wealth in some of the human towns. Since he took one rucksack of crystal, I'm sure he still intends to, though we don't know where," finished Carra.

Warlord Vorkus took a moment to consider. "What supplies do we require?" he asked.

"We have no food, and no charcoal for warmth," stated Carra.

"We don't have the strength to carry all the crystal rucksacks either," commented Vynocent.

"But weapons and shields we got plenty of," added Baltor.

With a grunt and a contemptuous scowl, staring at his audience with his glowing eyes, Warlord Vorkus issued his commands. The confidence in his voice rang throughout the cavern and stiffened the youths standing before him. "Our strength is limited by our numbers, and only eight of you are capable fighters." He glanced at the purple crystals scattered on the floor, then over to the improvised rucksacks. "Though the minerals that the humans trade for shall be used to our advantage, thus the four children will be of use as well."

He began pacing back and forth, thinking as he spoke, "I count thirty-five rucksacks here. We shall only bring enough crystal to purchase shelter and food, plus mules and charcoal. Once procured, the children will escort the mules back to this cave to load the remaining rucksacks to haul the crystal back into town. Meanwhile, I must find a way to speak to the human leader. He must be warned that Beknen Valley is now unguarded."

Everyone was shocked. They couldn't believe it when Warlord Dryden had said Clan Hortyr had abandoned post, but now it became all too real. The Soul Smith's demons could flood the land, unchecked and unchallenged. "I hope the humans are more capable warriors than I remember," The ancient Warlord's voice indicated low expectations in this regard.

Warlord Vorkus contemplated his Onyx armor, frowning at its putrid smell. "So pack with haste. I shall see to supplying our needs along the way. But first, I shall require a bath or my scent will attract unwanted attention."

He walked tall and confident to the hot springs. The rest of Clan Wyndlyn finished preparations already half-complete from having just transported the bulk of their remaining supplies from the crystal cave. Carra turned to watch Warlord Vorkus doff the torren dog hide and then wade into the warm pool, fully armored. He submerged himself for a quick moment, and then began unbuckling and unlatching the armor one piece at a time. Once it was all detached, he began scrubbing it with care, cleansing it of the vyceptor blood.

Carra wore her elegant pelt of a dire snow leopard. Soft and delicate, its fur was as white as a lotus flower, though speckled with dark spots; it was easy to conceal against the snow. It had been a gift from her father, but now she wished it didn't remind her of him. She approached Warlord Vorkus as he had finished bathing, and began donning the Onyx armor once more.

"Warlord Vorkus, what did you mean when you said we will use the crystals to our advantage? Why must we make a return trip for it?"

"We shall purchase swords for hire to supplement our numbers; possibly war beasts, if it comes to that."

"But Warlord Dryden is one man. Now with you and your knowledge of the runes, even our small retinue can handle him... can't it?"

"Not if he is in league with Clan Hortyr, as Erador suspected."

CHAPTER 18

Erador had arrived beneath a brilliantly white morning sun already threatened with a new storm front from the west. The last few precious hours of calm were lost by the time Clan Wyndlyn was able to depart, trading the familiar warmth of the cave for the unforgiving chill of renewed blizzard. They departed with a sense of determination, carrying dreams of vengeance and hopes of revenge fresh in their minds; nothing was more important than to seek out the justice that was due. The snowy tundra was dull, monotonous white; the blanket of snow was so seamless that it was difficult to notice edges in the landscape. They marched southward, paralleling the Jerackon Mountain range, a landmark difficult to miss even in a whiteout. There were no trails, no tracks to follow, only fresh powdered snow whirling and piling in drifts atop densely-packed older falls. They had left with almost no food, nor means of fueling a fire. They had brought three rucksacks full of crystals with them, enough to buy all the food they could ever dream of… provided that they get there alive. They would, at the very least, need to stay warm if they were to survive the journey; spare bear hides constituted the bulk of their burdens. Their fur wrappings could keep them warm only as long as they remained moving, while they had the energy to brave the blizzard; without food, they knew they couldn't keep it up for long.

They had also left the familiar cavern with a new unfamiliar friend leading the way. He called himself Warlord Vorkus, but it was difficult for the clan to acclimate to the difference, since he wore Erador's skin. The adolescents had been through a lot at the Willow Cave, surviving experiences that would have turned them into adults by other societal standards, but not elkin, for they were not yet adults by age. Those experiences shaped them, molded them into their true selves; now they found themselves leaving all that they knew, casting it all to the wind in the desperate ambition of staying Warlord Dryden's malevolence, pursuing him through the blizzard out of sheer will to see him pay for his actions. They risked much, but they had already lost greater. The Clan Wyndlyn heritage and secrets were forever lost to them, but the adolescents knew that Warlord Vorkus gave them a window to their past. So they walked in the footsteps of the elkin who wielded Herlidrek's spiked shield, who wore the Onyx Smith armor… and who wore their friend's body. The heavy, whirling snowfall cast an obscuring haze across their vision the same way the fierce howl of the wind drowned their ears. Carra would have been invisible in her dire snow leopard fur were it not for the Channeler's Staff.

He drove them forward without rest, their stomachs grumbling as they marched. After a time they could not measure—apart from knowing night could not be too far off—they discovered a small valley with a narrow opening, wedged between two large jutting ridges that ruptured the edges of the thick storm clouds, preventing them from coalescing. It was peaceful here, almost serene—a tranquil zone amidst the storm where its rage had relented, even if for but a moment, as if a break had been offered them by unseen hands. The dense, angry cloud banks swarmed the mountain range beyond the ridges, concealing the peaks from view. Clan Wyndlyn did not hesitate to take advantage of this halcyon breezeway that cut through the Jerackon Mountain range and the storm.

Warlord Vorkus led them to the fast-flowing river which carved the valley from the looming rock. It wasn't wide by any means, and looked to be only waist deep where they met it, but its pace had kept it ice-free. More, the valley walls had kept much of the ground free of heavy snow; in some places there was almost none at all. Patches of grass and various species of brush seemed to flourish here. He called a halt, and the elkin located a smattering of tall grasses along the snow-padded riverbank, brushed it clear and dropped down upon it. He waded into the river until he stood knee deep in ice-cold water. The others weren't even curious to know what he was doing, just content with resting their feet.

It was not too long, though, before Zimmerik began to lose his patience. "Why aren't we moving? We should be keeping pace if we are to catch Dryden by surprise!" he complained.

Warlord Vorkus did not respond, and no one else cared to take up the question. After another period of silence, he thrust his arm into the river and tossed a two-foot spotted salmon onto the land. Then another. And another. Everyone grasped at the flopping fish before they could escape back into the river.

Warlord Vorkus spoke with a commanding voice as he plodded back onto the land. "Need I remind you that we don't know where he is headed? Without sustenance, we wouldn't have the energy to fight him, even *if* we happened to be right on his heels. We will cook, camp, and rest. We still have much to prepare." Their stomachs acceded, and Clan Wyndlyn made camp.

The elkin chose a spot where the river had undercut a rock shelf in the past, where they would still have at least some shelter even if the wind turned and came up the valley, or the clouds overcame the resistance of the ridges. Gathering kindling and tinder from the brush were no problems here, even if the green wood was reluctant to catch at first. They lit their kindling from the sparks of their flint and steel, then slowly fed it progressively larger branches.

A water-logged branch the river had swept down from some upland tree, more than enough to feed the fire an entire night, remained obstinate, until Carra finally said, "Allow me. Abby, come watch." She first cut off a hand-span with a hatchet and laid it aside, then placed the Channeler's Staff lengthwise along the remainder of the branch and muttered some things only Abby could hear. The log emitted thick wafts of steam for several minutes, often popping and splitting along its sides. After Carra was satisfied, she turned the log over to the others to be chopped up and added to the fire. She took the piece she'd cut and walked a distance from the camp with Abby in tow, explaining something as they went. The chunk of branch was placed upon a stone near the river, then Carra and Abby returned. Carra was saying, "...told you *why* we dry wood from the outside in, but seeing is better than hearing." Carra pointed the Channeler's Staff at the wood and said the same words she'd said before. The result, magnified by the narrow valley, sounded like the bole of an ancient oak snapping. Brush and grass a dozen paces to either side jerked as splinters flew through them. Only a couple fragments of wood remained where she'd set the piece down. "And that's why I made sure the cut end was pointed our direction, too. I couldn't have done that at this distance without the Staff... but I *could* have done it when it was right at our feet, if I hadn't been careful to move the heat in slowly from the outside." Abby nodded solemnly, eyes huge. When Carra sat down at the fire and looked around, she noticed Abby's weren't the only ones.

One pair definitely wasn't. Even the Onyx helm did not conceal Warlord Vorkus' smile.

The cooked salmon was worth every bit of the effort.

Later, they burned pin weeble leaves, a yellow leaf much like any other, but giving off a curious scent in the fire. Warlord Vorkus explained: "The scent of burning pin weeble leaves drives animals to run away. It's the Gaia Smith's way to warn Her forest creatures from any of the Scorch Smith's wildfires before they can even see the flame, giving them a chance to flee before it is too late."

The clan was amazed. They wondered if this was something they may have learned from their elders upon their twentieth soul-keep, or if this was indeed a survival technique forgotten in time, much like the language of the Blacksmiths. Despite the protection it provided their encampment from the wild, there were always thieves to worry about, even out here in the winter. When one of the teens observed that the ongoing blizzard made those unlikely, Warlord Vorkus pointed out, "Unless, of course, the thieves know of the shelter this valley affords. The men who stole the antlers from Erador must have come from somewhere, and must have gone somewhere." The others nodded, cowed at having overlooked the obvious—and disturbed at him referring to their friend as if Erador were someone he had nothing to do with. "I'll take the first watch," he finished.

***

Carra awoke hours later to a cold gauntlet grasping her shoulder. "Wake up," she heard a voice whisper. She rolled, startled that someone might have snuck up while they slept. Wasn't someone supposed to be on watch? "Carra, it's only me. Erador."

She blinked a few times to allow her vision to awaken. She scrunched her brow and searched his eyes. She could tell: the light had receded, and Erador had returned. She lunged forward to hug him. "Erador, I had thought you had died inside," she exclaimed with joy.

"Died?" questioned Erador, puzzled. "What do you mean? I fell asleep in the cavern and awoke here. How did we get here?"

Carra's eyes glanced upward toward his metallic antler rack and back. "Erador, you were Vorkus. You led us from the cave after my fa—Warlord Dryden. You taught us things that you could not have known."

Erador seemed to drift into deep thought, as if trying to recollect a dream. "No, it can't be. The Fates. They said..."

Carra rubbed her eyes, trying to erase the last traces of sleep so she could think. "Go put another log on the fire while I try to figure this out." She sat up, drawing her layers of blankets around her.

Erador hunted up the pile of spare wood in the light of a dying, flickering flame. When he sat back down next to her, Carra continued, keeping her voice low so as not to awake the others. "You don't remember anything? What was it like? Try to remember, think back, see if you can recall anything."

Erador sat watching the flames dance around the new log. "I seem to remember talking to Vorkus, but all the details are eluding me."

Carra thought a moment as a sudden realization intrigued her. "Erador, you haven't slept at all. You were—that is, Vorkus was—standing watch. Aren't you tired?"

He shook his head once, with a smirk that challenged the intelligence of her question. "I feel like I've been asleep for half a day. I feel great."

She looked at him up and down, amazed. "Your body has been awake ever since you returned to the clan at the Willow Cave... I guess only the soul needs to sleep."

"What is that curious smell?" Erador pondered aloud. The scent was sweet, but had a tinge of vinegar to it and it seemed to be originating from the fire. It was as if the smell evoked a memory locked within his mind. "Wait. I remember something!" shouted Erador, ignoring her last statement. "I remember being in a fight. I think I fought Vorkus... But, why did I fight him when I need his help?"

Vivid memories flashed through Carra's mind: images of the metallic antlers glimmering and radiating with light after being fused to his head, of Erador writhing in pain on the ground, of witnessing Vorkus' consciousness emerge within Erador's eyes. "Erador, I think I understand what's happening to you. Since you and Vorkus now share your body, he is in all likelihood fighting you for control. You mustn't struggle over which soul controls your body, you must learn to work with him. If you keep fighting him… one of you might die."

Erador removed his helmet, and lifted one hand to massage his scalp around the base of his new antlers. He nodded in concurrence. "I seem to remember him telling me that there can only be room for one." His tone was stern; his words suggested a grim outcome, one few would dare to contemplate. Erador stood up, the light from the flame flickered against his dark Onyx plate. Carra dropped her head in concern as she mulled Erador's statement. He attempted to alleviate her despondency by changing the subject. "So where are we headed? Any news of Warlord Dryden?"

Carra shook her head. "We're traveling south. Vorkus claimed to know the way to a small human farm village. We're looking for some mules so some of us can take them back to grab the rest of the crystal."

Erador snorted. "What are we going to use all that crystal for?"

Carra took a breath to answer, then hesitated as her thoughts shifted toward the root of the problem. "Erador, the last thing Vorkus said to me in the cavern was that you suspected Warlord Dryden of working with Clan Hortyr. Is this true?"

"I don't suspect; I know. They were in league with each other, and they must have been collaborating for a while. He confirmed as much when he said he knew Clan Hortyr had abandoned Remaurus-Senti. The walls of our Armory were toppled over, and whatever was inside had been taken," stated Erador.

"Well, my father couldn't have stolen whatever was within the Armory. He wasn't carrying anything," said Carra, though she did not understand why she defended her father now. Her voice had risen, careless to those she *thought* were sleeping around her. The rest of the clan were motionless with the exception of opening their eyes. They were awake but had kept still, eavesdropping on their ongoing conversation.

"Except his travel bag. We don't know what was inside the Armory; it could have been small," exclaimed Erador.

Carra remembered seeing her father sleeping with his arm around his travel pack inside the crystalline room, as if guarding it. "Maybe," said Carra with reluctance. "Or Clan Hortyr could have taken it."

"Either way, they are working together. If Clan Hortyr did take it, it was some part of your father's plan." Erador could see the uncertainty in Carra's thoughts. "I need to be able to count on you in the battle against your father. We must be swift and without mercy if we are to best Warlord Dryden in battle. I can't afford any *more* hesitations out of you," accused Erador.

"What do you mean by that?" snapped Carra.

"It's curious how Warlord Dryden was able to conjure an entire tornado before you could blind him with a flash of light."

Carra's blood began to boil. "That's because—"

"Because he's your father!" shouted Erador, concluding Carra's sentence. There was a long moment of silence as they stared at each other, until she dropped her eyes, giving in to the truth. He began again in a calmer tone. "I know your father's betrayal is difficult to believe after you've known him for so long. But he is not that person anymore. You saw his defiance in the cave, you know of his treachery. He is not the same, and there isn't any piece of his former self remaining. You needn't defend him any longer. Your father seems arrogant, but not stupid. If he senses the slightest doubt in your commitment, he'll use it against you. And if he suspects that we are following him, then he will doubtless try to strengthen his numbers by meeting up with Clan Hortyr."

Carra let his words sink in before she began to answer Erador's original question. "Warlord Vorkus wanted to use the crystal to hire mercenaries and beasts if it came to a battle against Clan Hortyr. He also said he wanted to speak to the human leader, to warn them of—"

"The Soul Smith's demons," Erador concluded, finishing her sentence. "I'm aware. They go unchallenged and are free to roam the countryside. There were numerous vyceptors in the area already. We must get a move on. Wake everyone up, and let them know of everything we have spoken about."

"No need," said a voice.

***

Erador and Carra turned to see who had spoken. Zimmerik sat up. "We're already awake, and we heard it all. It's good to have you back Erador. We can't imagine the weight you must be shouldering with another soul inside you." Zimmerik got his feet.

"It's nothing, really," said Erador, rising as well.

"You're wrong. It's a huge deal because you did it for us. You did it even when we tried to hold you back, because you knew…" His voice trailed off, but he kept his gaze locked onto Erador's eyes for a brief moment, until he bowed his head and then knelt before Erador. "I will be the first to admit that you have not committed one selfish act. Everything you have done has been to protect us, at a great personal sacrifice to yourself. I'm sorry I didn't speak out on your behalf before your banishment. I should have gone with you, but I promise that I shall never leave your side again. I trust your judgment and your leadership with my life. I am proud to be serving under your command."

One by one, the other members of Clan Wyndlyn began kneeling before him, acknowledging his leadership. They bowed their heads to show their antlers to him, the elkin's highest sign of respect. All Erador could think was how proud his father would have been of him if he could have witnessed this moment. "Zimmerik," he said, "you are a good friend and an even better hunter. I can think of no one better to have at my side in battle. Join me as my wing-guard once more."

Zimmerik's words were as strong as iron. "I accept." Erador offered his hand, and they grasped each other's forearm to bind their contract. "Were it not that you must wait until the day of your twentieth soul-keep, when you ascend to adulthood, before you can bear the title of Warlord, I would call you that now," added Zimmerik. "That's not far out from now is it?"

"Not far at all," answered Erador with a smile.

Each elkin in turn welcomed Erador back. Wiltyn even offered to return the Sky Smith armor to Zimmerik, but he declined.

"The last time I wore it was during the loss against the gremlins. I think it may be a bad omen for me."

Tysyra approached Erador last, standing close and speaking quietly so the others would not hear. "I'm glad you returned to the cave when you did," she said in her sweetest voice. "We needed you."

Erador cracked an awkward smile.

"Who knows what Warlord Dryden would have done to us if it weren't for you."

Erador didn't know how to reply. Then Tysyra kissed him on the cheek. "I owe my life to you," she said. She returned to her place by the fire, leaving Erador a bit flustered.

While all of them were eager to rejoin the pursuit, only Erador felt rested. He seemed ready to assert his right to their newly-sworn obedience, but Carra cut him off. She pointed into the featureless darkness in the direction the valley's narrow opening, beyond which the winds could still be heard howling. "I'll be happy to follow you as long as you can see where you're going. But I can't light up the entire tundra, and I won't be able to do much of anything if I'm short on sleep all the time." Then, more gently, she added, "We'll all travel faster if we're rested." With obvious reluctance, he acceded. He went to the edge of the fire's light and stared into the blackness; the others settled back down, talking quietly amongst themselves or drifting back off to sleep.

Erador roused them at the first hint of dawn, and they broke camp without discussion. The clan continued its march south. The wind had fallen off in the early morning hours, yet it was still bitterly cold. Though the loose-packed snow was inches deeper than it had been before they camped and continued to fall, they made good time. Erador's return seemed to give them new vigor, and at first it was the talk of the trip, though the four youths couldn't quite grasp the concept of two souls in one vessel. Soon, however, that topic was exhausted—the more so because Erador was unwilling to contribute—and everyone turned to speculating whether Warlord Dryden could have survived on his own. They expressed hopes that venomous snow snakes had bit into his ankle, or that a stealthy glacial bat might have snatched him away into the sky, or that the bitter cold gradually immobilized his armor and then froze him to death. They kept telling tales of all the ways that could have brought death upon him, each one more gruesome than the last. The stories became alive in their minds, to the point where they took hold of their imaginations, convincing them that the likelihood of his survival was slim. After all, he was no native to this environment.

The high, rocky peaks of the northern stretch of the Jerackon Mountain range slowly transitioned to ones bearing heavy, snow-shrouded forest. The elkin walked with the river on their left, sticking to a ridge line that separated it from the rest of the tundra, where they could keep it within sight at all times—at least when the snow allowed them to, though this became more frequent as the day advanced.

Hammynt came up to Erador around midday, by which time only isolated flurries remained. "Erador, how will we know where to go when we don't have the mountains as a guide?" he asked.

Erador hadn't thought that far ahead, and now everyone was depending on him to come up with the answers. He wasn't a day into his new position, and he was already under pressure. He spent a moment taking in his surroundings. The ridge line was continuing to diminish, though it still ran as far up ahead as he could see. The cloud-covered sky had remained unchanging all day. The river flowed to his one side, with the mountains rising shortly beyond it, fast-falling streams swelling it to where it would already be hazardous to attempt any crossing. To his other side, only an occasional tree broke up the empty great expanse of land stretching without horizon. *Well, we can't just stop. We have to keep moving like the river or we'll freeze,* he thought.

Finally, Erador answered his friend, "It doesn't look like we're going to need to worry about that today. Our bigger concern will be finding a decent place to camp. Keep an eye out once it starts getting later."

"Don't suppose you'll be able to catch us some more fish with your bare hands?" Hammynt asked lightly.

Erador looked at him in surprise. Then he looked down at his plodding feet, anxious and glum.

"Sorry. Shouldn't have mentioned that." Hammynt looked away.

"No, it's okay. Something I have to get used to, that's all." Then he looked up and smiled. "Actually, that gives me an idea."

"Really?"

"You'll find out."

The clouds began to thin late in the day and the snow stopped; the price was the temperature dropping farther still and the wind rising once more. Erador called a halt while there was still plenty of light—which surprised the others. But he'd been looking for something specific, and had found it: a place where the river bed dropped enough to create shallows. As luck would have it, there were a couple scrubby trees within easy walking distance; he turned Baltor loose on those. Then he summoned his wing-guard.

Zimmerik came up to him—and almost took a step back when he caught sight of the grin on Erador's face. He wondered if Warlord Vorkus had returned. "Uh... Erador?"

Erador gestured toward the river. "I have a problem that requires your... finesse." He leaned a bit on the final word.

"My—?"

"With the javelin. I understand not all problems can be solved by strength."

Zimmerik stared at him, then shook his head and looked at the river. "You know, that looks awfully cold..."

"Does, doesn't it?" Erador chuckled.

"You're enjoying this."

"We'll both enjoy eating even more." He slapped his friend on the back, then went off to see about arranging the camp so they'd be out of the wind as much as possible.

Half an hour later, Zimmerik came back from the river with a pair of fish, each large enough to provide the clan a decent meal by itself, while the others were still getting a fire started. They'd have something to eat the next day. Even though Erador had arrived with an extra pack full of trail food, their reserves were dwindling rapidly as they struggled to maintain their strength for the journey.

Most of the clan were quick to forget about the absence of Warlord Vorkus, except for Carra, who kept a close watch on Erador. She was curious to see how long before Vorkus would try to regain control. She knew that Erador had maintained control over his body from the time he had awakened her early in the morning. She even volunteered to take a watch shift as the clan huddled together to share body heat, so that she could take special notice of Erador as he slept, though she could not watch him the entire night, needing sleep herself. Despite him seeming to have nightmares, he awoke the next morning untroubled and unperturbed. Still, she knew she needed to continue to observe him closely.

They rose before dawn; Erador had left orders for the watch to wake them if the sky cleared enough they could travel by moonlight. Which it did. They set off in a biting wind, but Erador knew their bigger danger was in running out of food. Apart from the fish left from the night before, they were out of reserves.

As they trudged on through the dawn and into the day, it began to seem to the elkin that the tundra was making a long, gradual descent the farther south they went. By the time the sun was falling, they had become certain of it: while it was not obvious looking forward, when they faced the way they'd come the rise was evident.

The next day was little different, including the early start. The land continued to drop in elevation as they went south. And the slope down to it from the ridge they walked upon was becoming longer as a result. Erador didn't want to surrender the river's sure guidance until he had to, but also didn't want to reach a point where they were obliged to descend a dangerous snow- and ice-covered slope or else be forced to backtrack. Worse, clouds began to gather ahead of them as the day went. They rose dark and massive on the horizon, threatening heavy rain or even heavier snow. In the distance, not yet engulfed by the clouds, they could make out what appeared to be the end of the mountain range, still far off but almost certainly within range of the morrow's march. Erador fretted about what they'd do then, but kept his concerns to himself.

The only food they had that night was a pair of rabbits from a burrow Gressyn chanced upon near their camp site. They split one of them between the four children, who needed it the most. The teens got about two bites each from the other.

An hour after dawn the next day—three hours after they'd resumed their trek—part of Erador's decision was made for him. The river turned a corner and headed east, drifting further and further away from them as it plunged into a non-traversable canyon. The mountains continued, though there was now no longer any question they'd soon end. With no more need to keep to the ridge line, the clan left it for the level of the still-descending tundra. In front of them the storm clouds loomed gargantuan and ominous.

Within another hour, the storm engulfed them. It seemed only steps between the first swarming flakes and getting hammered in their faces with the heaviest, wettest snow they'd ever endured in their lives. They'd become so used to the numbing temperatures of the past days that what met them now felt like a sudden onset of spring. Erador brought them to a halt long enough for them to tie themselves together with ropes around their waists. Inches of fresh snow already concealed what lay beneath; if that became ice before the transition point where it melted away, they'd need the security.

It did not, and while the slush they found instead was almost as bad, it soon washed away under the torrential downpour. The Flood Smith's rain came down in globules heavy enough to be painful. Even through coatings of oil, their fur coverings soon became drenched. They pressed on in sodden misery, trading slush for mud before reaching a point where the rain began to subside.

Here at least they began to encounter vegetation once more, even if much of it was pummeled flat. When they discovered some heavy bushes whose lower branches were still full of fresh berries, they decided to setup camp. Each berry was formed by a cluster of multiple black drupelets. The ripe juicy flavor burst in their mouths, making them crave more. They almost stripped the bushes bare before their stomachs were content.

No longer needing triple layers of fur blankets to insulate themselves from the cold, they unrolled the wettest ones and draped them over the bushes so they could have a covered space beneath in which to sleep shielded from the rain… if far from dry.

The elkin awoke to a damp and gloomy morning air that seemed to sit still across the land. The fog was so heavy they could almost stir it with their hands. They stripped the last few berries from the bushes and wrung what dampness they could from their furs. Without the river, with the mountains concealed by fog and the sun by the overcast sky they had no obvious natural landmarks left to guide them.

"Which way now?" asked Gressyn, searching the area for any clues.

"Downhill?" suggested Vynocent.

"Not much of a slope here."

"Tell the water that."

Erador agreed. "He's right. We go that way"—he pointed the direction opposite the one he reckoned they had approached the bushes—"until we hit a stream, follow it until the fog lifts. With luck, we'll be able to see the mountains then well enough to keep them at our backs. In the meantime, we'll still be moving."

The land continued to descend, and as predicted the elkin soon came across a stream, running through thick grasses, stout shrubs, and a plethora of leafy plants of all descriptions, most of which neither northern nor southern elkin could identify. Their stomachs would have been pleased for it to be otherwise, though in truth elkin ate little that was not flesh, and usually only at need. On any day they were well-fed, they would have plucked no more than a handful of berries as a treat, not stripped whole bushes as they had the night before.

Some hours later the stream they followed made a clear bend westward. By then, the overcast had lifted enough that they could see the end of the mountain range; they chose to put it at their backs rather than risk being diverted from their course... for as long as it would help them. Which would not be much longer, unless the clouds cleared off altogether, and not long at all if they became heavier.

It began to appear that they were. Between the clan's progress and the weather, what they could see of the mountains dwindled steadily. Worse, the ground they walked became damper, and grass and leaf held droplets signifying recent showers. A moist breeze was blowing from the southwest, not quite in their faces. They hoped it would be enough to keep any heavier rain from catching them from behind.

It was past midday when Hammynt hollered for everyone to halt. He turned in place, sniffing the air. "Do you smell that? Zimmerik?"

The clan's only Fates-chosen hunter copied Hammynt's actions. "Yeah. Animals. Big ones."

"Or lots of little ones," jibed Vynocent.

"Half the rabbits in Thornwall couldn't pile that much dung in one spot," Zimmerik replied. A couple of the others laughed and wondered out loud how much he knew about rabbits if he believed that.

Hammynt seconded him. "That's more like our goats after they've been penned up a few days. Though that's not goats…" He fairly danced with excitement. "I can't wait to get there to see what beasts they have tamed."

"Though not torren dogs. No one has tamed them," hollered Vynocent.

"Why is it that you have such an affection for animals, Hammynt? Were you a wolf in your past life?" teased Carra.

"By the looks of his unkempt hair, I'd say so," seconded Gressyn. He pulled out his milky white comb, made of bone, and offered it to Hammynt as guffaws burst amongst them all.

Hammynt waved it away. "No; it's due to my battle advisor—Klycik. He told me how the humans use beasts to amplify their effectiveness in combat. They ride horses to increase their speed, they used ospreys to watch over their flanks, and use dire arachnids to place blockades of webs. Some were tamed by hand, others by some Gaia Smith charm. Klycik said that animal training is one of the humans' strongest disciplines, and that there is something to be learned from it. The variations of utility in battle from one beast to the next are too numerous to count. He opened my eyes that day, and I've longed for the opportunity to see how beasts can improve *our* fighting prowess."

His wisdom lingered in the air until Zimmerik spoke up. "It couldn't improve by much. Races across Thornwall already fear the day that they find themselves standing against an army of elkin. We come from a long line of hunter-warriors and carry the blood of the Radiant Smith in our veins! Never mind ever facing one of our Warlords on the battlefield. They command the clan with unparalleled strategy and are regarded as the most skilled at their craft!"

Carra shook her head. "No one fears facing an army of elkin, Zimmerik—because there aren't enough of us in the world to *make* an army. You haven't seen the human lands yet. We number warriors by the dozen; they number them in hundreds—sometimes thousands, when their kingdoms hurl themselves at one other. We're good… but we're not that good. And talented as our Warlords are, they have no experience commanding numbers that large—nor confronting them. Which is why…" she trailed off. For a moment, it seemed she would not complete the sentence. Then, subdued, she added, "…why what my father is trying to do is… insane."

Zimmerik was about to respond, but Erador cut the argument short. "Well, the wind's from that direction." Erador motioned Zimmerik and Hammynt to take point. "Let's go. The mountains are pretty well out of sight now, anyway."

"I don't smell it," said Vynocent.

"You will," said Hammynt, leading them off.

Although the breeze remained in the same general direction, frequent minor shifts caused them to lose the scent, forcing them to slow down until they'd reacquired it. Sometimes, a shift would carry it, or similar odors, from a different heading as well.

"Baltor, you traveled through here with Clan Grondyr once. What do you remember of their lands?" questioned Erador.

"I'm sorry, but none o' this looks familiar. We passed by one o' the human cities an' it was amazin', with lofty towers made o' onyx, an' surrounded by a great bronze wall. A bunch o' humans rode out to meet us on horses to ask us our intentions with crossin' their land. We went past a bunch o' farms an' a whole lot o' grassland where their animals grazed, coupla villages." He looked around and shook his head. "Don't remember seein' anythin' like this."

Erador sighed. Leadership was not turning out to be the exhilaration his ambitions had made it out to be. He started to say, "We'll just have to keep mov—" then doubled over in agony. He groaned as he grasped his head, palms clamped against his helmet. "Get out of my head!" he shouted at the moist soil at his feet. The four children backed away, their faces twisted in fright.

Carra rushed to his aid. "Erador! Don't fight it! He's a part of you now."

Nothing but groans of pain emerged from Erador's throat. He threw off the dark Onyx helm, and began beating the side of his head with a fist. Carra persisted, "You mustn't resist! He could destroy you, or you him; and we need you both!"

Erador began to straighten from his cramped position, shuddering and straining against clenched muscles. His jaw seemed locked open, his face twitching spasmodically. As he stood straight, his head snapped back and faced the sky. A roar began to build from the depths of his throat, escalating from an indistinct moan until it croaked so loud it seemed supernatural. Beams of light burst out his eyes and shot into the sky; the ominous roar stopped, and all was silent. His head rolled back down to face his clansmen.

***

Warlord Vorkus stood silently, all but motionless as he took an assessment of himself and his surroundings. It was overcast and damp, and the long grass drooped over the water-soaked earth. He caught the faintest scent of manure on the damp breeze.

The adolescents were hesitant to interrupt his introspection. Ultimately, Carra did anyway. "Warlord Vorkus…? We're lost," she stated. Her voice was weak and fleeting. "We haven't a means to guide our path."

His deep voice commanded attention as he spoke. "Don't you smell that?"

Several of the others nodded. Hammynt mustered the courage to address this living legend. "The dung, you mean, Warlord? Yes, we've been trying to follow it. We were hoping it was from some human animals."

A corner of Warlord Vorkus' mouth twitched upward in approval. "You were correct. It's the smell of horse dung. You'll get used to it soon enough. Their farm villages are filled with it. The humans can't be far."

He began walking confidently in the direction of the wind, expecting the rest of the clan to follow. The adolescents exchanged glances with each other.

"Well, we have a new guide. We'd better get going before the wind dies and we lose our trail… or before he walks off and leaves us," grumbled Gressyn.

"I still don't smell it," comment Vynocent, followed by a few chuckles amongst the group.

The clan was disheartened by Erador's sudden departure, but they followed Warlord Vorkus anyway. Discontent found its way into their thoughts as they struggled with adapting to the change in leadership. The combination of the long, wearying journey and the cold gloomy weather seemed to make them lose sight of their goals, of why they were heading to the human farm

203

village, why it was important at all. They were reduced to following their inscrutable leader, going through motions that seemed increasingly purposeless... until they found a road.

Wet flat cobblestones, pressed into the earth until they were flush with the land, stretched in a line that receded into the distance as far as they could see in either direction. Small weeds took every opportunity to grow between the cracks in the stones. "The humans have improved their trails since I've last seen them. They used to be nothing but dirt," exclaimed Warlord Vorkus.

"That's what I remember them bein' as well, mostly, though we did see a road like this one," commented Baltor. "Though I still don't remember the land bein' like this."

Turning their heads each way, gazing down the empty length of the road, they contemplated which way they should head, until Tysyra broke the silence. "So do we turn left or right?" The scent they'd been following was barely evident: the wind crossed the road at an angle.

"Right," answered Warlord Vorkus. "The end of the mountains is farther east than the village we seek. And if we do not find it, this road must still lead somewhere."

As they travelled along the cobblestone road, a grey stone tower appeared in the distance atop a low hill. It wasn't grand. It stood just above the height of a stone wall which was itself little taller than an elkin hut. The walled structure sat adjacent to the passing road. They saw no movement as they approached; they heard no sounds apart from those made by untroubled nature, but they could all smell the scent of horse dung. The open gate from the road faced a small, rectangular courtyard. Beside the guard tower, they could see a stable and some sort of dwelling—barracks, an inn, or perhaps both. This structure seemed to be a small watch post to guard the road and to house weary travelers. Clan Wyndlyn warily circled the enclosure, but found no damage to the walls or tower.

"It looks intact," said Baltor.

"That means they were not forced to flee. They left this vacant for a reason," said Warlord Vorkus.

Clan Wyndlyn's curiosity had now been engaged by their first looks of what humans had wrought; the outpost was the largest building most of them had ever seen apart from the Armory, and the road must have required amounts of brick and labor beyond anything they could imagine. Even Zimmerik began to acknowledge that Carra might have had a valid point when she spoke of the power of humanity's numbers. Then they began to worry about where all these humans were. The guard post vanished behind them, and only the road broke the wilderness; they encountered no travelers, no other structures, no paths leading to one side or the other. They began to wonder if Warlord Vorkus had chosen correctly, or where else this road might be leading them.

The road they followed curved leftward to follow a shallow valley for a time. It climbed back out between two hills, curled again to the left around the hill's flank—and then ran down to and terminated in another cobblestone road a couple miles farther ahead. When the elkin reached the crossroad, they could see that its stones were far more worn than those they'd been walking upon. Theirs saw less traffic, it seemed… though since they hadn't seen any, the notion did not surprise them.

Once again they were faced with a decision. To the right the road passed through more of the same wilderness before curving out of sight, but to the left, on a far rise, they could make out another building, its outline resembling that of the abandoned guard post. The wind had long since stopped carrying clues to their noses; it now came from almost directly ahead of them. Even Warlord Vorkus seemed indecisive as to which direction was better. After contemplating for enough time the others grew antsy to get moving, he concluded that the other road had probably brought them far enough west that they ought to turn left, eastward, and that at worst they might be able to ask directions at the building they could see. When, however, they found it was another guard post identical to the first, likewise abandoned, he ignored it and pressed on. Before the post had been lost to sight behind them, the road made two switchbacks to drop into a narrow valley, cut by a brook mere inches deep where the road met it at a gravelly ford; then it made four more in the process of climbing back out the higher opposite slope. When the road crested that ridge, the elkin were presented with a spectacle that stayed their feet: a magnificent city, set in the midst of a broad, tailored valley.

An immense limestone wall wrapped the circumference of the city. Numerous tall towers pierced the sky, each flying a blue and gold flag atop its spire. Rooftops upon rooftops peeked over the wall, smoke billowing from chimneys atop buildings of all different shapes and sizes. The road ran down through farm lands where cabbage, wheat, and rye grew in long, narrow strips on either side, leading up to a large drawbridge gate that was open.

Peasants and cottars were scattered across the farm land, halting their labor one after another as they noticed the elkin, standing frozen in their fields and staring up at them. A few humans atop the wall saw Clan Wyndlyn standing upon the hillside and began pointing and shouting. Warlord Vorkus gasped in amazement. "Look at what the humans have built. The last time I passed their realms, there was nothing but wooden fences, scattered farms, and open land. I never imagined…"

Clan Wyndlyn was not sure if they should be reassured or terrified that even the legendary Warlord could be overawed. They noticed they were beginning to attract attention. With a grin of satisfaction, Warlord Vorkus added, "Although I can tell that they are just as enamored to see us as ever."

Clan Wyndlyn descended the slope, anxious as they walked, knowing they were about to step into a brand new world.

CHAPTER 19

The elkin could hear the city bustling and teeming with life, but the humans surrounding the gate were stunned, transfixed in awe as if they were staring at ghosts. "I'm getting the feeling that Warlord Dryden hasn't been through here yet," stated Zimmerik.

No effort was made to pull up the drawbridge or bar their way. The guards watching them from atop the wall wore pointed metallic hats, tunics that displayed a blue and gold checkered pattern across their chest and shoulders, worn over long-sleeved chain shirts. They held bows loosely at their side in an unthreatening manner. Clan Wyndlyn approached the entrance cautiously, intimidated by the grandeur of their limestone wall. Every step atop the heavy old planks of the drawbridge creaked and groaned.

The elkin realized that they appeared dangerous and formidable for being so well-armed, and that if it weren't for their small number and the four younglings, they may have been mistaken for a threat. Warlord Vorkus walked toward the gateway armored like a dark knight in the Onyx Smith plate decorated with golden runic inscriptions, his formidable metallic antlers protruding through his threatening helm. Wiltyn wore the armor of the Sky Smith, a blurry off-white with vibrant blue runes. Carra bore the unique staff forged from the warped antlers of Clan Wyndlyn's past Goma enchanters, while Baltor rested his oversized treblevine double-bladed axe over his shoulder. Despite Clan Wyndlyn's small number, the man standing above the entryway turned and yelled for support, his voice carrying a great distance.

"Why do they need a doorway this tall?" asked little Abby. She was apprehensive as she passed beneath the portcullis; the ends of its metallic bars were pointing down at her like daggers.

"For wagons, vehicles, and weapons of war," answered Vorkus, walking with a certain confidence in his step, as if expecting a royal reception.

They emerged into a busy jumble of buildings and streets, large enough to get lost in. They paused inside the wall, assessing the humans and their buildings that surrounded them. The well-constructed stone buildings in the immediate vicinity were immense and impressive in comparison to the elkins' simple individual stone huts. The adolescents were awestruck, yet Vorkus acted like he had seen it all before. He turned back to face his fellow elkin huddling close together, standing just a few steps inside the gateway. "Don't trust any humans with the contents of our rucksacks," he warned with a whisper. They all nodded and Vorkus seemed satisfied with that being the only cautionary warning he needed to give them.

Their arrival drew the attention of many bystanders, the watchman's call still more. Guards without bows came down from the walls to stand in loose formation around the elkin. The clattering of horseshoes upon the cobblestone street echoed as two men on horseback trotted forward. They arrived and faced the elkin, closing the semi-circle of guards around Clan Wyndlyn. They kept one hand upon the leather reins, and bore in their other long halberds pointed high into the air. Their saddles rested atop more blue and gold checkered cloth that draped over the horses. The guards peered at the elkin, assessing their group, their meager possessions and copious armaments, but most of all their rare runic armor.

"From what lands do you hail?" asked the older rider, perched atop his well-groomed amber stallion.

Vorkus didn't answer; instead he inspected the human pawns that had dared come to stand against him. With every moment of silence, he could see the fear creeping under their skin. They were but babes to his eyes: they couldn't have been older than fifteen—too young to fight.

How could you let such inexperience guard their home? he thought. The only exception were the two seasoned men on horseback, and only the one that spoke to him showed any sign of gumption. Vorkus' pride and honor would have otherwise forbidden him from answering to such low and youthful beings, but he knew the humans had food and bed for his clan within this city and so he would have to acquiesce. He decided to speak only to the horseman whose face reflected his years. "North of here, west of the Jerackon Mountains, across the open tundra," he answered.

"From Remaurus-Senti?"

"From Cerebus-Senti." Vorkus' scorn-laden reply drew a reaction from the guards, though he could not tell if they were curious or disturbed.

"Where are the rest of you?" asked the senior mounted soldier.

"This is all of us," said Vorkus. "The others are all dead, except for the traitorous one." The human guards exchanged uneasy glances amongst themselves, though they maintained their non-threatening demeanor, keeping their weapons sheathed but their vigilance high. He noticed the subtle head movements of the man atop the horse as he looked upward at something behind Vorkus' back. Vorkus turned to discover that the man was signaling to a guard atop the wall above the entryway. The guards along the wall and within the tower seemed to be scanning the countryside for any additional units, ensuring that their small group was not some trick. He grinned behind the Onyx helm, more amused than offended by the knight's precautionary measures.

No sooner did Vorkus look back upon the senior knight than a guard from atop the wall shouted, "It's all clear!"

"We don't want you bringing your troubles to our doorstep. We have enough troubles of our own already. What have you come here for?" the horseman asked.

"Food and shelter for just the night. Then we will continue on, if you can point us toward the village of Nolta," declared Vorkus.

"But this *is* Nolta," answered the young guard standing nearest to him. "Though it's called Nolta Tenoble, sir."

Vorkus' head cocked to his side in anger to look upon the so-called-man that had just spoken out of turn. He scowled at him, but managed to contain his pride. "Why the name change?" he sneered with his ominous voice as he stepped toward the young man.

The young man's face was cleanly shaven, his skin blushing a bright pink from the cool air, though it grew more and more uneasy as Vorkus stepped closer. "Tenoble means that this is a city within the King's domain, rightly named after His Majesty. No one has referred to this as an independent village for hundreds of years."

Vorkus let out a low groan, before muttering beneath his breath, "*Hrmph.* This place has changed much since I last set my eyes upon it." He became disinterested with the young man, leaving him in a state of utter confusion from his last statement.

The adolescents of Clan Wyndlyn were still gawking at the construction and stone architecture of the great towers and buildings, paying no mind to Vorkus' conversation. As their eyes roved downward from the rooftops of the two-story buildings that surrounded the entrance, the elkin began to look about at the commoners. There were a great many raggedly-clothed civilians, both dark and light skinned, passing by the gate; an ewerer carrying a bucket of water; a few dozen cottars and farmers transporting produce from the fields. All staring back at them, and whispers spread as a crowd bursting with curiosity began to form.

"He wears the Onyx armor!"

"He must be a Warlord."

"What is a Warlord doing here?"

"And the other wears the armor of the Sky Smith!"

"Is he a Warlord too?"

"Why have they left Cerebus-Senti?"

A man adorned in lavish attire, followed by an entourage of armed guards, approached at a rapid pace; onlookers backed out of the man's way to form a path as he and his cohorts advanced. As they jogged forward, Vorkus noticed that no human within sight wore armor as impressive or protective as the clan's Blacksmith armor. The guards surrounding them wore chain shirts and helmets, and in some cases bore shields; the henchmen surrounding the well-dressed man appeared to be unarmored beneath their gold tunics, wearing only dark metallic greaves and bracers, plus strange spiked, metallic scoop-like objects that curved from their weapon hands.

The man they accompanied dressed in a royal blue velvet tunic with white trim, and matching trousers. His head was bald and shiny, with a clean moustache trimmed to perfection; its grey whiskers matched his eye brows. He wore clean leather shoes and a simple sword at his waist, though Vorkus could tell by his soft hands that he never wielded it.

A man not able to wield a sword is a man not worthy of my time, he thought.

The whispers dissipated as the growing crowd became quiet so they could hear them speak. It was as if everyone in attendance was holding their breath; only the occasional snort from a horse or the clattering from their hooves could be heard.

The man dressed in the royal blue velvet bowed in respect before Warlord Vorkus. "My apologies for our precautions and the curiosity of our citizens. It is not every day that esteemed guests such as elkin come here to visit. You must have endured an impossible journey to get here this time of year. Allow me to introduce myself; I am Jon Rennly, Chamberlain of Knight Lord Lowry, Duke of Nolta Tenoble. And to whom do I owe this great pleasure?" He spoke with precise enunciation, an accent in his speech that alluded to high society and a sense of sophistication that the elkin lacked.

Vorkus, disgusted by this soft, pitiful excuse of a man standing before him, turned to address the crowd rather than respond directly to Jon Rennly. "I am Vorkus Wyndlyn, the first of my kind, the Chosen Champion of Brikken the Onyx Smith, Brandisher of the Onyx plate, Wielder of Wraith, Warlord of the West, and defender of its inhabitants."

Confused looks spread across the faces of the crowd. "First of his kind? What is he talking about?"

Jon Rennly kept a modest composure about him, only raising one eye brow at his claim, and let the crowd settle before continuing, "And for what purpose have you come?" Jon Rennly's eyes squinted as he peered at Vorkus with uncertainty and caution.

Vorkus matched his gaze, and stepped forward in an intimidating manner. Jon Rennly stepped back and his three guards stepped between them. "I have business to discuss concerning the safety of these lands. You would be wise to take me to your leader." Vorkus' voice sounded rustic and keen.

Worried whispers cascaded through the crowd and Jon Rennly did not look pleased by it. "Well, we have nothing to fear behind the safety of our walls," he replied. But Vorkus gave no response, and didn't move a muscle. He just maintained his threatening stare into the other's eyes. Eventually, the man went on, "Most certainly. Such a rare and distinguished visitor such as yourself may be granted an audience with Sir Duke Lowry. He shall be able to receive you at sunset on the morrow."

"That will not do. This is urgent!" flared Vorkus.

"Well, Sir Duke Lowry has been summoned to confer with His Majesty King Tenoble XLIII and won't return until the morrow, so it will have to do," stated the plump man in a calm tone, followed by a few nervous blinks.

Vorkus grew impatient, and knew this man was of no help. "Then who leads in his stead? I shall talk with him."

"The affairs of this city lie within my control until his return, as Sir Duke Lowry has no heirs," stated Jon Rennly as he mustered some courage. "So what concern do you bring?"

Vorkus sneered as he glanced at Jon Rennly's soft, plump hands and wondered how this man could ever command an army, "I shall wait for the Duke then. In the meantime, my clan requires food and rest."

"Excellent. Ang shall escort you through town," as he gestured toward one of his personal guards. "He will be able to help you find whatever you need to ensure that your stay here in Nolta Tenoble is satisfactory. Now, if there's nothing else, I'll see you at Sir Duke Lowry's keep tomorrow at dusk and I trust that your stay will be pleasant." Jon Rennly turned toward the crowd of commoners and shouted, "Everyone, go back to your business!" he said, waving his hands, motioning the crowd to disperse. As he departed, so did most of the crowd.

One of his soldiers stayed behind. "Warlord Vorkus, I see that you and your clan bore a great deal of equipment on your travels. Let's first get you rooms so you can leave your things and then we'll get some food. If your supplies are anything of value, you won't want to sleep anywhere in the slums, if you can help it. Do you have enough crystal to pay for a group of your size?"

Vorkus was already beginning to see the upside to having a guide, and nodded once. Ang was already on the move. "Follow me."

Ang led them toward their left, away from the poor citizens on the dirt road and toward the finer eateries along the cobblestone streets. The elkin trailed him through the city, their eyes continuing to fill with wonder at the size of the city and the vast number of people that lived within its walls. They passed horse-drawn carriages and wagons and many well-dressed citizens in silks and furs, liveried message-runners, clerks, apprentices and craftsmen from more trades than they could identify. The humans stared in surprise at the elkin as much as the elkin did at their surroundings. Echoes from smithies rang through the streets, and the smell of fresh-baked bread wafted through the air.

***

As they passed through the streets, Ang made eye contact with each of the stationed city guards. They responded with subtle nods verifying that they were ready to jump to his aid if he needed it, making him feel less alone. The elkin hadn't spoken a word since he began to lead them, and their silence was making him nervous. "The timing of your arrival is a strange one. You've come amidst a war, though it's good to know that you are no enemy of ours." Countless thoughts raced through his mind. He found himself unable to resist asking: "What brings you elkin to Nolta Tenoble? Must be important business."

Ang instantly regretted uttering the words as soon as they had rolled out of his mouth. He worried that he might have offended them. He kept walking, trying to remain casual, desperate for a reply. The seconds felt like hours. Finally, Warlord Vorkus' deep voice answered him, "First, you must tell me about that weapon you wield."

Ang stopped to turn and face his prestigious guests. He lifted his arm, twisting it back and forth to display his weapon. He could tell that the Warlord was fascinated by its unconventional shape. It looked like a long curved scoop extending from where Ang's hand entered at its base. Its interior was made of smooth polished metal while its exterior was fashioned with spikes along its backside. Ang's black leather belt held numerous bronze balls all around his waist.

"This is called a xistera. I can use the spiked backside to bash my enemies, or deflect their blows as a shield would, but its main purpose is to launch these projectiles with deadly speed and accuracy."

"Why not use a bow and arrow? Without a doubt they have a further range," inquired Carra.

"This weapon was born at the end of the War of the Wish and was responsible for turning the tide in our favor. Where our arrows could not fell the legions of walking skeletons, these metallic balls could crush bone. That, combined with its melee functionality, has made it my weapon of choice." Ang smiled, but was surprised to see only awkward stares. Ang grew very self-conscious. "So what business do you have to discuss with Sir Duke Lowry?"

"A traitorous elkin Warlord named Dryden has started a civil war. Now vyceptors scour the land unchecked and unchallenged," answered Warlord Vorkus.

"I don't see how the two are related," admitted Ang.

Zimmerik stepped forward and patted Ang on the back. "Don't worry, it will make sense tomorrow when we talk to the Duke." They resumed walking.

Two cross-streets later, Ang halted at a weathered oak door beneath a sign that read 'Brook Glenn Inn' in white lettering carved into an ornately hung wooden plank. He opened it and held it for them, gesturing for them to enter. As the elkin stepped inside, their fur boots tracked dirt upon a lavish runway rug woven in an elaborate pattern. He aided in negotiating a price with the owner, then left them to their relaxation and a fresh meal, promising he would come for them the next morning.

With room keys in hand and food stuffed into their bellies, Clan Wyndlyn was able to rest easy for the first time in a long time.

***

The next morning Erador awoke from another tormenting nightmare, discovering himself lying on top of comfy feather bedding. He rubbed his eyes and wondered if he had not yet escaped his dream, since he was in no place he's ever seen before. He panicked for just a moment as he strove to absorb his surroundings—all the wooden furniture, rich cushions, and paintings that seemed to swarm the room. Then he collected himself, realizing that the Onyx plate had been doffed and set carefully upon one chair and the floor. Erador went to the door and pulled it open. As the heavy wooden door creaked as it opened, he expected to see daylight and the open air; instead, all he saw was more walls and doors.

He stuck his head into a long empty hallway and was overwhelmed by a feeling that he was trapped. "Carra? Carra!"

After a minute another door opened and Carra looked down the hallway confused. "Erador? Are you all right?"

"No. I keep facing Vorkus in my sleep, still struggling to overcome him… What happened? Where are we?"

Carra's blank face began to smile as the humor of the situation began to sink in. "We're inside an inn within a human city. We're scheduled to speak to their leader tonight. Get dressed; our guide Ang will show us through their city. Don't forget to lock your door!"

All of Clan Wyndlyn was waiting for Ang downstairs by the time Erador had finished putting his armor on, except for the children, who were tasked with staying and keeping watch over the clan's supplies. As he descended the steps into the lobby of the inn, he tried to recollect the instructions his father had given him for conversing with humans. *Always introduce yourself as Erador Wyndlyn,* he remembered his father say. *The humans always have two names, sometimes more.*

His armor clanged with finality when he reached the last step. As his fellow elkin greeted him, a man dressed in a gold tunic threw open a door, through which Erador could see what *looked* like it might be the outside… though with another wall only a few paces beyond, he wasn't sure. The stranger approached him. "Warlord Vorkus, where can I take you today? Perhaps to see the finest smith in all of Thornwall?"

Erador at first wanted to correct him over his name, but decided to let it slide so as not to confuse him. "I think I'd like that, especially if you can take us to see your animals after."

The elkin followed their guide through the city while Erador attempted not to act surprised by the level of industrialization that the humans have achieved. Or the level of crowding. Or of odors. Ang led them to a crossroads, located at the heart of the city. "Welcome to Town Square," he said. "You will find every form of craftsmanship here at its four corners. The apothecaries to the south, carpenters and bowyers to the west, tanners, skinners, and leather workers to the east, and armorers and blacksmiths to the north."

Erador and the elkin stood at a distance to marvel at this center-of-creation. The apothecaries stored shelves of herbs and alchemical goods. The bowyers fashioned various crossbows and bows. The carpenters worked with large logs, constructing components for catapults and ballistae. The tanners and leather workers fixed belts, boots, clothing, leather jackets, and even the occasional lamellar vest. The blacksmiths and armorers took up the most space, forging swords, shields, scale mail, xisteras, helms, and many other manner of weapons and armor. The clang of their forging hammers against anvils seemed rhythmic, and smoke from their forges poured into the open sky. At the center stood a massive stone statue as a testament to the Old Gods. It depicted the old eight, some standing on top of the others' shoulders, some standing side by side, some leaping, composed in such a formation that together they formed the silhouette of one large man, representing the one true religion.

"Why is there still a statue of the Old Gods when they have abandoned us?" Erador questioned his guide.

"Because of King Tenoble XLIII. It is his family's divine right to rule, so he lives to undermine the Blacksmiths, to prove that they don't have control, to remind them that they are not true Gods. Even when the Chromium Smith who sits on the throne of the kingdom to our east threatens to invade us every day, His Majesty refuses to concede, just as he refuses to believe that the Gods will never return. And rightly so; these Blacksmiths have done nothing but make Thornwall worse," replied Ang. Erador sensed the emotion in his voice, rooted in anger toward the Blacksmiths.

As they stood at the edge of the square, they noticed a large group of humans moving toward the north corner of the square. "The Guillens approach," stated Ang. "They come to challenge Avatar Noren again." The title was foreign to Erador and he gave Ang a puzzled glance, but before he could ask, Ang answered him, "Avatar is the title given to the best blacksmith in the region, but he has to earn it. Besides being King, it's one of the best titles to have. Come on! Let's go watch! This is bound to be a great match!"

Clan Wyndlyn followed Ang closer to the north corner of the square to get a better view. The Guillens had large stomachs, curled red hair, and beards the color of leaves in the fall. They wore trousers and fur boots, but their chests were bare, covered with symbols drawn in orange body paint. Carra whispered to Zimmerik, "Their orange body paint is a sure sign that they worship the Scorch Smith."

The Guillens were led by a large man with a unique forging hammer strapped to his wrist. The surfaces of the flat ends of his forging hammer were oversized, while the body of the hammer slimmed in the middle between both ends. His entourage of followers, bearing bolos and mauls, seemed confident. As they walked, the Guillens drew an ecstatic crowd which fell to silence as the Guillen leader spoke, "I challenge Avatar Noren to a test of skill over a forging of breast and back plate." The crowd erupted in cheers at the prospect of witnessing such a great battle of their craftsmanship.

A black-haired man, slender at the waist but with broad shoulders and arms bulging with muscles, emerged from his forge. Soot and sweat covered his face and arms. He wore a black apron and carried black iron tongs in his left hand. "You know the rules, Horn. I must have time to collect my material, but as challenger, you must first reveal your metal to me."

Horn, a thick man that must have weighed twice the Avatar in stones, grinned with pleasure. "It is no metal." He waved his hand and a Guillen soldier brought forth a large sack and dumped its contents onto the ground. "It is the antlers of two dozen elkin. A rare collection," he said with pride. Gasps erupted through the crowd and a worried look crossed Avatar Noren's face. "They crossed our territory in the north and we taught them a lesson they will never forget, slew the lot of them with ease."

Erador grew furious at the thought of any elkin losing a battle against such inferior warriors. It would be a great discredit to his race, and he knew it couldn't be true. *Perhaps they come across Clan Hortyr while they slept?* he wondered. The thought of their demise brought a slight smile to his face, though he wished it would be by his hand.

"Impossible!" uttered Avatar Noren. "You can't forge a plate out of antlers."

Erador began to push through the crowd, with Ang and elkin in tow. "It isn't impossible," replied Horn with a cocky grin on his face that would have infuriated anyone.

"Believe it!" shouted Erador so all could hear as he emerged from the front of the crowd dressed in the venerated Onyx armor. "You can see that *we* have already mastered the art and forged a staff," as he gestured to Carra standing behind him holding the Channeler's Staff. "But what I can't believe is that you slaughtered the lot of them *with ease*."

Erador looked amongst the pile of antlers, searching for something… anything that he could recognize. Then he saw it. One antler rack amongst the pile had been capped with metal tips, and of all the elkin he knew only Warlord Brynn's rack had been mended in such a fashion. "In fact, I don't believe that you killed them at all, because I don't believe it possible for a human to best an elkin in combat. Put your best man against me in a duel, and if he wins I shall believe it. However, if I win, you must confess to everyone here where you really obtained these antlers."

Avatar Noren grinned with delight as he could see the confidence in Horn's eye begin to fade. "Surely, a Warlord such as yourself is a different beast in battle than the common elkin warrior, and with your runic Onyx armor, it would be unfair."

Erador removed his helm and said, "I am but a Warlord's son, and I will remove this armor if you wish to prove your claims."

Horn took a deep breath; his irritated frown showed through his thick beard. Then, to the astonishment of the crowd, he announced, "So be it." From the depths of his gut, he uttered a long powerful roar to summon his best man. "*Crooooox!*"

A giant of a human stepped forth wielding a crude double-handed blade as hefty as the Onyx blade. The man was almost as wide as he was tall, and the orange paint on his body formed odd, misshapen-looking runes.

"Teach this young man a lesson in pain," continued Horn, the Guillen blacksmith.

Clan Wyndlyn stepped in to help Erador doff his armor. Ang began to worry. "I need to alert the guards!"

As he spun to leave, a hefty hand on his shoulder held him in place. Ang turned to see who the hand belonged to, and Baltor looked down at him. "No need. This will be over in less than a minute."

Erador stood in his tunic and trousers and was handed a single-bladed axe and a plain rectangular wooden shield by his clan mates. He stood a few arm lengths from his challenger, surrounded by a circle of onlookers. Erador twisted the axe about in his hand so its blunt hammer-like side was facing his opponent.

"I don't want to hurt you," boasted Erador.

The crowd began to back up as Crox took a few practice swings, laughing in anticipation. Horn sat on the side lines, and his confidence began to resurface as he sized up Crox's opponent. "*Fight!*" he shouted.

Crox gripped his lengthy blade with two hands and pulled it back for a powerful swing. He took but one step before Erador landed a shield-lunge into his gut. Erador's powerful legs thrust him forward with such force that when the flat of his shield bashed against Crox's stomach, it knocked the wind right out of him. Crox buckled over from the hit, gasping for air while Erador twisted his body to bring his shield back, then with a nose-breaking uppercut, he swung his shield into the man's face. Crox toppled over backward to the ground. The fight was over.

"Now admit to everyone that you stole this sack of antlers from Cerebus-Senti," demanded Erador.

Horn's look of shame was as good as a confession. Erador stepped up and retrieved his father's antlers from the pile.

Avatar Noren stepped forth. "Great elkin, that was an impressive display of might. But Horn and I have a duel of our own." He turned his attention to his challenger. "I accept your challenge, and I already have my material." Horn looked up in disbelief.

"I'll forge a cuirass out of adamantium, a mineral that has never been used by man, stolen from the Chromium Smith himself!"

CHAPTER 20

With the heavy cacophonous chime of the bell tower ringing throughout the streets and alleys of Nolta Tenoble, the smithing duel commenced. Cheers erupted as the blacksmiths plunged their materials into their forges. Avatar Noren worked in the forge on the left, while Horn began heating the antlers in the forge on the right. It was a spectacle for the masses, seeing the skilled blacksmiths competing side by side. Spectators hung out of windows and sat on balconies of all the surrounding buildings, contesting for a better view.

The throng of onlookers watched in esteem as the blacksmiths removed their piping hot material from the fires, cheered at the clash of their skilled swings of their forging hammers smashing into their glowing red materials. Sparks and embers flew with every powerful strike against the unformed materials as the rivals began fashioning masterwork chest plates that were to be as unique as their hammers.

Avatar Noren's forging hammer was small, but accurate. Its handle was double-wrapped in a leather grip, while the head was designed in a cross shape, creating four square hammering heads. In between every swing he twisted his forging hammer in his hand ninety degrees so that his next strike would land on a new side of his hammer. His rhythmic form was mesmerizing to watch.

Opposite Avatar Noren was Horn of the Guillen tribe, using his custom forging hammer with an oversized face to flatten and bend the antlers, sometimes hammering three at a time upon his anvil. Horn's reddish, grizzled beard matched the body-paint of the strange swirled symbols of the Scorch Smith that spread along his shoulders, chest, and gut. While Horn's arms didn't have the muscular definition of Avatar Noren's, it was evident his swings carried with them a heavy force.

Tysyra, standing just before Erador in the crowd, was as interested in the blacksmith duel as the humans were. She was short and petite, though with an athletic build, and had to stand on her toes to see over the shoulders of the humans standing in front of her. She was enthralled by the competition and twisted around to face Erador. "We should have brought the children so they could see this and experience it firsthand."

Erador gave a slight grimace of doubt through the slits of his Onyx helm, followed by a throaty grunt. "I don't understand the human customs. They give praise to the best blacksmith instead of their best fighter. They say they worship the Old Gods, but they mimic the profession of the Blacksmiths."

Ang, dressed in the golden tunic and armor of his guard uniform, turned to look upon Erador and the elkin, his face wrought in disbelief at Erador's offensive statement. He took a deep breath to calm his nerves before attempting to rebut Erador, as he knew he shouldn't upset his guests. "You misunderstand, Warlord. It was the True Gods that saw greatness in eight human Blacksmiths, to whom they chose to impart their divine power. To be one of the best blacksmiths in all of Thornwall is to be the successor of the current Blacksmiths. It is the chosen profession of the True Gods, and when King Tenoble XLIII overthrows the Chromium Smith, it'll be the Avatar that takes up his hammer. We are ready to handle the responsibility of the power he wields."

"So tell me, Ang, if your True Gods are so responsible, why did they choose to give their godly power to such reckless humans, only to abandon the world after they realized their mistake?"

Ang was beside himself. "And you think the Blacksmiths are an improvement? When someone ascends to godliness, they don't just settle for being King. The Chromium Smith mocks the True Gods every day he sits in that throne!"

Erador loomed over Ang. "You are blind to what the Blacksmiths have given you. The Soul Smith created our race. Then the Onyx Smith saw greatness in the elkin, choosing us as His champions and giving us this runic plate armor to use to defend our clan and the inhabitants of these lands, including this city. We have defended you against threats for centuries, all manner of beasts and demons that you will soon know all too well."

"These monsters you speak of are the creation of none other than your Soul Smith, correct? Sounds like the Blacksmiths are doing a *great* job!" Ang said with a heavy dose of sarcasm. "And what do you mean we will know them all too well?"

Erador turned back, gripping his father's antler rack tighter in his hands. Its surface felt rough against his gauntleted fingers. "That will depend on how well the Duke defends this city."

"Is it serious? Should I alert the guards?"

"You are safe while we are here, but we won't be staying for long. We will tell the Duke what he is up against, and then we will get what we came here for: mercenaries and beasts."

A huge sigh of relief came out from Hammynt. "Finally! We've been here for two days and haven't even seen the handler's bestiary."

Clan Wyndlyn all grinned at how well Hammynt had remained patient this entire time. Then, in an eruption of cheers, the sea of people occupying the cobblestone center of the town square chanted and clapped as Avatar Noren began drawing out the form of his adamantium breastplate with a dexterous fury of blows. His hammer thundered against the piping hot metal from the full strength of his swing, making haste to strike the metal while it was still malleable. Worry mounted in his face as he realized the adamantium did not remain workable for as long as he'd expected it to. Avatar Noren shoved the partially shaped metal back into the fire, loaded more charcoal in and worked the bellows to increase its temperature.

Ang broke off his fixation with the contest for a moment and turned to Erador. "Why did you only take back that one antler rack from the Guillens?" he asked, gesturing to the rack in Erador's hands.

Erador held up his father's antlers with their metallic tips hiding broken and cracked tines. "Because these are the antlers of my father, and he deserves a Warlord's burial. The other antlers are serving a purpose now, like the antlers of our Goma enchanters. Even after a warrior's death, they still found a way to be in the thick of battle," he said with a sense of adoration. The Onyx helm masked his face from view as he smirked at how fitting a fate it was for his fallen clansmen. "They were murdered, taken by surprise by one of their own. Their antlers were almost lost in the snow, and then stolen from me, only to wind up right here, to be given a purpose beyond death, by protecting another warrior as armor, and the only surviving elkin of Clan Wyndlyn were here to watch it happen." *This has to be the work of the Fates*, he thought.

Erador leaned in closer to Ang to whisper into his ear. "How do you determine a winner?"

Without taking his eyes from the competition, Ang answered, "There is generally some clear component that brings a blacksmith victory over the other. If this were a duel of sword craft, victory might be awarded to the one that produced the best-balanced blade, or the sharpest one, or the lightest… whatever made that sword stand out over the other. In a duel over the forging of armor, it might be mobility, or lightness, or elegance of joins or articulation. In all cases, what material is used, or its overall appearance and perception on the battlefield might decide, should all other factors be equal. But the best part is when the pieces are both so superlative they must be put to the test."

"What test?" inquired Zimmerik.

"I don't want to give it away," voiced Ang in excitement. "You need to see it for yourself!" Ang vied for a better view.

Sweat streamed from the blacksmiths as they hammered their materials, drawing them out, dishing them, shaping them to perfection. "Hey Noren," cried the crude-looking Horn as he moved some smoldering antlers from the anvil and started pounding another set. "Sounds like you're having a hard time folding that metal," he mocked, followed by an evil laugh.

Avatar Noren shouted back, "I had been saving this for a special purpose." He grabbed the adamantium with his iron tongs and returned it to his furnace for further heating. "I'm hoping that once I craft the impossible, it'll shut you up for good," he said with a smirk.

The banter between the blacksmiths continued, and the crowd clung to every word, laughing and reacting with emphatic hurrahs. Their sweaty skin glistened in the glow from the furnace, highlighting streaks of soot across their brow and forearms. The cryptic symbols painted with orange body paint across Horn's shoulders, chest, and gut stayed intact despite the sweat and soot smeared across his body.

Avatar Noren seemed to be running into difficulty: working the adamantium was taxing even his strength. The metal was demanding increased amounts of time within his forge to soften the material enough to enable him to shape it, and he was clearly struggling to find an optimum temperature.

Horn hadn't even touched his bellows the whole competition. His lips were moving, as if he was mumbling something to the antlers he held over the fire of his forge. The orange symbols painted on Horn's body began to glow and radiate as the fire in his forge intensified. The change was subtle, but the keen eyes of the elkin noticed its radiance.

"He's using the symbols on his body to control the heat from the forge," said Carra. "Is that allowed?"

"Let it be, Carra," replied Erador with a heavy tone. "It is clear that we don't understand all the workings of the Scorch Smith, since those symbols don't even look like runes." The rest of the Guillens cheered Horn on as he found the perfect temperature to be able to mold the antlers. They had turned black as soot… but somehow had become malleable, not burning and breaking as bone normally would. Horn began weaving the antlers around each other, building an impressive chest piece, while Avatar Noren continued to struggle.

Shaping the adamantium was proving more difficult than he had imagined, and the crowd quieted down so he could concentrate. In the sea of people that were watching in silence, a single voice yelled out from the back, "You can do it, Avatar Noren!" Then the entire sea of people erupted in cheer. Avatar Noren pulled the block of scorching hot metal from his furnace and began striking it with his hammer with increased haste, gritting his teeth and groaning with every swing. He was using all his energy to keep hammering at such a fast pace.

Clan Wyndlyn began to realize why this was so appealing to the humans, as they were unable to avert their eyes from the action. The blacksmiths rotated work pieces from forge to anvil and back again with immense efficiency, each precise strike of their hammers drawing their materials a little nearer the desired shape.

Hours passed, and the overcast skies began to darken as the day turned to night. The crowd oohed and ahhed in an emotional turmoil that followed the successes and setbacks throughout the forging process, voicing an immense cheer when Avatar Noren pulled the final piece from his quenching trough, inspected it closely, and declared himself satisfied. Both blacksmiths had produced completed two-piece cuirasses with daylight to spare. Horn stepped forward to have his antler-woven armor displayed first on a Guillen volunteer. The antler armor had a chest piece and a back piece that were placed upon the wearer so that the antlers clasped and locked under the arms and over the shoulders. The thorns of the antlers sprouted up around the wearer's neck and flared out along the waistline in a fearsome display. The antlers had turned black as charcoal from the heating, and formed an intricate weave that left no exposed areas. However, the antler armor seemed more cumbersome and bulkier than Avatar Noren's pristine adamantine cuirass.

A lucky citizen in the front row of the crowd was chosen to don Avatar Noren's creation. The defending champion's breastplate was polished and stamped with the trademark etchings that only an Avatar can place upon an item of his craft, and only placed upon an item of his best work. Very few items carried the brand of an Avatar since so few customers had the resources to commission such perfection in a product. The only thing rarer than owning an Avatar's work was to possess an item forged by one of the Blacksmiths. The breastplate was hammered smooth, its surface pristine. While it did not carry the barbaric vehemence of the antler cuirass, it accomplished the same ends through its demonstration of wealth and technological achievement, deceptive in its simplicity.

A man advanced in years and with a slight hunch in his back, wearing a long wool cloak with a dark hood, approached each volunteer who had donned the sets of armor, inspecting the craftsmanship with meticulous detail. He walked in circles around the volunteers, but Erador couldn't catch a glimpse of his face beneath the concealment of his hood. He spoke clearly as he walked, letting his voice echo across the square so all could hear. "These are both crafted from rare and unique substances, demonstrating the masterful skill of each blacksmith. I see no imperfections in their work. Horn's cuirass is fearsome and intimidating, while Avatar Noren's plain design is light yet resilient. Without King Tenoble XLIII's divine right to assert the will of the Gods and pass judgment on these products of creation, we will attempt to commune with the Oracle."

As the hooded man stopped pacing and straightened to address the crowd, Erador noticed his face and hands seemed to be covered in fingernails, the way scales cover a snake. *Is that a mask? But it moves as he speaks... Smiths, they're part of him!*

"Place the armors upon the pedestal at the feet of the statue of the Gods. We shall receive judgment upon these master crafts, these worthy testaments of our devotion to the True Gods," he announced.

The two volunteers made their way through the crowd to the center of the square. "Who is the cloaked man issuing orders?" whispered Erador.

Ang's face twisted in disgust at the topic. "He is what we call a keratin, a perverse, pallid race of men that now live in bogs and swamps. Practicing the magic of old has cursed their bodies. Now even their children are born that way. Alas, they are the only ones that study the magic of old, thus they provide a useful service. He is going to pray and present these offerings to the Oracle, as a showcase of our achievements, the mastery of our craftsmen in their chosen discipline. If he receives no communications from the Oracle, then comes the test."

"Who is the Oracle?" interjected Carra.

"Legend says it's a gray mist that materializes before your eyes, remnants from the time before the Blacksmiths."

Carra lost her breath and couldn't find the words to say. She stuttered and stammered until she managed to blurt out, "Those are the Fates, not the Oracle!"

Ang turned to face the small group of savage elkin. "You've seen it?"

Erador intercepted the question. "When was the last time you've seen this... Oracle?"

A sudden appreciation opened within Ang's eyes as he looked upon the elkin with newfound awe. "Never. I mean, I've never seen them myself. But they appeared at the end of the first smithing duel to decide the winner. Now we do it out of respect to the Gods. But, I can't believe you've seen them! You have to show me!"

Carra formed a quaint smile at his enthusiasm, as if considering summoning the Fates, though she looked down at her arm to search for black veins. "I'm sorry, Ang, but we've summoned the Fates one time too many," she said as she glanced across at Erador. He made a small grunt and turned to watch the keratin covered in fingernail-scales strike flint against steel to ignite a small bundle of leaves inside a bowl.

Silence fell upon the square. The soothing smell of burning sage wafted through the air as the hooded man stared up at the heavens, waiting for the Oracle to arrive. Clan Wyndlyn grew nervous in the silence, waiting to see if the Fates answered the keratin's prayers. After several tense moments had passed, the keratin turned to face the crowd. "I'm afraid that the Oracle will not be judging this contest."

Disappointed exhalations from the crowd indicated just how many had been holding their breaths, but the Guillens seemed all too giddy in anticipation of the verdict. The wool-cloaked keratin lowered his hood and pulled up his billowy sleeves, revealing the fingernail scales that continued halfway down his neck, and extended from his hands to his elbows. The scales covered his head, displacing any hair he might have had. Small patches of the fingernail-scales were a rotten yellowish brown. Where his skin had no scales, it was forming small boils and bilious scabs.

"The armor shall undergo the judgment of the Old Magic soul-vessel spell. We must test the armor's bonds with the flame by testing its ability to vessel an evicted soul. Let us put them to the test!"

His words echoed throughout the square and were followed by the cheers of the crowd. Amidst their cheering, the keratin drew out a thin rectangular stone tablet from within his wool cloak.

***

Is that... a runic tablet? I have never heard of such a thing, thought Carra as she backhanded Ang's shoulder. "How is it that the humans have come to learn about Old Magic?" she asked.

Ang jolted in surprise at the strength her casual blow carried. "It is because we never forgot," he said, rubbing his shoulder.

Those few simple words spoke volumes and opened Carra's mind, showing her how much she had been sheltered while growing up in elkin clans, isolated from the rest of the world. Her perception of their clan's strength and power dwindled in her mind. *These humans worship the gods, the true gods that gave birth to Thornwall before elkin ever stepped foot into existence by the hand of the Soul Smith. They knew how to harness Old Magic while I had only just learned of it. The same powerful Magic that awakened a walking construct of crystal.*

"What do you know of this soul vessel spell? That is the test you were telling us of, correct?" she asked.

Ang's face grew irritated as she kept breaking his concentration on the preparations. "Humans were once tortured with this spell. It would tear a weaker man's soul from his body until he was just an empty shell. Some called it the Soul Rendering. Just before it was outlawed for being too severe a punishment, they discovered that this spell could siphon a lost, bodiless soul. The soul must bind itself to an object or else return whence it came, so whichever armor is chosen by the evicted soul is deemed the winner."

"Like the Armor of Souls? Where the helm needed a soul to power the armor's runes," stated Carra.

"No, Carra," Zimmerik chuckled. "It's like our antlers. If the lost soul needs an empty vessel, then Avatar Noren has already won!"

Ang looked cross and confused. "How so?" he asked, but the elkin only laughed in response, though Erador took no participation in it.

"Where do you siphon these souls from?" Erador asked with tense concern, hoping that Ang and these humans wouldn't be so naïve.

"From the Soul Smith," replied Ang with an unwavering voice, as if there was nothing wrong with what he had said.

Erador's disappointment showed in his stance. "That is why the Soul Smith has been summoning so many demons as of late. He is coming to collect." Erador took a deep breath and said, "You have brought this misfortune unto yourself. It seems the Old Magic didn't just curse the keratin; it has cursed you all."

The cuirasses sat perched upon the altars, lying in the faint shadow of the gigantic statue erected in the center of town square that depicted the compilation of gods. The keratin moved to face the front of the statue, and the crowd backed up to give him a wide berth. He made a respectful bow to the monument of the Gods, and then closed his eyes and entered a state of deep concentration. He held the stone tablet before him, its inscriptions facing outward. With a short low hum, he removed his hand from the tablet and it floated there, suspended in the air before him. He stretched his scaled hands toward the cuirasses upon the podium and began chanting beneath his breath.

The inscriptions upon the floating tablet trickled with a glimmering sheen, and then the keratin's eyes snapped open. Each cuirass began to radiate a low reddish glow that grew in intensity. A circle of light spread from the tablet, encompassing both armor-topped altars, beaming toward the skies in a pillar of radiance. Just then, a sharp flash of light broke out around the armor, and another, then another. It was as if light was tearing through the space that they occupied. The sea of onlookers was amazed at the magic unfolding before their eyes. Then two streaks of light ripped down through the sky until they connected with the earth. Those streaks brightened in intensity, and flickering bolts of energy surged earthward in increasing speed. Then, with a bone-rattling shattering sound, the very air ruptured open. A green essence began to emerge through the torn air, as if the pulsating streaks of light drew this ethereal essence from another realm.

The keratin began waving his hands in precise patterns in the air, and Carra noticed new scales protrude from beneath his skin, extending their coverage up his arms. *It's almost like we share the same curse,* she thought as she glanced down at her arms, hoping no signs of the Poisoning were present.

The green essence's brightness pulsated like the beating of a heart, and as the keratin lowered his hands the glare from the pillar of light diminished with them. Carra had never seen a soul before. Its energy danced and flickered as it hovered between the two armors. The green essence took no shape, just rolled in and out of itself like the waves of an ocean.

The green flickering moved toward the antler cuirass, brushing against it, and Horn's eyes grew wide with delight. Then the essence jerked away from the armor as if recoiling, threw itself at the adamantine plate forged by Avatar Noren, and vanished, along with all traces of the keratin's spell. The sea of people jumped and cheered in celebration that their blacksmith had defeated his opponent. Avatar Noren threw up his hands in victory, and grinned at his accomplishment, while Horn's face transitioned from one of blissful happiness to one of utter disbelief. The Guillens were furious in outrage.

"How did you know!?" demanded Ang.

Carra yelled into Ang's ear so he could hear her over the roar of cheering. "Every antler in that armor already has a soul in it."

Over the sounds of celebration, a clattering of horseshoes upon cobblestone streets emerged from the southeastern road, as a detachment of knights marched into the crossroads, led by a banner carrier displaying the city's colors, striped azure and gold. The crowd made way as the unit of knights fanned out into the town square. The knight in the back, displaying a brilliant set of scale armor marked with the etchings of an Avatar upon the right shoulder, halted his mount at the edge of the crowd.

"Raekor!" yelled the armored knight over the sea of people that filled the square. The scale-covered keratin looked up at him in response.

"Did the Oracle respond to your prayers?" the knight called. His keen scale armor shone in polished brilliance.

The keratin in the dark wool shook his head in response, then drew up the hood to cover his head.

"Who is that?" asked Erador as he stared up at the knight from across the square.

"That's the man you came to speak with. Knight Lord Lowry, Duke of Nolta Tenoble."

The Duke grimaced in disappointment at Raekor's reply. The Duke scanned the sea of commoners standing before him, and his eyes were drawn to the small grouping of men with antlers standing in the crowd. The elkin met his gaze, and his eyes stretched open with instant alertness. The bald and overweight Jon Rennly noticed this as well and approached the Duke, whispering up at him from the side of the Duke's horse.

"Avatar Noren!" the Duke shouted. "I require your counsel at an audience this night. May I request your presence at my keep?"

"You may," he responded.

"And I understand that congratulations are in order for yet another success. There will be a feast in your honor this night." His hand then gestured toward the elkin. "And to our esteemed visitors, I understand that we have an appointment. I bid you follow me to my keep as we have much to discuss over a feast of pheasant and wine." Duke Lowry then turned his gaze to the thickset bearded men. "And I trust that Horn and the rest of the Guillens will leave peacefully this time. I'm sure the guards will see to it."

Ang looked at the elkin. "Looks like this is where we part ways. If you need help finding anything else in the city, look me up."

***

The elkin were escorted through a massive double wooden door entryway into an enormous dining hall, just off the main entrance of the Keep. Erador was stunned at the absurd length of the dining table that filled this room. A long velvet running sheet ran the table's length, draping over the ends. The table was thick, and sanded smooth. A massive wrought iron chandelier hung from the high ceiling. Oversized wooden framed paintings covered the stone walls between torch sconces and windows.

As they sat down, plates of roasted pheasant breast were placed before them by numerous servants. The Duke sat across from Erador, each sitting at the middle of the length of the table. Avatar Noren sat to his right, and Jon Rennly sat to his left. Erador and all of Clan Wyndlyn sat along the opposite side, facing the three humans. Erador had removed his helm and gauntlets and placed them on the bench beside him. He and his fellow elkin grabbed up the succulent roast with their hands and tore into it, enjoying each juicy bite.

The Duke was the picture of wealth. His cloak, half blue and half gold, was fastened about his shoulders with two golden brooches the shape of the sun. His scale armor seemed pristine, polished enough to see your reflection in it. He had long golden hair that flowed down to the tops of his shoulders, groomed and cut with care. His clear blue eyes and handsome smile that revealed dimples in his cheeks bespoke an easy and long-practiced charm.

231

"So, Warlord Vorkus is it?" asked Duke Lowry, initiating the conversation.

Carra kicked Erador under the table. "Yes," he managed. Erador did not understand these human customs of discussing pressing matters while eating. It made him uneasy, and while he wanted to eat the juicy meat in front of him, he thought it best to wait.

"You look young to be a Warlord," commented Duke Lowry with a taste of curiosity.

Erador grunted in irritation. "We do not have time for such talk. We've come here with a warning."

The Duke took a last bite of his pheasant and dropped the roasted leg onto his plate as his attitude switched from blithe to despondent. "So tell me, what news do you bring?" His words were spoken in the most regretful manner; Erador could tell that he had already had earfuls of bad news.

"We are Clan Wyndlyn, at least what is left of it. We've traveled here from Cerebus-Senti. We have defended the inhabitants of this land from the demon creations of the Soul Smith for many years, but now we are too few in number, and a band of vyceptors are now roaming free, unchecked and unchallenged. I believe they are headed here and your watch posts along the road we approached from are vacant. You leave yourself exposed."

"Vyceptors? I thought those were only a problem to the men in the eastern lands," said Duke Lowry.

"What do you propose?" asked Jon Rennly as Duke Lowry began rubbing his forehead, tending to a headache.

"You must send troops to combat the vyceptors, away from your city. Your walls do not protect your farmers and their fields."

The Duke slammed his fist upon the well-worn table in frustration. "Our supply lines have been cut off to the east, most of my men have been repositioned to the front lines, and now you're telling me I'm about to get attacked from my flank? What proof do you have of this?"

Erador peered at him in umbrage, motionless, staring straight across the table at him in an intimidating manner, waiting for the Duke to see the truth in his eyes. Duke Lowry seemed reluctant to continue the conversation, but took Erador for his word. "I can perhaps send fifteen veteran soldiers."

"Only fifteen? We could handle more vyceptors than fifteen of your *best* men," boasted Wiltyn in his white runic Sky Smith armor.

"Our supplies are cut off. It would be suicide to send troops as far as Cerebeus-Senti," said the Duke.

"It would also be suicide to only send fifteen," rebutted Erador.

After much deliberation and bickering, the Duke came to terms with the threat at hand. "I suppose I could gather a reserve of fifty troops; ten cavalry, twenty pikemen, and twenty archers. But that's *if* I can scrounge up the weapons and armor. Avatar Noren, can you build the required equipment in time?"

"Not with the materials I have at hand. We'll have to purchase more from the miners up the road," said Avatar Noren.

Duke Lowry sighed. "This war is proving too costly. I'm sure the horses need hay and saddles, while the archers need more arrows... I can only afford to deploy them to the first watch post along the western road."

Erador leaned in. "It won't do you any good. The vyceptors need to be stopped at the source or else the Soul Smith will continue to summon more until you are overwhelmed. If finances are what you need, we will provide plenty of crystal to support this effort. Baltor and Tysyra, please go retrieve one rucksack for the Duke."

Baltor and Tysyra took one last bite of their pheasants and ran out the door.

"Why do you care so much?" asked the Duke with a bewildered look.

"We don't want to see this land ravaged by beasts in our absence. It is our home too, and we want to preserve it this way. Now, we have given you much knowledge—so we hope to gain some in return. Have you seen any other elkin on your travels back from seeing your King?"

"No, but some of my scouts working to the east of the city reported seeing some. They left them alone."

"How many were there?" asked Zimmerik.

"An entire herd," said Duke Lowry.

Erador snarled. "That many could only have been Clan Hortyr." He cursed them beneath his breath.

Carra interjected, "Which way were they headed?"

"South. Why? What's this about?"

Erador turned to look at Carra. "The jungle. They must be meeting him at Sonir-Senti." Erador still had no notion what his quarry hoped to accomplish, but it didn't matter. "Then that is where we're headed. If we find Clan Hortyr, we find Dryden." He looked back at the Duke. "Do not worry, your men made the right decision to stay back from that herd of elkin. They've betrayed our trust and slaughtered our clan when our elders were the most vulnerable, all at the behest of the one called Warlord Dryden."

Just then, Tysyra and Baltor returned, he carrying a sack over his shoulder. His thick muscular arm swung it off his shoulder and let it spill across the table. Hundreds of purple crystals skittered across the runner and amongst the platters and cups. Duke Lowry's eyes lit up in amazement as his mouth dropped in disbelief at the sight of so much crystal. He looked at the sack, still bulging with the majority of its burden. "All purple? *All* of it?"

Erador nodded. "One last question," he added, urgency tautening his voice. "Where can we purchase mercenaries and beasts of war?"

CHAPTER 21

"Why did you not ask the Duke about lending us some of his troops to go after Warlord Dryden?" asked Vynocent.

"We do not know for certain if Warlord Dryden still lives," Erador replied. "Plus, you saw how reluctant he was to send even fifty of his men to guard his western flank from vyceptors. I'm relieved to have asked for that first, or else we may not have received any help at all. We needed to find another means of gathering our troops to attack Clan Hortyr."

"Through mercenaries and sell-swords, right?" Tysyra asked as she playfully bumped against Erador.

Erador smiled and nodded his head. "It means that they won't be trained soldiers with reliable equipment. Any mercenaries we find will likely have a wide array of armaments, with no common weapon to mount any sort of battle strategy around."

Zimmerik joined in, "So instead, we're going to have to fight against trained adult elkin with a random selection of weaponry."

Erador buried his eyes into his hand and shook his head in disbelief. "This is why the elkin stick to a few select weapons, so that our strategies in battle can be adaptable to counter any surge. We're trained to place the right weapon in front of the right enemy."

"Perhaps we can use that knowledge to our advantage," suggested Vynocent. "Since we know the weaponry they possess, we know how they will fight. We need to come at them with surprise, to break their line of hunters."

"That's where the war beasts come in," exclaimed Hammynt. "We need to go see the Xyla Druids of the God-Spear Forest to assemble our horde."

"Yes, we must secure their aid! I'll be counting on you, Hammynt, to command the beasts, to launch the assault," said Erador.

"It's despicable for the Duke to have barred them from entry to this city due to their worship of the Gaia Smith. Perhaps that is the same hostility we sensed the Duke held against the Guillens too. These followers of the Old Gods are going to drive me mad," declared Wiltyn.

"Well, if we go see the Xyla Druids, I want to bring Abby with us," demanded Carra.

"Nightfall is already upon us. We must first head to the Stumbling Seer Tavern to find the one the Duke called Grindor the Ravenous," declared Zimmerik eagerly.

Erador was lost to his own thoughts and began shaking his head in disbelief. "Assembling an army in the black of night… Purchasing their services with crystal… We can only hope that their loyalty won't run dry," he muttered to himself.

Clan Wyndlyn could see the grief in Erador's expression. "What are you thinking, Erador? Do you think we can succeed?"

Erador let out a deep breath. "There's a lot to consider. Even if Warlord Dryden fell to the harsh blizzard of the Tundra, Clan Hortyr must still be confronted for their abandonment of Beknen Valley and their theft of the contents of our Armory! But if Warlord Dryden survived the blizzard, then we must compete with his sword Tempest as well. What if Clan Hortyr is waiting for us, and have set up their traps? What are the chances that our sell-swords can outmatch Clan Hortyr? What if the mercenaries don't join us? Or the Xyla Druids for that matter. The odds are stacking against us."

Despite hearing Erador's burdened thoughts on their seemingly insurmountable foe, Clan Wyndlyn was not discouraged. Listening to the concerns of their leader focused their ideas on strategizing ways to mitigate his concerns. Clan Wyndlyn never had to rely on the strength of others before, and it was a difficult concept for them to come to terms with. But their will to succeed was strong, and they knew they must see that their fallen were avenged. Lesser men would have misinterpreted their leader's concerns as fear, but the elkin had only vengeance on their minds.

They found themselves standing in the street under the starlit sky, and their voices were carrying farther than they would have liked. They couldn't help but feel a bit of paranoia that someone was eavesdropping. The empty streets were devoid of the horse-drawn carriages and the women dressed in corsets that bustled through them in the day. Just looking about the barren streets and dark alleys filled them with uneasiness, never knowing who might be lurking in the shadows at this time of night. They continued walking down the center of the torch-lit street following the instructions that Duke Lowry had provided. When they came upon a couple drunken commoners dancing in the street, the elkin knew they must be close.

"Erador," spoke Baltor in a low tone. "We wasted a night an' a day here in this city. If Warlord Dryden still lives, I think he's probably met up with Clan Hortyr already. They had a head start on us."

"Agreed, but did we have any other choice?" asked Erador. "We know nothing of Warlord Dryden's whereabouts, nor if he is even alive. All we knew was that Dryden himself wanted to go to the stone jungle. We did not know where Clan Hortyr would rendezvous with him until now. The Duke said that Clan Hortyr was spotted traveling south-east of here toward the Chyxurlgon Jungle; that is where the Duke said his supply lines were cut, is it not?"

"Indeed it is," voiced Vynocent. "What do you have in mind?"

"I imagine Clan Hortyr's chosen route will slow their speed, and possibly cause delays, as I am certain their path will cross with the human conflict in these lands. We may have faster travel, and might even catch up to them if we travel south-west. It would be best if whatever forces we can gather arrive at the Chyxurlgon Jungle healthy and unchallenged," Erador said.

"But humans would pose no obstacle to a herd of elkin. How do you figure that it would slow them down?"

"I do not think it was humans that had cut off the Duke's supply route—and it certainly wasn't Clan Hortyr. Though Duke Lowry did not say it out loud, his eyes alluded to something far more fearsome. Something far more dangerous," said Erador.

"Then we may stand a chance to catch them; but we can't spend any more time here if we want to have any hope of doing so," declared Wiltyn.

"Perhaps it is best we split up then," offered Hammynt. "I can take Carra and Abby to the God-Spear Forest with one rucksack of crystal while the rest of you track down Grindor the Ravenous."

"I'll join you," volunteered Zimmerik, evoking a smile from Carra. "We must heed Warlord Vorkus' warning and safeguard the crystal."

Erador's Onyx helm concealed his conniving glance at Zimmerik. "So be it. The woods are dark and Carra shall light the way."

***

Baltor threw open the heavy oaken door to the Stumbling Seer Tavern and the smell of musk and ale rolled out. Baltor's large stature filled the doorway, drawing the gaze of the tavern patrons one after another until he had captured all their attention. Conversation came halt, followed by the twangs of the bard's lute, plunging the tavern into an awkward silence; some men were astonished by the mere sight of an elkin, while most appeared to be waiting for something to happen. They watched in a drunken stupor as Baltor took a step backwards into the night air, making way for a figure as dark as shadow to step inside. It was as if the night itself had entered the tavern… wearing scythe-like metallic antlers upon its head. The heavy plate armor clunked with every step upon the tavern's wooden floor, which creaked beneath his weight. Fear spread amongst the patrons; many of them stood up in sobering surprise, while others backed against the walls.

Erador took a look about the tavern, trying to guess the identity of Grindor the Ravenous from everyone's reactions, the same way he used to guess the fathers of newborns during the Call of the Fates. The tavern was lit by candles, making Erador's Onyx Smith plate armor seem more silhouette than substance. Only on occasion would the flickering candlelight catch one of the golden runic inscriptions upon his chest or show his burning eyes within his helm. As he scanned the room, his unnatural antlers pointed at each man and woman like the finger of death, making him appear like some shade demon left by the Old Gods.

The tavern was furnished in a mix of wooden tables, square and round, freckled with knots. The wall behind the bar was lined with small barrels laid upon their sides, with bronze spigots protruding. In one back corner of the tavern, a large fire roared within a stone fireplace large enough for a man to lay in. Various animal heads decorated the walls, and many aged blue-and-gold flags hung from a ceiling darkened by the smoke of many years.

To one side of the door stood a man past his prime with a rugged unshaven face, dressed in a tattered tunic bearing the blue and gold clothing of the guards, though carried no weapons on his person. Behind the bar was a grotesque and overweight man who looked as though he had drunk away most of the tavern's profits. There was a wobbling drunken woman who braced herself against the bar table, dressed in dirty commoner's clothes that would have fit better on a bigger woman. A well-dressed man wore a fitted overcoat with an abundance of golden buttons and an upturned collar. The bard had a dark mustache that matched his wavy hair; he wore a clean silk tunic tucked into trousers held up by a thin leather belt. A group of toughs huddled around one table; each had burns or scars upon their face worthy of a long tale.

Numerous other less notable commoners packed the musky tavern, though Erador took little notice of them. His eyes were drawn to an avian in the far corner by the heat of the fireplace, sitting apart from the other patrons, as though separated from his flock. He was the size of a man, but most of his appearance was that of an eagle. Brown feathers covered his body, white ones from the neck up, where they peeked from beneath a silver coif. He had a short down-curved golden beak between solid black eyes. His studded leather armor was custom fitted to leave his enormous wings free, and his bird feet exhibited sharpened talons. The avian's only human features were his arms and hands.

Erador stared at the avian in curiosity. *He must be Grindor the Ravenous,* thought Erador, judging by his lack of reaction to Erador's presence, *except Duke Lowry made no mention of him being an avian, an odd detail for one to leave out.*

Erador took one last glance about the room. "I am looking for the one called Grindor the Ravenous," he announced.

Most of the humans' fear-riddled faces turned toward the avian at the back of the tavern, and Erador smirked behind his masking Onyx helm. But before he could speak, the avian responded in a defensive tone, "Are you a shade demon that has come to reclaim his life?"

"I am no demon. I am an elkin."

"You answered but half of my question," squawked the avian. "Have you come for his head?"

Erador was taken aback. *What type of man has the Duke sent me after? Why did he recommend him to me?* he thought. Erador then doubted if this was indeed Grindor or not, but he spoke on. "No. I have come to extend an offer to him. But I must speak to him this night."

The avian cocked his head to one side. "Grindor the Ravenous shares no interest in the affairs of an elkin. You waste your breath."

"But he would have an interest in the compensation we offer," countered Erador. "If you could arrange an audience with him for me, I will make it worth his while… and yours." Erador motioned for the rest of the elkin to enter the tavern. Baltor hefted a rucksack of crystal in one hand while his other held his axe over his broad shoulder. Wiltyn, Gressyn, Vynocent, and Tysyra followed, closing the tavern door behind them.

The avian's eyes blinked a few times, as if his curiosity was outweighing his caution. "Who are you, and who told you of Grindor the Ravenous?" he squawked.

"I am Erador Wyndlyn. Grindor the Ravenous was recommended to us… from a highly trusted source," lied Erador.

"Yah, and who's the brute behind you?"

"That there is Baltor Wyndlyn."

The avian tilted its head in perplexity as it glanced back and forth from Erador to Baltor and back. "You are brothers? I do not see the resemblance."

"Brothers?" winced Erador. "I do not know of that word."

The avian looked at Erador with skepticism and disbelief. He could tell that Erador was uncomfortable from his question. The avian sat there, looking upon the six elkin blocking the entry to the Stumbling Seer Tavern, two dressed in runic plate armor.

"Why should Grindor the Ravenous trust you?" he squawked.

"He can trust my word, but that can only go as far as he allows it. Otherwise, he can trust my payment, as I'll pay up front. But how will I know I can trust him?" answered Erador.

"Everyone out!" squawked the bird-man. The elkin stepped out of the way to let eager tavern patrons flee into the chill of the night, abandoning their half-drunk tankards. Once the Stumbling Seer Tavern was void of customers, the avian answered, "You can trust Grindor because you will know his face, and where he lives." The avian took a firm grasp on the table at which he sat and slid it away from the wall. The avian's talons sank into a small opening between the floor boards that had been concealed by the table, and pulled up a secret trap door entrance to a basement beneath the building with his foot.

"Follow me," he said and descended the hidden stairs.

The elkin looked at each other for reassurance, then followed the avian down the steps. The avian reached the bottom of the wooden staircase and arrived at a locked iron door. He knocked in a series of knocks the elkin guessed was probably not as random as it sounded. They waited in silence for what seemed a long time before they heard a metallic jolt from the other side of the door. The door eased inward slightly, then the avian pushed it wide.

They had walked so far down that they weren't beneath the floor of the tavern anymore. The room they found themselves in bore a resemblance to a mine tunnel. Thick, aged beams provided support all along the walls and across the ceiling, the height of which was just enough for an elkin and his antlers. There was nothing to the room but dirt and minimal furniture: a frame bed, barrels of ale, desk, and chair. The only attempt at decoration was a map that had been hung up like a painting.

A dark-skinned man, holding a torch and wearing mismatched leather armor and a sword sheathed at his waist, stood by the door in silence. The avian stopped half way into the room and spoke to the man sitting behind the plain desk. "Grindor, sire, I have with me Erador Wyndlyn and his fellow elkin. They have a proposal for you."

Grindor the Ravenous was sitting in his chair sideways so that his back was against the armrest and his feet up on the desk, searching for the last drop of ale at the bottom of his stein. He wore black leather boots and a lengthy heavy coat the color of charcoal. He had golden rings on almost every finger, and wore many golden chains around his neck. As he slammed his empty stein on the table, Erador got a good look at his face. His eyes were cold and bleak, as if they had seen too much for one lifetime. His nose looked as if it had been broken before, and his sideburns ran all the way down to the hinge of his jaw. His hands looked weathered and experienced with the sword.

Grindor got to his feet and adjusted his coat, relaxed in front of such unique visitors dressed in equally unique armor. "If you have been brought this far to see me, your situation must be dire." His voice was as coarse as a serrated blade.

"I am in need of a guide, along with a host of men as hungry for crystal as their swords are for blood, ready to march by daybreak."

Grindor ran one long-nailed finger across a bushy eyebrow. "That's a lot of men in a short amount of time. What might you offer for—?"

His sentence was cut short by the crash of the rucksack upon his desk. It elicited a reaction similar to the one that had been dropped on Duke Lowry's dining table. The eyes of the torch bearer, the avian, and Grindor all lit up in splendor at such a substantial amount of crystal, growing wider still as Grindor opened the sack to reveal its color. "It's yours. All of it. As payment in full, up front. As many men as that can afford," Erador summed up.

Grindor's greed did not overwhelm his prudence, even though he found it difficult to look away from such a pile of wealth. "You get straight to the point. I like that. But before I commit, I'd like to know where you need a guide to? And why do you require an entire host of men?"

"We must be led down a south-western route toward the Chyxurlgon Jungle. The larger our war band, the less danger we will attract during our travels. Once there, we plan to confront a traitorous clan of elkin to reap revenge for their murderous crimes against my clan!" Erador growled with indignation.

"An entire clan of elkin? The amount of men that I could gather in that time may not prove sufficient."

"We are acquiring other soldiers as we speak. If you decline, then this is the last you'll see of this crystal," stated Erador with finality.

"Calm yourself, friend. We take the jobs that no one else would, and have never turned down a fight. And we are still here! Which, I think, proves our skill. You have indeed come to the right place, Erador Wyndlyn. We make our living by getting paid to fight, so it makes no difference for us to know what you are fighting for.

There is no need to trouble us with the details of your concerns. So where shall we meet you tomorrow?"

For the first time that night, Erador gave a smile of confidence. "Outside of the city, near the edge of the God-Spear Forest."

***

Carra, Zimmerik, Hammynt and Abby had been wandering along a directionless path through the forest, guided only by a small lantern-like glow Carra had conjured atop the Channeler's Staff. The trees grew straight as poles and didn't bear a single branch until one hundred feet above the ground. These trees made pine trees appear dwarfed by comparison. Zimmerik rested his hand upon their beige bark, which was smooth to the touch. The high canopy blocked the moon and stars from view, enshrouding the forest floor with darkness. It was pitch black except for Carra's light.

The hoot of an owl kept Abby on edge. The acoustics of the forest made the sound seem like it came from everywhere and nowhere. "How will we know where to find them?" asked Abby, as Zimmerik hoisted her atop a tree which had toppled across their path.

"Duke Lowry said that *they* will find *us*," answered Hammynt.

"Abby, I chose to bring you along so that you could witness firsthand what the followers of the Gaia Smith are like," said Carra.

Zimmerik smiled. "You already missed an amazing blacksmith duel," he said, climbing last over the fallen tree.

Abby paused in shock. "You saw the Blacksmiths fight!? Was the Onyx Smith there?"

They all had a good laugh. "No, no," said Zimmerik. "*Human* blacksmiths had a competition to see who could make better armor. It was a big deal for them. One of them worshipped the Scorch Smith."

A gentle breeze rustled some leaves in the distance. "So what was it like?" asked Abby in her innocent voice.

Hammynt carried the last rucksack of crystal over his shoulder. "The humans here are stubborn and stuck in their old ways. They still worship the Old Gods; it is no place for an elkin."

"I'm sure they would say the same about us, Hammynt," retorted Carra. "The humans here have known how to use Old Magic for ages, while we only discovered it a few days before."

"Yes, but it turns their skin into scales. I don't see anything happen to you when you cast Goma incantations."

Abby turned to see Carra's reaction, as she remembered seeing the black veins in Carra's arm back in the cave. Carra said no more, but clutched her arm at the elbow. They had made their way deep into the forest, and every tree was starting to look the same. They heard another owl, closer this time, which made Hammynt stop and set his rucksack on the earth. He sniffed the cold night air, and crouched low to the ground. The other elkin did not speak, but turned their backs to each other to watch their flanks. Hammynt ran his hand across the ground as if studying its surface; he looked a few steps ahead and caught the slightest glimmer from Carra's light. A single strand, almost invisible to the eye, running taut a foot above the forest floor. A trip wire. He withdrew a javelin from the quiver on his back; his companions did the same. They knew something was lurking in the darkness just beyond Carra's light, watching them.

"We have come to seek the aid of the Xyla Druids of the God-Spear Forest," called Hammynt with brazen confidence. "If you are not them, then prepare to be attacked!" Silence followed the fading of his voice; they could hear their own hearts beating in their chest.

A large pair of eyes appeared in the darkness in front of Carra; she was amazed at how silent the creature had been. She could not tell what type of beast they belonged to, though they remained fixed upon her, hovering at her eye level, as whatever it was approached her with silent footsteps. She held out her hand in a defensive preparation. Something was odd about the eyes, a strange twinkle that seemed unnatural. Then a snarling brown head, as large as Abby, with jaws large enough to shatter bone, entered the light; a grizzly bear of monumental size… with a rider mounted on its back.

Carra gasped at how close the bear came to her face; she could feel its hot breath upon her. She turned her head and realized that they were surrounded by several more such bears and riders. The riders were human, but used no saddle like those she'd seen upon horses. Instead, they clutched slack fur at the back of the bears' necks, the way a mother would carry its cub. The riders wore leather, furs, and even curved patches of bark as shoulder plates and greaves. Their hair seemed stained black; their eyes were a faint lime green. All were slender of form; their immense steeds made them look almost childlike in contrast.

"You can put down your weapons," declared one rider. The elkin all obeyed. "What aid of ours do you seek?"

"We have come to purchase from you all manner of beasts that have been bred for war, and to hire trainers to guide them," said Hammynt, awe-struck at the command they wielded over such imposing beasts.

"Then it is not our aid, but war that you truly seek," said the rider. "Turn back. We cannot help you."

"No! Wait!" shouted Hammynt. "Please. This is your war too!" Tears began to well in his eyes, and his voice was full of emotion. "We are all that remains of Clan Wyndlyn, guardians of Beknen Valley and protectors of this land. Our elders were murdered by our neighboring clan. That clan has marched south, abandoning their post, and the Soul Smith's demons are already roaming unchallenged across the northern lands. If we do not achieve vengeance upon the traitorous Clan Hortyr, then evil and monstrous threats will spread across this land like a plague."

"I see that you speak from the heart, elkin warrior, and that you have traveled far to get here, but we cannot act upon hearsay. We have no means to validate your claims."

"Then don't participate. Just sell us your saber-tooths, your wolves, any beast that might aid in battle. We came with an abundance of crystal."

"We do not need your crystal. And if we sold you our animals, then we would still be helping your side. When it comes to war, we must remain neutral until action is necessary."

"Action *is* necessary!" responded Zimmerik in anger. "Allow us to plead with your leader. It's the least you could do."

"The least we could do is nothing. In speaking to you, we have already done more. I'm sorry, elkin of Clan Wyndlyn, but we are unable to help you," said the rider.

"Leave peacefully now," said another. "We will be watching you."

CHAPTER 22

Erador, Tysyra, and the other teens sat in unforgiving wooden stools in the empty lobby of the inn. Tysyra sat beside a table, her unbraided hair tied in a bun as she ran the edge of her spade-shaped blade against a whetstone. With the exception of the repetitive scrape of iron against stone, they all waited in silence for Carra, Zimmerik, Abby, and Hammynt to return from the God-Spear Forest.

The night only grew darker and quieter as time moved on. They waited a long while, knowing full well that their other group had to return from an excursion of unknown depth into the forest.

One by one, sleep overcame them, and their heavy eyes fell closed. Tysyra looked about at the sleeping Baltor, Gressyn, Vynocent, and Wiltyn, and stopped sharpening her blade. "Erador, I'm willing to stay up with you until Hammynt's return, but tomorrow we march. We should wake these four so they may retire to their rooms."

Erador nodded. Wiltyn, Gressyn, and Vynocent were able to wake and stumble up the stairs to their rooms; Baltor was so deep in slumber they thought it best to accompany him, to make sure he found his room. They slung his arms over their shoulders, guided him awkwardly up stairs never intended to take three abreast, dropped him onto his blanket-covered bed, tip-toed out of the room and closed the door, then waited a moment in silence, listening to see if their clamor had awakened anyone in the inn.

Erador tugged at the neck of his runic plate armor to readjust it after shouldering Baltor's weight.

"Here," stated Tysyra as she took his helm from him, steering him into his own room. "You shouldn't have to wear that any longer. Allow me to assist you."

"You're right. I can't remember the last time I slept without this armor on," said Erador as they entered his room. When she chuckled, he blushed slightly and amended his statement, "The last time I took it off to go to sleep, anyway." Tysyra placed the helmet upon the dressing table and then began loosening the buckles under his armor. As soon as the last piece of armor came off, Erador felt like he was lighter than air. He stretched his legs and arms and rolled his ahead around to crack his neck.

Tysyra watched him in amusement. "You know, it has been night for so long that I would bet it is more tomorrow than it is today," smiled Tysyra.

"What do you mean?"

"I mean, it is now your twentieth soul-keep… Warlord Erador." Erador had forgotten about his soul-keep, and was surprised at the mention of it. The sound of hearing the title of Warlord was savory to his ears. *I wish my father were here to see this day of my ascendance to adulthood.*

Tysyra continued, "And you know what every boy must do on his twentieth soul-keep to become a man, don't you?" Her voice was soft and affectionate and her hands began to massage and caress his muscular shoulders.

Erador turned to face her. "But you are not yet yourself an adult."

"I am only two years from it, and I don't mind sacrificing my purity for this. With you as the new leader and Warlord of Clan Wyndlyn, you must have the experience. We must keep with tradition." Her words were gentle and soothing. Tysyra placed her small hand upon the center of Erador's chest and pushed as she walked forward, backing him up toward the bed.

"You are a strong warrior; you will make strong children," she whispered into his ear as she let down the bun her hair had been gathered in. Unbraided, her hair flowed about her like a curtain of silk.

She slipped her furs and tunic off of her shoulders, letting them fall to the floor. She stood shirtless in front of Erador, who made no movements to stop her. As she continued to shed clothing, Erador responded in a heated, animalistic fury, and began tearing off his tunic and trousers. She pushed Erador over so that he fell flat on his back atop his bedding. Her soft, supple naked body straddled his and then their lips met with affectionate embrace.

Her curved athletic figure rocked in a rhythmic dance as they locked in lustful union. Instinct guided them as bestial passions took control. Erador began to twist his head from one side to the other in great strain, while Tysyra closed her eyes and rolled her head back. Their ragged gasps sounded in unison. Once the concupiscent dance was done, Tysyra smiled and opened her eyes and looked down at Erador to see an eerie glow emitting from his eyes; she realized in horror that it was Vorkus looking up at her.

Tysyra jumped to her feet, grabbed her clothes and clutched them against her body. Tears welled up in her eyes, and she threw open the door to run to her room, only to see Carra arriving at the top of the stairs, the others close behind her. They exchanged awkward glances, and the tears fell down Tysyra's cheeks as she ran in humiliation to her room.

Warlord Vorkus arose from the bed and looked out into the hall to see the tired and worried faces of Carra, Zimmerik, Hammynt and Abby. He stood in his doorway, his muscular physique illuminated only by the weak candle light; his radiant eyes cast a light of their own in the dimness of the corridor. He gave a pleased smiled, and closed his door.

Carra looked at her companions and watched as new worry replaced old. "I guess we don't have to deliver the bad news until morning," said Hammynt.

"What do we do with the extra rucksack of crystal, then?" asked Carra.

"Leave it here with the children. There is no place in battle for them," advised Zimmerik. "Let's all get what rest we can. Tomorrow is going to be a long day."

***

As the sun began peeking over the rooftops, Warlord Vorkus led Clan Wyndlyn from the city to meet Grindor the Ravenous and his host of men, patiently awaiting them on the outskirts of the God-Spear Forest beneath the open sky. The immense trees striped the ground with their monstrous shadows.

Grindor was dressed as he had been the night before, and by the looks of it, he hadn't gotten a wink of sleep. He had bags under his eyes, yet he was somehow wide awake and chipper.

Standing beside Grindor were ten soldiers in uniform, each wielding fearsome curved scimitars and sea-tortoise shells as shields. The shell's massive scales overlapped like snake's skin, and the shield was larger than the sap-coated wooden ones carried by the elkin. Accompanying them was a large unit of men, perhaps fifty in number, armed with all manner of weapons: spears, tridents, clubs, swords, and the occasional bow. They wore a variety of clothing, furs, and armor. Dispersed among their ranks were mules packed with rations and supplies.

"Ah, there you are," smiled Grindor. "May I introduce you to your band of misfits?"

Warlord Vorkus took in the handful of men standing before him and then turned to his fellow elkin. "This is all we were able to gather?" he shouted in anger.

Before Hammynt was able to speak, Grindor chimed in, "Oh no, there is more coming to augment our forces, I assure you. You will be surprised to see how much your crystal was able to afford. These are troubled times, and your generosity was well received. We were even able to procure provisions for our men. Food, blankets, tents and… other necessary supplies, carried by the mules." Grindor spoke very fast and enunciated every word.

"Who else is coming then? And how many?"

Grindor danced with excitement, his collection of golden necklaces jingling about his neck. "I stayed up all night, and this is all I could muster from the city in such a short amount of time. I had to send an osprey with a message to other mercenary leaders in order to summon more soldiers for this task. They should be arriving soon."

"You did not answer my question!" barked Warlord Vorkus.

"Ah! Well, the avian, Ocamyr, he will return with his flock… around two dozen. And Scokoo—the leader of the Brenzwik Tribe of erethizons; he was the only one to answer my osprey's call, unfortunately. Short notice, again. He should bring as many with him as I have."

All the elkin but Warlord Vorkus grew a little uneasy at thought of fighting side by side with a tribe of erethizons. Most remembered the battle, just a few years back, where Clan Wyndlyn defended Cerebus-Senti against an assault from the same tribe. It was Zimmerik's father who had felled their leader with a skilled javelin throw, which was how they won the Sky Smith runic armor that Wiltyn wore now.

Grindor continued speaking his thoughts, "This will be the most men I have ever summoned—dare I say, the largest gathering of mercenaries ever assembled. The best army money can buy!"

"I just hope it is enough," muttered Warlord Vorkus.

"But didn't you mention that you were also acquiring beasts of war too?" inquired Grindor.

Hammynt had been dreading this moment, but conjured the courage to speak up. "We were unsuccessful. The Xyla Druids did not wish to lend us their services, absolving themselves from a conflict they thought did not affect them, despite my attempts to convince them otherwise."

All Warlord Vorkus could manage was a glare of contempt at Hammynt.

Vynocent leaned over to whisper into his twin's ear. "I bet Warlord Vorkus wishes we had Sir Duke Lowry's fifty men now."

Wiltyn whispered back, "He wasn't the one who did the negotiations. They might be here if he had... well, some of them; I can't imagine cavalry being of use in a jungle. But then again, I'm not Hammynt." They both chuckled in spite of the gravity of their situation. "I get the feeling he would rather throw everything he can into this and worry about protecting against demon incursions afterward. He's even hotter to get at Warlord Dryden than Erador is... I wonder why."

The Brenzwik Tribe now joined them, emerging from the shadows of the forest. They looked like men with porcupine quills for hair. The quills ran down neck and back, and from shoulders to knuckles; even their shins bristled. They were dressed in uniform, wearing only an apron of leather scale, tied at the neck and covering their chest, then wrapping into a skirt about their waist, so as not to cover their quills. They bore lengthy halberds, and kept spiked flails at their waists. They even had a standard bearer at the head of their group, flying a flag depicting the glyph of the Brenzwik Tribe. Their tribe outnumbered the human sell-swords by a dozen or so. They came to a halt in precise formation; then their leader, Scokoo, approached the elkin. He carried a great quiver full of arrows slung over his shoulder, and held a great bow wrought with runic inscriptions running the entire length of its surface; upon his head was the helm of the Sky Smith.

Grindor advanced to greet him, "Scokoo! It has been too long, old friend."

Scokoo stood proud and arrogant. "Hold a minute, Grindor. I must have word with Clan Wyndlyn first."

The elkin couldn't believe their eyes. As Scokoo stepped past Grindor, his retinue came up behind him, halberds at the ready. Scokoo stared into the darkness of Warlord Vorkus' Onyx helm as he spoke, "When my tribe got the message of a chance to kill some elkin, we jumped at the opportunity. But when we heard who we had to fight alongside, we found ourselves in a predicament, given our history together. So I came here with this proposition: I will let you keep our portion of the payment if you hand over what is rightfully ours. Give me the Sky armor, or else my pikemen walk!"

Warlord Vorkus stood motionless, staring with menacing eyes at the erethizon who dared make demands of him. *To hand them the armor is to relinquish my control over them,* he thought. *We are the ones paying for service, it is we who should make demands and they should obey, not the other way around. Though what choice do we have? Without their help we would be lost... and he will be a powerful ally on the battlefield if he can wield that bow.*

"Wiltyn! Give him the armor," called Vorkus.

Scokoo's eyes lit up with pleasure and a grin broke across his face. His retinue of pikemen relaxed. The elkin gasped and grumbled, but they assisted Wiltyn in doffing the cloudy white runic armor. Piece by piece, they carried it over and placed it at the feet of Scokoo, who looked down at the empty armor as if his life's search had come to an end.

"Clan Wyndlyn, you have the aid of the Brenzwik Tribe in battle!"

"Good," intoned Vorkus. "Now take down your banner. We want to travel with as little fanfare as possible."

Scokoo gestured, and the banner was furled. As Scokoo began the delicate task of fitting armor over smoothed-down quills—with which he required considerable assistance from his tribesmen—a flock of avians arrived, swooping down from the sky. Their feathers were a mix of colors, some grey, others white, a few all black; their features resembled those of raptors. They wore silver coifs atop their heads and studded leather armor crafted to fit around their wings. Their feet bore dangerous talons, and they wielded two-handed hammers in their human arms. Ocamyr approached Grindor and asked for his flock's payment.

Vorkus assessed the mass of soldiers that they were able to gather, and his confidence began to grow. Grindor took pleasure at his ability to summon such an impressive retinue of troops. He seemed to wash his hands in the air in nervous habit, giddy from the sight of his sleepless night's work come to fruition.

"This is the stuff bards will sing about," proclaimed Grindor. "An army composed of four different races, wielding two complete full sets of Blacksmith runic armor, charging into the stone jungles of Chyxurlgon! Brothers, we'll be remembered in legend!" His host of men cheered and Vorkus removed his helm to make a speech of his own.

As soon as the cheers died down, Vorkus spoke up so all could hear; taking pauses in between his sentences to let his voice ring crisp and clear across the morning air. "We have a long march ahead of us. Take caution and keep your wits about you. I don't know how much you've heard, but we're headed to the stone jungles of Chyxurlgon. When we get there, we may catch our enemy by surprise. And if they're smart, they'll surrender—and each of you will have the easiest pay day of your lives. And if they don't, then we'll tear them apart limb from limb. And if anyone happens to slay Warlord Dryden before I do, they will earn tenfold their share of crystal!"

Roars, cheers, and squawks rang through the sky as the mercenaries and sell swords raised their weapons into the air and clashed metal to metal. Vorkus turned to Grindor with a smile on his face and donned the Onyx helm. "Now lead the way."

Grindor called the mixed troops to order. "Follow me. We have several days' march ahead of us. There's plenty of time for introductions and planning along the way."

Vorkus gave one last look back toward the outer walls of Nolta Tenoble where many men gathered upon the ramparts and watched them depart. They traveled southwest following the route Grindor had selected. The band of mismatched warriors marched in three regimented groups, segregated by race, with avians soaring above and pack-mules interspersed between them. They traversed great lengths of countryside, across dirt roads and rolling hills, fields of vineyards, grain and rugged ridges. The white sun beamed on their scalps, but the wisp of winter's cool air would bring goose bumps to their skin.

"Why are we stopping?" asked Vorkus, when Grindor unexpectedly called a halt.

"To rest," replied Grindor.

"Elkin do not take breaks on their travels."

"Well, humans, erethizons, and avians need a rest every now and then to catch their breath."

Vorkus grumbled as they all took a seat and broke out trail rations. The avians pulled out juicy, honey-filled melons of the leudinar tree. With their simple gesture of offering food, the three bands of mercenaries began to talk amongst each other, mingling more and more until the segregation was broken. After the introductions and small talk had run their course, Vorkus expressed interest in Scokoo's now-complete set of Sky Smith armor and bow.

"Can you read its runes?" he asked, nodding toward the ivory bow in Scokoo's quill-covered hand.

Scokoo held it in front of him to admire its craftsmanship. It was almost as long as he was tall, with lightning blue runes running up and down its length. He refrained from answering and looked at the massive blade that rested upon Vorkus' waist. "I should ask you the same about your blade."

Vorkus realized that neither one of them wanted to divulge his secrets to the other. "The reason I ask is because the elkin we aim to kill knows how to use his. His blade is named Tempest... though I shouldn't call it a blade, since the Sky Smith forged it out of the wind. Its vaporous shape passes through any armor, yet still cuts skin. And I think that Sky Smith runic armor of yours might be our only defense against it."

Scokoo took a long moment of silence to mull it over. "I can see that we will need to keep our distance from him. You will be pleasantly surprised to see what I can do with my bow. I can take him from a distance, and I never miss my mark," he said, unwilling to give too much away.

Vorkus gave a long sigh. "Warlord Dryden wears a suit of Sky Smith armor almost identical to yours. If I am right, and his weapon is useless against your armor, then your bow will be just as useless against his."

"What else do you know about them?" interjected Ocamyr.

Vorkus looked around and realized the conversation was drawing the attention of other knots of soldiers. He thought back to the detailed story that Erador had told him, and decided to tell it all, projecting his words so the entire army could hear. The details poured out of him as if they were *his* memories, as if it was *his* emotions. The soldiers were captivated. He told them of Clan Hortyr's betrayal, their robbery of the unknown contents of Clan Wyndlyn's Armory, and how Warlord Dryden orchestrated the whole thing. He detailed the battle strategies elkin employed, their use of javelin and atlatl, their vanquisher techniques for wielding axes, and Clan Hortyr's use of snares and traps.

"So, why are they headed to Chyxurlgon Jungle?" one soldier asked.

Vorkus was out of answers, and uncomfortable being forced to admit ignorance. "It was Clan Grondyr's home… Warlord Dryden's clan from Sonir-Senti… before it all turned to stone. What he hopes to accomplish there, I cannot guess."

A lingering silence followed his admission. Eventually, Ocamyr broke it. "How can we best be of use?" he squawked in a determined and chivalrous tone.

"We will need you to disrupt their javelin throwers. Swoop in from their flank, and crush them with your hammers. Be sure to make your first swing count."

Ocamyr nodded in agreement, and Vorkus turned his attention to the quill-covered leader of the Brenzwik Tribe. "We will need your unit of pikemen to time your charge. Your halberds will be a perfect defense against an elkin warrior's antler lunge. You will need to protect our avian brethren from Clan Hortyr's axemen."

Vorkus then turned toward the rugged-looking Grindor. "You and your elites will fight alongside us. The rest of your men will charge in to finish off whatever the avians don't slay with their assault." He considered the massive, antler-spiked shield Erador had carried with him, which had belonged to one of his dead clan mates. It meant nothing to Vorkus. "Here," he said to the mercenary leader. "A fortune-gift, and a token of my thanks for gathering our army. It belonged to one of the elkin murdered by those we seek. Perhaps seeing it will fill some of them with dismay. I shall have no use for it."

Grindor took the shield solemnly, turning it back and forth, testing its heft. He bowed his thanks to the Warlord. "Got it," he acknowledged his orders. "But what will you be doing?"

Vorkus withdrew the diamond-edged blade from its sheath, admiring the beauty of its power. "Wraith and I are going after Warlord Dryden."

They resumed their march, continuing until the sun began to fall into the horizon. They set up camp, and shared stories of war and honor, of bloodshed and heroism. The next day passed much the same way, and the next, and the next. The impact of humanity upon the land grew less pronounced and less frequent as they marched, until it had vanished altogether by the time they made their last camp but one.

The next day, they watched as the setting sun raised the silhouette of the petrified tree line of the stone jungle of Chyxurlgon. Its shadow crept ominously over their camp site before darkness consumed the land. The host of mercenaries would only get one more night of rest, one more night to fill their bellies with food and ale, one last night to pray to their Gods.

CHAPTER 23

Darkness faded as dawn broke across the land, illuminating the landscape as if awakening the world with the rays of the Radiant Smith's white sun. Abstract blends of burgundy and teal splashed across the light, fluffy clouds of the horizon. The grass stretched upward in greeting, the morning dew prismed miniature rainbows, gold and ochre leaves lifted on a fresh breeze as if to rejoin the branches and stems they once clad. Hundreds of dragonflies buzzed and hovered over the shimmering azure water of the pond, weaving iridescent patterns of green, yellow, red and blue. The vibrant immediacy of life compelled eye and mind to partake of and participate in its endless dance.

And then there was the stone jungle. Lifeless. Motionless. Colorless. Grim. It was a vast consummation of petrification: violated nature locked in eternal stasis. Only a few trees among the outskirts of the jungle remained untouched by the spell, tragic counterpoints already beginning to waste away from the disruption of the symbiotic intercourse upon which each individual life of a jungle relies. The sheer magnitude of desolated land was awe-inspiring and unfathomable. Such inconceivable power belonged in the sphere of the gods. But the gods were delinquent, and lesser hands took up their devolved powers... wreaking desecration.

In spite of such bountiful beauty and colorful life surrounding the company of mercenaries, not a single word was spoken. The inexorable presence of the jungle outweighed all. Warlord Vorkus and his army of sell-swords took a long look at the silent jungle of stone that awaited them before making their final preparations. He looked at the many faces of men that surrounded him, men with names that he would never know, some with families of their own, yet they were here to fight by his side. He met the eyes of each human, avian, and erethizon before him, one after another, signifying his appreciation. Words were unnecessary.

Warlord Vorkus turned to Ocamyr and pointed to the sky. Ocamyr nodded, holding his massive war hammer, and signaled his flock to rise. Their enormous wings spanned outward and began flapping in short, powerful bursts. As they took to the sky, the elkin, erethizons, and men began their march. The avians flew no higher than needed to reach the treetops, so as not to alert anyone of their presence. With branch and leaf turned to solid stone, the avians could walk across the treetops. Their vicious talons kept a firm grip upon the awkward, uneven surface, sometimes breaking loose small flakes of stone. Peering down through the canopy from their vantage point, fifty feet above ground, the avians could see little below them; all was consumed in shadow. Beams of daylight penetrating to the jungle floor were few and far between.

The elkin stopped as they arrived at the jungle's threshold, standing at the sharply-defined edge where earth turned to stone, peering into the darkness that awaited them within. No one was eager to enter. Carra stepped forward to stand beside Warlord Vorkus, the assemblage of intertwined antlers that formed the Channeler's Staff in her hand. "You think there's any chance we can draw them out?"

He shook his head. "Not without giving away our element of surprise."

Carra studied his impressive runic Onyx armor. "With your armor as black as night, you would be as good as invisible in there."

"I plan on it," he said in a calm voice. "Men fear what they cannot see."

Carra looked into the darkness with him. "So you know the language of the runes, right?"

He nodded.

"The Onyx Smith is the lord over stone and shadow. Within this environment, you will have unlimited resources to interact with."

He nodded again.

"But how can you fight in the darkness?"

"The Onyx helm lets me see," he said. He looked to the floor and began shaking his head.

"So why do you seem concerned? The power of the Onyx armor is legendary."

He clutched his helm as if his head ached. "I worry that it will be our men that fear what they cannot see," he said, tension entering his voice.

"What is it? What's wrong?" asked Carra.

"It's Erador. I can feel him… fighting me for control. But it's… different this time."

"Hold him off. We need the Onyx armor's power to win this battle, and you're the only one that knows how to use it. You let me worry about the darkness."

Carra turned to face the legion of warriors. "Everyone, I need you to focus on me!"

She closed her eyes and focused her thoughts, concentrating all her energy on one single incantation. The area surrounding the Channeler's Staff began to dim, appearing to draw in the light from the air. Carra's hands and arms tensed, as if the Staff grew difficult to hold steady as it drew more power. Carra felt her veins surge to the surface of her skin, but she no longer cared if anyone saw them. The black veins spread their way up her whole arm, up her neck and across her face. They spread down her shoulder and across her chest and back, covering the right half of her body.

Warlord Vorkus watched the progress of the Poisoning with great interest, the invasive black veins spreading through her body and into her mind as her powers flowed from her body into the Staff. Carra remained absorbed in her incantation, shutting out all else, gritting her teeth and straining against the Staff, which was now visibly pulsating and vibrating in her hands. Shimmers of light began to crawl between the twists of fused antlers.

Carra thought of her floating orb spell back in the cave within the Jerackon Mountains, of the green floating soul that the scale-covered keratin conjured out of the air, of the many souls that filled the Channeler's Staff, and of Abby's doubled spell casting upon her antlers. But most of all, Carra thought of Dorgeeryn's sacrifice, how he surrendered his soul to the Soul Smith so that Erador could summon the Fates.

Carra began to speak aloud in the runic language taught to her by Mother of Clan Grondyr, passed down from the ancients. The words she spoke had no meaning to her; they were just structured bits pulled together from other incantations. But as she spoke the forgotten language, conjuring the last of the magic within her blood, she could feel the power escape her lips as the archaic dialect rolled off her tongue. No man standing before her could understand the language that she spoke… except for Warlord Vorkus.

And then Carra let go.

As the Staff fell, lights continued to flicker from its surface. It made contact with the ground—and disintegrated into dozens upon dozens of hovering golden essences. They hung suspended in the air above Carra's head, expanding and contracting in size as if they were breathing. Their substance seemed to flow constantly around and back into itself, pulsating rhythmically. The mercenaries ogled the sparkling orbs, captivated by their beauty.

Warlord Vorkus leaned closer to Carra. "Do you know what the words that you just spoke mean?" he whispered.

She turned her gaze from the orbs to look upon him in confusion. He smiled and continued, "Your incantation translates to: Spirits of the Goma within this staff, use your powers of light to grant us vision within the darkness."

As if his words were a signal, the golden orbs scattered and flew into the eyes of every human, avian, elkin, and erethizon. Exclamations rang throughout the company at the resulting sudden blindness. It passed just as rapidly into a mere blurring, and they all began to blink and rub their eyes.

"Hey! Do you all see that?" cried one man. "I can see into the jungle as clear as day."

"Woah! He's right!" shouted another.

"What did you do to us?"

"I have granted us the sight of dark-vision," Carra called to the group. "We will stand a greater chance of taking our enemy by surprise if we have no need for a light source."

"What happened to your skin?" cried a man near the front line.

Carra looked down at her arms. Though her incantation had ended, her veins didn't recede. She felt as if one of her eyes had clouded black in entirety, and her skin was becoming pale as one who had never stood in sunlight. Warlord Vorkus looked at Carra with great admiration. "You have undergone the Poisoning and your powers have fallen to shadow."

It took Carra a moment to realize the implications of what he'd told her. "Does that mean I can keep us shrouded in darkness?"

"Only if you know how to harness its power," he said. "I can teach you, but only if you can learn quickly."

"How would you know anything of the Poisoning? You aren't of the Goma."

He put on a curious grin. "Oh, really? It's interesting that your elders have never mentioned it. You know far less than you think, but I am impressed at your grasp of the Radiant Smith's words."

Warlord Vorkus' comment lifted Carra's spirits, and a sense of pride overcame her. She sought out Zimmerik among the crowd and smiled at him when he met her gaze. He did not share in her excitement. Carra grew very self-conscious of her pale skin and her visible sinister-looking ebony veins. Zimmerik's expression was composed of disgust and reproach. He turned his back to her, and it was done. Carra's heart sank and filled with sorrow.

Sadness mounted across her face. Warlord Vorkus leant in again to whisper into her ear. "Remember this moment. How you feel. How you hurt. That is what you must draw upon if you are to control the shadow."

Carra looked down in contempt upon the stone floor where the Staff had fallen and saw nothing but a pile of dust. She kicked at it, scattering it, furious and angry at what she has become. She turned back at Warlord Vorkus, emotions naked on her face; hatred for her father's betrayal, anguish for her years of Goma-practice now wasted, guilt for failing to stand up for Erador when he faced banishment, and sorrow for the loss of Zimmerik. Her clouded black eye had glassed over and her only good eye dripped with a single tear. A faint darkness seemed to engulf her, as of a cloud blocking sunlight.

None of the others was willing to meet her tormented, disheartened gaze, either... none save Grindor. What she saw in his face made her wonder what his eyes must have witnessed in his lifetime, for him to look upon her with neither disgust nor pity, only... bleakness. It frightened her more than her own condition did.

Warlord Vorkus grunted. "You do learn quickly."

Carra peered at him. "Let's move out."

"This jungle used to be the home of your Clan, correct?"

Carra nodded.

"Then lead us to where you think your father is."

Carra faced the jungle, trying to recognize it as what used to be her home. It looked so different to her now, so devoid of life, but somewhere within that jungle lay the remnants of her clan's village. It used to be filled with pleasant memories of her father, of life in simpler times, but now those memories were gone. Tarnished by her father, by the very person that helped create them. This place was not her home. Not any longer. The petrification had tainted it, just as the Poisoning did to her by sucking out her life, her beauty. She looked back at Warlord Vorkus with a cold stare. "I'm ready to lead when they're ready to follow."

He looked across at his men. As he panned across the warriors, he could see that they had confidence in their hearts and carried dreams of glory. Their eyes were filled with a new-found courage

"They're ready," he said with a hint of pleasure. He raised his fist into the air and they all went silent. You couldn't even hear them breath. Only the sound of windblown leaves rustling across the stone floor, and a distant hoot of a late-returning owl could be heard. He drew his blade, clenched its hilt with both hands, and entered the petrified undergrowth. The avians were silent as they scrambled along the canopy to travel in tandem with the warriors, mirroring their movements below.

They had to move slowly, taking time to walk around even the smallest plants, as every twig and every leaf was now unyielding stone. Carra led the way, and the foliage was light at first but rapidly became denser as they progressed. As if a new spectrum of light had become visible to their eyes, the shadows under the canopy no longer held secrets; the rare streams of sunlight became mere ornamentation. All around them looked like an impossibly lifelike masterpiece of sculpture. They could see the detail of the bark upon every tree, the tendrils of hanging vines, the veins of every individual leaf, and the stamens and petals of every flower. Even birds, snakes, and leopards were consumed by stone. They trespassed through as silent as the wind, though the substantial undergrowth was becoming a great obstacle. They had to climb under and over low-hanging vines, evade the serrated blades of ferns, sometimes even walk atop broad, spreading leaves. The only moving thing they encountered was a stream, still running through its canal-like bed.

They picked their way through the jungle for hours, with no way for most of them to determine how far they might have come. Even Baltor seemed uncertain in this environment that appeared so different from what he'd grown up with. Carra never wavered. The sun was still high when the signal was finally passed back along the advancing troop: ahead, the column-like trees abruptly ended in an expansive clearing filled with daylight. Above, the avians hung back from its edge to keep out of view, while below the army of mercenaries filtered silently into positions arranged with a few hand signs, then waited within the concealing shadows. Most still could not see more than a few windows of daylight amid thinner cover. Carra looked over at Warlord Vorkus to learn what he wanted them to do next, but he was clutching at his helm, and seemed to be gritting his teeth in an effort not to scream.

***

By the time she could place a vein-covered hand upon his shoulder, it was too late. Erador had awoken, disoriented, looking all around him at the unfamiliar scenery. They could all hear voices from the clearing, and Carra pushed a finger across his lips so he knew not to make a sound. Which he nearly did when he took a look at her and reeled back. His eyes went wide with fright. He almost didn't recognize her, as her face looked only half alive and her skin was covered with the black webbing of her veins. She could see he was desperate to know what happened to her, but the voices grew louder.

"Why aren't the preparations complete? I won't keep General Dryden waiting," yelled a voice.

"Our men are chiseling the translation stone free as we speak, Soul Binder."

"Good. The General will be pleased."

"I know that voice," Erador murmured. Carra made to shush him, but he held up a hand. "That's Warlord Korin from Clan Hortyr! But why is the other man calling him Soul Binder?"

A third voice entered, "I haven't checked in with you since my return."

"General!" shouted the two voices in unison.

"And I see you've already given up your antlers to don the armor."

The first voice continued, "Welcome back home, sir. And yes, after the Soul Smith knocked over the stones and we brought forth the armor from the pit, I donned it immediately."

General Dryden began to snicker. "It's ironic how Mother fought against the Armor of Souls to end the War of the Wish, and now she will be at our side as we finish what was started so long ago. Are you ready to do your part?"

"Yes, General. I have mastered its runes."

"Good. As soon as my men have freed the translation stone, then the ritual can begin. The petrification will be reversed, Mother will be free, and soon the world will bend to my will," said General Dryden.

"Have you the Onyx Smith relic with you?"

"Yes, here in my travel pack. Clan Wyndlyn kept it at the edge of the world, near where the Gaia Smith built Her Wall of Thorns, at the sacred spot where Vorkus was crowned champion by Brikken the Onyx Smith. I obtained it while your clan was busy raiding their Armory."

"Excellent. Then we should be ready any moment now."

"Once the God-Dragon is free, let it come. I want Mother to watch."

Erador had to see what was going on. He snuck up as close as he could, and peeked through some stone leaves. They were all standing among the petrified village of Sonir-Senti. He saw General Dryden, still in the armor of the Sky Smith, holding his travel pack. He saw another elkin, dressed in the garb of Clan Hortyr, and a third person standing beside him. Erador almost mistook Warlord Korin for a man, for he bore no antlers. His head was encapsulated in the skull of a Cyclops. Every other component of his armor was composed from bones as well. The chest piece looked like a rib cage that encased his body. Long bones were splinted together to form bracers and greaves. The pauldrons might once have been pelvic girdles, elbows and knees the tops of skulls. A lengthy polished bone staff completed the collection. Every article of bone that covered his body had a unique runic emblem inscribed upon its surface. Erador knew he was staring at the Armor of Souls. Then

Erador noticed the three of them stood next to the most intricate and detailed statue of a female elkin, dressed in layers of robes, wielding a staff and staring up at the sky. The same unreadable runic inscriptions that could be found upon Blacksmith armor were etched from the base of her pedicle, up the beams, upon every fork, and all the way to the crown tine of her antlers.

General Dryden's voice raised in anger as he shouted at the petrified statue of Mother. "Did you hear that, Mother?! It is time for the elkin to rule this land! When I slay the God-Dragon with Tempest, you will wish you had listened to me! You thought the God-Dragon's scales to be impervious to our weapons; well, it is time I show you what Tempest can do!" He drew his sword, and a strong gust of wind began to blow about the dust and debris that littered the ground.

Erador had heard enough. He looked down at his father's antlers, which he had tied to his waist. "This one's for you," he whispered to them. His hate fueled his adrenaline. As he stood from his crouched position, his entire army rose with him. Wraith in hand, he stepped forward, and his entire army followed behind him until they stood at the edge of the wide clearing.

"*Dryden!*" shouted Erador from the depths of his lungs.

General Dryden turned with surprise, and his other two companions drew weapons in a panic. "Erador?" he asked in uncertainty. "Are those new antlers supposed to scare me?"

"I have come for your head on a plate! For everything you have done to my clan," bellowed Erador.

General Dryden grinned. "Their blood is all on the Soul Smith's hands; I was only allowed the great pleasure of slitting your father's throat."

"Traitor! I'm tired of your lies! Why would the Soul Smith ever help you?"

"Soon, you will see," teased General Dryden. "I am impressed that you have made it this far. You should join us, and we can rule the world together."

"Never! You will pay for your betrayal! I challenge you to a duel to the death!" Erador pointed his hefty blade at Dryden.

Erador began to notice more elkin entering the other side of the clearing. They all began to draw weapons except for the few who were carrying a large slab of stone. General Dryden turned to see the slab of stone and was wild with excitement, then turned back to Erador.

"What say you!?" challenged Erador.

"But I have already bested you in a duel. Where would be the fun in doing it again?"

Erador closed his eyes, and took one deep breath. When his eyes reopened, an eerie glow emanated forth from them. "You haven't bested me!" Warlord Vorkus' ominous, god-like voice rolled through the jungle.

Warlord Vorkus could see the terror run down General Dryden's spine. "Stop him! Keep him back while I cast the ritual!"

Warlord Vorkus roared to the sky like a lion. The golden runes across the chest of his black plate began to radiate power and he could feel the runes' magic surge through his veins. Huge chunks of stone began to crack and split underneath him, then break apart into sections and bend upward around him, curling inward as they encircled him. The stone clung to him as if drawn by magnetic force, encompassing everything but his antlers. The elkin facing him from across the clearing were so awe-struck at the spectacle that they could do nothing but watch. The rock compressed itself around his form, wrapping his entire body in an extra layer of stone atop his already formidable Onyx armor. Then, the face of the Onyx helm began to appear through the stone, and its eyes produced an eerie glow. Warlord Vorkus was now one with the rock, wearing it as if it were his skin.

Warlord Vorkus took one slow, thunderous step forward and shouted in a voice as deep as primordial caverns beneath mountain roots, "CHARGE!"

CHAPTER 24

General Dryden and the Soul Binder stared in disbelief as Warlord Vorkus, the Father of the elkin, proclaimed himself, returned within the body of Erador. But their disbelief turned to horror as he now stood before them encased in stone skin. They turned and retreated toward the elkin carrying the slab of stone, shouting as they ran, "Goma! Hold him back!"

Five Clan Hortyr elkin ran forward into the clearing to confront the giant man of stone wielding a blade as black as night. Clan Wyndlyn wanted to scream at their treachery: these had all been members of their own tribe once, come to be trained by the Channeler. They held out their palms and blasted the approaching stone man with light, but could not daze him. Warlord Vorkus gave a hearty guffaw in a voice that sounded as though it echoed from the depths of an abysmal bottomless pit. He advanced with slow, heavy strides, shaking the earth with every step.

One of the Goma enchanters tried a different tactic; as both of his hands were pulsating with light, he knelt and discharged his power into the ground. A beam of light appeared beneath the stone behemoth, trying to propel him backward into the sky, but the force couldn't lift his weight. Then the other four Goma echoed his action in unison, and their combined power conjured forth a pillar of ivory light beneath his stone-covered feet, lifting him off the ground and catapulting him backward into the stone trees behind him. The force of his impact shattered the petrified plant life as if he were a boulder crashing down from a mountainside.

"Archers!" yelled Warlord Vorkus, as he struggled to get back up to his feet.

The paltry handful of archers within his mercenary force unleashed a volley of arrows at the exposed Goma spell casters scattered across the open clearing. Ten barbed broad-head arrows laced the air, each displaying different colored fletching. Only one arrow found its mark, sticking in the shoulder of the center Goma wizard. Scokoo, standing beside the moving mountain of rock, readied his own bow. His black porcupine quills protruded from every crevice of his clouded-glass runic Sky Smith armor and helm. The Sky Smith bow he bore was crafted from the ivory heartwood of a great porg ambit tree, capped with cow horns at both tips, and was twice the girth of a regular bow. Scokoo placed three fingers upon the linen string drew it back until his right hand was locked at his anchor point at the back of his jaw. He had to utilize all of his strength just to draw the taut bowstring against the bow's massive resistance. He had no arrow nocked against the string.

Scokoo released a slow breath through his pursed lips, almost a low whistle. As his breath left his lips, the vibrant blue runes upon his bow began to glimmer with power. Just before the last of Scokoo's breath left his lungs, he turned his exhalation into a short phrase, "Luk. Cro!" He released the bowstring, and with a sharp *crack* through the air, a crooked lightning bolt struck down from the sky, striking the center Goma enchanter at the top of his head. The lightning-struck elkin was instantly crisped as a burnt log. The arrow protruding from his shoulder was smoldering, and he fell to the scorch-marked stone earth.

The other four Goma enchanters retreated behind a line of javelin-armed elkin that emerged from the edge of the stone tree line. Thirty elkin stood shoulder to shoulder, atlatls at the ready as they marched forward to get within range. Another volley of arrows was loosed and struck a few down. As they advanced, a retinue of elkin guarded General Dryden and the Soul Binder in a circular formation. The General withdrew from his travel pack an onyx tablet with rounded edges, as polished as a pearl. He then stood before the large translation stone and held the onyx tablet before him. He glanced back and forth from the translation stone to the onyx tablet as his lips began forming syllables.

Scokoo saw him begin his ritual and knew he had to be stopped. Scokoo stood exposed, and decided to use the last seconds of his time to get off one last shot before the elkin could strike him with their javelins. The stone canopy protected General Dryden protected from strikes from above, so he withdrew a long fork-headed arrow and nocked it. He began with another low exhalation, and the runes upon his helm illuminated with life. He murmured, "Varta sool," and the sharpness of his vision doubled.

With target in sight, he called upon his bow's power: "Ruk latma." As he spoke, he let fly his forked arrow. It zipped through the air with supernatural speed, crackling with lightning around its surface. General Dryden looked up with surprise as the arrow smashed into his Sky Smith armor, right above his heart. As it struck, it released a thunderous discharge of energy… to no effect. Runes upon his Sky Smith armor pulsed brilliant blue as they absorbed the charge. He saw the erethizon wielding the Sky Smith bow across the battlefield, grinned, and continued with the ritual.

"Damn!" cursed Scokoo as he retreated into the stone tree line to avoid the volley of javelins that were being launched his way. He and the archers vastly underestimated the distance that the atlatls added. One javelin glanced off the back of his armor. Others struck home into the stomachs and chests of all his fellow mercenary archers. The line of Clan Hortyr hunters drew fresh javelins from their quivers and reloaded their atlatls in the middle of the clearing. As they reloaded, strange shadows appeared upon the ground, as though a grouping of condors flew overhead. The elkin looked up in curiosity, only to realize that a flock of armored avians was diving down with their flesh-rending talons spread wide. The elkin had no time to get off another throw before the avians landed upon them.

The avians flew in like the wind, but landed like an avalanche. Their talons tore into the bodies of the unarmored elkin, sinking deep into their flesh, gripping tight as their force drove their foes down to the stone floor, landing atop their flattened bodies. Heavy, two-handed war hammers smashed down upon their foes, slamming into the chests, shoulders, and heads. The speed of their dive compounded the force of their swings, delivering instant death as they imploded skulls, shattered spines, and stove in ribs. Wherever an avian found an elkin laying upon the floor that still lived, he placed talons around the elkin's neck and squeezed.

It was a blood bath. A massacre.

The few elkin who survived the initial strike uninjured retaliated, thrusting their javelins like spears through the avians' thin leather armor. The Brenzwik Tribe charged out of the shadows of the jungle in three long rows, halberds leveled. Their vicious war cry rang through the air as they charged forth to protect the avians still fighting at the center of the clearing.

Clan Hortyr's warriors responded. Brandishing wooden shields and hand axes, they raced forth from the other side, rushing toward the mounting melee in the center of the clearing.

Grindor the Ravenous saw the elkin's counter-charge and, bursting with adrenaline, yelled at the top of his lungs, "*Attack!*" His band of human mercenaries surged forth, roaring with bravery in a wild, fanatical charge. Each man bore his own preference of weapon, ranging from clubs, spears, and tridents, to swords big and small. The armor they each wore was as individual as their weaponry; chain shirts, leather armor, shields and bucklers. They ran full speed in an attempt to catch up to the light-footed erethizons, but could not keep pace. The erethizons reached the center of the battle field just in time to produce a hedge of pole-mounted spikes to meet the oncoming charge of Clan Hortyr's warriors.

They set their feet firmly to brace against the powerful spear-headed lunges of the elkin. Scokoo paused as the melee made even his rune-enhanced sniping difficult. It seemed the plan was unfolding with near perfection… until he saw the Goma spell casters return. Just before the charging elkin reached the spiked tips of their lowered halberds, pillars of light burst beneath a few of the elkins' feet, propelling them over the front line of erethizons, and coming down upon the avians with vengeful chops of their axes. Scokoo nocked an arrow and dispatched an elkin in midair as a second wave were propelled over the tops of the erethizons, unleashing their vanquisher training upon the unfortunate avians.

The other charging elkin, unaided by magic, leaped high into the air with their powerful legs, or chopped at the halberd heads just before lunging forward with their antlers. Some elkin made it through their wall of spears, driving into the porcupine-quilled warriors. The elkin aligned their spines to derive maximum force for their full-bodied antler attacks. However, the braced halberds thwarted the charge of many elkin as they landed impaled upon the ends of their lengthy spiked tips. The Brenzwik Tribe dropped their two-handed pole weapons and drew flails from their belts, fanning out and striking about in a zealous frenzy.

THE SOUL SMITH

Ocamyr was locked in combat with one of the elkin warriors. He ducked beneath an axe swing, feinted with his hammer at his opponent's knee to force the elkin to lower his shield, then slashed into his opponent's neck instead with his razor-sharp beak. Ocamyr paused to assess the success of his flock. They weren't faring as well as he'd hoped. Numerous avians lay among the other corpses upon on the blood-soaked stone.

"To the skies!" squawked Ocamyr, as he threw open his great wings and began regrouping the surviving avians in the sky above the battlefield. As they escaped to safety, the legion of humans flooded the battlefield beneath them. Their numbers made up for their lack of coordination, but against elkin, they were proving of limited effect.

***

The mountain of rock that was Warlord Vorkus saw the avians take to the skies to regroup, and saw the humans falling victim to Clan Hortyr's superior fighting technique. As he glanced over at General Dryden, still surrounded by guards while performing his ritual, he knew he had to make a decision. *I want to slay Dryden, but the erethizons need my help. I can't risk losing any more of our forces if we want to control the battlefield.*

He bellowed into the sky, "Avians! Stop the ritual!" Then he jogged forth into the fray as fast as his stone-encased legs would move him. He trampled into the melee like a juggernaut, crushing all his enemies that stood in his path. He used one of his rock-encased arms to smash his foes into the earth, while in his other hand Wraith amputated limbs and impaled bodies.

The erethizons fought at his side, whipping their flails with ruthless accuracy as the metallic balls splintered the elkin's wooden shields and crushed their foes' bones. Backhanded swings of their empty fists left elkin with faces full of porcupine quills. It seemed that victory was in their grasp, but even as the line of elkin warriors succumbed to the assault, a barrage of javelins rained down upon the mixed army from ambush. Two broke against Vorkus' stone skin, but many more rained death upon the men and erethizons. They all turned in surprise to see more elkin standing at their flank in the tree line. Clan Wyndlyn was shocked to recognize their faces. They had

271

once shared a home together, but now they were enemies upon the battlefield.

"That's Clan *Grondyr*!" cried Carra. "They must have survived the blast in the tundra along with General Dryden."

Clan Wyndlyn, Scokoo, Grindor the Ravenous, and his ten elites wielding scimitars and tortoise shields were all that remained in the reserves—and they knew that they had to act now. While Vorkus positioned himself to shield his troops from the javelins, the reserves moved into flanking position. Scokoo emerged from the shadows of the stone jungle and let fly arrows in rapid succession toward Clan Grondyr with matchless precision. He felled several and wounded more. Clan Grondyr reloaded their atlatls and unleashed another volley of javelins upon the cluster of troops in the center of the clearing.

"Rally behind me!" bellowed Vorkus. He stomped his heavy stone leg upon the floor and a wall of rock rose up out of the ground before him. Most of javelins thudded against the wall.

The erethizons retrieved their halberds, and reformed their line. The remaining infantry grouped behind them.

Vorkus gestured; the wall began to crumble from center outward. He stepped through the middle even before the wings ceased sheltering his allies. He stared at his foes on the other side of Clan Grondyr's village and shouted, "Grek ruk buwok zek." As the magic's power rushed through his fingertips, the golden inscriptions etched upon Wraith shimmered, then were shrouded in shadow. A void encompassed the weapon; Vorkus swung the legendary blade through the air in front of him in an upward cutting motion. The shroud of shadow left the blade and surged across the stone floor of the clearing. As it passed beneath one of the elkin, the shadow lunged upward out of the ground, mimicking the upward slicing motion of Wraith, and split the elkin cleanly in two—as if Wraith itself had cut him from groin to shoulder.

"For Thornwall!" shouted Vorkus as the erethizons and humans rushed forward toward Clan Grondyr in ranked formation in an all-out sprint.

"For *victory!*" cried Grindor the Ravenous from his flanking position, as the elites and Clan Wyndlyn charged.

***

The avians, now reduced to half their original number, organized into a "V" formation in the sky. Ocamyr squawked to his brethren, "It is paramount that this ritual be stopped. Warlord Vorkus has entrusted this imperative task to us. We can't let him down! Let's show these bastards what happens when you mess with our flock! Leave Dryden to me!"

They swooped down toward the small gathering of elkin that surrounded the translation stone. Two avians were struck down by javelins as they dove beneath the canopy to execute their fly-by strike. Some of them experienced the familiar sensation of rending flesh with their claws, while the rest smashed into the shields of their enemy.

General Dryden was still reading the inscriptions upon the onyx tablet when Ocamyr's talons, in an attempt to grab it from him, knocked it from his hands. He turned in anger and withdrew Tempest from its silver sheath. Wisps of air outlined the wind-forged blade. He attacked aggressively, aiming vicious swings at Ocamyr, but Ocamyr was swift. He backed up just enough to dodge each swing of Tempest, then clawed back with his talons between Dryden's strikes. Ocamyr's talons scratched harmlessly at the surface of his clouded-glass armor until he got a lucky talon scrape down his face. The stone jungle offered little room for maneuvering, and the onyx tablet had fallen beneath some stone plants, beyond Ocamyr's ability to swoop and grab it.

Ocamyr hovered above the earth, flapping his wings, preparing for his next assault on General Dryden as his brethren were locked in combat all around him. Blood dripped from the lengthy gash down the General's face. The cloudiness within his Sky helm began to churn like a hurricane. A small bolt of lightning began to arc across the tips of his antlers. He leaped forward to try to swipe at Ocamyr again. After two more failed swings, Ocamyr's heavy hammer connected with the side of the Sky Armor with such force that it knocked his opponent to the ground.

In a fit of rage, General Dryden pointed Tempest at Ocamyr and roared, conjuring a tornado of wind from the tip of the weapon, sending Ocamyr flying backward and slamming into a stone tree. The General got to his feet, his clouded glass runic helm swirling with intensity. He roared again as bolts of lightning arced forth from his antlers and shocked the prone Ocamyr. Ocamyr felt weak and his feathers were singed, but he refused to give up. He clambered to his feet, standing tall and proud, remaining defiant against the other's onslaught. He caught his breath and shrilled, "Is that all you got?"

General Dryden lunged toward the avian, thrusting with Tempest. Ocamyr tried to time the swing of his hammer with the charge, but his opponent ducked beneath his sideward swipe, then launched himself forward and up, driving his antlers into Ocamyr. The avian fell again.

General Dryden stood over the wounded bird. "Come on! Get up!"

Ocamyr got to his feet one more time. General Dryden swung Tempest at the cornered avian; out of reflex, Ocamyr attempted to parry the strike with the shaft of his hammer. But Tempest's blade of air severed the war hammer's handle without pausing, then passed through the studded leather armor and body of the avian. Ocamyr's eyes widened in pain, and he gargled up blood. He took a last moment to look at his brethren fighting in the background.

They had fought valiantly, with every muscle, every ounce of energy, every fiber of their being and had slain many elkin this day… though at this moment, his eyes only saw defeat. He watched in a helpless stupor as one of his brethren fell to the thrust of a javelin, another to the chop of an axe, while another was gored by antlers. Ocamyr gave one final look at the bleeding face of General Dryden before he fell to the ground, dead.

***

General Dryden sheathed his weapon and recovered the onyx stone tablet. He looked at the tablet's smooth black surface, brimming with power from the partially completed conjuration. Several of its runes danced with flame; Dryden was choosing only a select few to read aloud to achieve his ends. With methodical persistence, he turned the translation stone to continue deciphering the runes upon the Onyx Smith tablet, unlocking the power contained within.

The slab of stone that rested upon the floor looked as if it had been separated from a larger stone, yet was still as long as a man. Its rugged surface bore writings in many different runic languages, displaying the markings of the common tongue, the words of the Sky Smith, the words of the Onyx Smith, the words of the Soul Smith, and of the Radiant Smith. Each set of runes bore just a fragment of the forgotten languages, relics of the time of the Gods, when they had summoned the best Blacksmiths from the eight corners of the world to pass them their power.

Dryden looked at his remaining handful of warriors, Goma spellbinders, and the Soul Binder. "This ritual must be completed. You know what you need to do." He resumed the ritual, reading aloud each new rune he selected. He could feel the tablet turn warm within his hands, as he knew he was close.

***

Carra rushed toward the Clan Grondyr elkin that had betrayed her as they waited braced for their charge. *Why are they just waiting there?* she thought.

Snap!

The metal jaws of a bear trap jumped from beneath a scattering of petrified leaves and clenched around her calf, half severing it. Pain seared up her leg. She saw Zimmerik, two of Grindor's elites, and a handful of erethizons get snagged in snares too.

Pain and hate churned inside of her for what they had done. Her skin turned pale, displaying her black veins even more prominently. As she tried to pry the metal jaws loose Carra yelled like a banshee at the top of her lungs, unable to escape its grasp. The hate and contempt boiled inside of her and she found power in her veins. As her emotions took control, her body began to act on its own. Her clouded black eye locked its vision onto the shadows within the canopy behind Clan Grondyr. Carra's hand stretched toward the jungle and then clenched into a fist. As she moved her hand, she dragged the darkness of the jungle with it. The shadows shifted, gathering about Clan Grondyr and consuming them within its void.

Clan Grondyr was blinded, helpless to respond as they heard the stampede of feet coming at them from both sides. Unhindered by the shadows, the erethizons drove forward with their halberds, watching as the spiked tips punctured the chests of their victims. Clan Grondyr swung wildly in desperation, but the erethizons and human elites easily evaded their blows and cut them down.

Clan Wyndlyn, the Brenzwik Tribe, and Grindor's band of humans cheered at their victory, but their celebration was short-lived, as they turned their attention to their wounded and to their trapped comrades. In the ensuing quiet, they could still hear General Dryden's voice as he continued chanting.

In the post-battle stillness, one figure strode toward the depleted mercenary force.

The man dressed in the bones of a black phoenix and the skull of a Cyclops approached casually, using his staff as a walking cane. He stared at the band's paltry survivors with pity. "Warlord Vorkus, your valiant efforts have proven futile. You should have known better. None can stand in our path."

He held out the staff and his eyes rolled back into his head as he opened his mouth to unleash an otherworldly cacophonic drone. The runes upon the Cyclops skull and upon the staff turned a jade green. As his groan turned into an unrecognizable chant, the bodies of all the dead warriors began to stir. The survivors watched in absolute horror as, in one synchronous motion, every fallen elkin, man, avian, and erethizon across the entire battlefield staggered back to their feet with weapons in hand. The eyes of the walking dead exuded the same jade green glow that flowed from the runes of his staff. The dead approached them in a brisk manner, encircling Clan Wyndlyn, the Brenzwik Tribe, and the humans until they were surrounded. Those stuck within the snares were unable to move, unable to flee. The legion of undead was so numerous that it drained all hope from the few still living.

The Soul Binder shouted, "You should have bowed to the almighty General Dryden when you had the chance. Now, prepare to suffer a fate worse than death."

CHAPTER 25

The dark lord within the Armor of Souls stepped toward Warlord Vorkus with brazen confidence. "Hand over Wraith and surrender now, or I'll make you watch as my army tears your brethren apart."

Vorkus stood tall and fearless, still encased in his stone skin. He looked at the man before him, surrounded by a legion of undead warriors, a man that had given his soul to the Cyclops Helm for power and greed. The image conjured old memories, and like a reflection upon the water's surface, his enemy stood before him yet he saw only himself. History was repeating itself.

"Don't do it!" shouted Scokoo. "He'll kill us anyway, to make us into his puppets. We will fight to the end!"

Vorkus nodded at Scokoo's words, maintaining his mountainous gaze on the necromancer. "You're going to have to take it from me, if you can," he said. The stone surrounding his sword-hand altered and reformed to become a solid block hardened around the handle of Wraith.

The other man steamed with rage as he pointed the tip of his bone staff toward Vorkus and shouted, "Tro marac kee!" Jade energy surged about the runic inscriptions of the staff as he pointed a finger at the stone behemoth.

Vorkus felt a tug on his spine, and then felt every part of his body lock stiff, as if his body had entered the state of rigor mortis. He tried to move, but his body would not respond. He found it hard to even breathe, and began to wheeze.

"I… can't… move," he said gritting through his teeth. He glanced to his right and saw Grindor's hesitant courage from his apprehensive stance. Grindor the Ravenous looked at the legion of undead that swarmed around them. Many of them were men he knew; now their cold lifeless stares filled him with uneasiness.

Vorkus used all of his energy just to gasp out, "Protect the wounded… that are stuck… in the traps."

Grindor acknowledged the command, and responded with integrity and honor. "If we don't make it, it's been an honor to fight at your side."

Seeing the undead elkin set javelins in their atlatls, Grindor called to his troops, "Elites! Form a shield wall! Protect the wounded!"

The eight warriors wielding heavy tortoise shields formed a long line, shield to shield, holding the blades of their scimitars above the tops of the turtle shells like the menacing stinger of scorpions' tails. The other two elites, who were locked within the steel jaws of the snares, tossed their shields; two of the surviving human mercenaries retrieved them and joined the elites to extend the length of the shield wall.

The Soul Binder smiled with pleasure at the human's feeble efforts. "Your soul is strong, Vorkus, but it can't resist my paralysis. Now I will make you watch your friends' pathetic attempt to fight for their lives."

Vorkus' deep voice clawed its way through his throat, "This is… the War of the… Wish all… over again! You're… making the same… mistake… I did!"

"No!" he shouted back. "This time will be different. This time, not even *you* can stop us!"

Vynocent and Wiltyn looked at each other in bewilderment. "Is Warlord Vorkus…?"

"…The elkin that defeated the Soul Smith and started the War of the Wish?"

All of the elkin of Clan Wyndlyn exchanged looks of surprise and dismay as they realized that the true history of their heritage had been kept from them. Their whole life they'd worshipped Vorkus as the Father of Clan Wyndlyn and of the elkin. To them, he was the Champion of the Onyx Smith. The wielder of Wraith. Defender of the West! But now, the truth has been revealed. He was the selfish, power-hungry warmonger that almost drove Thornwall into oblivion.

"I'll end this right now!" shouted Scokoo, drawing his bowstring back, without an arrow nocked, and aimed at the man within the Armor of Souls. He spoke the cryptic words to invoke the power of the runes and released. The bowstring flung forward, a bolt of lightning jolted down from the sky… but struck down an undead erethizon instead, leaping from upraised halberd to quill-covered head, leaving a giant seared mark across its face and neck before it fell dead at the dark lord's feet. Scokoo's mouth dropped agape. "How did I miss my mark?" he said in incredulity.

"Lightning is attracted to metal, of which the Armor of Souls has none," mocked the Soul Binder. He spat at the charred corpse. Then he pointed to the wounded soldiers still stuck in the traps. "*Kill them!*" he commanded his slaves.

"*No!*" Vorkus choked in impotent fury.

Carra looked up at Warlord Vorkus with calm dignity, as if she had already accepted her fate. Clan Wyndlyn watched frozen in horror as the undead moved in on Carra and Zimmerik, raising their weapons high above their heads. With Carra's last breath she looked upon her fellow elkin and said, "For Dorgeeryn." As the axes and flails came down upon the defenseless victims of the snares, they delivered quick, clean deaths. The other mercenaries felt powerless as the legion of glowing green eyes that surrounded them began to close in.

The young warriors of Clan Wyndlyn cast glances at one other, knowing the same thoughts were racing through all their minds. They remembered the life Dorgeeryn had given, so that Erador could find a way to protect the Clan, so that they could stop General Dryden. Gressyn's eyes went red as he strained to hold back tears. "For Dorgeeryn!" he shouted at the top of his lungs.

"For Dorgeeryn!" echoed the others, cries merging into an inarticulate roar. Their roar was long, and powerful; it would have stolen the courage away from a living man. Their hearts were filled with rage, their minds were free from the fear of death, and they were one with their weapons. As they hacked and slashed, they left a wake of destruction in their trail.

The blood of the undead had turned black, and their eyes beamed a necrotic green glow. The blood of their death-wounds covered their pale skin. They didn't breath, they didn't show pain, they just… were. In an eerie synchronicity, they raised their weapons and marched fearlessly against what remained of the forces Clan Wyndlyn had gathered. Wounded warriors from both sides struggled to crawl away, lest they be added to the indifferent, cadaverous horde.

Vorkus struggled to move against the arcane hold that paralyzed his soul, and he spoke through gritted teeth. "Erador... if you're there... I need... you... *now!*"

Vorkus felt the presence of another, and his legs began moving without his command. It was as if he had become a detached observer as his body responded to an unseen essence. He could still feel the paralytic grip restraining him, yet somehow his stone-encased legs were being forced to step forward toward his tormentor.

"Impossible!" uttered the Soul Binder in disbelief as the stone giant continued his unrelenting advance. "What magic is this?"

Vorkus muttered in defiance, "Looks like I won't... be watching them die... after all."

His opponent spewed irritation. "General Dryden is almost finished with his ritual, and soon his plans will be complete!"

Vorkus watched his own arm raise Wraith into a striking position. The Soul Binder stepped back as it advanced, focusing his concentration, still trying with all his might to stop the stone giant from moving. Vorkus' arm swung and cleaved a scar into the stone floor as the other side-stepped the blow. Wraith swept back and forth, again and again, to no avail. The dark lord tightened his eldritch grip, choking him, and it took all of Vorkus' energy just to stay conscious. With a gasp, he uttered one last, powerful word. The forgotten tongue energized a rune upon his chest plate, commanding the stone of the earth to fold upward and collapse around the necromancer. Huge slabs of stone broke free and contorted around the dark lord, swallowing him inside a twisted orb of rock. As the spherical rock constricted its prey, Vorkus fell to the floor unconscious.

The Armor of Souls and its profane wearer were imprisoned inside a ball of stone.

***

Scokoo began unleashing heaven's wrath upon the undead, striking them down with repeated bolts of lightning. Each discharge

280

drained the jade green glow from the eyes of another animated cadaver. The stench of burnt flesh filled the air. The glimmer of hope his assault brought was offset by a rain of javelins upon the last remaining mercenaries. Cries of agony filled the skies as only the shield wall and a very few others remained.

The heavy swings of the elites' scimitars dismembered and decapitated their enemies, while the elkin lunged with piercing antlers, driving the undead to the ground where they became easy prey for their weapons. The twins, Vynocent and Wiltyn, dealt their dance of death in mirrored teamwork. Baltor's massive double-bladed axe hewed animated corpses in half with each stroke. Tysyra flowed like a breeze around the edges of the battle, distracting her opponents, fouling weapons, slicing tendons whenever an opening presented itself; her clothes were tattered and she was covered in shallow nicks and cuts from the many lethal blows she evaded. Gressyn's war cry became a howl of pain when the halberd of an undead erethizon smashed his upraised shield into his collar bone, but his axe never slowed. Hammynt bled profusely from a scalp wound.

The issue remained in doubt for a long time—whether the elkin and their allies could destroy the tireless undead before they succumbed to exhaustion and wounds. Gradually, the assault began to founder against the rock of the elites' shields, while it was torn apart from side and rear by the elkin and by Scokoo's archery. Bereft of command, the undead began to falter, becoming ever easier prey. The odds narrowed. Then they became even. Then it was over.

The survivors could do nothing but gasp precious air and marvel that they still stood.

***

Warlord Vorkus regained consciousness and turned his eyes toward General Dryden, who was still reading aloud as he continued to glance from the tablet to the translation stone. Then, with finality in his tone, General Dryden shouted the final words loud enough all could hear, "BEL LOK!"

The runes upon the tablet were billowing with flame, and the tablet glowed red-hot in General Dryden's hands. He dropped it and let it burn on the ground as the power of the runes mounted into an aura of elemental authority. The tablet rattled upon the petrified earth as a thing alive. Then the runes could no longer contain the accumulated power. An explosion of wind and sound burst from it in a booming dome of sorcery across the land. The wave of sortilege swept outward in all directions, followed by another, and another, each burst radiating further than the one before it.

General Dryden watched in elation as the petrification of the jungle began to reverse. The dull stone greyness began to fade, the ground and the trees to regain their colors. The ground turned soft underfoot. Swathes of vegetation began to sway, flutter and swing in the wind, freed from the petrification, from high, graceful leaf and dangling vine down to every weed and blade of grass. The near-silence following the invocation was rent asunder by countless cries, calls, hisses and hums of animal, bird, reptile and insect.

Warlord Vorkus' stone skin began to slough away, revealing the Onyx Armor beneath. The stone orb that enclosed the Armor of Souls turned to dirt. General Dryden approached the elderly female elkin as color began to return to her face and robes. She moved her eyes, her lips, her fingers, and then with a jolt of life she gasped for air. Her rune-inscribed antlers returned to their natural bone color, and her billowy clothes flowed about her.

General Dryden stood tall before her. "Hello, Mother," he said with pleasure and arrogance.

Her eyes darted around at her surroundings, witnessing the pulses of sortilege still sweeping from the Onyx tablet as the petrified jungle came back to life. She saw the sweep and wrack of the battle that had raged through Clan Grondyr's village. It was when she saw the pallid, black-blooded corpses of undead elkin that tears began to fall from her eyes. To have sacrificed herself to save the lives of many, and then awaken to see so many dead, afflicted her spirit. The sight of all those souls that were not allowed to rest brought her heartache, but the realization that the Armor of Souls had been worn once more brought her torment.

"Dryden, what have you done?" Her scratchy voice was composed of wisdom and despair.

"It's General Dryden now," he said with bitterness. "I will show you that you were wrong not to trust me. I will prove to you that the elkin were meant to rule this land, instead of serve it. That even the great Blacksmiths will come to fear us. And I did it all for you, so that you may rule at my side, as my Queen."

She began shaking her head. "But what about the God-Dragon?"

She was answered by a voice resounding from a league away, a primal roar reverberating through the very earth that they stood upon. Birds fled treetops as it echoed within the jungle. Trees rattled, huts shuddered, and bone-tingling terror seized the hearts of the living. So much fear filled every fiber of their being, that many dropped their weapons, lost all ability to speak, even lost control of their bladders. The God-Dragon screamed its offended wrath somewhere off in the distance, then…

Clan Wyndlyn and their allies watched transfixed as the dragon rose from the horizon, gargantuan beyond anything imagination could paint. The colossal creature swept an arc high overhead, swerving and diving as its eyes locked on to the humanoids occupying the clearing. As the flying leviathan approached, its immensity blocked out the sun.

CHAPTER 26

The Soul Binder retreated to General Dryden and the handful of remaining elkin from Clan Hortyr. He bowed before Mother. "My Queen. You must be protected."

Warlord Vorkus lay upon the ground, struggling to move as he regained control of his body one limb at a time. He closed his eyes as the God-Dragon eclipsed the sun and cast its shadow across the jungle. As it landed at the edge of the clearing, it crushed and splintered trees like twigs beneath its enormous feet. It snarled malevolently at all that still stood within the clearing, baring its monstrous teeth. Its breath sounded like an avalanche within its throat. Its scales were like thousands of overlapping sea-green shields, many sporting patches of moss that had grown during its slumber. Thorns protruded from the scales of its brow. Its rich amber irises surrounded the tall, narrow slits of pupils glaring at its prey. Its snout was long and pointed, its lower jaw spiked. Two devilish horns swept back from its skull. A spiked ridge ran the length of its spine. Large brownish spikes protruded from elbow and knee. As it flapped its vast leathery wings, gusts of wind blew the leaves from trees. Its tail writhed back and forth like a serpent waiting to strike. The God-Dragon looked as old as time itself.

A devilish grin crossed General Dryden's face. "This will truly be a fight worthy of legend. Goma spell casters, follow me."

The God-Dragon looked down upon the jungle clearing, glancing around the stone huts of the village to inspect the small creatures below. Amongst them, there was only one that dared challenge it. He walked calmly, decked in clouded glass armor with shimmering blue runes dancing its surface. He withdrew Tempest from its silver sheath. He looked up at the colossal God-Dragon before him, ready to exert the full power of his runes upon the deadliest creature his world had ever known. The three remaining Goma incantatory wizards followed behind.

The God-Dragon opened its maw and drew in a deep breath. General Dryden could see the flames flickering within its mouth. As the God-Dragon roared with rage, it blew a barrage of flame just as General Dryden yelled with power and released a tornado straight toward the Dragon's mouth. The twisting tunnel of wind smashed against the God-Dragon's gushing pillar of fire. The wind deflected the flame, yet General Dryden began to sweat from its heat even from such a safe distance. Tongues of flame were thrown in all directions by the spinning wind, scorching and igniting the surrounding plant life. Plumes of smoke began to rise through the air as the trees crackled in the conflagration.

The God-Dragon looked down at its challenger with a new, analytical eye. General Dryden began whirling Tempest in giant circles above his head, stirring the surrounding wind as it gained speed. As the wind twisted and churned within the clearing, smoke and debris circled around him, forming the makings of a new, more powerful whirlwind. The clouds within his helm began churning also, and his antlers sparked with lightning, sending lashes of energy into the growing spiral. In one powerful, howling rush, air was sucked into Tempest with such speed that the surrounding fires were snuffed out. For a brief moment, Tempest's blade looked as if it contained all of that compacted smoke-filled churning wind. General Dryden pointed his blade toward the ground; as he thrust the blade into the earth, a pillar of churning black wind riddled with bolts of lightning dropped like a hammer from the sky and smashed against the head of the God-Dragon, slamming it to the earth.

General Dryden removed Tempest from the earth, and the lightning-riddled cyclone ended. His helm was churning like a hurricane, arcing bolts of energy from his antlers to his blade, charging it with lightning. Tempest's blade was vibrating with concentrated lightning dancing about as if trying to escape. The burgeoning blade lengthened until it was twice his height.

The God-Dragon shook its head to shrug off the blow from the crushing tornado. It peered down at the puny elkin who dared defy it and raised one massive arm to swipe at General Dryden with its man-sized talons. The three Goma spellbinders blasted its eyes with blinding light. The God-Dragon jerked its head back and blinked its eyes furiously. General Dryden thrust Tempest's elongated energy-filled blade at the God-Dragon's hand. The blade passed straight through its scales, sending a shocking surge through its arm and body. The God-Dragon snarled as its muscles clenched and spasmed.

General Dryden withdrew Tempest and the God-Dragon was released from the shock. It snarled in madness as it stood up on its hind legs, arching its long neck downward and sweeping its head to expel a massive burst of fire in all directions. The searing flames blackened the village's stone huts, charred the earth, and melted two of the Goma enchanters alive. General Dryden and the remaining Goma dove out of its path to save their own skins.

The God-Dragon spread its enormous leathery wings and began to flap them, generating huge gusts of wind as it rose into the sky. The elkin had to shield their eyes as the gusts blew burning embers and smoke their way. The God-Dragon circled the clearing, roaring and breathing pillars of fire all along the edges of the clearing before rising higher.

Warlord Vorkus yelled above the roaring fire, "Dryden! You're going to get us all killed!"

"We're trapped! Surrounded by fire!" shouted the last Goma spellbinder.

As the God-Dragon stooped to make another pass over the clearing, Scokoo, Warlord Vorkus, the elkin, and the humans hid inside the blackened stone huts of Sonir-Senti. The ancient God-Dragon swept the clearing with fresh waves of incinerating breath. The dead bodies of the brave warriors who had given their lives were reduced to ash as smoke billowed toward the sky in huge dark clouds.

Grindor the Ravenous yelled out from his hut, "We're going to die in here!"

Gressyn shouted, "We've got to do something."

"But how do we defeat somethin' that big?" asked Baltor.

Warlord Vorkus called back "By using its own strength against itself. Scokoo! I need you to take out its wings! Are you with me?"

"To the end, Warlord Vorkus!" he shouted back.

They left the safety of the huts, only to see a feeble female elkin stand before them. She blocked their path as the flames burned with uncontrollable hunger all around them. She looked at the surroyal metal antlers atop the head of the man wearing the bulky runic plate armor of the Onyx Smith. Her scratchy voice spoke in a tone of disbelief, "Vorkus? Is that really you?"

"The very same," he said as her familiar face brought a smile to his lips.

"How…" she stuttered as she stared into the face of a young adult that somehow bore Warlord Vorkus' familiar antlers. "How is this possible? I killed you to end the War of the Wish."

"When Erador donned my antlers, he told me that Dryden would lead me to you, so I gladly played along."

She paused, as if considering whether his statement was intended as a threat. "I'm more powerful now. I've killed you before, I can kill you again."

"I don't think so; I like the skin I'm in. Plus, I wasn't wearing my Onyx armor then!" The glow in his eyes brightened as a shroud of darkness covered Wraith. He sliced through the open air, sending a shadow surging across the ground toward Mother. She flicked up her hand and a beacon of light gushed out of it as bright as the sun, squelching his shadow attack into nothingness. As her light diminished, they peered at each other with burning animosity.

"Warlord Vorkus! The God-Dragon returns!" shouted Scokoo.

They dove out of the way as a wall of fire came scorching down between them. As the blaze came pouring out from the God-Dragon's gullet, Scokoo called the lightning from the sky with a flurry of shots from his runic bow. Every bolt struck straight to the earth as the God-Dragon flew between the lightning-strikes with surprising dexterity and speed, then shot high into the air.

As soon as it was safe, Gressyn, Baltor, Hammynt, Tysyra, Vynocent and Wiltyn approached Warlord Vorkus with determination. "Hey!" shouted Gressyn. "What do you mean that you like the skin you're in?!"

"What do you care if I stay? Dryden will be dead, Mother will be dead, and we'll both have our revenge!"

"We want Erador back!" shouted Tysyra in a fit of rage.

"I bet you do, you harlot! Now get back, the lot of you!"

The God-Dragon swept back over the clearing, an enormous boulder in each of its claws. It released the boulders from its grip upon the paltry creatures running about below and arced away. They thudded down, rolling across the clearing from their momentum. The first crushed the last Goma spell binder into a bloody pulp, while the other three landed with near misses—as their intended targets used their powerful elkin legs to dive out of the way.

General Dryden's Sky armor was covered in streaks of smoke and soot. He watched the God-Dragon ascend higher into the sky. "Let's take the wind out of your sails." He called out the runic power of Tempest, "Soo nok ri." He swung Tempest down in a chopping motion, pulling the air from the sky, creating an enormous downdraft. A vacuum formed beneath the God-Dragon's massive, billowing wings. It flailed in futility at air too thin to support a sparrow. As it fell, it screamed fire, dropping like a meteor from the sky.

Standing at the edge of the Clan Grondyr village, the Soul Binder shouted in horror at Mother, "My Queen! Get to safety! The God-Dragon is going to fall right on top of us!"

Everyone else heard his cry of warning as well and scrambled in all directions in a panic, jumping and lunging through walls of burning flame... everyone but Warlord Vorkus.

Without hesitation, Warlord Vorkus positioned himself in the center of the village, surrounded by the stone huts, and held Wraith above his head, pointing it straight toward the plunging colossus. He shouted, "Ag xor brek chouq!" Golden runes lit up, first at his feet, then spiraling up his legs, across his chest, along his raised arm and up the Wraith's blade to its point, until every rune was glowing with power. The huts of the village all leaned toward him until they toppled in his direction. The stone blocks rolled toward the Onyx armor as though it were some sort of magnet; they surrounded him and stacked upon themselves, building a new structure around him with incredible speed. The glow of the runes could be seen through gaps between the rocks until they began melding together into a single, solid piece of stone. They continued to rise around him, covering his face, his antlers, his arms, and covering Wraith until they had converged into one giant stone spike.

No sooner did the giant stone spike finish solidifying than did the tumbling mass of beast impale itself upon it. The beast slammed to the ground with earth-quaking impact, driving it full upon the spike and extinguishing its fiery breath. The spike protruded through its ribs from belly to back, and a pool of green blood began to spread about it. The God-Dragon lay sprawled across the clearing, reaching nearly from one side to the other; its wings draped trees to either side.

General Dryden approached the enormous head of the creature warily, as he could still hear breath within its nostrils. He stood only as tall as its longest tooth and little larger than its eye. He leapt up upon its upper jaw. As he walked the ridge of its snout, its glazed eyes opened, its tail slithered across the ground, and it began to move its feet firmly underneath itself one after another.

He lunged forward to grasp the spikes atop its head. With an ear-shattering yowl, the God-Dragon began to stand to push itself off of the spike upon which it was impaled. As it lifted its body, its green blood raced down the surface of the stone spike. The God-Dragon removed itself from the pointed object and clumsily sidled away from it, then began to gather its wings.

General Dryden knew he had to act. He raised Tempest high into the sky and stabbed the wispy blade straight through its thick, moss-covered green scales at the center of its skull. The eyes of the Dragon rolled inward as its entire body toppled sideways into the jungle canopy, crushing and splintering trees beneath it. General Dryden was thrown from its head into the charred, smoldering jungle.

***

After a long, tense silence, the elkin of Clan Wyndlyn emerged from whence they had ran. General Dryden stood by his kill, sword sheathed and armor covered in soot. Mother and the Soul Binder approached him. Warlord Vorkus rose from the strewn pieces of his pointed stone obelisk, covered in the stone's fine gray dust.

Then, to the bewilderment of all, an unknown man walked into the clearing. Every step he took across the blackened jungle floor left a glowing amber footprint that dissipated behind him. The man's head was bald, except for a single patch at the back of his head that dropped in a long black pony tail. His black eye brows were wild and bushy, while his goatee was neatly trimmed. He wore heavy silver chains that crossed his chest and clinked against bronze half-plate armor. The armor's plating was pronounced on his left shoulder and arm, guarding his flank like a shield. His muscular right arm was bare; in his hand was a hammer with a head that appeared to be made of flesh.

Everyone gravitated toward his approach. Mother knelt and bowed her head in his presence, though General Dryden and the Soul Binder remained standing. Warlord Vorkus hastened over, so Clan Wyndlyn followed him.

Warlord Vorkus approached the man, shouting in an anger, "What is the meaning of this?"

The man turned with a very calm demeanor to face the hulking elkin in Onyx armor. He spoke the common tongue with a heavy accent, as if he had come from a faraway land, "Who is this who dares to not address me as god!... wait... I remember forging those antlers... over two thousand years ago."

Mother rose from her kneeling position. "Soul Smith, Warlord Vorkus has returned to us in the flesh of another."

The Soul Smith grew intrigued as he stared at the raging elkin. "I've been looking for your soul, Vorkus. How did you manage to remove it from the Cyclops Helm from when you wore the Armor of Souls?"

"Using Old Magic. I had a keratin perform the Soul Rendering ritual so that I could escape your hell."

Mother stared at Warlord Vorkus with hatred. "How dare you insult the gods in their presence!"

The Soul Smith held up His hand. "Now, now. You two can settle your quarrels after I leave." He looked at Dryden with a stern gaze. "I dispatched the elkin of Clan Wyndlyn so you could get your prize." The Soul Smith gestured toward the Armor of Souls and then to Mother. "And in turn, you have slain the God-Dragon so I can have my prize."

"Not. So. Fast!" shouted General Dryden with a wicked grin.

The Soul Binder stepped back and began the chant to raise the dead. The ground quaked and rumbled as the jade glow rippled through the runes of his bone staff, conjuring an emerald essence that began to swim around the enormous body of the dead God-Dragon. Its dripping blood turned black, and even its sea-green scales began to lose their color, turning dark as night. The undead God-Dragon opened luminous green eyes, spread shadowy wings over the clearing and rose to its feet. Pestilence gargled at the back of its gullet where its flames used to be.

"I have usurped the God-Dragon's soul. It is under my command," smirked the man within the Armor of Souls.

"Now, give me your Forging Hammer… or die," demanded General Dryden.

The Soul Smith's eyes grew wide with disbelief as He assumed a defensive stance. The Forging Hammer's heartbeat raced as He readied to strike.

CHAPTER 27

Mother of Clan Grondyr was shocked, astonished at the sight of the undead God-Dragon. Its dark wings spanned the horizon, jet-black blood seeped from its wound, its hollow gaze rested upon its master. She marveled in reverence at General Dryden's cunning—to steal the Soul Smith's prize out from under Him, to force Him to surrender when He was most exposed.

Before the Soul Binder raised the God-Dragon, she had thought all hope was lost, that the Soul Smith would use the God-Dragon's remains to construct an even deadlier creature—as was clearly His intent, from his words. She stared enraptured at the undead God-Dragon, admiring the stratagem of General Dryden's contrivance come to fruition. And its eyes, those green glowing eyes now seemed to be staring right at her, yet she felt safe. She turned to her adversary, her former lover, Vorkus. He stood before her in a fit of rage, swearing he would have his vengeance, yet she felt safe. She saw the Soul Smith standing before her too, a God, or as close to a God as any man can get, and could see the worry mount across His face. Standing before the God-Dragon He was as frightened as a squire first learning to wield a blade against a knight. She felt safe. *It seems like a dream*, she thought. *To be called Queen, to have been rescued from petrification, to have slain a dragon, all for me.*

She turned to the Soul Smith and spoke with a cold, coarse, and confident voice, "Hand us your Hammer, or else you are going to die this day."

The Soul Smith scrunched his brow at her disrespect, injured pride displacing fear. "Speaks the one who bent knee to me the moment before. Your soul will be the first that I torture for your insolence!"

Warlord Vorkus interjected, "Mother! How can you stand by Dryden in all this? I implore you to find reason. You're breaking your oath. Dryden is just repeating history. It's the War of the Wish all over again!"

Mother turned her cold stare upon the youthful guise that Warlord Vorkus' soul occupied. Her voice was harsh and bitter, vile and shrill, and filled with grit. "You know nothing of oaths! Elkin swear an oath to defend the land, *never* to cast it aside for pursuit of selfish ambitions! I had been wrong about General Dryden, underestimating what he was capable of. I knew not of the power he commanded with Tempest, and I knew not of a better way to keep the Soul Smith from acquiring the remains of a deceased God-Dragon. That's why I sacrificed myself and petrified the entire jungle.

"But I see it now. General Dryden has found a better way to defend the land. To rule over it, to unite the realm under his command, to crusade against the Soul Smith's demons, is to protect it. But General Dryden went straight to the source. To take the power from the Soul Smith is the same act as defending the land. This is very different from you, who were too selfish to destroy the Soul Smith when you had the chance. You chose to keep your soul instead of saving others, and that's when I stopped loving you. That was the day I knew you had to be killed. I did it to protect this land. And that is what I intend to do again today."

"Dryden killed his own kind!"

"We all make sacrifices. Those that have fallen did a great service for Thornwall. Even the Fates would agree. You must sacrifice a few in order to save many."

"A few won't be sacrificed. This is the War of the Wish all over again. Armies will rise to resist Dryden's tyranny! A great many lives will be lost unless he is stopped now."

"A *great* many *more* lives will be lost if the Soul Smith lives to see another day. Whatever ungodly monstrosity He forges from the God-Dragon's carcass will unleash countless more deaths than what is needed to make the people of this land obey," said Mother with certainty.

What few remained of Clan Wyndlyn began to back away from the black, tainted God-Dragon, never taking their eyes from the hulking beast. As if it were preparing to charge, the God-Dragon began to scratch at the ground in anticipation, its enormous claws plowing the earth, waiting for the command to attack. Warlord Vorkus held his ground in an audacious display of courage.

General Dryden and the Soul Binder stared at the Soul Smith, relishing watching Him sweat. General Dryden gave an evil grin. "So what will it be?"

"You will never have my Hammer, you arrogant rok kvian qo pasd!" cursed the Soul Smith in His native tongue.

"Then, your time here is done."

The Soul Smith shook His head, and said in a quiet, heated whisper, "No. I will have *all* your souls by the end of this day."

The undead God-Dragon spread its enormous wings in a display of power, plunging the clearing into shadow as it shrieked an uncanny cry that rang through the jungle. The Soul Smith whispered to the Forging Hammer; His words charged its pumping heart as it began to beat even faster, swelling with power. He flexed His bicep with all his might to hold the Hammer steady. The Soul Smith's muscular arm looked as strong and chiseled as stone as the power of the Hammer surged through Him. He cried in agony as the sound of rending flesh and bones snapping burst from His back. As the Hammer of Flesh continued to beat ever faster, dark bat-like wings began to emerge from His spine. At first disfigured and distorted, they evolved in mere moments into grand sweeps of flesh and sinew. He spread his demon wings and took to the sky toward the undead God-Dragon.

General Dryden drew Tempest, and he and the Soul Binder stepped forward against Warlord Vorkus. It was two against one, and Warlord Vorkus was hesitant to make the first strike. Eclipsed within the shadow of the God-Dragon's wings, he whispered, "Sry alum." A single golden rune upon the center of his black Onyx armor shimmered for a split second; as he took a step backward within the shadow, it was as if the shadow consumed him as he disappeared in thin air, hidden from sight.

***

Scokoo waited a safe distance back, his bow at the ready. *I got to take down the man in the Armor of Souls*, he thought. *But I'm going to need some arrows.* He scanned the battlefield, searching in frantic anxiety for any arrows that survived the Dragon's breath. He sidled toward some elkin cadavers near the edge of the clearing; their charred remains rendered them indistinguishable from one another, though when he saw two elkin stuck in steel bear traps, he knew they were of Clan Wyndlyn. He retrieved two fork-tipped blackened arrows that had escaped the God-Dragon's wrath. Scokoo brushed ash from their charred shafts, determined that they were good enough for reuse and placed them in his quiver.

He nocked a blackened arrow and took aim at the man in the Armor of Souls. He drew back the bowstring, the runes upon the bow-staff lit up as he spoke, and he released the shaft. The arrow streaked through the air with supernatural speed, crackling with lustrous blue bolts of energy. As the splintering sound of the arrow piercing through the air reached the ears of the necromancer, he ducked out of reflex. The fork-tipped arrow zipped past him and slashed through Mother's carotid, lodging in her spine. Blood gushed from the wound and out of her mouth as the lightning discharged along her spine. She gave one last glance of incredulity at General Dryden before she fell limp upon the ground.

***

General Dryden gave a bloodcurdling yell, and the skies replied with dark, thunderous clouds. The Sky helm's clouded glass appearance was now surging with a whirlwind of fury while bolts of energy bridged his antlers. Their charge flashed into Tempest, rebuilding the crackling blade of lightning. "Where are you, Vorkus? Come out and fight, you coward!"

With its claws clutching the earth ready to pounce, the undead God-Dragon watched the Soul Smith fly towards it on demonic wings. Its dead lungs drew in air, and it blasted purple and black noxious fumes into the sky. The Soul Smith twisted and turned in the air, evading the pestilential cloud. As He flew closer, the God-Dragon lunged and snapped at Him with its powerful jaws, missing by narrow margins with each strike. As the Soul Smith maneuvered through its relentless assault, the undead God-Dragon reared back upon its hind legs, towering over the land and thrashing its wings, buffeting the Soul Smith with turbulent winds before blowing another blast of its macabre black gases across the sky.

The Soul Smith dove through the roiling air and beneath the undead God-Dragon's noxious cloud. He shouted words in His long-forgotten tongue and a jolt of green energy surged out of His Hammer and struck the scales of the God-Dragon in a massive explosion of sparks and screams. He swooped toward the exposed rupture in the God-Dragon's belly; as it flapped its enormous wings and took to the air, He went after it.

The shadow of the God-Dragon was gone, and Warlord Vorkus appeared out of thin air, standing behind General Dryden with his eyes glowing white. He raised Wraith high into the air to deal a lethal blow, but as he brought down the pendulum swing, it was parried by the bone staff. General Dryden kicked backward at Warlord Vorkus like a bucking bull, knocking him away with surprising force. He charged after him, and their swords clashed and flickered with blinding speed as they dueled for their lives. General Dryden swung his surging lightning blade in reckless fury, sending sparks flying with every warding block of Wraith. The Soul Binder fired a ray of energy and knocked Warlord Vorkus onto his back. General Dryden cursed in the language of the Sky Smith as his lightning blade shifted its shape into a whip of surging energy. He slashed at Warlord Vorkus as he laid upon the ground, thunderous *cracks* sounding with every lash. Warlord Vorkus rolled backward to avoid the shocking lashes that seared the earth. He continued his advance, slashing and attacking with a berserker rage as Warlord Vorkus scrambled to his feet.

The Soul Binder spoke in the ancient tongue of the Soul Smith, evoking the power of the runes to paralyze Warlord Vorkus once more. General Dryden approached the immobilized Warlord and spat in his face. Then a lightning-filled blackened arrow flew into the smallest gap between the rib bones of the Armor of Souls, sending enervating surges through its wearer's body.

***

The black-scaled undead God-Dragon glared at the Soul Smith with its evil jade-green eyes. It swung a massive claw at its adversary. The blow sent Him tumbling down like a comet from the sky. As He fell to the earth, the undead God-Dragon followed. He crashed into the ground amongst the masses of burnt bodies near where Scokoo stood. The God-Dragon landed and unleashed its pestilence breath right on top of Him.

The Soul Smith raised his Forging Hammer. Its beating heart extracted the souls from the dead that lay around Him, glowing green wisps swirling inward toward it. Their energy converged about Him, building a protective wall of whirling, wailing souls, dispersing the toxic fumes in all directions. Scokoo tried to flee, but the pestilence breath spread too rapidly. As the black cloud engulfed him, it seeped through the cracks of his Sky armor and he gave a hideous, final scream as his skin began to slough off his bones. The Soul Smith got to His feet as He drove the shield of souls outward against the undead God-Dragon's breath. He held the glowing green bubble of souls about Him as He ran toward its belly within the obscuring cover of the billowing black clouds. As He closed, He flapped His demonic wings and surged toward the God-Dragon's open wound.

***

I emptied my lungs, but the presumptuous mortal's swirling green ornament dispersed all my efforts. My whole being demanded its destruction, to pulverize its bones within my grasp, to watch its flesh liquefy and soak into the tormented earth. I would not be assuaged by anything less. When the cloud finally cleared, my foe was nowhere to be seen. Where did—? *I arched my long neck to inspect the gaping hole in my belly.* There! *The winged man was trying to climb inside my wound! Its defense was withdrawn now. I blasted my life-consuming breath at the wound... too late; it had found shelter within my flesh. I raised my claws, scratched at the wound... the thing was already beyond dislodging. The sensation of it worming its way ever deeper into my chest evoked responses within my center-of-self that were ... unpleasant... and, worse, attending them only gave them added strength. This was unacceptable. This must end. Now. I thrust talons inside scales never breached since the dawn of dawns, ululating my agony as I picked and probed through my own being to pluck forth this annoyance, end this impossible invasion, so that I may return to the tasks my master wishes me to—*

***

An explosion of coruscating green energy burst open the God-Dragon's chest from where its heart would have been. The Soul Smith flew out of its body, drenched in its black blood. The eerie jade green glow of the God-Dragon's eyes dwindled as the colossal creature toppled to the earth.

Warlord Vorkus rose to his feet as Scokoo's arrow broke the Soul Binder's concentration on his paralytic spell. He glared in contempt at General Dryden. He rumbled a single word in the language of the Onyx Smith, and swung Wraith in a powerful sideward chop. Dryden brought Tempest's surging blade of lightning to parry the blow, but where he expected the crushing swing of Wraith to connect with Tempest, Dryden felt… nothing whatsoever. He realized that he'd just blocked a projection, a false copy of Warlord Vorkus— a shadow.

Dryden saw the real strike come at him from the other side. He called out the fastest of the Sky armor's protections he could invoke, yelling, "Vu esh!"

Nothing happened. No runes lit with power. In that fraction of a second, all of Dryden's confidence left him as, in a flash of memory, he was taken back to the Willow Cave. To when he demanded his Sky armor back from that fool who'd had the audacity to wear it. To how his armor didn't fit properly as he donned it… which he'd attributed to amateurish adjustments and inexpert assistance, then had dismissed from his mind. *This is not my armor,* he thought. All this passed in a moment's review as the heavy blade of Wraith crashed against the Sky Smith armor like a battering ram. Dryden flew across the clearing and slammed against a tree trunk, then slumped limp as a rag doll. Tempest's lightning-blade dissipated as it flew into the jungle, leaving a trail of severed foliage drifting down in its wake.

***

Before Warlord Vorkus could follow up his attack, the Soul Binder swung the bulbous end of his bone staff into his face. His nose was broken and his blood spattered the bone staff. He fell hard to the ground, trying to breathe through his blood-filled mouth. The

Soul Binder staggered to recover from his own blow, the arrow still in his side.

He stood over the defeated Warlord Vorkus, planting the staff to remain upright. "This armor thirsts for your soul. I can feel it. I am *one* with this armor as you once were all those years ago. How fitting that your soul shall be the first that I absorb. To mend my wounds, to never grow old, to become immortal."

He murmured beneath his breath. A single rune upon the bone armor of the black phoenix burned with jade green energy, and so did his eyes. He held his hand, quivering with power, over Warlord Vorkus' chest. Warlord Vorkus' back arched upward. He screamed as the white glow departed his eyes and a green luminous essence was drawn from his chest. The Soul Binder guided the pulsing soul toward his own chest. As it flowed into the runic armor, he could feel the power surge through his body in a tantalizing tingle. The blackened arrow stuck in his side eased back out through the wound and fell to the ground. The wound closed. He stood straight, weight no longer against the staff, rejuvenated.

***

As if awakening from one of his nightmares, Erador became once more conscious of his own body; his nose was throbbing in pain and, when he tried to breathe through it, blood trickled into his throat. He was prone at the feet of the man in the Armor of Souls, who was for some reason paying no mind to him. Without hesitation, Erador rolled to his feet and swung Wraith with such force that the diamond-edged blade sheared through the ribs of the armor and then those of its wearer. The Soul Binder's blood ran from his half-severed torso down the grooves between the joined bones of his armor. For a moment, a flicker of green mist played about the wound, but then it was gone. Erador watched the life drain from his eyes.

Erador looked up from his foe. And wondered once again if he had truly awakened, or if he had descended to an ultimate nightmare hell he was doomed to inhabit forever. He recognized that the jungle was no longer stone—since stone did not smoke and smolder. He recognized that he was in a clearing, though all sign of Clan Hortyr's village was erased. He saw the ground littered with

299

corpses, most charred beyond the ability to recognize what—who—they had been in life. He beheld a black behemoth that could only be the God-Dragon… unmoving. Dead. But it was only when he saw the few members of Clan Wyndlyn still standing at the edge of the clearing that his heart skipped a beat. All six of them. Carra and Zimmerik were not standing among them. Emotion pierced a numbness he had not been aware had engulfed him. Once again, he had been unable to defend his clan.

He began breathing in a panic as his eyes searched the battlefield for them, but his gaze stopped when he saw the body of an elkin wearing Sky Smith armor laying against a burnt tree. Erador walked up to the battered body, watching for motion, for breath, to see if he still lived. The Sky Smith armor's breastplate was cracked and broken, and his clawed face was dripping with blood, but as Erador neared, General Dryden began to blink. Still proud, still defiant—or, as Carra had said, insane—his eyes met Erador's without the least trace of remorse. Erador reached back for his father's antlers and then knelt down to General Dryden's level. Without a word, or a change of expression, he shoved his father's antlers into his enemy's eyes. He kept pushing them in as General Dryden's body twitched with random convulsions, then finally went limp.

Erador removed his father's antlers and returned them to his belt, then rose and stood looking down at his defeated foe. "I have avenged you, father," he muttered. Then he wondered, *But then why don't I feel it? All I feel is… a hole, as if I've lost something, not gained it. Where is the victory?*

As Erador stood there, a man with bronze half-plate armor and demonic wings approached on foot, bulky chains rattling against his breast plate as he walked. When Erador saw the legendary Forging Hammer he wielded, he knew that he was in the presence of the Soul Smith. The Soul Smith had a look of hatred upon His face as He walked up to the lifeless body of Mother. He held the Hammer over her body, and a brilliant verdant essence swirled upward into it.

Erador didn't know what to do, what to say. *Should I kneel?* he wondered. But before he could gather his thoughts, he blurted the first thing that came to mind, "Did you kill my entire clan?"

The Soul Smith nodded in affirmation as He looked at Erador with contempt, but then His expression shifted to curiosity. "Your voice is different," said the demi-god, in a thick accent Erador did not recognize. "And your eyes. The essence of Vorkus is no longer within that body."

"I am Erador, Warlord of Clan Wyndlyn."

One corner of the Smith's mouth twitched upward for a second. "I would advise you to be wary of who you give your name to. Names have power. I shall remember yours."

Erador looked away from the Smith's disquieting gaze. His eyes fell on the rune-inscribed antlers of Clan Grondyr's Mother. "How did she get her antlers inscribed with your runes?"

"After the War of the Wish, I decided to commend her for her victory over Vorkus by inscribing runes upon her antlers. The runes I placed are the reason she has lived all these centuries. But don't expect any sort of reward from me today," said the Soul Smith. Fatigued and bruised, Erador watched as He gathered Dryden's soul, then the soul within the Armor of Souls—or souls: it seemed to Erador's eyes that the green spiral that rose from it seemed to be composed of slightly varied hues that refused to blend into one.

The Smith met his gaze once more. "So, are *you* going to try to kill me too?"

Erador straightened his battered body, and spoke through his fatigue, his shock, his pain, his bereavement and horror and failure and still-unresolved anger, somehow managing to locate a glimmer of pride: "Are you going to try to take the souls of my clan?"

The Soul Smith raised an eyebrow at Erador's quiet, desperate defiance. He seemed to consider for a moment, then gave a mocking bow. "Well spoken, young Warlord. I believe there is enough here to content me that I can spare you that much." Then He added, severely, "Today."

Erador's stance sagged, relieved of any need of continued effort. He nodded once, acknowledging the Smith's concession.

"Smart." The Soul Smith looked about the devastation they stood amidst. Even He seemed affected by it… saddened, perhaps.

"So what happens now?"

"I will collect my prize and you will go home," said the Soul Smith as He walked toward the carcass of the God-Dragon. Standing next to it, He turned and added, "And I *will* remember your name, Warlord Erador of Clan Wyndlyn."

Erador watched as the amber glowing footsteps of the Soul Smith fade upon the charred ground of the clearing. The last surviving members of Clan Wyndlyn came out from the canopy to regroup with Erador. Tysyra rushed over to tend to his broken nose. Erador sat on the battlefield, and they all watched as the Soul Smith placed His hand upon the God-Dragon; then they both vanished.

"Now the Soul Smith is going to augment the God-Dragon into something even more terrifying," stated Gressyn.

Erador looked over at the translation stone and then glanced up at the white sun shining through the thinning smoke of dying fires. "May the Onyx Smith protect us all."

End

ABOUT THE AUTHOR

Adrian V. Diglio received his Bachelor of Arts degree from California Polytechnic University Pomona in music business, then received his Master of Business Administration degree from San Diego State University in information systems. He is a systems engineer and resides in San Diego with his wife and two daughters. For more information about the author and his works, Adrian V. Diglio invites you to visit his web site at adriandiglio.com.